grand...
jobs have included working as a qualified nurse and a civil servant in the Prison Service. When her children were young she successfully completed an Open University B.A. degree studying psychology and sociology. She was a member of the Romantic Novelists' Association for four years and is now a member of ALLi (the Alliance of Independent Authors) and Goodreads.

As well as writing she loves country walks and travelling abroad (she adores bus stations, railway stations, airports and ferry ports – any place where people are on the move).

Contact the author by email at
Julia@JuliaBellRomanticFiction.co.uk

or visit her website at
www.JuliaBellRomanticFiction.co.uk

ACKNOWLEDGEMENTS

I would like to thank:

Amanda Lillywhite for the excellent work she did creating the front cover. Amanda can be contacted via her website at www.AJLIllustration.talktalk.net.

I would also like to thank Rob White for all his technical know-how, moral support and encouragement for which I am very grateful.

Hazel Garner. Her wonderful proof reading kept me on track and her sensible advice was invaluable.

Cover re-engineered for paperback by
Beenish Qureshi   www.fiverr.com/bqureshi

First Published as an ebook UK 2012

Published in paperback UK 2018

Copyright © 2012 by Julia Bell Romantic Fiction

No part of this book may be used or reproduced in any manner whatsoever without written permission from the Publisher except in the case of brief quotations embodied in critical articles or reviews

Names and characters except for the historical figures are purely the product of the author's imagination.

JuliaBellRomanticFiction.co.uk

First Edition

For my daughter-in-law, Shazma

DECEIT OF ANGELS

by

Julia Bell

JULIA BELL ROMANTIC FICTION

To Dorothy
Best wishes
Julia Bell
22/6/2024

CHAPTER ONE

The train slowed down as it reached the outskirts of Bristol. Anna pulled on her coat, ran a comb through her hair and checked her makeup in her compact mirror. Pulling a face at her image she glanced once more out of the window, noticing the customary large warehouses and business premises that often littered the area surrounding a mainline station. Passengers stood and gathered their belongings, but Anna remained seated.

The platforms and buildings of the station finally came into sight, the train sliding to a stop. As passengers scrambled to get out of the doors first, Anna decided to take her time and wait for the carriage to empty. There didn't seem any point in hurrying. But once on the platform, the walk to the exit seemed interminable, her heart racing with a mixture of excitement and fear. She took a deep breath, trying to soothe her guilty conscience at deceiving her family. Perhaps she should have been honest with them? She shrugged knowing it was too late now.

Outside the station, her eyes swept around the rushing melee of moving figures and traffic, searching for the vehicle that was to pick her up. She was about to give up and try and contact someone on her mobile, when a pleasant husky voice came from behind.

"Mrs Stevens?"

Anna spun round and came face to face with a man smartly dressed in a chauffeur's uniform. He raised his hand to the peak of his cap as he smiled and asked her name.

"Yes. Yes, I'm Mrs Stevens."

"My name's Ben. If you'd like to come with me, I'll show you where the car's parked."

She followed him, trying to keep up with his long strides by skipping every other step and then raised her eyebrows at what awaited her in the car park. Ben opened the door to a sleek, grey limousine and Anna slipped into the back seat, falling against the luxurious black leather of the interior. She watched him take his place behind the wheel and skilfully pull out of the congested car park. As their journey started, Anna looked around the inside of the car, feeling impressed. She noticed a small hatch and pulling it down revealed a whole array of drinks and liqueurs.

"Very nice," she murmured.

"If you'd like a drink, miss, please help yourself. Mr Harrington never minds."

Anna felt embarrassed and shut the hatch with a slam.

"Actually, I don't drink much alcohol. Is it very far, this place we're bound for?" she asked, running her fingers through her hair.

"It's near Bishop Sutton, about twenty minutes drive. Why don't you just sit back and enjoy the ride."

She didn't answer, but watched the houses and shops pass her by, smiling to herself. For the first time in weeks she felt relaxed and strangely contented. She decided to let the coming events unfold naturally. After all, she was only doing this for experience. Her eyelids felt heavy and she tried to blink away the sudden tiredness that overcame her. But then her head nodded in sleep.

She jerked awake when the driver's door slammed shut as Ben jumped out and came round to her side.

He opened the door.

"Here we are then. You seemed to have dozed off." His eyes crinkled with amusement. Anna gave him a wry smile and stepped out of the car. "If you'd like to follow me, miss. We need to go round the back to the kitchen entrance. It's been decided that applicants wait in the kitchen with Mrs Wilby and have a cup of coffee, until their turn comes to be interviewed."

"Have there been many applicants?" she asked.

"Well, you're the sixth, I believe. Mr Harrington wanted all the interviews out of the way by two as he's rushing off to a meeting in London this afternoon. I think you're the last."

As she entered through the kitchen door, her gaze took in the back of the house and she gave a low whistle. It was a large building in mock Tudor style with many rectangular windows staring out over the lawn and flowerbeds. The garden was beautiful, with a manicured lawn and borders full of lily of the valley, primulas and a few late tulips. The trees groaned under the weight of the pink cherry blossom and at the far end she could see an area set aside for barbecues. Ben led her into a spacious and well-organised kitchen, where a stout, middle-aged woman hauled herself to her feet to greet her.

The chauffeur gestured with a casual wave of his hand. "This is our Mrs Wilby, the cook-cum-housekeeper of our happy home and the only one who can keep us all in order. Mrs Wilby meet Mrs Stevens, the last applicant for the post of PA."

Mrs Wilby gripped Anna's hand. "Come and sit down, my dear. You've come all the way from West Yorkshire, haven't you? My late husband came from Leeds, so we often came your way when we visited the in-laws. That's when I was a young bride, of course. They died within six months of each other, did my in-laws, just five years after I married. It was so sad. Would you like a cup of coffee?" Anna felt overcome by her friendly manner and could only find the strength to nod. "Sit down. Sit down and we'll soon have you all sorted out."

She bustled about the kitchen setting out crockery and filling the cups with the sweet aroma of freshly ground coffee.

Ben took off his cap and threw it on the pine kitchen table. Turning a chair round and sitting astride with his arms across the back, he winked at Anna.

"She's a bit of a chatterbox, but she's the loveliest person you could ever meet," he said in a low voice.

Three cups of coffee appeared and Anna sipped hers, gathering her courage for what lay ahead of her. Mrs Wilby lowered her large bulk into a pine chair with arms and scrutinised the young woman sitting across from her.

"Now then, my dear. I hear you're a widow like me. Although you're so young to be without a husband. Has he been gone long?"

Anna started visibly and Ben broke into the conversation. "Do let her catch her breath, Mrs Wilby. She's not been here five minutes and you're giving her the third degree already."

Anna took another sip of her coffee. She felt as though her secret was there for all to see and a terrible feeling of uncertainty washed over her.

The housekeeper's face flushed red with embarrassment. "I'm sorry. I do talk, I know."

Anna's heart went out to her. "It's all right, really it is." She took a deep breath. "My husband died six years ago."

There, it was said! Hang on in there girl, she told herself, you'll never see these people again after today, so it doesn't matter what they hear.

Mrs Wilby's face became sombre. "Oh, how sad. Were there any children?"

"Twin boys, but they're hardly children," smiled Anna, concentrating on her cup of coffee.

They were interrupted by the entrance of a slightly built young girl, in her early twenties, with long brown hair plaited at the back.

She glanced towards Anna and smiled. "Ah, you must be Mrs Stevens. I'm Sharon O'Reilly, Mr. Harrington's personal assistant. We're ready to interview you now if you'd like to come with me."

It wasn't difficult to recognise the soft southern Irish accent of the woman on the phone, although Anna couldn't help feeling surprised at how young she was. She stood up and thanked Mrs Wilby for the coffee. Ben put his thumb in the air and mouthed 'good luck'.

Anna followed Sharon out of the kitchen and across a spacious hallway. Making her way to the furthest end of the hall, she opened the door and stepped through. Hard on her heels a very nervous Anna tried to take in huge gulps of air to calm her racing heart.

"Jason, this is our last applicant, Mrs Anna Stevens. Anna, this is Jason Harrington, the Managing Director of Harrington Rhodes Shipping Agents."

Anna entered an office that was a good size with a huge window that filled the room with bright light. A large desk dominated the opposite side of the window and sitting behind it was Jason Harrington.

Sharon gestured to the chair in front of his desk and then went to sit down a short distance away. As Anna walked towards Jason, he stood up and held out his hand in greeting. He's certainly attractive, thought Anna, with dark brown hair and deep blue eyes, but it dismayed her how his manner seemed to be brisk and efficient. Taking his hand, she realised she probably wouldn't meet his specifications for a personal assistant. She licked her lips and tried to relax. How ironic, she thought, believing this was such a clever idea, but now feeling like a trapped animal. Her grim thoughts were arrested by his smile. It was a wonderful smile that lit up his face and seemed to convey a warm feeling of genuine friendship. She shook his hand, hoping hers wasn't trembling. Sweat started trickling down her back.

"Mrs Stevens, I'm so pleased you arrived safely. Did you have a good journey?"

"Yes, I did, thank you."

They made themselves comfortable.

"Splendid! Well, let's get down to business." He paused for a moment before continuing, "I run a busy shipping agency, exporting and importing a variety of goods. You've met my present PA, Sharon, who unfortunately is leaving me to go back to Ireland to get married. I'm looking for someone who can run this office, whether I'm here or not and generally take care of things at this end. I can be away quite a lot as I have business interests in London and...."

Sharon pulled a face. "And Paris...and Brussels...and..."

He gave a chuckle that made Anna smile. "Anyway, you get the picture, I'm sure. I travel a great deal and sometimes I need to attend meetings at our main office in Bristol. However, I do work here at home most of the time. The person who runs this office, would have to be efficient and willing to work the hours that suit me. I'm not a bad boss, at least I hope not, but I am demanding. I expect my PA to be here when needed. And to make things easier, I do provide food and accommodation."

Anna stared at him. "I would live here?"

"You would be given a comfortable room and enjoy the benefit of Mrs Wilby's excellent cooking."

"I will certainly miss that," Sharon sighed.

Jason grinned at her before turning his attention back to Anna. "When I'm away, my PA would have to work on his or her own initiative. Are you OK about working on your own?"

Anna nodded. "Yes, I'm quite happy about that."

"Good. Now then, let's see what we know about you." He looked down at the open file on his desk and Anna's mouth dried up. She licked her lips as she watched him scan down her CV. "I see you're a widow with twin boys."

"Yes, they're eighteen and just about to go to university."

He nodded. "Does that mean you haven't any family responsibilities as such?"

"I have a mother, stepfather and younger sister living in Wakefield. That's all."

She felt a great urge to sit on her shaking hands, but instead, she held them in her lap, locked together. Keep a grip on yourself, she told herself, this will soon be over.

His eyes searched her face and then rested ever so lightly on her clenched hands.

"I see you achieved good 'A' level grades and you've been employed for the last four years as a school secretary?"

Anna's spirits soared as she explained her ambitions to him, her face becoming animated. "Yes, I decided to go back to college when the twins were twelve. I thought a secretarial qualification would help me go further in a career. As you can see, I worked for the Prison Service for two years as a typist and then I started working as a school secretary."

She felt an enormous sense of relief that for once, she was telling the truth.

He smiled in admiration. "You've certainly worked hard to look after your children."

"I...I married young." He was watching her and before she knew it she had blurted out, "I spent many years caring for my husband. He was ill with...with multiple sclerosis. He died..." What had she told Mrs Wilby? With great relief she added, "six years ago."

Anna's spirits sank, her brief moment of truth had ignited and burnt out so quickly.

Jason nodded. "That shows a great deal of dedication for one so young. That's the sort of loyalty that can only be commended." Anna tried to fight the waves of sickness. He pressed on with his interminable questions. "You understand that this position is immediate? How will your sons manage if you come to work in Bristol? You say that they're not leaving home until after the summer? In fact, isn't Bristol a long way from your family and friends?"

"My mother will take care of the boys until they leave." She swallowed with difficulty. "I want to get away from my home town." She hoped she didn't sound selfish and added, "Memories, you understand."

His expression softened. "I can understand why you're looking for a fresh start. Life can sometimes hit below the belt." Anna kept her expression impassive. Jason sighed as though reflecting on his own sorrows before saying, "I don't bother with shorthand. I much prefer to dictate into this little machine." He tapped the recorder on the desk.

"Audio typing would be no problem for me," she said quietly.

He carried on talking; explaining the work conditions and salary, but Anna had stopped listening. She wanted to go home. She had said too much and the sooner she was on that train the better. The elated feelings she had had when setting off that morning had evaporated. It was only a matter of time now. Soon he would say, "Thanks, but no thanks," and she would be on her way.

Anna glanced towards the window, noticing how the trees in the garden were already starting to shed their blossom, the tiny petals fluttering down in delicate flurries. Another month or so and it would be summer. So absorbed was she in her own thoughts, she failed to hear Jason Harrington's next comment. It was only when she realised the room had fallen silent and Sharon was rising to her feet, was she able to pull herself back to reality.

"Would you like to follow me, Mrs Stevens. I'll take you back to the kitchen and with any luck, Mrs Wilby will have another cup of coffee for you." Dazed, Anna followed her from the office and across the hall to the kitchen. Mrs Wilby was bustling about preparing lunch, but grinned when she saw them. "Look after her, will you? I'll be back shortly."

"Sit down, my dear," said Mrs Wilby. "No doubt they're going to put their heads together and decide on the best person for the job." She poured out the coffee and Anna took it in her hands, gulping it down.

"Well, it certainly won't be me. I was terrible!"

"Now, don't talk like that," laughed Mrs Wilby. "You never know what's going to happen. Better to wait and see."

"But I was awful. All nerves and prattle," said Anna. "I can't believe that the other five candidates were worse than me."

Mrs Wilby threw back her head and her laughter echoed round the large kitchen. "You have no idea, my chick, no idea at all. The first one turned up an hour late and from what Sharon told us, didn't stop chewing her gum all through the interview. The second one looked down her nose at us as if we were far below the likes of her and as for the third…!" Anna began to laugh and it eased the discomfort. "The third one was plainly after the boss rather than the work. I've never seen so much thigh or bosom." Tears of laughter streamed down her fat cheeks. "Poor Ben didn't know where to look."

"I bet," giggled Anna, putting her cup down on the table. "Where is he, by the way?"

"Oh, he's gone to tie up the daffs. He's the gardener and handyman too, you know, as well as the chauffeur."

"And what about the fourth and fifth?" asked Anna.

Mrs Wilby thought for a moment. "The fourth rang up to say he had had a better offer and we're still waiting for the fifth! So, you could be in with a chance after all, my dear."

Before Anna could reply, Sharon appeared. "Could you come back to the office please," she said.

Anna tried to read her expression but it was obvious she wasn't going to give anything away. She followed her once more across the hall and into the office, where Jason was leaning back in his chair, tapping his pen on the desk. His expression was serious as he told her to take her seat.

Anna sat down, her body calm, her thoughts quiet. She knew what was coming and she was ready for it.

"Well, Mrs Stevens. The job is yours," said Jason without any preamble.

Anna stared at him. "I'm sorry, did you say I'd got the job?" she stammered.

"Yes, I did and I'm hoping you can start within the next few weeks. Sharon has agreed to spend time with you, teaching you the ropes and getting everything sorted out." Turning his head, he directed his next remark to Sharon. "Has your father given you a date for starting?"

She shook her head. "No, he's leaving it up to me, but it would be helpful if I could have a good five days in the office with Mrs Stevens." She looked across at Anna and a smile spread across her face as she realised Anna's utter bewilderment. "I think you've taken Mrs Stevens by surprise, Jason."

"You're offering me the job?" repeated Anna.

Jason laughed. "If you want the job, it's yours."

"But...I never expected!" Her voice faded as she glanced from Jason to Sharon and then back to Jason.

He shook his head in amusement. "Are you accepting the job or have you come all this way just to turn it down?"

"I'm sorry. What I mean is...I'd like the work very much. It's just that your offer has come as...actually, I'm gobsmacked." Her voice shook as she scanned the expression of the man sitting opposite her.

He threw her that disarming smile of his, understanding her confusion. "Well, Mrs Stevens...Anna. May I call you Anna?" She nodded. "I'm always delighted when I catch people unawares. But I'm sure you'll do very well as my PA. Your work as a school secretary has given you the right experience. Of course, Sharon will have to train you in the way I want the office to run and we'll have to sort out your references." He glanced down at her CV again. "I see you've put down your referees as the headmistress at the school and your boss in the Prison Service." Anna nodded again and he added, "So, when can we say you'll start?"

"I must give four weeks' notice," she answered slowly. "The headmistress will be surprised but understanding. She knows my boys are going off to university in the autumn."

"Good. Then let us know," said Jason, a bright smile lighting up his face.

Anna nodded and murmured a soft, "Thank you."

Jason rubbed his hands together as if he had just completed a satisfactory business deal and stood, holding out his hand. She took it reluctantly. "Good! Welcome to the family, Anna. I hope you'll be happy with us. Now then, Sharon, where's my damned briefcase!" Sharon jumped up, collected a black leather bag from the chair by the wall and placed it on his desk. He opened it with a sharp snap of the catches and started flinging in papers. He closed the case and picking up his mobile phone, attached it to his trouser belt. "Will you tell Ben I'm ready to leave for the airport." Sharon left the office en route to the kitchen. Jason straightened his tie, all the time his eyes fixed on Anna's white, pinched face. "Are you all right, Anna? You look pale."

She shivered. "Do I? I suppose I must be in shock."

He gave a jolly laugh. "Don't worry. I'm sure we'll work very well together. I'm not usually wrong about people. I'm a fairly good judge of character; I have to be in my line of work. Goodbye until I see you again." He strode towards the door, but then stopped on the threshold and after a moment of consideration asked, "I know this is going to sound a bit of a cliché, but have we met before?"

Anna shook her head. "I don't think so. It's the first time I've been to this part of England."

He smiled and left the room.

The quietness seemed to suffocate her. What had she done! Of all the idiotic things to do, to go and accept a job that was out of the question. Sharon returning interrupted her confused thoughts.

"Now then, Anna. Would you like to look round the house first and then have some lunch with Mrs Wilby and me? Ben will be back in about an hour and then he can take you to the station."

The barrage of questions made her head throb.

"I'll do whatever suits you," she smiled.

Sharon looked round the office, her eyes filling with tears. "We really are like a family," she sighed. "There isn't any 'them' and 'us' to speak about. We all kind of pull together to get the work done. I'm going to miss everyone to be honest, but I'm going to work for my dad in Dublin. My fiancé, Aengus, wants us to get married this year as he's fed up of waiting."

Anna's heart softened at her sad expression and she reached out to squeeze her hand.

Ben arrived back from the airport when they were halfway through their meal.

"Well, that's got him away to London. Tell you something, you wouldn't catch me going up in a helicopter. Bloody dangerous, I say!" He shook Anna's hand and added, "By the way, welcome aboard."

Later that afternoon, Anna left with Ben to catch the train home, opting to sit in the front seat this time and keeping up a friendly banter all through the journey. At the station, they said their goodbyes.

As Anna watched him drive away, she felt her heart break in two. She would never see him again, she was sure of that, just as she would never see Sharon or Mrs Wilby or Jason ever again. How a group of people could gain her friendship in so short a time she would never know, but it had happened.

If the journey to Bristol had been full of excitement, then the journey home couldn't have been more melancholy. Anna sat with her head leaning against the window, her mind dull, her feelings torn. She would ring tomorrow and make some excuse. She was getting good at lying. Tears stung the back of her eyes, her mind spinning at how easily she had got herself into such a mess.

At the station, she caught a taxi and was relieved to arrive home. Turning the key, she stepped into the hallway, only to be greeted by the blast of heavy metal from the rooms above. She flung her jacket over the banister and climbed the stairs. In Christopher's bedroom she came upon a scene which made her smile, even if the din was ear-splitting.

The boys were dancing about in a wild jig, tins of lager in their hands. Anna stepped across to the stereo and turned it down and then stared at them, her expression demanding an explanation.

"Sorry, Mum. Were we making too much noise?" said Martyn, his eyebrows raised in innocence. Anna grunted in reply. "We were just celebrating."

"Celebrating what? You haven't started your exams never mind getting the results."

Christopher pulled a face. "We're celebrating the fact our school days are over and after our 'A' levels it's goodbye Wakefield."

Anna found it difficult to swallow at the thought her boys were leaving home. "Well, I don't mind a little fun, but keep the noise down. They can hear you in Doncaster."

Martyn grinned and crossed the room to place his arm round his mother's shoulder. "You're going to miss us, aren't you?"

Anna's expression was one of complete indifference. "I certainly will not! Can't wait for you to leave. The sooner you go, the sooner I'll get a bit of peace and quiet."

Downstairs she headed for the kitchen. Hands wrapped round a cup of tea, she contemplated this extraordinary day. Now she was home, the interview seemed unreal, like a dream…or a nightmare. The opportunity would have been wonderful though. New place, new people, new experience. Never mind, she sighed, it was only an experiment after all. She thought of her boys. How was she going to manage without their presence, the house filled with their noise, their mess? After their exams they were off to Romania for a month on a life experience expedition organised by their school. They were to help out on a farm and in an orphanage and although they were travelling with a group of eight boys and girls, Anna knew that it would be a worrying time for her. Sighing in resignation she decided to have a long soak in the bath.

Dave arrived home later that night, smelling slightly of alcohol. He spoke hardly a dozen words, before falling exhausted into bed. Anna turned her back on him, angry that he had stopped at the pub when he had promised to come straight home after work. The guilt that had plagued her throughout the day began to lessen and as her eyes closed in sleep she thought of the folk in Bishop Sutton, of Jason

Harrington and the life she could have if she could only muster the courage.

CHAPTER TWO

It was the day after her job interview that Anna decided to visit Elaine.

"So where were you all yesterday?" The question from her sister startled her.

Anna licked her lips. "Do you remember Susie Kimble? I used to run the playgroup with her?"

Elaine frowned. "Can't say I do remember," she said.

Anna eased herself onto the barstool and helped herself to a biscuit.

"She...She invited me to an Ann Summers' party, but she lives in Bradford now so I made a day of it."

"Buy anything interesting?" asked Elaine, trying to suppress a cheeky grin and failing miserably.

Anna shook her head. "No, I didn't." She gave a wry smile.

"You should have told me. I'd have come with you."

"Didn't think." She paused before adding. "Would you have gone?"

"Certainly! It would have been interesting. Might have found something for me and Terry." She winked. "There's one thing about my Terry, he certainly knows how to push all the right buttons."

Her confession caused Anna to purse her lips despondently. Dave had always had a selfish attitude to sex, never considering her feelings or desires. It had been the same story since that foolish night in the back of his mini nearly nineteen years ago. Anna wrinkled her nose at the memory, one night of carelessness and she had lurched from virgin to motherhood.

It wasn't as though it had been pleasurable for her, it had been uncomfortable and over in five minutes. As they had quickly straightened their clothing afterwards, Dave had laughed at her embarrassment. They had been going out together just six months and she had never let him go all the way in their petting sessions, since in her inimitable way, she had always dreamed of a white wedding in the true sense of the meaning.

Anna sighed, remembering how 1977 had turned out to be a terrible year. They had married quickly, at her mother's insistence. Anna winced at the memory of her mother's harsh comments about the shame, the disappointment at having a daughter 'in trouble'. The worst aspect was the ache she felt as her friends left to go to university or start careers. How could a moment of carelessness have ruined her future?

"Are you going to see that counsellor I recommended?" said Elaine, breaking into Anna's melancholy thoughts.

"I don't think so. Doesn't seem to be any point."

"Look Anna, I know you and Dave are still having problems. Please go and see her!"

"No, I'm not going to wash my dirty linen in public! We'll sort ourselves out," said Anna adamantly.

Elaine gave a resigned sigh. She always knew when she was beaten and decided to change the subject for the rest of Anna's visit.

Anna drove home, her mind filled with conflicting emotions. She needed to ring Sharon, but as yet had done nothing about it. It was as if she was still hanging onto the dream, the hope of a better life. There was no denying that working for Jason Harrington would have been terrific experience, but it had come at the wrong time. How could she leave the boys just as they were sitting such important exams? She should be there to see them off to Romania. And when they returned, she wanted to be around when they collected their exam results, before their departure for university.

For all that she distrusted Dave, her husband worked hard in his career as a structural engineer, often called to meetings until the late evening and his success had meant a move for the family to the more affluent area of Sandal and to a house that even her mother admired. But she hadn't thought married life would turn out like this. When the twins were placed in her arms she had smiled at them and made her plans. There was no reason why she couldn't have it all, motherhood and a career. She would care for her boys and when the time was right she would go to university and get her degree. But the years had flown by and by the time she reached her thirties she had started to panic.

Elaine was right, she and Dave had had problems from the start of their marriage and it was senseless to say that everything was OK. For a while she had ignored the difficulties, concentrating on her plan to study at college and mastering typing and office administration, getting excellent grades. The certificate she had earned for all her hard work had filled her with a certain amount of satisfaction. Her work in the Prison Service had been satisfactory and her four years at the local primary as school secretary had been rewarding. But all she achieved, couldn't erase the fact that her husband had a roving eye.

Sighing rebelliously, she pulled into the drive and jumped out of the car. She took the shopping from the boot and carried it into the house, dropping it onto the kitchen table. Pulling her tongue out at the pile of ironing, she started sorting the shopping before thrusting yet another load of washing into the machine.

As she waited for the kettle to boil, she reached inside her bag and pulled out the newspaper cutting. She had seen the job advert when the boys had finished school for the Easter holidays. Even now, reading it again, made her smile. The advert had appealed to her immediately, although she realised it was a long way to go for a job interview. It was after the third reading that Anna had had the crazy idea of applying. It would be an experiment. Not for one moment did she think she would get an interview, but that didn't seem to matter at the time. All she wanted was to give it a try. She would send them a CV and leave it at that.

She had used the computer in Martyn's bedroom, trying to ignore her elder son's domain that resembled a battle zone. Christopher was a lot tidier, for all he was just ten minutes younger than his brother. They were not identical twins and their personalities were very different, even though they were devoted to each other. And yet Anna hadn't been surprised when they had chosen different universities. She knew they felt it was time to go their separate ways.

It was while sitting at the computer that everything went almost supernatural. When she reached the part about marital status, her mind had rebelled. She sat back in the chair, staring at the screen. She wanted more, she wanted it to be so different. Her dreams had vanished like sea mist at the age of eighteen and perhaps it was time to redress the balance. Give fate a hand. Quickly taking the cursor back to where she had typed 'married', she typed 'widow'.

She remembered feeling appalled and sitting back in the chair, pushing her hands between the knees of her jeans and biting her lip. Why had she done that? It was such a terrible lie.

"But it's only a little lie that won't do any harm, nothing to worry about really," she had whispered.

She had posted her CV and letter never expecting to hear anything, so when the reply arrived two weeks later inviting her for an interview, Anna had almost fallen off the kitchen chair.

Yes, she had had to tell a lie to gain one precious day of freedom but as she had boarded the train bound for Bristol Temple Meads that Thursday morning, she had felt it was all worth while. It had been exhilarating, the wonderful sense of freedom and independence accompanying her all the way to Bristol.

But everything had come crashing round her when Mrs Wilby, the housekeeper, had asked such personal questions. She hadn't realised that her lies would have to be qualified since she had naively believed that no one would be interested in her private life. Multiple sclerosis! Where had that come from?

Suddenly, Anna remembered Jason Harrington's expression as he had shaken her hand, his wonderful smile and his friendly manner. A feeling of longing swept through her and she wandered over to the window. The next door neighbour was in the act of chasing a cat from his immaculate garden and she sighed sadly. She must make that phone call soon, it was only fair to Sharon and Jason. Looking down at the crumpled advert in her hand, Anna read it once more and then threw it in the kitchen bin.

"I'm not sure what to pack for Romania?" said Anna, folding yet another pair of jeans.

Martyn looked over her shoulder. "The weather is a bit like here, I think. Better to take warm stuff while we're working on the farm."

"Yes, but our oldest things," added Christopher. "The place will be full of sh...manure."

Anna chuckled and studied her two sons who were already taller than her.

"You'll take care of each other, won't you?" She slipped her arms round their waists. "Keep in touch and...Oh, God, I'm going to miss you both."

They hugged her close. "You mustn't worry about us and we'll send you texts every day," said Martyn.

"Yeah, and if anything goes wrong...," Christopher started and received a warning glance from his brother. "But nothing's going to go wrong, of course. We'll be fine."

"I expect you to take charge." Anna turned to Martyn.

"Why must he take charge?" asked Christopher indignantly.

"Because your head's always in the clouds," scoffed Martyn, grinning.

Anna smiled through her lonely tears.

And she was lonely after they had left. How still the house was. At first, it was hard to get used to it and often she would wander around the quiet, tidy rooms like a ghost. The emptiness she felt was made worse by the fact that usually a married couple would feel delighted to have the house to themselves, but there was no comfort in her marriage and she knew why. Dave had destroyed her trust in the early days when she had found out about his first affair. That's if it had been his first affair, since she had never been sure when the betrayal had begun. The twins were just over a year old when Elaine had discovered it and reluctantly told her, hoping that their closeness as sisters would soften the blow.

Although denying it at first, she had been dumbstruck when he had confessed.

"But it meant absolutely nothing," he had said. "You're my wife and I love you."

"Then why did you sleep with her?"

"I've no excuse. It just happened, that's all."

At the time, she was too weary, too burdened down with motherhood to argue and his contrition, his reassurances that it would never happen again convinced her to persevere with her marriage. It was a sad fact that even if she wanted to leave him, she would have nowhere to go, no money to live on. She could have taken the twins to her mother's but her mother was seeing Greg at the time, the man she would eventually marry and it seemed unfair to palm herself and two small babies onto her.

The next time she discovered his infidelity, the boys were twelve and the incident had spurred her on to study for qualifications and enter employment. She had to plan her own future, knowing that if her husband betrayed her once more then she would leave him without a thought.

The pub was full and finding a place was difficult. Anna wondered if going out on a Friday night was a sensible thing to do, but Dave had insisted that a night out would do her good. The boys were away, he told her and they could go out when they wanted to now. They met Elaine and Terry inside and were relieved that two seats had been reserved for them. And it turned out to be a pleasant evening, Anna finally relaxing and enjoying herself.

"Heard from the boys yet?" said Elaine.

Anna nodded. "Yesterday. Just a postcard from sunny Romania. Seems they're working hard."

"It will do them good. If anything they'll come back with a load of stories."

"Three weeks two days and then they'll be home."

Elaine looked at her askance. "You're not counting the days, are you?"

Anna couldn't help giggling. "No not really. But I do miss them."

She looked across to the bar where Dave and Terry where waiting to be served. Terry suddenly left, obviously on his way to the toilet and Dave gave their order to the barman. It was then Anna noticed a woman with red hair to her husband's right, a woman with her back to him and yet seemed to be intruding into his space. Anna shook her head and wondered at the rudeness of some people. And then she saw Dave reach out and grasp the woman's hand, almost nonchalantly, both he and the woman only briefly turning to each other before resuming their back-to-back position. It was just a fleeting gesture, but Anna knew what Dave was doing. She gave a gasp and a pain shot through her chest, making it hard to breathe.

"Are you OK?" said Elaine. "You look pale."

Anna didn't dare look her in the face. "I can't take any more," she whispered.

Anna boarded the train and found a seat. As the doors shut and the engine started to pull out of the station, a rush of excitement gripped her insides. She was on her way, no turning back now. The trees and houses flashed by, her thoughts tumbled in her head and she remembered the agonising decision she had made over the last ten days. It hadn't been easy at all.

The day after the terrible revelation in the pub, she had phoned the house in Bishop Sutton, hoping that she could speak to Jason and ask if the position was still available. She guessed it wouldn't be, but she had to give it a try, before searching the paper for another place to live. One thing she was adamant about and that was she would not stay with her husband, even if it meant the boys had to come home with her gone. Her heart ached at the very idea, but it couldn't be helped, she refused to put up with his behaviour any longer.

She was more than surprised when Sharon answered the phone.

"Anna, how lovely to hear from you again."

"Goodness, what are you doing there? I thought you'd be long gone by now."

Sharon giggled. "The person we finally hired decided she didn't like the idea of working on her own and quit after the first week. So, I'm here for a little while longer."

"I'm so sorry. But I bet Jason was pleased."

"Well, he was glad for himself but sad for me. So, why are you ringing? No, let me guess. You've changed your mind and want to take the position?"

Anna bit her lip. "I know I have an unbelievable cheek…"

Sharon chuckled again. "I think the luck of the Irish must be with me. I really must go back to Dublin and I've decided to leave in two weeks' time. Jason has asked me to sort out temporary cover from the Bristol office. Now, how surprised would he be, if he found you here instead?"

"He would be surprised," laughed Anna. "But would he be pleased about it? After all, I did turn down the job in the first place."

"Well, he was very disappointed about that, so I think he'll be delighted."

"When shall I start?"

Sharon paused for a moment. "It will have to be sorted quickly, I'm afraid. He's away for five days the week after next, so could you manage a week Monday?"

The headmistress was not pleased at all.

"You're leaving me, with still a month to go before the end of term? You really should give me four weeks' notice."

Anna's face blanched as she tried to explain, "I must take this job now or I'll lose it again."

"Again?"

"Yes. I went for an interview a few months ago, but turned the job down. I'm so sorry to leave you in the lurch like this, but I have no choice."

The headmistress shook her head. "Well, I'm very sorry about it too, but Phyllis can fill the position until I find another secretary." She eyed Anna curiously. "Isn't Bristol a long way to go for a job? What about your family?"

Anna's mind began to spin, the last thing she wanted was folk to know where she was going and regretted that the location of her new job had slipped out. "That…That's only the head office. I shall be working at their branch in Leeds. They're shipping agents."

A look of surprise passed over the headmistress's face, but then she sighed. "Well, I suppose you must take every opportunity that comes your way. I guess this company will have links with Hull and Grimsby. Sounds very interesting."

Anna murmured a reply and stumbled to the staff toilets. There she stared at herself in the mirror, noticing her sickly complexion. All this subterfuge was taking its toll. She couldn't tell Elaine what she was doing and every minute she was afraid that Dave would find out.

But the decision was made and she spent the following week secretly packing her case, hiding it in the cupboard under the stairs where she kept the vacuum cleaner.

On Monday morning, she saw Dave off to work as though it was another day. The taxi arrived and Anna placed the letter on the kitchen table, the one she had written only that morning. It was short and to the point, stating that she had had enough and the redheaded slapper in the pub could have him.

Now she was on the train and speeding along the tracks southbound, her heart thudding in her chest. When she reached Sheffield, she almost lost courage and decided to get off and return home, but something compelled her to stay in her seat. Deep inside her, she knew this endeavour was important. It was a pilgrimage of faith and despite her fears, destiny was drawing her down to the south-west of England.

The journey was very much straightforward, except the nearer she got to her destination, the weaker her resolve became. By the time she emerged from the station, her legs felt like jelly, her heart pounding like a drum roll. And then she saw Ben. It was like meeting an old friend and greeting him with a big hug, she allowed her emotions to bubble to the surface briefly, before climbing into the Mercedes. She listened with joy to his gossip about Mrs Wilby and how they were planning a surprise party on Friday for Sharon. Mr. Harrington had left that morning for New York and had no idea what they were up to.

Once in the house, she was almost squeezed to death by the forceful greeting from the housekeeper, who couldn't stop talking. Sharon rescued her and laughing with delight, urged her out of the kitchen and up the stairs, with Ben carrying her case one step behind. Although qualms about leaving her boys surfaced momentarily, Anna knew she must be positive. She would let them know her situation before they returned home so that they would be prepared and then arrange to meet up with them before they left for university. And if they asked why she had separated from their father, then she would avoid the absolute truth. Why burden them with the sordid details?

Sharon led her into a large and tastefully decorated bedroom, overlooking the back of the house and hence the beautiful garden. Anna almost let slip that it will be lovely to have her own private space, but stopped herself just in time and realised she must watch her tongue carefully, in case she inadvertently mentioned her husband. This could be a problem. She must somehow, think of herself as a widow.

"Well Anna, I'll leave you to get settled in. I'm pleased you like your room."

"It's perfect and it'll be very easy to keep clean."

Sharon giggled. "You're employed as a personal assistant, not a cleaner! We have a lovely lady from the village who comes every day to clean the house. You're not expected to do it. The only thing we do, is our own washing, but there's a washing machine and dryer in the utility room for that. You'll find an iron and ironing board in the cupboard."

"Does Jason do his own washing?" Anna asked curiously.

"No, Mrs Thompson washes and irons his clothes. She'll do anything for him. But that's the way it is with Jason. He has a fatal charm about him."

Sharon left her to settle in and Anna unpacked her clothes, placing underwear and woollens in the drawers and hanging up her skirts and blouses in the large cupboard. And then she checked her phone and saw that Martyn had sent her a text. They were fine and had just returned from a wonderful visit to Bucharest. She quickly replied and then switched it off. Dave was bound to phone her as soon as he read the note she had left, but she was determined that the only calls she would take would be from either her sons or her sister. She went downstairs for lunch.

While they ate, she found out some very interesting information regarding her new employer. First of all, he was married but was now going through a divorce. It seemed the marriage had been perfectly fine, even happy, but then events had turned sour.

"She's a lovely lady is Mrs Harrington," Ben admitted sadly. "Always laughing and such fun to be with. You always knew when she was around. And as for Jason, many thought him the luckiest man alive."

"So why did it all go wrong?"

Mrs Wilby and Ben exchanged wary glances but then Sharon spoke up. "It's better that she knows. We're not tittle-tattling just getting her acquainted with the situation." She waited for them to agree before continuing. "We don't know why things went wrong. Kiera was the accountant for Harrington Rhodes and sometimes she would accompany Jason on his business trips. It seems she fell for one of the executives at a client company."

"It's as simple as that. We were all surprised but I guess these things happen," said Ben.

"And I suppose, that was the end of their marriage?" asked Anna matter-of-factly.

Sharon nodded. "They separated a year ago."

"She's Canadian, you know," said Mrs Wilby and then added quietly, "But it was a very bad business. He was married too, so that meant two innocent people got hurt."

"And there's no chance of a reconciliation?" Anna asked.

"Unfaithfulness can rot a marriage," said Ben. "Even if they tried again, it would never be the same. Better that they divorce and start afresh."

"Where is she now?"

"She went to live with *him* in an apartment in Bristol. Jason agreed that she should take their little girl with her," said Ben.

Anna felt startled. "Goodness, they have a daughter?"

"Yes, Hollie, she's seven. A beautiful child and the apple of her daddy's eye," said Mrs Wilby. She suddenly glanced around the kitchen. "I really miss her coming in here and pinching my baking before it could cool down."

"But Jason will see that they're both OK," sighed Ben. "Kiera will have a good divorce settlement and Hollie will be able to stay at her private school."

"Does he see his little girl often?"

They all nodded, but it was Sharon who explained, "She comes to visit every Sunday and Jason really looks forward to her visits. But sometimes when he has to be elsewhere or she can't visit because of circumstances, then you just know his heart's breaking."

That afternoon, Anna was keen to start work, although Sharon insisted she must be too tired from the journey. It was finally agreed that they would spend just a few hours in the office so that Anna could familiarise herself with the routine. By the end of two hours she had regretted her hasty enthusiasm. Her head ached, her brain whirled from the confusion of trying to understand everything. She felt at home on the computer and the fax and photocopier were simple enough. But she wondered if she would ever sort out the intricacies of the paperwork. By the time they had decided to call it a day, Anna began to have doubts about her capabilities and it crossed her mind if she had made a terrible mistake. Sharon, with her wonderful Irish humour, didn't seem to care when she made an error, but simply grinned and told her not to worry. Anna hoped that the following day would be better.

After their evening meal, she went out for a short walk in the wonderful June sunshine in an attempt to clear her head. She thought of Dave and wondered how he had taken the news of her leaving. She suspected he wouldn't take it too well. And then her feelings sank as she thought of the boys and the fact she would have to tell them soon that she no longer lived at home. Anna breathed in the fresh air and turned back towards the house that would be her home for the duration.

The next few days seemed to fly by. Anna concentrated her energies on learning the new routine and to her delight, discovered she was improving. When she eventually completed a whole series of jobs without a single flaw, events began to take on a new meaning. She began to enjoy the work and as Sharon gradually relinquished the responsibility, Anna knew her decision to come to Bristol had been sound. All this was valuable experience and one she wouldn't have missed for the world. The invoicing, ordering and numerous phone calls became less of an ordeal for her and as she gained in confidence, she even discovered she had a good rapport with the office in Bristol.

"He sounds very nice," Anna said to Sharon after a lengthy phone call.

"That's our Mr Rhodes, Jason's partner," said Sharon with a twinkle in her eye. "You'll meet him eventually. Very straight-laced is our Mr Rhodes. Graham is a lot older than Jason and does the financial side of the business. It's Jason who goes to all the meetings and sorts out the contracts. That's why we have this office, so that he has somewhere to work when he gets back late or at the weekends, when the Bristol office is closed."

"He seems to work very hard."

"He certainly does."

As the days progressed, Anna started operating the small Dictaphone and type the constant letters that flowed through the office. Jason's voice was warm and friendly, reflecting his smile, and listening to it, she suddenly felt excited at actually working for him once he arrived back from New York.

During her first week, Anna posted letters to the boys and to her mother. In them she said that everything was fine, she had found a job and a place to live and would keep in touch no matter what. Dropping the envelopes in the post box, she hoped they would understand.

On Friday morning, Jason arrived back from New York. Ben had gone to fetch him from the airport and Sharon mischievously forced Anna into her chair and told her to look busy while she hid in the downstairs toilet. It all seemed very childish, but Anna went along with the joke.

Jason entered the room. "Sharon, I need..." Anna turned her head and smiled. "No, you're not Sharon," he said, frowning.

"Tell me what you need and I'll see what I can do for you," said Anna, sporting her most efficient voice.

"Erm," he coughed nervously. "I need to talk to Graham."

Anna picked up the phone and dialled the number. Soon she was talking to Graham's secretary who put her through. Anna transferred the call. "Graham's on the line, Jason."

Jason sank down in his chair, his eyes never leaving Anna, who had turned to the computer and carried on typing while trying to keep her face straight. Sharon returned from her hiding place and walked across to her boss, who had finished his call.

"So, what have you been up to?" he asked, his eyebrows raised.

Sharon giggled. "Jason, may I introduce you to your new PA, Mrs Anna Stevens."

"Welcome to Harrington Rhodes, Mrs Stevens," he murmured.

Despite the practical joke, Anna was keenly aware that Sharon would be departing for Ireland the following morning, leaving her entirely responsible for running the office and working with her new employer. The thought of it made her feel nervous, but she constantly reminded herself she had set this chain of events in motion, she sank or swam by her own actions.

The three worked together for the rest of the day, until about four in the afternoon, when Sharon brought some letters over to Jason for signing.

He took them from her, put them on his desk, then stood up and tucked her hand through his arm. "Never mind about those. Come with me. You too Anna."

Slightly bemused, Sharon allowed herself to be led across the hallway and into the kitchen, followed by the equally delighted Anna.

The room seemed full of people. The table groaned under the weight of an elaborate buffet, Ben stood by the sink pouring out wine, while Mrs Wilby handed round the glasses. Everyone clapped and cheered as Sharon came in, her cheeks tinged scarlet with painful embarrassment at all the attention.

Jason quickly introduced Anna to the guests. Many of the people from the village she already knew, but it was interesting to meet some of the personnel from the Bristol office. Then she noticed a tall woman with long, dark hair and large, brown eyes, the colour of melting chocolate. And she knew beyond any doubt that she was looking at Kiera Harrington.

Jason gave a short speech, very much the usual words an employer would say when losing a special and valued employee. Sharon responded with a shy, quick 'thank you'. It was obvious the whole occasion was too overwhelming for her and as she opened her presents, she wiped tears from her cheeks.

Eventually, Anna found herself in Sharon's company and felt the need to add her own sentiments to the occasion.

"I know we'll all miss you, especially me. You've been so patient this last week and a marvellous teacher. Thanks for everything."

"I think you've done very well. You've certainly picked it up quickly. All you need is more practice. Jason will look after you though. Oh dear! I didn't realise how much I'd miss everyone." Tears appeared in her eyes again and Anna squeezed her hand.

"When are you getting married?"

"At Christmas and I'm inviting everyone here, including you now you're a member of the family."

Anna turned slightly and could see Jason and Kiera talking together. It was good to see that they were trying to remain friends and now and again Kiera's warm laughter echoed across the room. But it was obvious that Jason was still hurting and seemed tense standing next to his wife. Suddenly he caught Anna's eye and smiled. He took Kiera's arm and guided her in Anna's direction.

"Anna, I'd like you to meet Kiera. Kiera this is Anna my new PA."

They shook hands.

"I've been hearing a lot about you," said Kiera giving Anna a friendly smile. Anna smiled too detecting the strong

Canadian accent. "But let me give you some advice. Don't let him bully you and never, never let him take you for granted."

"Oh, I don't think he'd do that," laughed Anna.

"Well, not consciously. But he has a way about him and before you know it, you're under his spell." Jason gave an embarrassed cough and Kiera cast him an enigmatic smile.

How sad, thought Anna, in better circumstances we could have been the best of friends.

An Italian restaurant in Bristol was the venue for that evening and Anna finally met the financial director of Harrington Rhodes Shipping Agents. Graham Rhodes was tall and lean with greying hair and an almost military bearing and asked in a very concerned manner, if Anna was settling in OK. When she answered that she was, he impressed on her that she mustn't be shy about phoning him if she had any problems when Jason was away. Anna answered him with a smile.

But the smile faded when he began to question her about her financial plans. Did she own her own house back in Wakefield? Was she considering selling it and buying a house in this area? If so, he certainly knew the contacts that would give her a good deal. Anna began to feel uncomfortable, although she realised he wasn't being nosy, just acutely interested in all matters financial. She stuttered a reply behind her glass of wine.

Working for Jason was all Sharon said it would be and Anna found that each day seemed to get better. During her time in the office, she could forget that she was married; that an angry husband was sitting stewing at home. And there was no doubt that he was stewing. Every night she would turn on her phone and there were at least fifteen missed calls and texts waiting for her which she immediately deleted.

Her sons had received her letter and after a few days, a short text arrived from Martyn saying that they would ring soon. She answered just as briefly, stating the time she would be alone in her room and they could talk in private. And when that call came one sunny evening, Anna had decided how she would deal with her sons. She would be firm but gentle and hope they were mature enough to understand.

But one thing was certain, she refused to assassinate her husband's character even though he deserved it. She was acutely aware that her boys loved their father and regarded him highly. His infidelities had been kept from them and Anna didn't think it her place to tell them unless it was absolutely necessary.

"You must ask your dad why I left," she told her elder son. "He knows the reason why."

"But why can't you tell us?" asked Martyn. As was the case on a mobile, he sounded a long way away and Anna's heart ached that he wasn't in the room with her.

"If you don't get a satisfactory answer from him then I'll tell you."

There was a pause at the end of the line. "You won't be home when we get back?"

"No, I won't. I'm so sorry, sweetheart. I really wish I could be, but you'll be fine. If you have any problems, your grandma is there to help and we'll meet up when you get your results and go out and celebrate."

"It won't be the same without you there."

Guilt tore through Anna. "I know, but I had to do this. And please, Martyn, don't tell your dad where I am. I don't want him to find me."

"OK. Chris wants to talk to you."

It was good to hear from her sons, but after the call, Anna felt slightly sick that she had done this terrible thing to them. Perhaps she should have waited until they had left for university? But this wonderful job had happened along and she had to grab her opportunity when it came. It might have been too late if she had waited until the boys had left home. She wouldn't hurt them for the world and when she met them again, she would try and make up for it. Although how she would do that, she had no idea, how do you compensate children for breaking up their family? The house filling with noise and laughter interrupted her troubled thoughts. Jason had brought Hollie to stay for the weekend and for the next two days, there would be chaos.

Hollie was the spitting image of her mother with long dark hair and the most beautiful big brown eyes. It was obvious that everyone doted on her and Anna soon realised why. She was a happy, contented child, but loved playing pranks on those she cared for. Anna found the charming nature of the little girl hard to ignore and was amused and secretly pleased when Hollie included her in her naughty pranks.

One exceptionally hot Sunday in the middle of July, Anna came into the kitchen to be greeted by Mrs Wilby filling a large wicker hamper with all manner of fare; pies, sandwiches, containers of salad and flasks of coffee. Anna stared in bewilderment.

"Oh, my dear!" gasped Mrs Wilby, rushing from cupboard to cupboard. "Could you get your own breakfast this morning? I'm so busy preparing for this picnic. Jason's idea, with it being such a beautiful day. We're just waiting for him to come back with Hollie then we'll be on our way. Ben is bringing the car round in twenty minutes."

Anna poured herself some coffee. The thought of a picnic pleased her and she smiled as she watched Mrs Wilby scurrying around the kitchen. Jason arrived back with Hollie who bounded into the kitchen excited by the news they were going on a picnic. Within the hour Anna was sitting beside the fidgety little girl and Mrs Wilby in the back of the Mercedes, with Jason up front with Ben.

"Where are we going?" Anna asked, trying to remember when she had last been on a picnic.

"Oh, it's our usual place," said Hollie with a bright smile. "You'll really like it. And we can play tennis. Can you play tennis, Anna?" Anna smiled and nodded.

"It's just in the foothills of the Mendips," said Mrs Wilby. "Such a wonderful spot to have a day out. We often go there if the weather is fine. It doesn't seem to matter what the season, the scenery is always so pretty."

They parked the car and climbed a small hill. Jason and Ben carried the hamper while Anna clutched a folding chair in one hand and with the other helped Mrs Wilby to puff and pant her way to the top. Hollie ran ahead looking for the best spot. The view was glorious. Spread before them were the meadows and woods of the valley, sparkling in the warm summer sun. Mrs Wilby made herself comfortable in the chair and after shuffling about, pulled out her knitting from a huge canvas bag.

Hollie unzipped the racquets from their bag and Jason threw her the ball that he had tucked in his pocket.

"Play tennis with me, Anna," she said, pulling at Anna's hand.

"Hey! What about me?" shouted Jason.

"No, Daddy! I want Anna to play. You hit the ball too hard and it goes down the hill."

Jason gave Anna a resigned smile and lay down on the rug, staring up into the vivid blue sky, his hands behind his head.

Anna and Hollie started their game and in moments there were squeals of delight as they ran backwards and forwards. After a while, Hollie had had enough and went to join the others on the rug. Anna felt the need for solitude to put her thoughts in perspective. Making her way further along the hill, she finally reached a spot that was absolutely breathtaking. The peace and quiet seemed to ease her mind. Her sons were coming home in a few days and she had made plans to meet them. She hoped Dave would tell them the truth and not leave the terrible burden to her.

"It's lovely isn't it?"

Anna turned to find Jason standing behind her. "I've never seen anything so beautiful. You're very lucky to live here."

Jason came to her side. "But you're not far from the Yorkshire Dales or even the Lake District, surely?" he queried, frowning slightly.

"Oh yes! But we...I mean.... I never seemed to have the time to go anywhere."

"I suppose you wouldn't, with nursing your husband."

Anna tried to change the subject. "I'm having a wonderful time. Thank you for suggesting a picnic."

"I'm glad you came. All the way from Bristol, Hollie kept asking if you were coming with us. I wasn't sure if you'd want to so I had to tell her so. She seemed very disappointed with the idea you might not come."

"I wouldn't have missed it for the world."

"She's very fond of you and that's good considering the circumstances."

Anna paused for a moment before asking, "Is the divorce really definite? You seem so suited when you're together."

Jason glanced away and then looked towards his daughter who was now making a daisy chain and insisting that Ben try it on.

"Appearances can be deceptive. But we decided to stay amicable for Hollie's sake. Kiera has settled down with…Well, she's decided she wants to marry and who am I to stand in her way."

"It's so sad."

Jason shrugged indifferently. "No, it's just life."

Hollie called to say it was eating time and they joined her for the picnic.

CHAPTER THREE

The letter arrived for Anna two weeks later, when she felt at her happiest. The boys had returned home and she had managed to meet up with them. Elaine had brought them down and they had had a wonderful lunch together at a pizza restaurant in Bristol. They had talked endlessly of their trip to Romania with just a slight hint of worry about their impending exam results. Anna wasn't surprised when they said they had decided to work for the rest of the summer.

"Marks and Spencer's have taken us on," said Martyn, almost in amazement.

Chris nodded. "We stack the shelves but I've been on check-out and I'm quite brilliant at it."

"The trouble is we can't help spending what we earn. Working in a shopping centre like the Ridings is too tempting," complained Martyn.

There was uncomfortable silence until Anna asked, "Have you spoken to your dad?"

The boys glanced at each other before Martyn replied. "We asked him why you had to move out and he said that there were problems in the past, but you were making a fuss over nothing."

Anna felt her blood boiling. "He said what!"

Elaine reached out and squeezed her hand. "I told them what those problems were." Anna looked at her in horror. "I felt it only right that they know and since Dave wasn't going to deliver the goods, someone had to say something. They're not children."

Anna sat back in her chair. "Well, now you know. So, what do you think?"

Again Martyn answered for them both, his lip curling slightly. "We asked Dad if it was true and he admitted that ages ago he..." He looked at his brother. "We've decided to move in with Grandma. She said it would be OK."

"Yes, that might be for the best," breathed Anna with relief. "She'll look after you." She gave a bright smile.

"When you get your results, then we'll meet up again to celebrate."

She didn't want to think about her husband and her life in Wakefield so the rest of the meal was spent in telling them about how much she enjoyed her job, the wonderful atmosphere that permeated through the house in Bishop Sutton as the summer wove its magic. She had helped Jason plan the trips to the seaside with Hollie and organise the barbecues that were held in the garden and were presided over by Ben. Anna had watched with delight as he cooked the sausages and burgers over the flames, sporting the rather risqué apron depicting a nude man with a fig leaf over the necessary parts of his anatomy.

Mrs Wilby was always busy in the kitchen, preparing salads and quiches, the mouth-watering smell of baking sausage rolls, bread and strawberry tarts sending enticing invitations around the house.

At the end of the visit, Anna walked with her family to the car and after giving them all hugs, she watched with her heart in her mouth, as they drove away. Sadness stayed with her in the taxi back to Bishop Sutton and she was glad to arrive home and join the others for coffee in the kitchen.

All the talk that afternoon was of their visit to the Grange, which was about ten miles away on the other side of the Mendip Hills. It seemed it was a tradition to spend a week each summer at the Grange with Jason and his mother and this year was very special since it was her seventieth birthday. She intended to hold a celebratory lunch followed by a party and everyone was invited, including Anna, much to her surprise. It was then that Jason remembered a letter had come for her.

He had dropped it on her desk and after their coffee, both she and Jason went back into the office to finish off for the day.

He nodded at the envelope. "It's been re-directed from the main office."

She picked it up, immediately recognising Dave's bold handwriting. A sharp intake of breath took her by surprise as her mind reeled in horror at the thought her husband had found her address. She knew Jason was watching her and she was well aware of why, since she had felt the colour drain from her face. She gave Jason a weak smile and murmured a 'thank you'.

"Aren't you going to open it?" he asked rather bewildered.

"It's only from a…friend. It's probably just full of gossip. I can read it later."

She went back to her work, but she could feel him watching her and she was conscious of her neck and face burning. For the first time since meeting him, she began to feel indignant and wished he wasn't in the room.

Anna slipped upstairs just before the evening meal. Locking herself in her bedroom, she opened the letter with trembling hands.

Anna,

I'm sure you're going to be surprised as hell to get this letter, since you've never bothered to tell me where you are. I found out by accident. You left the info on the computer and I was very surprised to read it. What do you mean you're a widow? Is that some way of saying you wish me dead?

I know you're angry with me, but I don't think I deserve this from you. I don't know what you're talking about when you mention a redheaded woman. What redheaded woman? I think it's just an excuse, as I won't believe you went down there just for a job. I know there's another bloke involved and if I ever get my hands on him then he'll answer to me for his actions.

Dave

Anna held the letter in a limp hand as the enormity of its contents sank in. Leaving her CV on the computer wasn't the problem, it was the changes she had made. She lay back on her bed, her thoughts and nerves a jangled mess at her husband's threats. How could he accuse her of having someone else after the affairs he had had? But that would be so typical of him. One rule for him and one for her. Thank goodness she had left him and although she had probably lost her home, she didn't really care. Her children and family were supporting her and that was all that mattered.

She pulled herself up into a sitting position and remembered the day of the picnic. It had been a wonderful day and as her emotions became calmer, she wondered how her future would be. Divorce would be the next step, she supposed. It seemed that she and Jason would be going through similar experiences. Sniffing into a tissue, she remembered that Jason knew nothing of her husband, he still thought of her as a widow. She carried the letter to the wastepaper basket and crushed it into a tight ball before flinging it in. Feeling much better, she went to tidy herself up.

In the kitchen, Anna ate her evening meal with the others. She guessed her eyes must still be a little red, since she had spent a good part of five minutes crying. But Ben and Mrs Wilby didn't seem to notice and chatted away throughout the meal.

Only Jason studied her, his eyes narrowed. "Well, Anna. Have you decided to come to the Grange with us?" he asked, as they finished their coffee.

"What do you mean!" Mrs Wilby broke in sharply. "Of course she's coming with us."

"Now, now, Mrs Wilby. Let's not jump to any conclusions. Anna is new to the job and she might have made her own plans. After all, she has got family in Wakefield." He turned to her. "If you want to spend a few days with your sons, then it's OK by me."

Jason's voice had been gentle, almost comforting and as she searched his expression, her mind raced with the thought of telling him about her husband. But then he might react badly when he discovered her lie and would be disgusted with her. He had already gone through so much with Kiera's betrayal and he surely wouldn't tolerate an employee's deceit. Would he sack her? But worse than that, much worse than that, was the humiliation she would feel when his eyes told her he was disappointed and hurt by her deception. She knew he regarded her highly and she couldn't bear the thought that his respect would disappear with one swift blow.

Anna licked her lips and tried to answer calmly. "I thought I might go back up to Wakefield, to visit my boys when they get their exam results."

"Well, if that's what you want to do, then you must do it," said Jason.

She scrutinised their faces for reassurance and found it. She turned to Jason. "But that's not until mid-August and there would be no problem seeing your home and meeting your mother before that, if you don't mind me coming."

"Great!" said Ben.

Anna tried to read Jason's expression, but all she saw was his wonderful smile.

"It'll be lovely us all going there together," said Mrs Wilby. Turning to Anna she added, "I hope you've got a posh frock for the birthday dance!"

Anna almost choked on her coffee. "Birthday dance?"

Jason gave a chuckle. "Remember? The dance my mother is holding at the Grange."

"Well, I've got a few nice evening dresses but they're back in Wakefield," said Anna.

"They're no good there, my dear," laughed Mrs Wilby.

"I didn't think to bring anything formal," said Anna pulling a face.

"Well, it's the one time we can all get dressed up," said Mrs Wilby.

"Oh dear, then I suppose my clogs and shawl will be out of the question."

Jason and Ben exchanged amused glances.

"Not to worry," said Mrs Wilby. "We'll go into Bristol tomorrow and spend some time shopping. I do love shopping."

Back in her room, Anna tipped out the rubbish from the wastepaper basket and found the crumpled letter. She smoothed it out and read it again, anger pouring from her as the words stung her once more. And then she decided to destroy it, after all, she couldn't let Mrs Thompson find it and burning it would make her feel better. Anna made her way down to the kitchen. There was no one about since Mrs Wilby always took herself off to the lounge to watch telly after their evening meal and Ben was working in the garden.

She stooped down and took an ashtray from the cupboard. Putting the ashtray in the sink, she dropped the letter in the base, collected the matches and set fire to it. As the orange flame consumed each part, she felt purged from all the pain.

Anna smiled as she rinsed the black flaky scraps down the plug-hole.

"Good riddance to you," she said, grinning. It was then she heard the high pitched wailing noise coming from the left-hand side of the kitchen. At first she looked up in bewilderment at the round, cream coloured box, situated to one side of the cooker and then realisation dawned on her. "Oh, bugger!" she said and looked towards the hallway knowing that Jason would be able to hear the smoke alarm in the office.

Anna dragged a chair across the floor and jumped up onto it, grabbing the folded newspaper from the work surface and using it to cause a draught.

Jason burst in at the door. He glanced around the kitchen and then at Anna. "What are you doing?" he shouted, trying to make himself heard above the din.

Anna suspended her actions and stared down at him. She could barely hear him. "This stupid alarm went off. I'm trying to stop it," she shouted back.

Suddenly the alarm did stop and a wonderful silence filled the room. Anna stayed up on the chair wondering how she was going to get out of this one. Jason strode across the floor and helped her down.

"And why was the alarm going off?" he said. Anna shrugged her shoulders and pressed her lips together in a non-committal grimace. Jason glanced around the kitchen. "Something has been burning, I can smell it. What on earth have you been doing?"

"It must have been the toast I made myself. Never was any good at cooking." She began to feel silly.

He narrowed his eyes. "Toast! But we've just had dinner." He moved the chair back to its place and spotted the ashtray in the sink. "What's this doing here?"

"Mrs Thompson must have left it there until she had time to wash it," said Anna, her mouth drying somewhat.

"Who would have used one today? No one's been to the house."

Anna thought rapidly. "Must be Ben's."

"I don't think so. Ben can only smoke outside or in his room and he has to clean his own ashtrays."

Anna thought again. "Mr Tyler came yesterday. I remember having to get him one. I must have forgotten to take it out of the office and Mrs Thompson probably found it this morning when she came to clean." Jason was about to make another comment when Anna said hurriedly, "I think I'll go for a walk, unless you want me to do anything for you?"

Jason didn't answer so she decided to make her escape.

As she turned to go, he caught her by the arm and put his hands on her shoulders. "Anna, I hope you regard me as your friend as well as your employer."

"Of course I do. You're a very kind and generous man and I've enjoyed working for you."

"Oh! A very kind and generous man. Is that how you think of me?"

"Well, yes. Also considerate and pleasant and..."

"Very nice into the bargain! How boring," he interrupted her. "Look Anna, I know lying is sometimes necessary, I've been in business long enough to know that. But what I want to know is why are you lying about the ashtray?"

Anna felt the colour rush to her face and she gulped down a large lump in her throat. "What do you mean?"

He paused for a few seconds. When he answered he spoke gently, as though he didn't want to hurt her feelings. "You were right, Mr Tyler did come to see me yesterday and he has smoked heavily for years. However, I happen to know he's under strict instructions from the doctor to give it up. So, yesterday he didn't smoke for the whole two hours he was with me." Tears were stinging Anna's eyes, but she shook them away. Jason pressed home his argument. "What I'm trying to say, is that I know you were burning something and a good guess would be the letter that came this morning. Now

I don't understand why you would want to burn a letter, unless it's caused you a great deal of pain. As a friend, I'd like you to know that I'm here, if you have a problem you would like to talk about. We think of ourselves as a family, Anna. That means we care for each other."

"I know. And thanks for the offer, but, honestly, there isn't anything that needs talking over." He gave a sigh and dropped his hands from her shoulders. "I'll go for that walk now, if you don't mind."

After she had left, Jason stood in the kitchen for a few minutes longer, deep in thought. He looked up at the smoke detector. "Toast, indeed! But we shall see. We shall see."

The walk to the village took ten minutes, but for Anna it seemed like a few seconds as her mind spun with her tumbled thoughts. She must be careful in the future, otherwise Jason would become suspicious that she was hiding something. Perhaps he already was? She heard the hooting of a car horn and turned her head to look, surprised and delighted when she saw Kiera sitting in her car on the far side of the road.

She ran across and Kiera opened the passenger door. "Jump in. I'll give you a lift home."

"Is everything OK?" asked Anna, sliding into the seat and buckling her belt.

Kiera visited the house only when she came to collect Hollie and Anna had got into the habit of sitting in the kitchen with her while she waited. Hollie always left it to the last moment to collect her things together so there was ample opportunity for a chat. Anna found Kiera a fascinating person and was bowled over by her stories about her childhood in Canada, her education at Berkeley College in California and the year she had backpacked around the world with three friends. In contrast, Anna's life seemed very domestic.

"I've come to see Jason," said Kiera. "To talk about the divorce."

Anna glanced at her and noticed her features turn grey, her eyes become even darker. It must be an awful business going through a divorce, thought Anna grimly. She wondered what her experience would be if she and Dave ever divorced. She knew it might be worse, since Dave could be very vindictive when he wanted to. For a terrible brief moment she really wished she were a widow.

But then sanity returned and she dismissed the thought from her mind. "Is Hollie looking forward to visiting tomorrow? Jason is thinking of taking her to the zoo," said Anna, smiling.

Kiera paused for a brief moment before answering. "Actually, she's gone there today." Seeing Anna's expression she gave a gentle chuckle. "Don't worry, I'm sure Jason will find somewhere else to take her."

They had arrived at the front of the house and Kiera parked the car. They decided to walk round the back since Anna knew that Mrs Wilby would have the kitchen door open and it made for a much easier access. As they entered the garden they saw Ben engrossed in putting a coat of creosote on the fence. His expression showed surprise when he saw Kiera, but he waved his arm in a warm welcome.

Mrs Wilby was just putting some maids of honour in the oven in readiness for Hollie's visit and was equally taken aback as the two women stepped over the threshold.

"Kiera's here to see Jason," explained Anna.

"He's still in the office," said Mrs Wilby. "Would you both like some coffee? Or there's cold drinks in the fridge."

They declined the offer and Kiera followed Anna through the hallway and into the office. Jason was on the phone as they entered and his flow of conversation abruptly stopped at Kiera's entrance.

Making a polite excuse to the person at the end of the phone, he replaced the receiver. "This is an unexpected visit," he said dryly.

Anna wasn't sure if he was pleased or angry, but she didn't wait to find out. Closing the door behind her, she made her way back to the kitchen.

"Well, I'd like to be a fly on the wall in there," said Mrs Wilby, laughing.

CHAPTER FOUR

Jason felt irritated. There was no reason for Kiera to visit him like this, their solicitors were in negotiations and everything would be sorted out in due course.

"Would you like to sit down?" he said quietly.

She took a seat opposite him and realised with some amusement that he preferred to stay behind his desk. How typical, she thought, he has to stay in control, as though he was still the boss.

"I've come to discuss the divorce settlement and I want to…"

Jason didn't let her finish. "For goodness sake! Did you have to drive all the way from Bristol to talk about that? We've already discussed the terms and I've instructed my solicitor. You should hear…"

This time it was Kiera's turn to interrupt. "You don't have to jump down my throat! Anyway, I don't want your damned money!"

He sat forward in surprise. "What on earth are you talking about? What are you going to live on if you don't accept the settlement?" Suddenly he realised. "Oh, I understand. Peter wants to look after you. Well, good for him! However, I would like to support my own daughter, if you don't mind."

Kiera looked down at her hands clenched together on her lap. "Of course you must support Hollie," she said softly.

Jason let out an exasperated breath. "OK, if that's the way you want it, I'll tell my solicitor that the arrangements have changed." He watched his wife curiously for a few seconds before asking, "I suppose you and Peter will marry as soon as the divorce goes through?"

Kiera looked up and he was stunned to see large tears brim from her eyes and roll slowly down her cheeks.

"Peter's gone back to his wife," she said almost in a whisper.

At first Jason felt elation but then realised that that was unworthy of him.

"I see," he said. He puzzled for a moment. "I don't understand. Then you'll need the money. Unless you're thinking of going back to work full-time?"

He knew that Kiera had found herself a part-time job as an accountant at a building society, but he couldn't imagine that she was earning enough money to keep herself in the manner she liked.

"No, I'm not thinking of going back full-time. In fact, I'm contemplating giving up work altogether."

Jason shook his head in bewilderment. "What's this all about, Kiera? Why have you come to see me? Do you want sympathy for the way Peter has treated you? Well, I am sorry but I can't do anything about that."

"Jason, I'm ill and I might die." Her voice was almost inaudible, but he heard.

It was as if her statement had hit him physically and he jerked back in his chair.

"What…?"

She gave a faint smile. "I've been diagnosed with a brain tumour. It's inoperable, so they're going to try alternative treatment."

She said it in such a matter-of-fact way that at first, he found it difficult to speak. After a couple of stunned seconds he rose slowly from his chair. Taking another one from its place by the wall, he dragged it across the carpet and came to sit closer to her.

He leaned forward and took her hands in his. "I'm so very, very sorry," he said gently.

She looked down at his hands closed round hers. "It's a long time since you've held my hand."

"Well, I think the occasion demands it."

She let out a breath. "We need to talk about Hollie. I have to go into hospital on Monday to start treatment. I thought that she could come to stay with you while I'm there? Perhaps she could stay from tomorrow?"

"Of course she can stay," he said and then added quietly. "Does she know?"

"She knows I've been sick, but I thought I'd tell her on a need to know basis. It might be easier for her to understand that way. She's broken up for the summer holidays but there's still Brownies and her ballet classes."

"I can sort that out. What about your parents?"

She gave a bright smile. "They arrived yesterday. They've taken her to the zoo today. They wanted to look after her themselves but Dad's health isn't brilliant and I don't think he could cope...with everything."

"Well, it'll be no problem for her to stay with me."

"Thank you," she whispered.

"Don't be silly. She's my daughter." He squeezed her fingers. "I hope you don't mind me saying it but I think Peter has picked one hell of a time to leave you."

She gave an ironic laugh. "It was my illness that drove him away. It frightened him witless." She glanced down at his hands still gripping hers. "Isn't it strange, the events that bring out a person's true nature."

After Kiera had left, Jason told the others everything that had happened in his office. Anna didn't take her eyes from his face the entire time, Ben stared down at the table and Mrs Wilby was unable to focus on anything except to dab at the corner of her eyes with a lace hanky. At the conclusion, Jason suggested that they postpone their visit to the Grange until further notice. In the end this didn't cause a problem since after a brief telephone call, his mother was in complete agreement that her birthday celebrations should be put on hold for the time being.

The following day was very strange. Jason went to collect Hollie as usual and when she arrived, she crashed into the house pulling a small trolley containing her possessions and causing Ben to wince at the chipped paintwork on the doorframe. She was keen to tell everyone that Granddad and Grandma Macintosh had come to visit all the way from Canada.

"But Mummy has to go into hospital tomorrow," she added sadly. "She's very sick and the doctors are going to make her better."

The adults made no comment.

Anna followed her upstairs to the small room that had once been her nursery and then her bedroom until she had left with her mother. Now it was set aside for her occasional visits. Although the smallest bedroom in the house, it had been decorated in Hollie's favourite colour, pink and the bed sported a Barbie cover that matched the curtains. Anna helped her unpack and noticed that her Brownie uniform was rather crumpled so she decided to take it to the utility room and run the iron over it.

Leaving Hollie to sort out her things, Anna spent the next ten minutes busily removing the creases from the dress and pressing the collar back into shape, delighting in the tiny garment that seemed to be made for a doll rather than a child. She cherished her boys and wouldn't change them for anything, but she would have loved a little girl, to dress in pretty clothes, to brush her hair and do all the things a mother could do for a daughter. She sighed sadly. If Dave hadn't been the way he was, she might have contemplated a second pregnancy, but the way things had gone it was out of the question.

When she reached Hollie's room, she found father and daughter sitting on the bed, deep in conversation. They both smiled as Anna entered the room. Hollie had unpacked the rest of her things so Anna found a hanger and hung the dress on the door of the cupboard.

"All right, young lady," said Anna turning to the little girl. "I know you've finished school, but if I remember rightly, the teacher often gives homework for the summer."

Hollie's expression became doleful. "I suppose."

"What is it?"

The little girl shuffled about on the bed. "I've got to read two pages of my book and write down five things I like about the summer."

"Well, that sounds easy enough. Shall we do it now?"

"What now!" said Hollie in disgust. "But the holidays have ages to go yet."

"If you get it done now, then you'll have the rest of the time to do fun things," Anna insisted, holding out her hand. Giving a sigh, Hollie collected her books and took her hand.

Anna laughed and turned to Jason for support. "I'm sure your daddy didn't leave his homework until the last minute."

"No, I didn't. But there again, I was a boarder and the school had strict rules," he smiled, rising to his feet.

"Martyn tended to leave his homework until Sunday afternoon," she said, thinking back. "But Chris was very diligent and got his out of the way on Friday night."

"What are they studying at university?"

Anna bristled with pride. "Chris is studying electronic engineering at Loughborough and Martyn economics at Warwick." She gave a giggle. "I think my elder son has ambitions to become Chancellor of the Exchequer."

"I'd like to meet your boys one day. They sound like fine young men. Your husband must have been very proud of them."

"Yes, he is…was," said Anna, her cheeks flushing slightly as she saw Jason frowning.

Hollie pulled on Anna's hand. "Can we go and do this silly homework now?"

The following week was a whirl of activity as they all adjusted to their new routine and it was during that first week and afterwards that Anna would often accompany Jason and Hollie to the hospital to visit Kiera. It was at one of these visits that she met Fergus and Gaynor Macintosh, Kiera's parents. They were constantly at the hospital and although in their sixties were determined to be with their daughter and see her through her illness. When Jason and Hollie arrived, they would take the opportunity to catch up on some chores and allow Hollie to have some time with her mother. Anna didn't want to intrude and would often find a seat and watch Jason and Hollie slowly walk round the hospital garden helping Kiera along, their arms round her to steady her faltering footsteps.

It was obvious her illness had rapidly taken a dramatic hold on her. The medication was alleviating the pain but the progression of the tumour was profound. Jason, who was still her husband and therefore legally her next of kin, had had long discussions with her consultant. His prognosis was bleak and he had to admit that all they could do was make the patient comfortable as Kiera might have only a matter of weeks.

It was the middle of August the day Anna received two contrasting phone calls. Jason had left for a meeting in Birmingham early that morning and hoped to return later that night.

The first call came about lunchtime and was from Chris.

"We got exactly the same results, Mum, even though we did different exams. Two As and a B." His voice at the end of the phone was excited and filled with delight.

"That's wonderful, sweetheart. So, your places are confirmed?"

"Yes, everything's sorted. Grandma said she'll help us pack all the stuff we'll need to take with us for living in halls." He paused for a moment. "But we have something to tell you and we don't want you to be upset."

"Why should I be upset?" she laughed.

"Dad was dead pleased, of course and he's given us some money, so we're off to Ibiza for two weeks. We got a great last minute deal."

"That's fantastic. You enjoy yourselves."

"The trouble is you wanted to celebrate our results, but we're going on Sunday so there'll not be time and also we'll be gone for your birthday."

"Don't worry about that. I think I'd rather forget my birthday." She grimaced. "Thirty-eight is not exactly a birthday to celebrate."

Chris chuckled at the end of the line. "Can't imagine being that old."

"Cheeky sod!"

Anna smiled to herself as she resumed working. It seemed her boys were doing fine without her and in a way she felt relieved. In early October they would leave home to start their degrees and who knows where they would end up after that?

The second call came mid-afternoon and was from Gaynor Macintosh who told Anna that Kiera's condition had worsened and she was asking to see her. Although very surprised at the request, she could do nothing else but comply. Ben drove her to the hospital and while he waited in the car, Anna made her way through the corridors to Kiera's room.

Her parents were at her bedside as usual and as Anna entered the room she gave them a smile and then winced at the figure lying in the bed. Kiera was propped up on two pillows and now and again her eyelashes flickered as she drifted in and out of consciousness. Her pale, sunken features seemed in sharp contrast to the dark hair that had been tied back out of the way.

"We'll pop out for a coffee," said Mrs Macintosh. "There's a snack bar just down the corridor."

Anna took a seat and reached across to hold Kiera's hand. The movement disturbed her sleep and she slowly opened her eyes.

"Anna, is that you?" Her voice was so weak it could hardly leave her throat.

"Yes, I'm here," said Anna.

Kiera struggled to sit up further and Anna eased her into a more comfortable position.

"I'm so glad you came. I want to ask you something." She started coughing and Anna held a cup to her lips while she drank. "I need to be...sure of something...before it's too late."

"You're very tired. Do you want to leave it until you feel stronger?"

Despite her illness, Kiera gave a hoarse chuckle. "I don't think I'm going to get any stronger, " she said.

"Then what do you want to ask me?"

"It's about Hollie. Anna, please, please promise you'll take care of her for me."

Anna gripped her hand tighter. "Of course I'll look after her. You don't need to ask me that."

Kiera shook her head slowly. "No, you don't understand. I mean, always be there for her. I want you to marry Jason and be his wife and then care for my Hollie as a mother."

Anna almost stopped breathing. "Kiera, I can't promise that! Jason might not see it the same way."

"Oh, but he does. I know he thinks a lot about you."

"Yes, as his personal assistant. But marriage is a completely different thing."

"As Jason's assistant you could leave at any moment, then my little girl will be on her own."

Anna became alarmed and bent closer to her. "No, Kiera, you're wrong. Hollie has her father and her grandparents and Mrs Wilby and Ben to take care of her. She doesn't need me."

Kiera closed her eyes for what seemed a long time, but then her eyelashes flickered once more.

"Her grandparents are too old. Ben and Mrs Wilby are fine, but you're a good mother…and you know how to bring up kids. I need to know that she'll be OK." Her eyes opened wide and seemed as black as night. "Please don't… let me down." Anna could hardly speak. "Promise me."

Anna opened her mouth to answer, tears filling her eyes. "I…promise," she said hesitantly. "I promise that I will do everything I can for Hollie."

Kiera smiled and closed her eyes.

It was nearly midnight and Anna was sitting alone at the kitchen table. Everyone had gone to bed, but she had insisted on staying up until Jason came home. It had been a hot day and she left the door open to let any draught enter the house and bring in its wonderful coolness. Her mind was troubled. She had promised a dying woman that she would do all she could for her little girl and she would keep that promise to the best of her ability. But to marry Jason was out of the question. She had too many marital problems of her own to sort out and to marry a second time was a thought that had never entered her head.

Jason appeared out of the darkness, startling her out of her grim thoughts. "Goodness, what are you doing still up?" he asked, giving her a smile. He came into the kitchen and flung his briefcase onto the table.

"Would you like me to make you some coffee?" she said, ignoring his question.

"No, I'll have a quick drink of orange and then I'm off to bed."

"How was Birmingham? Did it go OK?"

He opened the fridge and poured himself a glass of juice smiling triumphantly. "Well, I got the contract. Has Hollie been good today?"

"Yes, but…" He turned to face her and his smile faded. Anna swallowed hard. "It's Kiera, Jason. Her condition became critical. She died just before nine o' clock tonight."

There was so much to do the following week after Kiera's death that Anna could hardly remember what happened from one hour to the next. Jason spent the next few days at Kiera's apartment, helping her parents sort out the furniture and private effects. Kiera had requested that most of her jewellery be returned to Jason, since they had been his gifts and it was one morning, shortly after Jason had completed all the arrangements for Kiera's funeral, he came into the office and went straight to Anna. He placed a box on top of her desk. Anna picked it up and stared at it. It was a square shaped jewel box, with a plush pale blue covering. It had the name *Tiffany & Co* embossed on the front.

"What's this?" she asked in surprise.

"Why don't you open it and see." She did so and let out a gasp of delight. Inside was a gold bracelet of small diamonds and sapphires. "It's for you. Kiera wanted you to have it," he said, watching her lift it out of the box and hold it up to the light, so that it sparkled in the rays from the sun. She knew it was very expensive, the name on the box told her that.

"But I don't understand why," she said puzzled.

"I'm guessing they're a 'thank you' for being a friend."

"I was hardly that, Jason! We talked together and I visited her in the hospital. I can't accept something as expensive as this! Besides, didn't you say you'd bought Kiera most of her jewellery?"

Jason nodded. "Yes, that was my wedding present to her."

Anna couldn't hide her horror. "Then I can't possibly take it! What will Ben and Mrs Wilby say?"

"Does it matter what they say? Kiera wanted you to have it and I'm OK with that."

Anna shook her head. "But…!"

He didn't let her get any further, but took the bracelet from her and clasped it round her wrist.

"Take it, Anna, I want you to wear it. It seems so right for you."

She couldn't answer; her thoughts were so confused. He smiled at her bewilderment and continued holding her hand. Suddenly he raised it to his lips and softly kissed her fingers. It was the first intimate contact they had had and the gesture made her heart jump into her throat. She knew that Kiera had a good reason for wanting her to have Jason's wedding present.

The days leading up to the funeral proved a very difficult time for Anna. She thought of her sons constantly, pinning their postcard from Ibiza next to the one from Romania. Their photo, in a wooden frame, stood on her desk and Anna would often stop working to stare at it. It was her favourite one showing them with their arms round each other and sporting cheeky grins. Martyn, with his dark hair and hazel eyes looking so like his father, while Chris, blond and blue-eyed, took after her.

She missed them terribly and sought refuge in keeping her promise to Kiera and helping Jason with Hollie, even taking the little girl to the florist and allowing her to choose the flowers.

Hollie had had her bath and was sitting at the dressing table in her room while Anna brushed her hair.

"What will it be like tomorrow?" the little girl asked seriously.

"How do you mean?"

"Is it going to be very scary saying goodbye to Mummy?"

Anna stopped her brushing and put her arms round her. "No, it won't be scary. You've worked very hard to make it a special day. The flowers will be lovely."

"But Mummy will be in a coffin and people will be crying."

"Yes, people will cry because that's what happens at a funeral, but they're crying because they love the person who's died and it's a way of showing that love. And yes, I know your mummy will be in a coffin but that's only her body. Her soul has gone to heaven. She's happy now and she isn't sick any more."

"But I miss her."

Anna hugged her closer. "I know you do." She paused, remembering. "You know, Hollie, my daddy died when I was just a bit older than you. I was twelve and I missed him so much."

"Was he very sick too?"

"No, he died in a car accident. It all happened very suddenly. My mum and my little sister and me were left on our own. It was very difficult to be without him but we managed and we never, never stopped thinking about him or loving him."

"Even though he wasn't there any more?"

"Oh, Hollie. You never stop thinking of someone just because you can't see them any more. They're here." She put her hand over the little girl's heart. "And that means they're always with you every single day of your life."

"And I can look at her photo," she said, pointing to the silver frame on her bedside table.

"Of course you can." Anna kissed the top of her head.

Jason suddenly appeared. "Are you ready for a story?"

Hollie jumped into bed, pulling the covers up to her chin. "Yes! Yes! Yes!"

"So, what story do you want," he asked, walking over to the bookshelf.

"*The Selfish Giant*," yelled Hollie.

Jason gave a groan. "Oh, not again! I've read it hundreds of times!" Anna kissed Hollie good night and made for the door. As she past Jason, he gave her a grimace. "Oscar Wilde has a lot to answer for."

Anna settled down for the evening, curled up on the couch, reading a magazine. Jason came into the room and took a seat next to her.

"Thank you for talking to Hollie about tomorrow. I really appreciate it."

Anna gave him a bright smile. "She told you about it?"

"No, I was listening outside the door," he admitted with a grin.

"You were eavesdropping!" She hit him playfully with the magazine.

He blew out a breath. "Couldn't help it really. I was just coming to her room and I heard you talking and I just had to stop and listen."

"Well, it's a good job we weren't talking about you! You might have heard something you didn't want to hear."

He gave her a sidelong glance. "That's true, but it would have served me right." He paused slightly before adding, "I'm sorry about your father. I didn't know he'd died. I assumed your parents were divorced."

"Why should you have known? I never told you, because I didn't think you'd be interested."

"I'm very interested in your life." He tilted his head. "You never talk about your husband. What did he do for a living? I mean, before he fell ill."

Anna swallowed hard. "He was a structural engineer." She tried to go back to her magazine, but knew his eyes were still on her and although she tried not to meet his gaze, she found she was compelled to look up once more. He was smiling.

"I know how it feels to have your heart broken. I don't blame you for not wanting to talk about him."

She was alarmed to recognise something in his gentle tone, his soft expression that made her think that he knew the truth about her. But how could he? She absorbed herself in her magazine, convinced that she had imagined it; he was making polite conversation that was all.

The day of the funeral dawned and it seemed the weather was going to be kind. Throughout the next few hours, Hollie positioned herself between her father and Anna, holding their hands firmly. Her courage astonished Anna and it was only when the curtain finally swished round the casket that Hollie needed a gentle hug from her father.

While they were standing outside the crematorium, Anna noticed an elegant woman, sporting a large hat and sunglasses. She wondered if she was a relative or perhaps, a family friend. Whoever she was, Jason would probably introduce her when they all went back to the house. Then Anna remembered Kiera's lover, Peter, and guessed he must be somewhere about. Surely he would want to attend the funeral, even if the situation might be a little awkward between him and Jason.

The wake afterwards was pleasant and Anna helped Hollie to pass round the plates of food. Again, Anna searched for the woman she had seen outside the crematorium, but she obviously had not wanted to come to the house. Also, there didn't seem to be any sign of the mysterious Peter. She sighed despondently. Poor Kiera, after everything she had been through, he couldn't even be there for her. Thank goodness she had had Jason at the end.

A few days later, Jason collected Kiera's ashes. It was nearing the end of August and Jason had made arrangements with his daughter's headmistress that she should accompany her grandparents back to Vancouver and spend a few weeks with them.

It was a cloudy day as they made their way up the hill to where they had spent the picnic. Since it was Hollie's favourite place, it had been decided that that was where they would scatter the ashes. Anna, Mrs Wilby and Ben walked with Jason, while Hollie and her grandparents went on ahead. And it was these three only that took part in the actual act of finally laying Kiera to rest. Even Jason stood back, knowing that this was a very private moment.

They looked on from a distance as her grandparents took Hollie to the brow of the hill and kneeling down they allowed her to lift the lid off the small silver urn and then helped her shake the ashes into the wind. Everyone watched as the grey flakes drifted and danced in the light breeze to join the elements and return at last to the earth.

"Goodbye, Mummy," whispered Hollie. "I hope you like living in heaven."

Anna was standing next to Jason and she felt him suddenly tense. She glanced at him and noticed the muscles in his jaw tighten and realised that this was the hardest part for him. She knew it wasn't sorrow for Kiera, but for his little daughter who now was without her mother. What made Anna do the next action she couldn't imagine, but suddenly she slipped her hand into his and was surprised when he responded by clenching it tightly as if he never meant to let it go.

Two days later, Jason drove Hollie and her grandparents to Heathrow to board the flight for the long journey to Vancouver. After they had left, Anna joined Mrs Wilby in the kitchen.

"Well, I suppose that's that," said the housekeeper taking a sip of her tea.

"It went well and I thought Hollie was so brave," said Anna.

"Yes, such a determined little soul. But now we have to think of the future," said Mrs Wilby. "We're going to the Grange soon for Mrs Harrington's belated birthday celebrations. So, we must go into Bristol and buy you a lovely evening dress for the party." All the conversation since the funeral had been about the delayed visit to Jason's boyhood home.

The telephone started ringing in the office and Anna stood to answer it. Yes, she thought grimly, it was time to tell Jason about her husband and the dreadful state of her marriage. But how she would explain everything she couldn't imagine.

CHAPTER FIVE

A few days after Hollie had left for Canada, they all piled into the Volvo Estate and set off for the Grange. Ben drove and it was hoped that the journey would be trouble free. They travelled first through heavy city traffic and then into the countryside. It was going to be a hot day and as they drove along Anna insisted on winding down the windows even though Ben complained that that wasn't necessary since the car's air conditioning was in good working order. Anna would have none of it. She didn't want to be closed in on such a beautiful day and wanted to feel the breeze in her face. Her excitement at spending time at Jason's childhood home had made her feel carefree and contented as a small child and she had decided to enjoy herself.

The journey took longer than expected, as they were forced to stop while a farmer and his herdsman rounded up about a dozen cows that had escaped from the field and had wandered onto the road. The cows seemed to want to go anywhere but back to the meadow, the antics of the two men causing a great deal of amusement for the people waiting patiently in the car. Until one beast attempted to push its head through Anna's window causing her to squeal.

Finally, they reached the gates that stood tall and proud at the end of the drive and Jason jumped out to swing them open. As the car passed through, Anna's mouth nearly fell open in surprise. She had assumed that Jason's childhood home was just a large house called the Grange, but it was obvious that it was much, much more. She noticed the wonderfully entwined leaves in the elaborate ironwork of the gate and then the drive up to the house. Closing the gates after them, Jason got back in the car and they drove up the drive and into the forecourt at the front of the house.

It was an impressive building, in the style of an Elizabethan manor with ivy growing along the walls. But the most wonderful adornment was the boxes and baskets filled to capacity with lobelia, geranium and chrysanthemums. The main entrance was set back in a substantial porch-like structure, above it three more storeys, with windows of small panes of glass. But to the left and right of the main door the building extended a good hundred metres in each direction as three storeys, until finally becoming four storeys again at each end. Anna smiled as she surveyed its expanse and wondered if it had changed much since it had been built. Somehow she felt very little had been done to the external structure except for the necessary repairs and maintenance.

"It's wonderful," said Anna, peering upwards. "It's as though time has stood still."

Jason responded with a chuckle, as he helped Ben to empty the luggage from the back of the Volvo. "That's been said many times before."

She followed Mrs Wilby through the sturdy oak door and into the main hall where a small figure with short, curly hair greeted them.

"My dears, you've arrived!" she smiled. "I was getting quite worried. The travel news seemed to say there were hold ups everywhere." Suddenly a golden retriever appeared and made its way straight to Anna. She backed away alarmed at its wet, inquisitive nose that nuzzled her hand. The woman stepped forward briskly and caught hold of its collar. "Come away, Tess! People don't want you slobbering over them."

Anna felt embarrassed. "I'm so sorry. I'm not really a dog person. My mother wouldn't have one in the house."

"That's perfectly OK, my dear. Please don't worry about it. She's very friendly though, so I'll put her in the kitchen."

"Oh, please don't do that," said Anna in alarm. "It's her home not mine."

Jason suddenly burst through the door with Ben hot on his heels. They dropped the luggage on the floor and Jason flung his arms round his mother, nearly pulling her off her feet.

"We would have been here earlier, but we got held up by a herd of cows," said Jason, winking at Anna. He bent towards the dog. "Hello you old thing," he said vigorously rubbing her ears, before gesturing to Anna. "You've met Anna, Mother?"

Jason's mother gave a bright smile and held out her hand. "Jason has told me all about you. I'm so delighted you decided to spend my birthday with me."

"Thank you for inviting me Mrs Harrington. I'm so sorry you had to delay all your celebrations."

"It couldn't be helped and please call me Margaret! Now, let's go into the parlour and have coffee. Leave the luggage there and I'll get John to take it to your rooms."

Anna looked about her. She was standing in a spacious hall, with a marble floor and large chandelier secured to the centre of the ceiling. On the oak-panelled walls were an assortment of antique weapons and there was even a suit of armour standing in the corner. By the stairs an exquisite grandfather clock ticked the hours away.

This was Jason's childhood home, Anna thought, as a boy he had most probably slid down the banister and played in all the rooms. She watched his animated face, aware of his happiness and a sudden thought crossed her mind. Perhaps her revelation wouldn't be such bad news for him, perhaps she was overestimating its importance to him? After all, it didn't threaten her position, she could still remain his PA and even if she had put herself down as a widow on her CV, that still didn't change anything. Except the fact she had lied. She swallowed and tried to shrug away her guilty feelings.

After their coffee, they all trekked upstairs to their rooms, the hub of their conversation and laughter echoing round the walls. Halfway up the grand stairway, Anna turned to survey the immense hall below her and then continuing her climb, was surprised to find Jason waiting for her at the top.

"I'll show you to your room. It's just along the corridor next to Ben's and Mrs Wilby's."

"Thank you. There seems to be a lot of doors in this place," she laughed. "Knowing my luck I'm sure to get lost."

"You'll soon find your way around."

At the door to her bedroom, he left her. The room allocated to Anna was facing south-west, so receiving a great deal of the day's sunshine. As she entered the room, she gave a cry of pleasure, for standing against the wall was a wide four-poster bed. She made her way round the room peeping into the cupboards and opening the drawers. Against the wall was a long mirror in which she could see herself from top to toe. Suddenly she spied another door and opening it, found herself in a wonderful Victorian bathroom with a large cast iron bath standing on claw feet. It had large brass taps and attached to the wall was a matching showerhead. Anna traced her fingers along the intricately decorated glass shower screen that covered half the bath. The sink and toilet were of the same design as the bath and positioned over the rails were freshly laundered towels. Margaret had even peppered the shelves with pot-pourri and bottles of bubble bath and shampoo.

Anna left the bathroom and ran over to the bed, launching herself on top of the duvet. The mattress was soft and huge enough to get lost in. She lay on her back and looked around her. The room created the impression of days gone by and it wasn't only because of the bed, since the furniture seemed relatively old too. The carpet and curtains were quite new, she guessed. But the wallpaper was a good twenty years old.

There was a brisk knock on the door. She scrambled off the bed, tucked her shirt into her jeans and went to answer it.

"Is your room OK?" asked Jason.

"It's absolutely wonderful."

"Oh, good. I've come to say that lunch will be served in the dining room at one o'clock."

She nodded. "That sounds great, but I'd love to have a bath first."

"Feel free, but be warned! There's plenty of hot water but the plumbing is a bit temperamental. It will probably spit at you."

"Then I'll just spit back," she said crisply, closing the door on him.

After her bath she changed into something more presentable and made her way along the corridor to the head of the stairs. She met Jason coming the opposite way.

"I thought you might not find the dining room," he said, smiling. "As you said, there's a lot of doors in this place."

At the top of the stairs was a large portrait and her eyes were drawn to it.

"Are these your ancestors?" she asked, gesturing towards the painting.

"Yes, they are. May I introduce you to Frederick and Elizabeth Harrington." The portrait depicted a middle-aged man in long tailed coat, waistcoat and cravat standing behind a chair on which sat an attractive woman with fair hair and dressed in late Georgian period. Her blue dress was pinched tight at the waist and then flowed out in endless silk and lace. The elbow length sleeves were gathered with wide, ruffled lace and round her throat she wore a white, silk ribbon. Her smile was barely perceptible, but there was a glint in her eyes as though she was amused at something just said to her. In the background Anna could just make out the fuzzy image of the Grange. "He's the Harrington who bought the place. My grandfather about six times removed, I think, but the lady is my favourite. When I was a young boy, I would stand for hours looking..." His abrupt break in conversation, caused Anna to glance quickly at him. He was staring at the painting with a bewildered expression. Then he turned to look at Anna before returning to gaze at the woman in the portrait. "Good God! It's you. It's definitely you."

"Me? Oh Jason, I don't think so!"

"It is you! Same eyes and colour hair, same face and figure!"

Anna began to feel cross. "Oh, don't be silly! I'm nothing like her!" She ran trembling fingers through blonde hair that was cut in a neat bob.

"Take a look for yourself."

She studied the portrait closely and saw that he was right. She did bear a resemblance if a person looked hard enough. Suddenly Anna closed her eyes in shocked awareness.

"That's why you thought you knew me the day of my interview! I'm the lady in the portrait. The one you've admired since you were a boy."

"Maybe. But I didn't connect you at all with this painting, when I first met you."

A terrible thought came into head. "Oh God, you didn't employ me because I fitted a boyhood fantasy, did you?"

He swung her round to face him, his hands gripping her shoulders firmly. "No, I did not! Don't you dare start accusing me of ulterior motives. I'm a businessman and I run my business with logic and a great deal of acumen. I do not go around making decisions based on whims and speculation."

"Then why did you employ me, if not because I reminded you of her?" She nodded in the direction of the portrait.

"Because you had the right qualifications and the right experience." He paused slightly. "I felt that we would work well together and..." He licked dry lips. The time wasn't right to tell her how she had affected him the moment she had walked into the office, walked into his life. He had been so pleased that she fitted his specifications for a PA and then been bitterly disappointed when she had turned down the job. For weeks afterwards he had felt a melancholy that had stifled his thinking and made him restless. When he had come back from New York to find her sitting at Sharon's desk, he actually believed jet lag was causing him to hallucinate. He would tell her how he felt, but he would choose his moment. "After all, I was right, wasn't I? You turned out to be an excellent personal assistant," he added, watching her.

"You're a smooth one," Anna muttered.

"Thank you, kind lady!"

She knew by his smile that he hadn't taken offence and looked at the portrait once more. "I can see a family resemblance in both of them. You have Frederick's eyes but Elizabeth's smile. But she is lovely."

"As I said, just like you," he grinned. She ignored him and Jason decided that they had spent enough time looking at his ancestors. "Come on, let's go down to lunch before Mother sends someone to search for us."

Margaret Harrington put down her cup and glanced towards her son.

"You must give Anna a tour of the old place."

"Would you like to look round?" he asked, halting Anna's advance on the bookshelf where she intended to examine the reading literature.

"Yes, please, I'd love to," said Anna eagerly.

He opened the door and both passed through into the hall.

Margaret smiled after them. "She seems so nice and Jason told me how wonderful she's been, through Kiera's illness. And a widow too. I wonder if they…Oh, never mind. I'm just a silly old woman matchmaking again."

Mrs Wilby chuckled, her eyes bright with enthusiasm. "You're not a silly old woman at all. And as for those two, well, I wouldn't be surprised if Jason has got something on his mind. I've worked for him for nine years and I know him well."

"I suppose we'd better start in the hall." Jason looked around the great expanse. "Although I must warn you, the east wing is closed up now and the rooms there are given over to storage and the stables are full of old junk from the farm."

"When did the horses go?"

"My father sold them about twenty years ago. Then the stables were made into a garage. Now, people tend to park in the drive."

"I guess you can ride."

"I can, but I much prefer to drive. I find riding a little wearing on the…clothes," he chuckled. "Have you ever ridden a horse?"

"Goodness no, I don't think I've been anywhere near one. This is an enormous place. Do you have many staff?"

"Well, John and Irene 'live in' with their daughter Fran. They have an apartment above the kitchen. We have six part-time ladies who come from the village, but we have more outdoor staff as the grounds are open to the public in the summer."

"Doesn't your mother get lonely, living in such a big house on her own?"

"Not at all. She's turned it into a thriving business. The Grange has been catering for business conferences and seminars for years. And she's just recently got a licence to hold weddings here."

"Oh, Jason, that's lovely. Imagine getting married here."

He nodded. "They're intending to hold the ceremonies in the morning room and then the receptions can be in the ballroom. That's the only room that leads out onto a veranda and from there a flight of steps takes you outside to the gardens. There's a good two acres of garden for the photographs."

Anna looked about her, imagining the brides floating through the grand hallway to get married. So different from her own functional register office wedding.

"How old is this place?" she said, her gaze searching the ceiling and examining the magnificent cornices.

"Well, it was built in the sixteenth century, by one of the noble lords at the court of Elizabeth the first. It's had quite a few owners since then but it was bought by my ancestor, Frederick Harrington, at the end of the eighteenth century."

"He must have had quite a bit of money. This place would have cost a fortune in those days."

Jason looked away in embarrassment. "He was already a wealthy landowner, but I'm sorry to say he increased his fortune with the slave trade." He saw her shocked expression and nodded. "I know, it sounds dreadful. But in the eighteenth century, Bristol was heavily involved in such business. My ancestor jumped on the bandwagon, I guess. There was money to be made and he saw his opportunity."

She grimaced. "Oh well, it's not fair to judge them by today's standards. It was a different time and different thinking. I suppose a man had to make a living or his family starved to death."

"I'm glad you understand."

"Did his children join him in that business?"

"He had about four children, but only one survived to adulthood, a son, who followed him into the family business. If I remember rightly he was injured in a duel and walked with a limp from then on."

"And I expect the duel was over a woman!"

"Most probably."

She sniffed with disdain. "Why do men have to make fools of themselves over women?"

"Oh, testosterone, I should think. It's a natural process," he said, his lips twitching slightly.

"But marriage should be…" She stopped, horrified, before saying, "Let's get on with the tour."

Jason walked across the hall and opened a door. Anna preceded him and entered a room that filled her with delight. The sun streamed through long windows, sending shafts of light bouncing off the furniture and walls. She looked about her in wonder. This room was similar to the parlour, although slightly larger and boasted a huge fireplace and oak panelled walls. Dotted around were armchairs and couches, of which there must have been a complement of at least three suites. In the corner was a small mahogany desk.

"This is a gorgeous room," she said.

"Yes, it's the morning room and where the marriage ceremonies will be held. After it's been decorated, of course."

They moved back into the hall, where he continued to guide her through the remaining rooms, the library, Margaret's study and the games room that sported a snooker table, before taking her down to the kitchen to introduce her to the staff that helped Margaret to run the Grange. He informed her as they walked about the history of each room, his love for the house so apparent.

Wonder and awe engulfed Anna as she followed Jason into the final room on their tour. She made her way to the centre of the floor and stared about her. She was in the most magnificent place she had ever seen, obviously the ballroom, since it was spacious and light with five great windows set in bays. Two chandeliers hung from the ceiling and the floor was polished wood covered with a thick burgundy carpet. On the walls was plush red and gold wallpaper and a sculptured gold frieze depicted birds, foliage and fruit. But the most impressive feature was the huge white marble fireplace, one at each end of the room.

"Jason. I'm speechless. I've never seen anything so...so..!" She began to giggle at her inept attempts to find the right words.

"It is lovely, isn't it."

"Do you ever use it for a social occasion?"

"Oh yes! Whenever it's thought appropriate. It's been used for business dinner dances and award ceremonies. And it's used for family functions. We'll be in this room for Mother's birthday dance and she always organises a party on New

Year's Eve. We'll all be there so if you'd like to come too, you'd be very welcome." Anna didn't answer. Instead, she circled the room and drank in its wonderful splendour. "Would you like to see the estate now? I can take you to the farm, if you wish."

"That would be lovely. Has it any cows?"

They spent a wonderful afternoon together. As they drove to the farm, Jason pointed out the main features on the estate, telling her that there was over a thousand acres of land consisting of parks and woods as well as some very profitable farmland. For Anna, the lands belonging to the Grange seemed to stretch in every direction.

Mr Durrant and his wife were overjoyed to see 'Master' Jason and his young lady friend and spent a good hour telling Anna of all the scrapes he had got into as a boy. Eventually, feeling completely embarrassed, he decided it was time to go. As they drove back in the warm evening sun, Anna found it difficult to keep back her giggles as she remembered the stories she had heard.

Jason became exasperated. "If you don't stop laughing, I'll pull over and throw you out!"

"Never! And make me walk back?" she chuckled.

"I wouldn't give it a second thought!"

The evening was spent in the parlour, Mrs Wilby and Margaret catching up on news while Ben engrossed himself with the crossword in his paper.

"Anna, do you fancy a game of whist?" Jason asked, opening a drawer in the wall unit and getting out a pack of cards.

"Yes. But don't we need more players?"

"Everyone seems otherwise occupied, so I'm afraid it's me and thee." She sat down opposite him and he held out the pack. "You choose trumps."

She split the cards and turned them over. "Hearts are trumps," she smiled.

An hour passed quietly until Margaret ordered some coffee.

Anna picked up a card and held it to the light. "Are these cards marked?" she asked scornfully.

Jason feigned indignation. "Certainly not! Are you accusing me of cheating?"

"Well, I'm finding it difficult to beat you," she said, pulling a face at him.

"I think you're doing OK."

"If I'm doing OK, then how come you're winning!" She gave him a sly grin. "You seem to forget I know the little tricks you pull with your clients."

His lips parted in order to protest but he was saved from answering by the arrival of Fran with the coffee.

"Would you like to go out for a stroll?" Jason asked Anna, after they had finished their coffee.

Anna nodded. "Sounds wonderful. I'd love to see a bit of the garden before the light goes."

Tess rose to her feet, sensing a walk was being offered. She yawned and stretched.

"No, you stay here," ordered Jason. "I want Anna to myself for a change."

Tess pricked her ears and tilted her head to one side. At eleven years old, her old bones couldn't cope with much strenuous exercise and the soft rug was more tempting. She resumed her place, resting her chin on her paws.

Outside it was very mild. The stars shone brightly in a clear sky and the air was heavy with the scent of late summer flowers and newly mown grass. They walked along the drive and Anna turned to survey the building they had just left. Light poured from the windows and the ivy caught the glow and shone with a luminescence all of its own. Anna gasped at the sight.

"It's so pretty," she said. "It looks like a totally different place in the evening than it does during the day."

Jason nodded in agreement. "It's always the same. It seems to change with the seasons and the weather. But then Mother does it credit with her gardening skill."

At the end of the drive they followed the path that skirted the lawns and yew topiary bushes making their way round to the rose garden. As they talked together, Jason suddenly reached out and took Anna's hand. His touch was like an electrical charge shooting up her arm and she jerked away in surprise.

He stopped walking. "I'm sorry. I didn't mean to cause you any offence," he said. "I remembered how good it felt when you took my hand the day we scattered Kiera's ashes."

Anna's reaction had been instinctive and the last thing she wanted was to hurt his feelings. But the sensations she had experienced had been too much for her. She slipped her hand through his arm and smiled.

"It's OK. It just surprised me for a second." She was answered by his hand covering hers. They continued their walk, until eventually they found themselves back at the entrance. She looked around her once more. "In the twilight it looks like a fairytale castle from one of Hans Christian Anderson's stories. You can almost imagine a beautiful princess and a handsome prince living in it." Anna let her imagination run away with her, as she took in the vision of the windows filled with a soft glow.

"Well, we've got our beautiful princess. All we need now is to find the handsome prince," Jason answered, smiling.

"Don't be silly. I'm far from being a beautiful princess!"

"Beauty is in the eye of the beholder, Anna." He kissed her hand. "You have a wonderful innocence about you that I find very appealing." She turned her head away to hide her embarrassment. He lifted her face towards him with the edge of his forefinger and murmured softly, "Have you had a pleasant day, your first day in the fairytale castle?"

"Oh, yes, except for meeting Elizabeth Harrington, who I shall hate for the rest of my days."

"Why, for goodness sake?"

"Because I'm not totally convinced you employed me on my own merits. I'm sure she had something to do with it."

He shook his head. "She didn't, I assure you," he whispered.

His arms came slowly round her, pulling her nearer, his face pressed against her hair. When he started to brush his lips gently on her cheek, Anna felt herself melting. The thrill that ran down her spine was something she had never experienced before, but then a terrible thought came to her that she was behaving little better than her husband and for a few seconds she tensed. Even so, the emotions that were overwhelming her and making her legs go weak, had an irresistible force which compelled her to remain still. No, she wasn't like her husband. Dave was not part of her life any more, they had separated and she wasn't hurting anyone by her conduct.

Ignoring her mind, she focused attention on her body, welcoming his caress until gradually, his lips moved closer to hers and when they finally met, her feelings surrendered.

Anna couldn't remember how long they kissed. She didn't even care. She was only aware of her palpitating heart and the blood surging round her body and the knowledge she wanted more. His tongue explored her mouth tenderly, causing her to sink against him, her arms reaching up to encircle his neck. Dave had never kissed her like this. This was so different. More sensual and demanding and somehow, more fulfilling.

Jason lifted his head, his eyes shining with relief and excitement at her response. He was certain of one thing; he wanted Anna in his bed.

"If you only knew how long I've wanted to do that," he murmured, holding the side of her face and stroking her lips with his thumb. "I've fallen in love with you, Anna."

She couldn't believe what she was hearing. "Jason. I don't think I..." Her voice faded into space.

"I realise you might think it too soon after Kiera, but let me assure you, it was over long ago between my wife and me. However, if you want more time then I don't mind waiting."

It sounded wonderful, his soft words mesmerising her, and yet deep within her soul was such a terrible, black secret, she thought it would surely rise up and choke his words forever.

She tried to see his face, but the gloom was too intense. "You've no idea what you'll be taking on!" she said.

"Well, I've always enjoyed a challenge," he said and in spite of the shadows she knew he was smiling.

"I need some time to think."

"Of course." His fingers caressed her cheek, before he added, "Would you like to go to the golf club tomorrow? I could teach you how to play golf and then we could have a spot of lunch."

"That sounds wonderful. But what makes you think I can't play golf?"

"Can you?" he said.

His surprise made her grin. "I was only captain of the ladies team for twelve months."

"Well, goodness me! You never mentioned it," he said. He gave a low chuckle. "What's your handicap?"

Anna thought for a moment. "Shan't tell. I wouldn't want to put you off your game knowing you had such a formidable opponent."

He pulled her more closely towards him. "I think tomorrow is going to be very interesting. Come on. Let's go inside. The temperature seems to be dropping."

She took his hand and they started their way back. "Strange. I don't feel cold at all," Anna sighed, as they climbed the steps to the main door.

CHAPTER SIX

It was early when Anna awoke the next morning and she immediately remembered the previous night. Jason had kissed her and told her he loved her. He had aroused passions in her that she never knew existed. Dave had never done that. Never whispered how much she meant to him, or that he needed her. Jason's endearments had come from his heart, she was sure of it. He had meant what he had said and what's more, he had asked nothing of her, prepared to wait and give her time.

The thought of Dave made her heart leap and she sat up in bed, clutching a pillow tightly to her breast. She must do something and quickly. Events were moving too fast and the knowledge they might get out of control, frightened her beyond belief. Swinging her legs over the side of the mattress, she came to a decision. They would have their game of golf and during lunch she would tell him about her husband and why she had lied on her CV. He would understand, she felt sure of it, but if he was upset, then she only had herself to blame.

Anna made her way downstairs to breakfast. Halfway down she heard laughter echoing from the dining room and stopped momentarily. She took in a large breath before continuing her descent and walking briskly into the dining room. A chorus of 'good morning' greeted her. It was apparent Jason hadn't come down yet, since there was an empty seat at the table.

Margaret caught her quick glance at the chair and smiled. "I'm afraid Jason has had to go back to Bristol, my dear."

Anna's heart sank. "But why? I thought the office was closed on a Saturday."

"It is, but this morning he received an urgent phone call, to say that a ship has been held up in port. I'm not quite sure of the exact details but there seems to be a hitch with customs."

"Will he be long?"

"It depends on how quickly he can clear up the problem. He said he would phone later and let us know how things are. Don't worry, he's sure to return as soon as he can."

Margaret watched her face as she spoke. There was definitely some warmth and affection in her eyes when Jason's name was mentioned. Perhaps Mrs Wilby was right, perhaps there was something more between these two than a simple employer-employee relationship. It would be good if this turned out to be true, her son needed a wife at his side.

Margaret sighed and thought of Kiera. She realised she shouldn't think ill of the dead, but it was obvious why her son had chosen her. She was so beautiful and charming and had the ability to capture everyone's heart. What a pity she had the ability to break a heart too. Anna was different, she had the steadfastness needed in a good marriage. Margaret had been told that Anna had nursed her husband for many years through a long and debilitating illness whilst caring for twin boys. That showed a great deal of determination and yet having lost her husband, she had supported her boys and then made a new life for herself with new people in a new place. Any other woman would have stayed in their hometown with their next of kin, but Anna had journeyed forth into the unknown.

The sadness on Anna's face moved her. "I'm sure he misses you as much as you miss him," she told her soothingly.

Anna blinked in horror. "I don't miss him! I just wanted to know when he'll be back."

Margaret patted her hand and gave her a knowing smile.

Later that morning, Margaret had an official engagement as guest of honour at the primary school, planting a tree in memory of her late husband. Mrs Wilby and Ben had decided to join her, but Anna had declined the invitation wanting to stay behind so that she would be ready to play their game of golf when Jason came home.

She made herself comfortable in the parlour and absorbed herself in a book. Eventually she wandered over to the window and looked out at the grounds of the Grange. The vivid blue sky had disappeared and it had started to rain. She sighed sadly when she realised that they would have to cancel their round of golf. But lunch might still be possible if Jason returned early enough.

She walked round the room, scrutinising the photos on the unit and smiling at one in particular, showing Jason on his graduation day. She picked it up and examined the robe he was wearing and his look of absolute pride. He must have been in his early twenties and she noticed with amazement that he had attended Cardiff University.

How she found herself in the kitchen she couldn't remember but she strongly suspected that the sound of laughter had drawn her down the stairs. Irene and her daughter, Fran, were busy cooking the lunch for that day as well as making the final preparations for the birthday meal. Anna asked if she could help.

"Oh, no! miss, it wouldn't be right. You being a guest and all. And besides the rest of the staff will be here shortly to give a hand." The broad, flushed face of the cook smiled at her over the steaming pans.

"Well, I have peeled a fair amount of potatoes and carrots in my time. Please let me help."

In the end, the cook relented and set Anna on the sprouts. As it neared lunchtime, the sherry was brought out.

"I generally don't drink alcohol! Only at weddings and funerals and special occasions," said Anna.

"Well this is a special occasion, ain't it?" said Fran, drinking down her glass quickly.

"It doesn't hurt to have a tot, once in a while, my dear," the cook laughed as she sipped her drink. Anna picked up her glass and the thick liquid slipped down her throat, making her radiate with warmth to the very ends of her fingers and toes. Somehow, it reminded her of the feelings Jason had aroused in her, when he had kissed her the previous night. She wanted more and finished the whole glass. Taking the bottle she poured herself another measure. "Steady, my dear. It'll go to your head quite quickly if you're not used to it," said the cook.

Anna ignored her and drank it down.

She finally left the kitchen when the part-time staff arrived. Lunch would be ready soon and as Anna made her way up the kitchen stairs to the hall, she was conscious of her head feeling extremely light. She tried to shrug it off and went into the dining room. Taking a seat, she watched as the tureens of food arrived and the diners helped themselves. As Ben passed the peas to Anna, he noticed she missed the target and her hand shot to the left. He placed the tureen down in front of her and watched as she scooped the vegetables unsteadily onto her plate, mostly tipping them on the tablecloth.

"Are you OK, Anna?" he asked, suddenly feeling concerned.

Anna grinned. "I've been helping the cook and she brought out the sherry bottle."

Margaret smiled. "I didn't know we had an alcoholic in our midst."

Anna jerked her head in her direction. "Oh, no, I'm not a drinker. Really, I'm not. It's just that…please excuse me."

She headed for the door before Margaret could explain, "Oh dear, I was only joking, but I seem to have offended her."

"She wanted to make a good impression," nodded Ben. "She was worried what you'd think of her."

Margaret sighed. "I think she's a lovely girl, but a little too sensitive perhaps."

"I'll go and see how she is," said Mrs Wilby, rising from the table.

"And tell her I apologise," Margaret called after her.

Mrs Wilby rejoined them at the table after a couple of minutes.

"She's fast asleep. The poor girl was already out cold when I got there."

Anna slept for an hour and when the events at lunch finally sieved through her memory, she let out a groan and jumped to her feet. She visited the bathroom and hurriedly did her face and hair, smacking her cheeks to make herself more alert.

She found Margaret in the study, hammering away on an old-fashioned typewriter. "Jason wants me to get a computer, but I find this much more convenient," she grinned.

Anna gave her a half-smile. "I'm so sorry for my appalling behaviour at lunch. I don't know why I drank all that sherry. It was very wrong of me, but I'm not an alcoholic, really I'm not."

Margaret turned a good-natured face towards her. "My dear, don't worry about it. I was just having fun at your expense. Of course you're not an alcoholic and I do apologise." Anna grimaced. "By the way Jason phoned."

"What did he say?"

"It seems that things aren't going too well. He's going to try and get here by this evening, or later tonight. If it's too late he'll go back to his own house and make the journey tomorrow morning. He said he'd ring if he has to do that. He asked to speak to you."

"Oh, and I missed him!"

"Don't worry, he'll ring again. Or why don't you ring him on his mobile?"

"Better not if he's having a difficult time."

Anna decided to go for a walk since the rain had stopped and the sun had come out again. If anything, it would clear her head that still felt terribly fuzzy. She made her way into the hall to collect her jacket, which she knew she had left over a chair. The chair was gone. Thinking her jacket might have been put in her bedroom she started upstairs, when the downstairs door opened and Fran came bustling through carrying a vacuum cleaner.

"You haven't seen my jacket have you? I'm sure I left it over a chair in the hall," asked Anna.

Fran thought for a moment. "I think that chair was put back in the morning room, miss. Sorry, miss, I should have told you."

She found her jacket still hanging over the back of the chair and was just putting it on when she spotted movement by the bureau. She quickly turned as Tess's large bulk came bounding towards her, making her cry out in fright. Tess had been sleeping in the warmth of the sun coming through the window and Anna's entrance had startled her. She ran into Anna's legs and then barked loudly before running through the door and out into the hall. Sudden contact with the dog had made Anna back up against the occasional table and she stumbled. Reaching out to steady herself, she felt her hand brush against the crystal vase. The vase rocked for just a few seconds and then fell towards the carpet, hitting the floor with a crash of glass, scattering the flowers and splashing water everywhere. Anna stared down at the broken vase in dismay. It looked expensive.

When Margaret rushed through the door moments later, she found Anna kneeling on the floor, picking up the shards of glass, her hand bleeding.

"Oh, my dear! What have you been doing?"

"I knocked the vase over. I'm so sorry."

"Oh, don't worry about it. Come to the kitchen and let me bathe your hand. The cut isn't too bad. Nothing that a little antiseptic and a sticking plaster will put right."

During the evening, Anna played snooker with Ben in the billiard room and then they joined the others in front of the television, an activity to which she felt unable to give her undivided attention, so absorbed was she in keeping her eyes on her watch.

Margaret patted her knee. "You're worrying too much."

Anna gave a smile. "Have I been that transparent?"

"Yes, you have. My philosophy is why worry unnecessarily about it. Of course, I used to worry as all mothers do, but then I came to the conclusion that no news is good news. He hasn't rung to say he's staying somewhere else tonight, so let's assume that he's on his way home this very moment. It's only nine-thirty and he said ten or eleven, so there's plenty of time yet."

Anna smiled sadly. "We were going to play golf today."

"There's always tomorrow."

"Yes, there's always tomorrow," Anna repeated.

There was no sleep for Anna when she finally went to bed. No matter how hard she tried to keep her eyes closed, they would open and fix on the curtain for the beam of headlights that she knew would have to shine past her window. Her ears strained for the sound of a car. Eventually, she looked at her watch. It was midnight. A new day and Jason still hadn't returned. Agitated and concerned Anna jumped out of bed. Slipping into the silk kimono dressing gown that her husband had brought back from Japan, she pulled back the curtains and leaned her forehead against the window.

The rain seemed torrential, coming down in sheets that she could hardly see the lamp glowing in the drive never mind the second one in the distance by the gate. The wind bent the trees and howled through the chimney pots. But there was no sign of a vehicle. Margaret was so right; worrying didn't help matters one bit. Jason was an excellent driver, of course he would take care, nothing was going to happen to him. Pulling a seat up below the window, she sat down and rested her arms on the window-sill, her chin on her hands, her eyes fastened on the hazy sheen at the end of the drive, its radiance, a beacon guiding Jason home. But as yet it had only succeeded in illuminating the trees, making them appear ghostly and forbidding as they swayed in the wind. Her eyes slowly closed in sleep.

When the noise of crunching gravel finally came and the beam of car headlights swept across her room, Anna wasn't awake to see or hear. It was only when the barking of a dog filtered into her exhausted brain that she slowly surfaced from sleep. Then her precarious position of leaning on the window ledge proved to be the hazard it was. Her slumbering unsupported body slid gently off the sill and she fell sideways, almost tumbling onto the floor. Jerking awake, she rubbed the elbow that had banged on the edge of the chair. Was that Tess she had heard? She couldn't be sure but glancing at the clock she saw it was half-past twelve.

She stood and stretched and then started walking about the room, knowing it was impossible to settle down properly until she knew Jason was safely home. There was nothing for it, but to go and see. Anna sneaked out of her room and tiptoed past Ben's and then Mrs Wilby's. She knew Jason's room was on the next landing and up a short flight of seven stairs.

She reached the door and listened, but detecting no sound, turned to go back along the corridor. It was then that she noticed a small sliver of light under the door. Her heart leapt and she knocked very gently. There wasn't any answer, but wanting to be certain that Jason was actually home, she twisted the handle and put her head round.

The room was empty, but there were signs of occupation, since the small bedside light was on and Jason's watch lay next to it. His jacket hung on the back of a chair and on the seat lay a buff folder. Looking around, she suddenly realised she could hear the noise of running water coming from an adjoining room and the knowledge he must be taking a shower, made her smile with relief.

She crossed the room, picked up the folder and made herself comfortable in the chair, waiting patiently for him to finish. The folder intrigued her and although not wanting to be inquisitive, she opened the flap and slipped the papers out. After all, she was Jason's personal assistant and they would probably land on her desk sooner or later.

All of them were about the merchant vessel The Lucky Lady just arrived from Iran with a cargo of carpets and leather goods. Most were customs and excise documents and various other permits relating to the shipment and as Anna read them, she realised that Jason must have had a nightmare of a day, trying to sort out the problem.

She grimaced and looked towards the bathroom, where the noise of running water had now stopped. If he was totally exhausted and chances were he would be, then he would want to sleep as soon as possible. Her presence was going to delay this and anxious not to cause him undue fatigue, she decided to go. Now she was satisfied that all was well, she was content to leave their reunion until the morning.

As she reached out to turn the handle, the bathroom door opened and Jason strode into the bedroom, a towel round his waist, another one about his neck. At first he didn't see her, since he was busy drying his face, but then his head turned and he gave a cry of delight.

"My goodness! You're a sight for sore eyes. Come here!"

She was propelled towards him as though he were a magnet. Her arms entwined round his neck, and he covered her face and lips with wonderful warm kisses.

"I thought you were never coming home. I was looking out of the window, but I fell asleep for a few minutes and didn't hear your car."

"So you thought you'd come and track me down. Oh, it feels so good to hold you close after the day I've had!" His arms tightened round her as he pulled her nearer.

"Was it very bad?" she asked breathlessly.

"Well, it could have been better. Who would have thought a ship named The Lucky Lady could be so unlucky."

"Why was she held up?"

"Just red tape, really. You'd have thought we were gun running instead of importing carpets and leather goods. But things are so tense in the Middle East that everyone gets jittery. The client was with me and he was getting very annoyed. I thought he was going to punch one official on the nose."

"Would you have stopped him, if he'd tried?" said Anna, smiling.

"No way! He had a great deal of money tied up in the shipment and his lorries and men were standing around idle, so he had a right to lose his temper. We were all relieved when the cargo was released for unloading." He gave a small chuckle. "And none more so than the captain and his crew. They were keen to get home to their families as soon as possible. Anyway, enough about me. What have you been doing today?"

"Just this and that really. I missed you so much."

His lips brushed hers briefly, before he lifted his face and smiled mischievously. "Hey! You're in my room!"

"I know that. So what?"

"But wasn't that a dangerous thing to do? Coming to my room in the dead of night."

"Well, my intention was to make sure you were home safely. I don't know what your intentions are." He raised his eyebrows, but disappointment crossed his face when she added coyly, "But I know that a gentleman like you, would never take advantage of a lady just because he had the opportunity."

"Then you'd better go back to your own room, before I forget I'm a gentleman!" In spite of his words, he didn't let go.

She swallowed painfully. The thought of going back to her lonely room didn't appeal to her at all, now that the anxieties of the day were finally at an end. She wanted to stay with him, to feel his body close to hers, to satisfy the deep yearning that had been building up inside her. She pressed her cheek into his shoulder and hung onto him for a few seconds more. Tomorrow she would have to tell him everything, but until then there was still tonight.

"Jason."

"Mmm!" Eyes closed, he was resting his face on top of her head.

"Can I stay with you tonight?" she whispered.

He stood quite still as if contemplating some insurmountable problem. "Do you really mean that, Anna? I told you I can wait." He rubbed his cheek against her hair.

"I want to stay with you. That's unless you don't want me to. I mean, you've had such an awful day and you must be tired out."

His hand moved gently down her back and he gave a low moan. "Sweetheart, invitations like that have a habit of chasing away any tiredness a man might have, believe me!" His arms tightened as he pressed light, soft kisses on her face and neck. "Lord, you smell nice. I could eat you!" Clinging tightly against him, her body started to tingle as he manoeuvred her over towards the bed. Once there, they both toppled on top of the duvet and she peeled off the kimono, letting it fall to the floor. His kisses became more demanding and spread to her shoulders and arms and then finally back to her lips. They slipped between the sheets. Jason threw his towels across the room and helped her out of her nightdress. "You're so beautiful," he moaned, his mouth moving to her breasts, his tongue stimulating her nipples so they hardened under his touch. His arm slid under the small of her back, raising her up, as his kisses spread to her stomach.

At first everything seemed so wonderful and she drifted along with the sweet sensation of being loved and desired, responding to his caresses. It was only when his lovemaking became much more sensual and intimate, Anna heard the voice of her husband screaming inside her head, *"How dare you criticise me, when your behaviour is no better!"*

She stiffened and put her fist to her mouth, pushing the knuckles against her teeth. Tears began to trickle into her hair and she let out a mournful sob. Jason had felt her body tense and stopped his caressing. Taking her in his arms, he let her work the tears out of her system, while he kissed her.

"I knew it was too soon," he sighed.

She sobbed into his shoulder. "I did want us to be together tonight. I don't know what's the matter with me."

They clung together, while he stroked her shaking body and murmured words of comfort in her hair. Eventually, she became still. When he raised his face to look at her, he found she had fallen asleep with complete exhaustion.

He kissed her lips gently. "I know you have a secret, Anna. When are you going to tell me?" he whispered.

CHAPTER SEVEN

In the early hours of the morning, Anna suddenly awoke and was horrified to see she was lying naked in bed next to Jason. She remembered the previous hours and the disaster of their lovemaking, but most of all she was filled with a great sense of propriety and the desire not to be discovered in such a compromising situation by Margaret and the others. His arms were still tightly round her and although she wanted to stay warm and comfortable, she decided she must go. She leaned over and tenderly kissed his sleeping eyes before slipping out of bed. She found her kimono and wrapping it round herself, left the room, closing the door quietly.

The journey back was filled with shadows that jumped out at her as she groped her way along the wall. Only the small night-time noises could be heard, but they were enough to cause her to hasten her steps. Once in her own room, she jumped straight into bed. The sheets were cold against her bare flesh and she shivered. And then she closed her eyes.

It was nine o'clock when Anna finally stirred from sleep. She jumped out of bed and crossed the room to open the window and breathe in the cool, fresh country air; the glory of the day spread before her. The rain had stopped and the sun shone brightly in a brilliant blue sky. The branches on the trees swayed slightly with the breeze and she could smell the sweet moisture of the grass.

There was a knock on her door. Closing the window, she reached for her robe and covered herself, since she was still in the same state of nakedness she had been in when returning to her own bed. Jason was standing in the corridor, already up and dressed and carrying an oyster-pink nightgown over his arm.

"You left this last night."

"Oh, you haven't come here carrying my nightie, have you!" she cried in alarm, looking out to see if there was anyone about.

"Everyone's at breakfast, Anna. They'll be off to church soon. It was quite safe."

"But what would've happened if your mother had seen you!"

"You do worry about what people are going to say, don't you. Is that why you left me last night? Because you didn't want anyone to see us in bed together."

Grabbing the nightgown from his arm, she pulled him into the room, astonished at his brashness.

"Shhh! Someone might hear you!"

"We are consenting adults, you know. What we decide to do is nobody's business but our own."

"I know it is, but I'd feel embarrassed if they found out."

"Really? And there's me thinking of telling them at breakfast." He was teasing her, but Anna stared past him, her expression serious.

"I don't want to offend your mother. She's been so good to me," she explained anxiously.

"And she likes you a lot."

"When did she tell you that?"

"Yesterday morning, before I set off for Bristol. In fact, she said I should consider settling down again since being forty, time is not on my side."

"You're having me on! She wouldn't say that so soon after Kiera."

"Well, Mother has a habit of moving on with life."

Anna felt a coldness pass over her. Was he going to ask her to marry him? The explanation of her situation was awkward enough as employer and employee, but after last night it had become distressing now they had become romantically involved.

She decided to get rid of him. "Go away, Jason! Let me get dressed. I'll be down in ten minutes."

She pushed him out of the room, but failed to avoid his sudden grasp and the kiss he placed firmly on her mouth. Then he was gone.

Anna took her time getting dressed and before she left her room, she scrutinised herself in the long mirror. She pulled out her tongue at her reflection and sighed sadly. It was a special day in more ways than one, but who would know that? She went down to breakfast. Margaret, Ben and Mrs Wilby were leaving for church. They all kissed her and wished her a good morning, before disappearing out into the sharp morning air.

In the dining room, Jason sat on his own, reading the paper.

"Don't you want to go to church?" she asked him, as she took her place and poured herself some coffee from a silver pot.

"I only go if I'm forced to. Anyway, I've more important things to do today."

Anna felt overwhelmed with disappointment. After the events of the previous day, she had hoped to spend a little time with him and get this awful business out of the way. If it had to be delayed any longer, she would become a gibbering idiot.

"Do you have to go somewhere?" Her question came in a small voice, her eyes not daring to meet his.

"Not exactly. I want to give you your birthday present," he said nonchalantly. He looked up and smiled. "Happy birthday."

Anna almost choked on her coffee. "How on earth did you know it was my birthday?"

"First of September. It was on your CV," he said turning the page of his newspaper. He took her hand and kissed her fingers. "After you've had your breakfast we'll go and find your present."

Her mind started spinning. What did he mean 'find it'? She nibbled some toast and held back the overpowering desire to ask him more questions. He, on the other hand, became absorbed in his paper and didn't look up once.

Breakfast over, they stood and he took her hand. "You'll need your jacket. We're going outside and it's a little chilly this morning."

"What's this all about, Jason. You're not playing a joke on me are you?"

"Certainly not! I don't go around playing practical jokes on people." She squinted eagerly at his expression, trying to understand, but all she saw was his charming smile and an intriguing glint in his eyes.

They left the Grange through the main entrance. She followed Jason along the drive that led to the far end of the building, her thoughts in confusion and yet, excitement made her tingle. As they rounded the corner, the stables came into sight. These were a row of low structures with half a dozen split doors opening onto a large cobbled area, where riders used to mount and dismount. However, standing in the centre of this courtyard was a brand new Peugeot, its red paintwork gleaming in the bright morning sun.

Jason slipped his arm round her waist. Anna looked to left and right in bewilderment.

"I don't know what you're up to, but I'm starting to get very nervous!" she muttered.

"Nothing to get nervous about, we're here now and there's my present to you."

She glanced at him and then her eyes followed his line of vision to the new car.

"You're looking at the car," she commented dryly.

"I know. That's my present."

"You've bought me a car?"

He didn't answer, but his smile showed his delight at her total surprise. They walked towards it, Jason sweeping his eyes over the sleek bodywork, making sure it was exactly to his specifications. Anna couldn't speak. Her heart thudded loudly and she found it hard to catch her breath with excitement.

"Well! Do you like it?" he asked giving her a huge squeeze.

"How can I not like it! I don't understand, why did you buy me a car?" She narrowed her eyes at him. "Is this a company car? Do I have to return it when you sack me?"

He chuckled. "I thought it time you had your own transport and it's yours for as long as you wish."

She grimaced, knowing her own car was still parked in the driveway of the home she shared with her husband, but then she smiled. "I love it. I really, really do. But I can't accept it."

"Why not? And if you so much as mutter, 'what will people say', I'll pick you up and throw you in the stable. With any luck I might even find some manure to drop you in!"

"I feel embarrassed. It's so lovely. How can I thank you."

"A kiss will suffice for now."

She entwined her arms about his neck and only after the lingering kiss had floated away, did she suddenly remember she still had to tell him about her husband. Nausea gripped her insides, since now the guilt she carried had been compounded by the giving of his marvellous gift. She held him close and took in a deep breath.

He didn't say anything, but tenderly moved his hands down her back and over her buttocks.

After a couple of minutes, he dipped into his trouser pocket and pulled out some jangling keys.

"Well, milady, where are you going to take me?"

"You want me to drive now?"

"Of course! This is your car so let's see how you can handle her."

"But I don't know any places to drive to."

"Then we'll go up to the lake. It's only about three or four miles. I'll direct you."

Excitedly, Anna took the keys and opened the driver's door. As she climbed in and unlocked the passenger side, she looked around. Everything was spanking brand new, with shining knobs and an intoxicating smell of leather. They started their excursion, a journey that only took about ten minutes along the twisting country roads.

By the time they reached the lake and parked, Anna's spirits had started to soar and she believed that whatever the outcome of the next hour or two, at least she would have the most wonderful memories to take back to West Yorkshire with her.

Hand in hand, they started their walk round the lake. It was a popular spot for families and courting couples and the weather had brought many people out of doors. The sun felt gloriously warm on their faces and occasionally they would stand and watch the glittering lake with the boats and windsurfers gliding across the surface, the sails a riot of colour against the blueness of the water. At one point, two young boys came screeching past on bikes. They found an empty bench and took a rest. They didn't speak for a while, their eyes drinking in the beauty of the scene before them.

After a couple of minutes, Jason pointed to a young man wobbling about in a canoe. "I hope that young man can swim. It looks as though he might go over any minute. Whoops! There he goes!"

"Shouldn't laugh, really. After all, it looks fairly difficult to do."

"Just technique really. After a bit of practice, it's quite easy."

"Can you canoe?" Anna asked incredulously.

"Yes. We did it at school. I used to come here with my friends when I was a boy. I've had a great deal of fun here. This is a special place for me. That's why I wanted to bring you."

She sighed. "It's very beautiful. A place where you can forget all your problems."

"Have you any problems?"

"Why do you ask?"

"Just wondered." His eyes remained fixed on the boats.

Casting him a sidelong glance, she bit her lip nervously. "Are you talking about last night? I'm so sorry about that, I really am. It must have been the ghastly day I had."

"What happened that was so ghastly? Mother didn't say anything when I phoned. In fact, she gave me the impression you were absolutely fine."

She paused slightly before continuing. "To begin with, I found out you had gone to Bristol. That was a good start to the day!"

"No one was more disappointed than me, I can tell you. But that's the business I'm in."

Then Anna took in a deep breath and began to tell him of the incident in the kitchen and how she had disgraced herself so miserably.

"I didn't realise that a few glasses of sherry would affect me so much and I was sleeping it off when you rang the first time. I felt so ashamed, but your mother was charming about it all."

All through the narrative, Jason had listened with great delight, bursting into laughter when she came to the part about misunderstanding Margaret's comments.

"My mother has a strange sense of humour," he smiled.

"If that had been all, then I would have got over it, only something else happened and this one scared me a little." Anna continued, telling him about the events in the morning room and how Tess had rushed at her, making her knock over a vase. "I'm not used to dogs and for one dreadful moment I thought she was a wolf or something."

Jason grinned. "There's been no wolves in England for quite some time and Tess won't hurt you." Sitting forward in the seat, his elbows resting on his knees, he couldn't hold back his amusement. "I'll ask Mother to keep her in the kitchen for the duration of your visit. I want your stay at the Grange to be pleasant…and comfortable."

"You'll do no such thing! I'll get used to her." She looked away for a moment and then smiled. "A wolf! How ridiculous is that. My husband always tells me I have a lively imagination!"

Jason paused for a second, his eyes searching across the surface of the lake. When he spoke it was quiet, almost a whisper. "Your husband always 'tells' you?" She looked at him puzzled, not understanding. He decided to make it clearer. "You've done this before, used the present tense when referring to your husband. Surely if you're a widow, it should be your husband always 'told' you."

Anna sat still, barely daring to breathe. She turned her head away so she couldn't see his face. She blinked hard, fighting to control the surge that was threatening to spill over at any minute. The moment had finally arrived. "I'm not a widow," she said quickly. "I have a husband in Wakefield. I left him to come and work for you."

She stared down at her fingers clenched so tightly the white of her knuckles showed and waited for Jason to say something as she gulped hard and tried to steady her breathing. She felt him lean back on the bench and take in a sharp breath. But he remained silent and the silence cut through her and made her wince with the pain. It was then she realised she had been right all along. He was disgusted with her for her deceit; he hated her for her betrayal of his trust. She couldn't bear it any longer and sprang from her seat. Without daring to look back she hurried towards the car her only thought to get away from him. She didn't want to see the anger and disappointment in his eyes.

It was when she reached the car that he caught up with her, grabbing her by the shoulders and bringing her to a sudden stop.

"I hope you're not thinking of leaving me to walk back?" he asked.

She didn't dare turn round, tears ran down her face in an endless stream. "You take the car. I'll walk home," she sobbed.

"Now, that's being silly." He offered her a white folded handkerchief. "Give me the keys."

She passed them to him and he opened the door and put her in the passenger's seat. Walking round, he got in behind the wheel.

Anna lifted her head and was surprised to see his expression passive. There was no hate in his eyes just a look of resignation.

She began to talk quickly. "If you take me back to the Grange, I'll pack my things and leave. I'm sure Ben would give me a lift to the station and I'll send for…"

She got no further. To her utter amazement he suddenly reached out for her and before she could catch her breath his mouth was on hers, pressing down with the passion and intensity he had shown her the night before. At first she struggled, not understanding, almost frightened of him. But then his kiss became gentler and she relaxed, sinking against him. It seemed a long time before he finally released her. And when she opened her eyes, he was smiling.

"I don't understand," she said, shaking her head.

"Well, if you'd given me the chance, I would have explained."

"Explained what?"

He waited a few seconds, before pulling her close once more and kissing her hair.

"I know, Anna. I know about your husband. That's why I hesitated. I was trying to pluck up the courage to tell you," he whispered.

She jerked her head round to look at him. "You...You knew! But how?"

He smiled meekly. "Oh, little clues you kept giving away. I told you, I'm a good judge of character. I also have an instinct about people." He saw the blank look on her face and took in a breath. "When you came into my office for your interview, I knew you were hiding something. That interested me. A woman with an intriguing secret! There's not many about, I can tell you. And it was so obvious you were watching your every word in case you let something slip."

"You could see all that?"

"It wasn't very difficult." He held her closer a small smile hovering around his lips. "Did you know that when a person lies, they can't look you in the eye? You averted your gaze so often, I knew you were...what should I call it? Stretching the truth somewhat."

"That's an understatement! I've been lying through my teeth since the day I read your advert!"

He threw back his head and gave an incredulous laugh, before saying, "Anyway, by the time you received the letter, the one you burnt, I knew that things were very, very wrong."

"So you put it all together and worked out that I wasn't a widow after all and that I did have a husband tucked away somewhere," she said crisply.

"In actual fact, I knew the real truth about you long before that. A month after you arrived I discovered all about you."

"A month!"

"I had a phone call from a...well, suffice it to say I ended up speaking to your husband."

Anna opened her eyes in horror, putting her hand to her mouth to stop the scream that wanted to make itself heard. "You spoke to my husband!"

"You're starting to sound like a parrot," he chuckled, but then continued more seriously, "I found myself talking to a very angry, rude guy. At first, I didn't know who he was, but then when he said your name, and how you'd run off and left him and the boys, his words not mine by the way, I got the general idea. He was very furious about the fact I'd taken you away from him. You see, sweetheart, he thought I was the 'other' man. I found that quite interesting at the time. Of course, after I discovered I really did love you and after what nearly happened last night, I suppose I am the 'other' man now."

"But I had to leave him, Jason. Please understand. I told you I was a widow, because I didn't think you would give me the job, if you knew I had responsibilities in Wakefield."

"Why did you turn the job down and then change your mind?"

She swallowed hard. "I felt I had to turn it down, because of the twins and their exams, but then they went off to Romania and I discovered..." She gave a sob and put her hand to her mouth. "I discovered Dave had been up to his old tricks again. I think he's cheated on me from the day we married, perhaps even before. And I couldn't take any more." She tried to pull herself together. "I was so happy working for you, but then came the letter."

"I assume it wasn't very pleasant?"

"It was upsetting because he seemed to be blaming me for our separation. He made me feel guilty when I hadn't done anything wrong." Moments of silence passed between them. "Jason, why didn't you tell me you'd spoken to him?" she pleaded in desperation.

"What would you have done, if I had?"

"Been shocked, but at least things would have been straight between us."

He sighed sadly. "Many times I came close to saying something, but I decided not to. I believed you would tell me sooner or later. Of course, I didn't realise you would hold out for so long, even though I could see it was a huge strain. I gave you one more day, if you hadn't said anything by tomorrow, then I was going to say something to you! I can't understand why you didn't tell me sooner."

"I thought you'd hate me and send me packing."

"Even after I told you that I loved you?"

"That was when you thought I was a widow. Or at least, I thought you thought I was a widow. Oh dear! This is getting complicated. You'd gone through such a lot with Kiera and I couldn't bear to add to your problems."

"Do you believe me when I tell you that nothing has changed and I still love you?"

"But Jason, I just up and left my husband one morning. I abandoned my two children. Doesn't that worry you about the sort of woman I might be?"

He chucked her under the chin. "Your sons are no longer children so you've not abandoned them. And what kind of woman are you?"

"The kind that runs away when there's any kind of problem."

"Infidelity is not just any kind of problem. How you put up with it all those years is beyond me. It shows incredible courage."

"Or stupidity," she said, puckering her lips. "But what about my lies? Dear Lord, I shudder to think of what I came out with. To tell you that my husband had died of a terrible illness and then your own wife dies. I feel so ashamed."

Jason frowned. "Then you mustn't."

"You're so good to forgive me," she sighed.

Jason took his arm from her and put both hands on the steering wheel as if trying to summon strength from gripping it tightly.

"Anna, I don't think you understand. I was trapped in a nightmare of a marriage too, so I understand. Kiera and I…disintegrated. Oh, I know we tried for Hollie's sake but it was becoming more and more difficult to live together and finally we had to separate."

Anna felt stunned. "What about Peter? I thought she left you for him?"

He gave a caustic laugh. "She did." He rubbed his forehead, trying to ease the tension. "Our marriage was over and as soon as she met Peter, then that was her 'get out of jail' card.' I allowed Hollie to go with her because she was always an excellent mother."

"Kiera doted on her," Anna smiled.

Jason nodded and dropped his hands from the steering wheel. He took in a breath before turning to her again. "Did Kiera, by any chance, tell you that she'd like us to marry? Then you could look after Hollie?"

Anna's mouth went dry. "Yes…Yes she did."

"She told me that too." Jason put his arm round her. "And that's exactly what you've done. You've been a second mother to Hollie."

"Have I though?"

"You certainly have! Anyway, it wasn't Kiera's place to put that kind of responsibility on your shoulders." He held her closer. "And you've been a wonderful support to me through all this. I don't think I could have managed without you."

"But marriage?"

He gave a half-smile. "I would ask you here and now to be my wife and not because Kiera wanted it, but because I do."

"So Kiera was right. You did have feelings for me, although I didn't realise."

Jason smiled and kissed the top of her head. "We're a fine pair. Both trapped in a loveless marriage."

Anna pressed her face against his shoulder. "I lived with Dave for nineteen years. I gave him two sons. Surely it means something?"

"It means that you persevered against all odds."

"I did love him. Well, at the beginning I certainly did. And I was always faithful to him. That's why last night was such a disaster. I couldn't bring myself to behave the same way he did."

"You have quite a traditional view of marriage, haven't you? Fidelity and loyalty figure highly in your notions of marriage. I feel so sad that it wasn't returned, because you deserve better."

Anna looked out of the window and across the lake. "Yes, I did expect more from my marriage," she said dejectedly. "But there again, I had expected much more from myself before I got married. Oh Jason, I had such dreams, so many plans. I wanted to go to university and study English. Then I could train as a teacher. I wanted to work abroad, even go to the States. But instead I got married." She searched his expression for reassurance. "I thought that I could still do it after the boys had left home. Still do all the things I'd planned. I thought that if I got a qualification in office work, it would give me a start. But it all got out of hand when you offered me a job. My application was supposed to be an experiment."

"Some experiment," said Jason, smiling. He added, "So, what do you want to do next?"

"I need a little time to work things out."

"Take all the time you need. I want us to be together, but only when you wish it too. I want you to be comfortable with the situation."

"How long are you prepared to wait?" she giggled and then became more serious. "Life can be so complicated. I'll be glad when the boys have left for university, then I know I'll feel more settled. My ties with my husband will be finished."

He gave a sigh as he thought this over. The morning was almost gone. "Then I'll leave the decision to you. Come on, Anna, let's go home for Mother's birthday lunch. Shall I drive?"

"Certainly not! This is my car!" As they changed places, Anna flung her arms round his neck and kissed him full on the lips.

It had been the most wonderful birthday of Anna's life. Not only because of Jason's gift of the car, but also the tremendous relief at confessing her dark and dismal secret. Knowing he understood and still loved her, filled her with joy. As she drove back for lunch, she felt as though a hundred years of guilt had slipped from her shoulders. Jason clicked on the radio and they sang along to the songs.

She parked in the drive and with their arms round each other; they strolled through the main entrance and into the large hall. They could hear laughter coming from the parlour and the clinking of glasses.

"I think Mother is serving cocktails before lunch. Would you like to try one?" Jason cast her a mischievous sidelong glance. "Or you can have lemonade if you're worried about getting tipsy." She gave him a withering look and he gave her a quick kiss. "Come and meet our lunch guests."

They entered the parlour and were greeted by Margaret, who had been waiting to introduce Anna to the motley group of people from Wedmore Village and surrounding neighbourhood. Taking her arm and whisking her away, she guided her round the room for ten minutes, intent on getting her acquainted with everyone. At the end, Anna's head buzzed with all the names she had heard and her hand ached from the force of so much shaking. By the time she had circled the room, she was relieved to be back where Jason waited with a cocktail for her.

"Goodness me!" she exclaimed with delight, "they all seem to be clergymen and generals and judges and lady this or that!"

Jason chuckled. "Mother does have rather influential friends." He pointed towards a stout gentleman with a white beard. "That's Doctor Orchard. He's been the family doctor for as long as I can remember."

Suddenly another guest swept into the room, causing all eyes to turn in her direction. Her head crowned with thick, black hair, her face enhanced with dark, seductive eyes, it was little wonder she immediately became the focus of attention. Anna's gaze took in the stylish clothes definitely bought at only the top fashion houses in Milan and London. Tall and slender, with an elegant walk, she moved with the confident air of someone who knew she had the power to dominate.

Seeing Jason, she glided towards him. "Jason, it's been ages since I last spoke with you!"

Anna noticed he had become uncomfortable.

"Oh, hello Deborah. Didn't know you were coming today. May I introduce you to Anna Stevens? Anna, this is Deborah Gilbert-Hines, an old friend of the family."

Deborah held out a limp hand and Anna took it politely, knowing she was being scrutinised from head to toe.

"Hi there. You're Jason's new secretary or something aren't you? I love the way he brings his employees to the Grange on special occasions." Anna cast him an incredulous look of amusement, but her smile faded as she saw his black, thunderous expression. He didn't answer. Deborah continued, "You don't mind if I take him away from you for a few moments, do you? I've something I must discuss with him!"

Without waiting for a reply, she manoeuvred Jason to the corner of the room and they became absorbed in forceful conversation.

Margaret had seen all this happen and came to Anna's side. "Oh dear, I don't think it was a good idea to invite that woman, but I wanted to invite her mother and it seemed impolite not to invite the daughter too."

Anna swallowed a lump in her throat. "Were they ever serious? They're talking as if they know each other very well."

"My dear, Deborah is the sort of woman men always fall madly in love with. She's already had two husbands."

"Perhaps she's looking for a third."

"You mean Jason? That was over long ago, I assure you. We did think there was something there to be honest, but it was just after Kiera had left and I think he was on the rebound."

"She has the same kind of beauty as Kiera. Dark and sensual."

The description caused Margaret to laugh. "Now, come with me. I want to introduce you to Doctor Orchard. You'll find him a lovely man and so interesting." She guided Anna over to the gentleman with a white beard. "Colin, this is the young lady I told you about. This is her first visit to the Grange. Will you take care of her, while I sort out my other guests?"

Anna tried to concentrate on the conversation, but found her eyes drifting frequently to the corner, where Jason was still engrossed with Deborah. There was something very familiar about this woman in the way she held herself and the cut of her clothes. Anna wondered if she had met her before. Suddenly, she remembered the woman at Kiera's funeral, the one standing outside the crematorium wearing a large hat and sunglasses. If it was the same woman then had she been there for Kiera's sake or Jason's? The thought made her bite her lip anxiously. The morning had turned out so wonderful, surely it wasn't going to be spoilt. Not now, Anna groaned to herself in despair, not after all we've been through.

"Colin, you've had a call from Mrs Turner," came a voice from Anna's right-hand side. Anna turned to see a tall, lean woman with rather protruding teeth. "I'm sorry to butt in. I'm Sarah, Colin's wife. And you're Anna, Jason's new secretary?" They shook hands and she turned to her husband once more. "It seems Mrs Turner's mother has taken a turn for the worse."

"Oh dear, I did expect this," said the doctor. He smiled ruefully. "Looks like my lunch will have to be kept warm as is often the case."

"Shall I come with you?" said his wife.

"No, no, not necessary." He kissed her warmly on the cheek. "See you later."

"I really hoped he would have a day free from patients," said Sarah wistfully, watching him leave the room.

"The trials and tribulations of being a doctor," smiled Anna.

"Not to mention a doctor's wife," nodded Sarah.

Jason appeared and placed his arm round Anna's waist. Sarah said a brief 'hello' to him and then moved on to talk to another guest.

"Sorry to leave you like that. Mother says she loved our gift. But I told her it was your idea."

"Oh, Jason, we decided together. You thought of lunch and a shopping trip to Harrods and I suggested including tickets for a West End show!"

"Well, she was delighted with it and she's looking forward to going with Sarah Orchard, they've been friends for years."

Anna paused a moment before saying, "Have you finished speaking to Deborah?"

Her strained voice told him everything and he sighed. "That woman is evil and I rue the day I ever set eyes on her!"

"Margaret said you had a thing about her once."

"Mother told you that, did she? Well, yes, I did go out with her when I was at university. After Kiera left, we started seeing each other again. But then I realised what a fool I was and finished it."

"Did you ever think of marrying her?"

"Everyone seemed to expect it. Said we made a lovely couple, or some such rot. However, I knew she was a leech. Takes a man for everything he has. There's no giving, with a woman like Deborah. You know she's had two husbands already?" Anna nodded. "One is now bankrupt and the other is in a psychiatric hospital."

"But that might not have been Deborah's fault!"

"Anna, you're too understanding. Anyway, I don't want to spoil the day by discussing that dreadful woman."

The gong sounded for lunch.

The table looked marvellous, gleaming with bright silver cutlery and cut glass goblets. Flowers and candles decorated the centre making the whole array a dazzling invitation.

Jason took Anna's hand. "I sit at one end and Mother at the other. And you're sitting next to me."

The diners took their seats and the first course was served. Anna felt relieved to see that Deborah was down at the far end of the table, which meant there was no danger of having to make conversation with her. She felt uneasy in her presence and for some inexplicable reason, she knew it was more than the fact she was Jason's former lover.

Anna turned her attention back to Jason who was engrossed in conversation with a certain Lady Manville who had been seated on the other side of him. She smiled to herself at how the elderly woman would often reach across and pat his hand.

She caught Anna's eye. "I've known this boy since he was born, my dear. He's a credit to his mother and late father and I'm so delighted to see that he has such a charming young lady in his life."

Jason nodded. "I can't believe my luck, Lady Manville. Anna arrived just when I needed her. Perhaps it was our destiny to meet since she travelled a fair distance to come and work for me."

"Only three hours by train, Jason," said Anna, laughing.

"It still meant a complete change for you. A different life." He winked at her. "And a life that I hope will bring you a great deal of happiness."

"Yes, I hope so too," she whispered.

Lady Manville watched them for a few seconds, her brow creased in a frown. "My dear, I was told that your husband died? And you nursed him for many years?"

Anna took a large gulp of wine to steady her nerves. "I was married...for quite a long time. My husband..."

Jason interrupted her. "Lady Manville, I don't think Anna wants to be reminded of what she's been through. Not today of all days," he said kindly.

"Of course not. Oh dear, how unfeeling of me. Do forgive me, my dear."

"It's OK," said Anna. "It's all in the past."

She glanced uneasily at Jason and tried to smile. She had told the most terrible lies about her husband and the day of reckoning would come sooner or later. How was she going to explain everything? Suddenly, she felt tempted to tell Lady Manville that she wasn't a widow at all. She wanted to stand up and tell everyone, to clear the air and set everything straight. But in her mind's eye she saw the horror on the faces of Margaret, Ben and Mrs Wilby as they learnt the truth. But worst of all, was that she knew Deborah would lap it up. She would enjoy seeing Jason's new girlfriend falling from grace. Anna pressed her lips together and slipped her hand under the table, caressing Jason's leg. And when he reached to squeeze her fingers in response, she took in a huge breath and smiled.

Margaret rising to her feet and banging a spoon on the table, interrupted everyone's conversation.

"Ladies and gentlemen, could I have your attention please." Having assured herself that all were listening, Margaret continued. "I'd like to thank you all for coming to my birthday lunch and I do hope you've enjoyed yourself as much as I have. Goodness, am I really seventy? The staff have worked very hard and I'm sure you'll agree with me when I say they have surpassed themselves in making this a wonderful day for me." Everyone clapped and cheered. She went on, "As you know the village is holding a special fete today in honour of my birthday and some of you have expressed a wish to attend. So if those of you who would like to go would assemble in the drive after lunch, we can all go together."

"Would you like to go?" Anna whispered to Jason.

"I've got other plans for us," he whispered back.

"What are they?"

"Wait and see," he smiled.

She grimaced and glanced down the table. Deborah's hostile eyes met hers and she shivered.

CHAPTER EIGHT

After lunch, the guests milled about, some taking the opportunity of thanking Margaret, before starting their journeys home. The rest collected together for the excursion to the village fete. Jason disappeared upstairs. Anna went to find her jacket from where she had placed it after returning from their trip to the lake.

While she was slipping it on, Deborah walked through the hall, her expression breaking into a sardonic smile when she saw Anna. Her voice resonated off the oak-panelled walls like gunfire.

"Are you going to the fete?"

Anna shook her head. "Jason has something special planned for us but I don't know what it is."

Deborah pursed her lips. "Yes, I remember his surprises. Watch yourself with a man like Jason, you might find yourself out of your depth."

Her advice was not well-intentioned and anger boiled up in the depths of Anna's stomach. She was tempted to answer with an equally vindictive retort and opened her mouth to speak. But then she remembered her father telling her that dignity is always maintained with silence and pressed her lips together. But she couldn't help raising her index fingers and putting them in the sign of a cross as Deborah disappeared through the door.

"What are you doing?" said Jason, grinning. He had just appeared at the bottom of the stairs and had witnessed Anna's strange action.

"Just warding off the evil eye," laughed Anna. He shook his head in exasperation, knowing exactly what she meant. She noticed he was carrying a bag containing golfing irons. "We're going to play this afternoon?" she said in amazement. "Is there time? The party's at eight."

"I'm sure there'll be time. For half a round at least. And if I'm on top form, we should be lucky enough to get round the entire course." He didn't notice Anna's smug smile.

His mother appeared hauling along another bag of clubs. Jason hurried across and took them from her.

"I think these should be OK for you, dear. They've served me well for many a year," said Margaret.

Anna smiled and took out one of the irons. She balanced it in her hands and then took a firm swing at an invisible ball.

"These will be wonderful. I should be able to do them justice."

Jason took the bags out to the Volvo and put them in the boot. Within minutes they were on their way to the golf club, a distance of about eight miles. They didn't speak for several minutes, until Anna decided to bring up the subject of his former lover.

"I don't think Deborah likes me and I can't work out why. I've hardly spoken to her since we met."

Jason sighed. "She thinks you've come between us."

"Oh, no, have I?"

"No, you haven't! There was nothing there, for you to come between. That's why she cornered me in the parlour before lunch. She wanted to know why I wasn't answering her emails or returning her phone calls. I told her it was because I wasn't interested in her and hadn't been for the last ten months."

"Did you love her, when you were interested in her?"

"If you're asking if I enjoyed sleeping with her, the answer is yes."

"You're very honest with your answers."

"In this instance, it's better to be honest. Besides if we're to have any kind of relationship, then it's better if we know the truth about each other."

"She's very beautiful."

"Now what are you trying to say?"

"Oh, that you're able to make comparisons. I just wondered what score out of ten I would get from you."

He smiled at the idea. "I don't give scores to the women I've slept with."

"Have there been many?" she asked quietly.

Jason's smile faded as he pulled the car over to the side of the road, stopped and pulled on the handbrake. Anna glanced out of the side window. She shouldn't have asked him that, but she had felt compelled to know.

Jason touched her cheek gently. "What's this all about?"

She turned to face him and was surprised to see his concerned expression. "Sorry, I had no right to ask you that."

He pursed his lips. "I disagree. Why shouldn't you know how many women I've slept with." He thought for a moment. "Well, I did have a few girlfriends before I married, but I don't think it was excessive. I was totally faithful to Kiera while we were living as man and wife, then I had a brief affair with Deborah after my wife left. I didn't keep count, but at a rough estimate I should say about seven, no perhaps eight relationships in all and that includes my wife and Deborah. Now, does that put your mind at rest?"

Anna felt uncomfortable. "Thank you for telling me, but it's none of my business who you've been out with in the past." She grimaced. "Except you can make comparisons. If Deborah and your wife are anything to go by, you've chosen some very beautiful women to share your life."

Jason smiled, aware that Anna didn't realise what she had just said. He decided to have some fun at her expense. "Oh, and you can't understand why I've now chosen a plain Jane? Well, I guess I'll just have to grin and bear it." She widened her eyes in surprise and he continued, "Anna, I'm not making any comparisons. Deborah might be beautiful, but she's rotten to the core. I shouldn't have got mixed up with her in the first place. And as for Kiera, I had a few years of happiness and then it evaporated. You've given me more joy and contentment in two months than I've known for a long time. You've helped me through a very difficult time and I love you for it." He grinned cheekily. "And the minute I get the chance, I'll show you how much!"

"If last night's anything to go by, you might have a difficult job."

"Last night was different. You had a great deal on your mind, but now you've unburdened yourself from your guilty secret, there's no reason why we shouldn't be very happy. Come here, you silly girl." He enclosed her in a warm embrace.

She gave a sigh. "I'm afraid Dave was my first and last boyfriend. I got married because we were careless and I found I was pregnant. I was so naive."

Jason began to laugh and pulled Anna closer to him. "It looks like the sooner you can make a comparison, the better it will be for both of us. Perhaps we can plan something for tonight?"

"No way! I'm going to sleep! These last forty-eight hours have been too much for me."

Jason feigned disappointment and then holding her tightly, he lightly brushed his lips against hers, before pressing down with passionate intensity, forcing her lips apart with his tongue. His hand crept up her body and slipped inside her jacket, resting gently on her breast. Anna felt herself sinking into that void of abandoned pleasure that Jason always seemed to arouse in her.

When they finally parted from the kiss, she pressed her face against his shoulder and groaned. "Oh, God! You make me ache in places, I have no right to!"

"We could always forget the golf and climb into the back seat," he murmured into her hair.

"Yes! Oh, yes," she murmured in reply. Suddenly, she realised what she had said and opened her eyes in fright. Pushing him away she countermanded it sharply. "Not on your life! I did that when I was eighteen and it got me into a great deal of trouble. I'm old enough to know better now. Let's go and play some golf!"

Jason shook himself back to reality. "Yes, ma'am."

They finally arrived in the car park belonging to the golf club. It was an attractive, modern building, two storeys high with large windows and white painted walls. Jason signed her in as a guest and the receptionist gave her a bright smile and welcomed her.

Anna had never had so much fun in years. She had always loved golf and was determined to give Jason a hard time. At the first tee, she hit the ball almost onto the green with her first shot, while Jason went into a bunker. From that moment on it became a battle of wills and skill and with her heart singing, she knew that he was forced to give everything he had just to keep pace with her.

"The winner buys the drinks," he said, as they reached the eighteenth hole.

"You never said that when we started!" she remonstrated with him. "Hope you're not going to be a sore loser."

"I haven't lost yet," he said, smiling. But he did lose and as they walked back to the clubhouse, Jason was obviously impressed. "Well, done. Perhaps you'll tell me your handicap now?"

Anna hesitated for a moment but finally said, "Five."

He let out a groan. "I should have guessed. Mine's seven. I didn't think for one minute that yours would be better. How arrogant of me."

"Never mind, I'll let you win next time."

"You will not! We play fair or not at all!"

The club seemed to be very full when they arrived back and it was difficult to find seats. Then Anna spotted an empty table in the corner and headed for it. Despite saying that the winner would buy the drinks, Jason didn't hesitate in going straight to the bar. He brought back their drinks smiling brightly.

"When shall we have a return match?" he asked, putting her drink down in front of her.

"You're a glutton for punishment."

"No, just keen not to be beaten." They talked for the next thirty minutes and Anna told him about the golf club in Wakefield and the many tournaments that she had taken part in, including the medals and trophies that filled an entire cabinet at home. "It's a good thing I didn't know this before we started playing," said Jason. "I might have suggested a game of scrabble instead."

Anna sighed. "Your birthplace is so lovely. But why is it called the Isle of Wedmore?"

"A throwback from the Saxon times, I believe, when Wedmore was completely surrounded by wet marshland."

The club was beginning to empty and Anna glanced across the room. "Talking of marshland, Deborah whatshername is sitting not too far from us."

"I've never heard Deborah compared to a marshland before."

"Well, I get the feeling she can suck you down, if you let her."

"I forgot she was a member too. How awkward."

"I don't think she's seen us. She's very engrossed in talking to an attractive young man." Anna gave a grin. "For all her declarations of love, I believe she's forgotten you already."

"That's Deborah for you."

"What does she do for a living?"

"She's in marketing. Got a steady little business herself in Bristol with about six employees. Would you like another drink?"

Anna nodded and he stood, collected up their empty glasses and carried them to the bar. When he returned his face was grey. He put their drinks on the table, almost spilling them with his shaking hands.

"What's the matter?" said Anna. She reached out and touched him gently.

"That man Deborah is talking to, is called Peter."

"What! The Peter! Kiera's fiancé…?"

"Yes. I wonder how she knows him."

"Well, it looks like Peter's heart has mended quickly."

Jason bit his lip as he suddenly remembered. "Oh, of course, you won't know. Kiera told me that Peter had left her as soon as she discovered she was ill. He went back to his wife."

"How cruel! I wondered why I never saw him at the hospital. And he didn't seem to be at the funeral. I didn't like to ask you about him." She peered over Jason's shoulder. "They're in deep conversation."

"Probably planning some treacherous plot!"

Anna couldn't help smiling at his expression of contempt.

It had been a wonderful afternoon, but it was time to go. Before leaving the clubhouse, Anna decided to visit the ladies. She entered a room she could have lived in. Comfortable and plush, it was designed so that any woman would feel perfectly comfortable as she went about her business. The room was empty and Anna selected a cubicle and closed the door. She had just thrown the small bolt, when someone else came in. This individual was obviously using the ladies to make a call on her mobile and Anna was surprised to hear Deborah's husky voice.

"Hi, Ellen, it's me. Have you any more info?" Anna stood perfectly still not daring to move. She couldn't bear the thought of coming face to face with Deborah. "Peter's here with me now and you won't believe it but so is Jason Harrington with his new *amour*, his secretary of all people." Anna almost stopped breathing. "Yes, I quite agree. He's really scraping the bottom of the barrel now." Anna gritted her teeth and wondered if she should go and punch her lights out. "I'm very suspicious about her, though. She's too good to be true. I've got a feeling that there's more to that woman than she's letting on. Some dark, terrible secret in Yorkshire, no doubt." Deborah gave a mischievous laugh. "Must go. See you tomorrow."

After she had left, Anna came out of the cubicle and stood quietly for some moments. She looked at her reflection in the mirror and saw that her complexion was as ashen as Jason's had been when he had discovered that Peter was talking to Deborah. She felt numb with shock. Deborah suspected something about her and her suspicions could only be proved correct. Telling Jason her secret was only the beginning, others would find out eventually and then what would people think of her? Feeling slightly sick, Anna left the ladies room and made her way to the foyer where Jason said he would wait for her.

Anna sat at the dressing table assessing the situation. They had arrived back from their game of golf just fifteen minutes before and she had gone straight upstairs. Now she sat wondering what she should do. All through the journey home, Anna had tried to tell Jason what she had overheard in the ladies room. But somehow she couldn't find the words.

Suddenly she remembered that Margaret had organised coffee in the parlour. Within minutes she was downstairs sitting next to Jason who was wolfing down a large piece of apple pie.

After they had had their coffee, Margaret excused herself and disappeared, only to appear again with a pile of brightly coloured presents.

"These are for you, Anna. And a very happy birthday."

"Oh, goodness!" Anna cried in delight. "I didn't think you knew."

"A little bird told us," said Mrs Wilby, beaming from ear to ear.

"Yes and he's sitting right next to you," said Ben.

"You rat!" said Jason. He turned to Anna. "I noticed the cards from your family before we left Bishop Sutton, even though you tried to hide them from me. I thought it only right that your birthday should be celebrated too."

Margaret gave a chuckle. "Well, it's been a special day all round, I think."

"Hear, hear," said everyone together.

Anna opened her presents, touched that time and energy had gone into buying them and as she opened each parcel; perfume from Ben; a beautifully patterned woollen hat, scarf and gloves from Mrs Wilby and a promise of a year's subscription for the golf club from Margaret, she let out a cry of delight.

"What fantastic things! You're all so kind and thoughtful." She stood up, gathering her gifts to her. "I'll take them upstairs. I want to take a bath before the party."

Jason stood also. "And I must check my emails before I get ready."

But once out in the hall, Jason pulled Anna towards him. "So, will you give me the first dance tonight?" he murmured softly.

"I'm not sure. Perhaps I ought to check on the other talent first."

"If that's the case, then I don't stand a chance the way you are."

Anna thought for a moment. "What do you mean, the way I am?"

Jason gave a chuckle. "Have you any idea how seductive you are?"

"Me? You're joking."

He looked at her seriously. "I'm not joking, Anna. Haven't you noticed how men watch you as you walk by?"

Anna couldn't help seeing the funny side of this. "Oh yes, they're probably thinking the same things my husband thought."

"And what was that?"

"That I'd be OK in the dark. At least, he never said anything to the contrary, so that's what I always imagined."

"Do you mean he never told you how beautiful you are?"

"He never once said that. Am I beautiful?"

"You're a very beautiful woman. And I'm so proud that you're mine."

Anna touched his cheek gently and smiled. "Well, you did say that beauty is in the eyes of the beholder. Perhaps my husband never saw me that way. And I must admit, I never felt beautiful."

"I didn't realise your self esteem was so low!" He held her close and brushed his face against her hair, before they continued upstairs and Jason followed her into her room so that they could continue the conversation. "And yet why am I surprised that you have such a low opinion of yourself? I remember how I felt when Kiera told me she was leaving me for Peter. I felt humiliated and rejected, even though our relationship was over."

Anna nodded. "It's even worse when a person is betrayed over and over again. I began to feel used. In fact, Dave made me feel foolish." She dropped the presents on the bed. "We'd been together six months and I lost my virginity and became a mother in one fell swoop." She paused before continuing, "I don't think we were really suited to each other. In fact, I doubt we would have married if I hadn't been pregnant in the first place. Perhaps I shouldn't have married him, but my mum would have felt ashamed if I'd been an unmarried mother. It wasn't so common as it is today."

"You didn't think of having your pregnancy terminated?"

"It never entered my head. It wasn't the baby's fault." She smiled wistfully. "We didn't find out we were having twins until three weeks before the birth. Chris was hiding and then one day, the midwife heard two heartbeats."

Jason smiled with her. "It's sounds wonderful but a lot of hard work."

"I hope they're OK. They'll be flying back from Ibiza today and once again, I won't be home to meet them, just like I wasn't there when they came back from Romania."

"You didn't abandon them, Anna. You had to get away from an impossible situation. No one would blame you."

Tears appeared on her lower eyelids, trickling slowly down her cheeks. "I did abandon them, though," she murmured guiltily. Jason made her sit on the edge of the bed. She leaned against his shoulder, drawing on his strength, her thoughts on her family. She gave a sad smile. "They were so good about it all, when I met up with them in Bristol. Despite being so young, they seemed to understand. I was surprised at that."

"Why? You've brought them up very well. You've encouraged them to be independent and taught them to be considerate and always do their best."

"That's why I encouraged them to go to Romania on that life experience expedition. I thought time working on a farm and in an orphanage would be character building. But they are so different in character. Chris has astounding mathematical ability. He loves anything to do with aircraft. In his room he must have fifty models of different makes. He knows everything about them. When they were built, where they were built, when they first flew, what battles if any, they flew in. He knows every air combat in history, from the Red Baron right up to the Falklands. He's already a member of a gliding club in Rufford and after university he wants to join the RAF as a pilot." She suddenly gasped and hid her face, trying to fight back the devastating emotions that threatened to choke her with pain. "I wanted to see him through it all. And Martyn too. He loves to wheel and deal and used to talk his brother into investing his pocket money in all sorts of business ventures, from car washing to gardening."

Jason pulled her closer. "Oh, Anna, you'll see both your boys again very soon. I'm sure they'll want to visit before they go to university."

Anna dried her eyes and looked at him. She frowned slightly. "How can things be so wonderful and yet so terrible at the same time?"

His expression softened as he caressed her cheek gently with his finger.

"Because you're going through a big change in your life." He took in a breath. "Anna, I'm asking you formally to marry me. I want you to be my wife."

"But I'm already married."

"In name only."

"I suppose I should divorce Dave."

Sighing heavily, he spoke in a soft hushed voice. "That's for you to decide, but it'll be difficult for you to become my wife if you don't."

"It seems such a final step to take, especially after nineteen years."

"Yes, it is, but you've already made the first step. You've been brave enough to walk away from an impossible marriage and that's a start. From what I can see your marriage was over long ago."

"But he hasn't mentioned divorce."

"Then perhaps it ought to be mentioned and pretty quickly too!"

She eased herself away from him. "For a short time, I saw you going through hell. It scares me to think that I might have to go through the same thing."

"Whatever happens, I'll be with you all the way. You supported me and now it's my turn to support you." Seeing she wasn't convinced, he pressed home his argument. "All I'm saying is that I want to give you my love and my name and I want to spend the rest of my life with you. If it's going to be a fight between your husband and me, well, I'm ready and willing. Although, he'd better watch out because I usually get what I want!"

He gave a whoop of joy and pulled her up onto her feet. He gathered her up in his arms so tightly, she was almost swung off the ground.

Despite his exuberance, Anna began to feel uncomfortable. "You make it all sound so easy."

Jason became still for a moment and studied her expression. "But it is easy. You just find a solicitor and set the wheels in motion."

"It doesn't seem right to say that half your life didn't mean anything. If something is a problem, then just dispense with it."

"Are you saying you want to go back to your husband? Are you saying you want to try and patch things up with him, forgive him once more for his behaviour?"

Anna turned away from him, her thoughts confused. "No, not that. It's just that you're talking like a businessman."

"What on earth do you mean!"

"You said it yourself. Find a solicitor and set the wheels in motion. Deal's done! Sorted! But it's my life we're talking about. I have a lot that needs to be considered. I must talk it over with the boys."

Jason realised he had put pressure on her, when he had been determined to give her space and time. "Yes, of course you must. I'm sorry. I'm too eager for you to make up your mind where you want to be and who you want to be with."

She struggled to understand her feelings and shrank away from him.

"I feel confused. Leave me alone, please."

He held out his arms in a vain attempt to comfort and reassure her, angry with himself for causing an awkward situation. "Anna, I only meant to..."

Her eyes flashed with an annoyance he had never seen in her. It made him catch his breath in dismay. "Jason, I need to think!"

He stood for a while studying her, the pain on her face sending rivers of alarm coursing through him and the knowledge he had exacerbated the problem by trying to persuade her to divorce her husband. She needed more time, he thought ruefully, he had rushed her into things she wasn't ready for. And then nodding in defeat, he left her.

Anna watched him go with longing. She couldn't understand why she had spoken to Jason in that way. Hurting him was the last thing she wanted. It was as though she was angry and afraid all at the same time and yet there was nothing to be angry about. On the contrary, he had given her nothing but happiness, since the first day she had met him and she blessed the day he had entered her life. The same sentiments applied to her sudden irrational fear. Jason was right; divorce was the next step, however painful.

Anna went over to a box of tissues and quickly dried her eyes and blew her nose. She ought to apologise straight away, that was always the best thing to do. But at the moment she longed for some peace and quiet. Filling her lungs with air and letting it out slowly, she closed her eyes and searched for some tranquillity for her troubled thoughts. She noticed her birthday presents on the bed and carefully removed them, placing them on the floor. Kicking off her shoes, she lay down, curling up into the foetal position on the duvet, her knuckles pressed against her lips. Jason had offered her everything he had, she thought sleepily. She mustn't lose him because she lacked the courage to end her marriage. Not now, after she had come this far.

Jason finished his emails and looked at his watch. Anna had remained upstairs for the last hour. Perhaps she was getting ready for the party? He wandered out of the parlour and stood at the bottom of the stairs, looking upwards. He couldn't decide whether or not to check on her. He didn't want to intrude on her privacy, but it seemed callous to leave her on her own when she seemed so upset. Finally, he gave in to his feelings and taking the stairs two at a time, he was soon at her door. He knocked quietly but there was no answer. He opened the door and peered round. Anna was lying on the bed, fast asleep.

Jason crossed the carpet and sat on the side of the mattress. Her expression was peaceful, her body relaxed, her breathing soft and rhythmic. He tenderly brushed the hair from her eyes and bent to kiss her lips. She awoke and stretched herself.

"Did I fall asleep?"

"You certainly did."

"What time is it?"

He looked at his watch. "Just gone six." He smiled at her. "It's time to get ready for the party."

"Yes, I want to take a bath first."

"There's still time. The revelries don't start until eight."

She giggled and grabbed his clothing, pulling him down. He tumbled on top of her and then he rolled to lie by her side. For a few moments they both stared up at the ceiling.

"I'm sorry," she said softly.

He turned over and raised himself up on his elbow, looking down at her. "I shouldn't have put pressure on you. It was very wrong of me."

"Everything you said was true. And my answer is yes."

"Yes?"

"Yes, I will marry you." She paused for a moment. "You haven't changed your mind, have you?

He answered her, smiling. "No I haven't and I would like to make it official by getting you a ring."

Anna felt startled. She and Dave had never bothered to get engaged or buy a ring. It hardly seemed worth the bother.

"That would be lovely," she whispered.

"Well, that settles it."

Anna pulled herself back to reality. "No, you mustn't buy a ring just yet. As wonderful as it sounds, you must remember I'm still a married woman." She raised her left hand and wriggled her fingers. "And I'm still wearing a wedding ring."

"You could take that off," he said quietly.

"I will when the time's right. And I promise you that when I take this ring off, I'll replace it with yours."

"Fair enough," he smiled and kissed her hand.

"What are we going to tell the others?" she added, frowning.

"About what?"

She sat up and pulled the pillow across her, holding it close. He sat up with her, putting another pillow behind his back.

"Your mother! And Mrs Wilby and Ben! All this time they've thought I was a widow. How can I explain all this?"

He thought for a moment. "I suppose they'll need some kind of explanation. So, we'll tell them the truth. We'll explain your circumstances and that's all. You don't need to justify your actions."

"Do you think they'll understand?"

"Sweetheart, it doesn't matter if they understand or not. And besides they all love you and in the end, I'm sure they'll want us to be happy."

Anna gave a sigh. "And I'll have to explain everything to the family too. About you and my intention to end my marriage."

"I'd really love to meet your family," he smiled.

"You might find my mother rather daunting," she laughed. He gave a chuckle and jumped up, pulling her onto her feet. He wrapped his arms round her and she closed her eyes, pressing herself against him. A peaceful contentment settled on them. And then Anna remembered her encounter with Deborah and summoning her courage she told him what she had overheard in the ladies room at the clubhouse. "She suspects something, I know she does."

His brow creased in an anxious frown. "How can she? Whatever she's implying it doesn't matter. It's none of her business."

Anna had to admit he was right, even though she dreaded the thought that people would soon know how she had lied in order to pursue her own ambitions.

"Now, shoo," she said, laughing. "And leave me to get ready."

Anna prepared for the party by having a long, luxurious soak in the bath, before dressing her hair and applying her makeup. This was the evening she had been looking forward to since arriving at the Grange and she wanted to look perfect. Her belated shopping expedition to Bristol had finally located a dress that pleased her. It was a long black evening dress in the classic style, but with a slit on the left side reaching from hem to knee. The edges of the slit were embroidered with silver, as were the edges of the bodice and straps that crossed at the back. When she had stepped out of the changing room in the shop, Mrs Wilby's mouth had fallen open in astonishment.

"My, you do look a picture. I think that's the one, my dear. It will certainly make Jason's eyes pop out of his head!"

At the time, Anna couldn't understand why Jason would be interested in what she looked like or if she would care anyway. But now everything was so different. Now she wanted to look special, she wanted to be the 'belle of the ball'.

Anna fastened her earrings in place. The white gold set off the cascade of three beautiful small diamonds and for a brief moment she held the matching necklace in her hands, turning it about and watching it sparkle. This was the only jewellery she had brought with her from Wakefield, as they had been a twenty-first birthday present from her mother and stepfather. For some strange reason she hadn't been able to leave them behind, although as she had tucked them in her case she couldn't imagine when she would wear them. Smiling with amusement she fastened the clasp round her neck and then eased on the black high-heeled sandals she had bought. Anna picked up the shawl and evening bag that completed the ensemble and stood in front of the long mirror. She scrutinised her appearance, turning to left and right. For the first time in years she didn't grimace at her reflection, but instead, nodded with satisfaction.

She descended the stairs to the hall where the rest of the party was waiting. Margaret and Mrs Wilby looked wonderful in their evening dresses and Jason and Ben looked smart in their dress suits. But the look on Jason's face told her everything.

"Wow!" he murmured. "Looks like I really will be fighting off the other guys tonight."

Anna took his arm. "I've decided you can have the first dance," she said, smiling.

"Can I have the second?" chimed in Ben.

Margaret glanced at Mrs Wilby. "It seems we'll be dancing together."

"Speak for yourself," said Mrs Wilby, with a twinkle in her eye.

They made their way to the ballroom where the carpet had been removed revealing the beautiful polished wood flooring. As Anna promised, she and Jason had the first dance and Ben had the second. And as Jason surmised, every man then queued up to have his turn with the 'belle of the ball'. In the end, Jason had no choice but to sneak in and steal Anna away if he thought she was being overwhelmed.

For Anna it was a wonderful evening and the dances with Jason proved to be very special. At ten o'clock, the live band retired and a buffet supper was served, before a DJ took his place for the disco; the dancing becoming a lot livelier. The older folk took their seats round the room, chatting and watching the gyrating of the younger ones, only the brave few venturing out onto the floor to join in. And then finally, it was time for the last dance and Anna and Jason found themselves in each other's arms once more. As they danced slowly round the floor, they became oblivious to the other partygoers, or the satisfied smiles from their closest friends. They were lost in each other and for all they cared, they could have been the last two people on earth.

It was late when the guests left and the household went to bed. Anna waited a short while and then skipped barefooted down the corridor and up the short flight of stairs to Jason's room. He was waiting for her and laughed softly as she closed the door behind her, ran across the carpet and slipped into bed beside him.

This time was very different from the previous one and very different from anything Anna had ever experienced before. Jason murmured endearments as he made love to her and she cried out with the emotion that made her tremble with ecstasy. For the first time, Anna reached the height of sexual arousal and afterwards, Jason stroked her hair and kissed away the tears that spilled onto her cheeks. Anna couldn't believe that she had been a married woman for nineteen years, for that night she might as well have been a young girl in the throes of her first love affair. She now knew the true meaning of being loved and as she fell asleep in Jason's arms, the world was wonderful and life worth living.

CHAPTER NINE

The following day, everyone awoke to a heavy, leaden sky filled with rain. The sun made a valiant effort to put in an appearance whenever a gap opened up in the clouds, but it seemed that the end of summer was determined to enter into battle with the start of autumn.

Anna tied up her hair with a band, lowered herself into the hot water, lay back and relaxed. She closed her eyes and smiled as the bubbles tickled her chin. How she would miss this wonderful bathroom when they left the Grange on Sunday. Her thoughts drifted back to the night before when she had gone to Jason's room. The feelings he had awakened in her had been unbelievable; emotions that she had never known existed.

She opened her eyes and held up her left hand, moving her fingers so that the water ran over her wedding ring. Why in all the years she had been married, had she never experienced an orgasm with her husband? And yet she knew the answer was simple, she didn't trust him. And the distrust didn't just stem from his suspected infidelities. She was anxious for her sexual health. Although she had visited the clinic regularly and thankfully had been reassured that all was well, advice that her husband should use extra protection went unheeded. Dave was furious, telling her it was unnecessary and an insult, since it insinuated his guilt.

Anna sighed. Why had she persevered for all those years? Jason had made her see sense and when he looked at her, she felt like a desirable woman, a woman to be cherished. If it hadn't been for her boys and the need to give them a stable home, she would have left Dave years ago. Suddenly she felt angry and tore the ring from her finger flinging it across the room. She heard it clatter into the sink and wondered if it had gone down the plug-hole. Never mind, she thought, the sewer was probably the best place for it.

Jason had woken her in the early light of dawn, kissing her eyes and lips and throat. His love making that morning had been gentle but much more ardent and Anna had responded with a passion that seemed almost frenzied. Afterwards, she had felt embarrassed at her loss of control but he had whispered his wonderful words of love and reassured her that it was nothing to be ashamed about. He had not wanted her to leave when the time finally came, but Anna still hadn't the courage to stay and be discovered by the others. He had let her go reluctantly, catching her hand and kissing her fingers as she left his bed.

There was a gentle knock on the bathroom door. Anna sat up, startled out of her reflections.

"Sweetheart, are you in the bath?"

"Yes, I'll be with you in a moment." She went to stand up and then realised with a grin that Jason was familiar with every part of her and it would be silly to be shy in his presence. She sank back down into the bubbles. "You might as well come in. The door's unlocked."

He came in and gave a cheeky smile. "Now, that's what I call a lovely sight." He bent to kiss her. "I've come to tell you that my solicitor wants to see me. I guess about Kiera's will." He sat down on the edge of the bath.

"I thought that was all sorted."

"Kind of. But Kiera had shares in the company and she's probably willed them to me. I've just had a phone call from Nigel Barnes. He's an old school chum and also my solicitor. He wants me to go and see him." He stared down at her. "Fancy coming with me?"

Anna smiled but then gave a sigh. "Will you be gone long?" she asked.

He shrugged. "A few hours perhaps. You could shop while I pop into his office."

She suddenly felt cold. "Could you pass me a towel, please."

Jason went over to the rail by the sink and brought back a large bath sheet. Anna stood up and he wrapped it round her and steadied her as she stepped out onto the mat. His arms came round her.

"Dear lord! The things you do to me," he murmured, kissing her wet shoulders.

She made a decision. "No, I won't go with you. I want to tell the others, Jason. While you're away, I want to tell them my true situation and why I had to leave my family."

"Are you sure? It can wait."

"I don't think it can."

"Would you like me to tell them? I can explain it from my point of view and then it might sound more rational."

"No, I must do it and it must be done today."

"OK, but I know they'll take it well."

"If they don't, then I'll escape in my new car!"

He grinned and chucked her under the chin. "As long as it's only as far as Bishop Sutton." He contemplated her for a few moments. His voice was hesitant as he added, "If you're going to spill the beans, then perhaps I should speak to Nigel about starting divorce proceedings? I could pave the way for you. You don't have to do anything yet, it's just…."

She smiled at his difficulty. "Yes, do that, please. In fact, make an appointment for me."

He sighed with relief and then he was gone and Anna was left to get dressed. Before she made her way down to breakfast, she searched the bathroom for her wedding ring. It wasn't in the sink or on the floor. Oh well, she thought, someone in the sewage works will get a surprise when they find it.

No one was about in the dining room and Anna ate her breakfast alone. Fran bustled in carrying a pot of fresh coffee.

"Where are the others?" Anna asked.

"Oh, they've gone to the farm, miss. Farmer's just bought some heifers and Madam has gone to look them over. They said they'll be back about ten."

Anna decided to walk round the garden, her thoughts on what she would say to them when they returned. She must be clear and logical, she told herself firmly, they would understand if she explained it all in an intelligent manner. The sky was still very grey, but now and again the sun would break through making the various shades of green shimmer. She passed the flowerbeds of pink and red busy lizzies and blue lobelia, the colours vivid. By the time she went back to the house, she had perfected her speech word for word.

Fran was bringing the tray of crockery from the kitchen in readiness for morning coffee, so Anna settled herself in the parlour. When she finally heard the front door open and a draught of chilly air swept through the room along with the noise and laughter of the others returning, she took in a huge breath. She was ready and after it was done, she would set the wheels in motion to end her awful marriage.

Jason sat back in his chair and stared at his friend in disbelief. He was in the office of Nigel Barnes, his solicitor, and he had just listened while Nigel had read from the document in front of him.

"Kiera didn't leave the shares to me?"

"I'm afraid not. It seems that she left them to Peter Shelby."

Jason blinked hard. "Why, on earth would she do that?"

"I drew up this will for her when she was planning to marry."

"But he left her! The bastard didn't even stick around to help her through it."

"And her illness was quite short, mercifully. It could be that she simply forgot about the shares."

Jason shook his head in resignation. "Well, there wasn't many, if I remember rightly." Nigel looked uncomfortable. "Is there more to this?"

Nigel nodded. "I've heard that Shelby is planning to sell them."

"That's his prerogative!"

"And I've also heard that Deborah Gilbert-Hines is keen to invest in your company."

"Never knew she was interested in stocks and shares."

"Well, she's become very interested in Harrington Rhodes Shipping Agents."

Jason couldn't help smiling. "Investment is a good thing and can only help the company grow. As long as Graham and I have the major shareholding, I don't care what she does."

"Yes, but be warned. She might attend the shareholders meetings and make a right nuisance of herself."

Jason's smile turned into a grin. "As long as she gets her dividend, I'm sure she'll have no quibble with us."

Nothing more could be discussed and Jason decided to take his leave. The two men stood and Nigel walked round the desk to shake Jason's hand.

"I was sorry about Kiera. She was a lovely woman."

Jason sighed. "Yes, it was a sad loss to her family and especially for Hollie."

"How is the little monkey?"

"She's gone to Vancouver to stay with her grandparents."

"Oh, good. Well, when you see her next, tell her it took me ages to get the talcum powder out of my car!"

Jason couldn't suppress a smile. "Sorry about that."

"I also hear you have a new lady in your life?"

"News does travel fast!"

"I also hear she's a widow. Annie is it?"

"Anna. And about her being a widow, well, that's not strictly accurate. Actually, she is married, but now wants a divorce."

Nigel raised his eyebrows. "And she wants me to act for her?"

"Absolutely."

"Then we'll make an appointment for her on the way out."

After Jason had left, Nigel went back to his desk. He had known Jason Harrington for twenty-five years and had never known him to back out of fight in his entire life. Nigel smiled as he remembered his first meeting with Jason. They were at school although Jason had been in the year above him. Bullying had never been allowed at their boarding school and could be severely punished by expulsion. However, Vickers didn't seem to care if he was expelled and had picked on the weaker, younger boys mercilessly. Not that Nigel had thought himself as weak, it was just that his height and slight stature had made him a target for Vickers and his sadistic ways.

Nigel had been cornered in the prep room one afternoon and Vickers had held him up against the wall in a vice like grip that could have squeezed the life out of him. He had done his best to punch and kick his assailant but Vickers was too big and strong for it to have any effect. Suddenly, Nigel had dropped like a stone to the floor and had watched in surprise as his tormentor was dragged backwards and then sent flying across a table as a fist hit him full in the face with a resounding crack. And that's how he and Jason had first met. They had become firm friends after that and Vickers was shipped back home. It was Jason who had encouraged Nigel to take up kick boxing as a means of self-defence. And he had done well at it, achieving black belt second dan standard by the time he was in his late teens.

He lost touch with Jason after they had left school and it was years later that they met up again, in a restaurant, when Kiera was heavily pregnant with Hollie. And so they had resumed their friendship and Nigel had become Jason's solicitor. Nigel closed the file in front of him and sighed. It was sad about Kiera, but there again, Jason had found someone else and seemed quite smitten. Nigel thought over what his friend had told him. Her name was Anna and she wasn't a widow after all. He shrugged indifferently. Stories along the grapevine always became distorted.

The others joined Anna in the parlour for coffee. She listened to their happy banter about their visit to the farm and smiled when they mentioned how the rain had made the smells more pungent forcing them to leave earlier than expected. And then came a lull in the conversation.

"I've something to tell you all," said Anna, putting down her cup and noticing that her hands were shaking. Three pairs of eyes turned in her direction. "And I really, really hope that when I've finished you'll understand."

Margaret smiled and raised her hand as if to stop her. "My dear, if it's about you and Jason, and the fact you've...well, fallen in love and intend to get married. Then we already know."

Ben jerked his head round to her. "Since when did we know? I didn't know!"

Mrs Wilby gave him a playful slap on the hand and told him to 'shush' since now he did know. Anna felt as though her heart had stopped beating with the shock.

Margaret was aghast at her pale expression. "I'm so sorry, my dear. Perhaps I've been too blunt but I wanted to spare you the need to go into any details. I realise that you'll probably feel it's rather unseemly to announce your engagement so soon after Kiera, but please remember that she and Jason were already separated and would have divorced if she'd lived. We..." she indicated Mrs Wilby and Ben, "are very happy for you both. Jason deserves a wonderful person like you after all he's been through."

"How did you know?" asked Anna, colour flooding her face.

"Before Jason dashed off this morning, he mentioned that you had something to tell us and we guessed that must be it."

Anna opened her mouth and then closed it sharply. Margaret's statement had thrown her completely off her guard and she felt a wave of horror pass through her.

"That's not what I was going to tell you," she whispered.

"Oh, it's not?" said Margaret.

"Well, it is... but not exactly...We are in love and Jason has asked me to marry him...and I said yes...but that's not all of it." Anna's mouth dried up as the three people sitting opposite her gave her their undivided attention once more. "I need to tell you..." Suddenly she realised that her carefully prepared speech had completely disappeared from her memory. "You need to know...that I'm not a widow...I'm married...and I've been married nineteen years...but I was unhappy...so I had a plan to come and work for Jason...and we fell in love...I told him I was a widow because I wanted to get away...from my marriage...because I was unhappy."

She couldn't continue. The expressions on the faces of the people she had grown to love dismayed her. Margaret had momentarily closed her eyes in shocked awareness, Mrs Wilby stared at her as if she was something from outer space and Ben had a look of absolute bewilderment. Anna's thoughts screamed inside her head. Jason had been right, this could have waited. Oh, why hadn't she listened to him? She should have left it to him just as he had suggested.

It was Margaret who finally broke the silence. "You left your husband in Yorkshire, to come and work for Jason? And you told him you were a widow but you weren't?"

Anna nodded. "I thought it would be a way of giving myself some space so I could think things through. I never realised for one minute that we would fall in love. It just happened. I was so grateful to be Jason's PA, while I decided what to do next."

There was a brief moment of silence as the others absorbed this.

"And what have you decided to do?" asked Margaret.

"Oh, it's quite clear. I must end my marriage and Jason is going to help me with the divorce. My feelings for Jason are absolutely real. I've never felt like this about any other man." She felt compelled to justify the last statement. "Not that there's been any others...My husband is the only man I've known...if you see what I mean...and...and...please forgive me. Please don't hate me for what I've done." Tears brimmed over her eyelashes and trickled down her cheeks.

Ben rose to his feet and came to sit beside her. He placed a fatherly arm round her shoulders.

"If you ask me, Anna deserves all our support in this." He gave the other two a piercing glance. "I left my wife when I couldn't bear my marriage any longer. I just packed my bags and left without saying what I was doing or where I was going. I was gone six years before I heard she'd died and I was finally free."

Mrs Wilby and Margaret opened their eyes wide in astonishment. "Well, this certainly is a day for revelations!" said Margaret. "But I don't think you left any children behind, did you Ben?"

"No, I didn't have any children. Even so, Anna's boys are due to go to university soon and as far as I'm concerned, they're independent adults. And she's kept in touch with them."

"Yes, I will always be there for them," said Anna in desperation. "I've not abandoned them simply because I don't want to be married to their father."

Margaret stared across at the photos displayed in the wall unit. "I'm thinking about my son. I don't want him to be hurt again," she said sadly.

"But I don't want to hurt him either," said Anna. "I'll do anything to make him happy."

Ben rounded on Margaret. "You weren't there during that awful time when Kiera was so desperately ill! And then afterwards! You didn't see the wonderful support Anna gave Jason through it all."

"That's very true," murmured Mrs Wilby. Up to that moment she had remained silent, her thoughts quietly forming. She turned to Margaret, her expression serious. "As I see it, we two are extremely lucky. We had very happy marriages and I think we should thank our blessings for that. But Anna and Ben and Jason too haven't been so lucky. Since Anna arrived, Jason has been a changed man. He's happy and he wants to start afresh with her. And yes, things aren't all packaged up neat and tidy, as you would want. For a little while longer it's going to get messy while Anna sorts herself out and ends her marriage. But it will pass with time. I think we should give them a chance."

Ben nodded. "There's something else we must remember. Anna has told us this because she has the good grace to believe that we should know. But Jason would be the first to say it's none of our business. That it's up to him and Anna to decide their future."

"I completely agree," said Mrs Wilby.

Margaret stared at them for a while. She was stunned at their loyalty to her son and yet inwardly felt pleased. But even so she had really hoped that all the pain was behind them now. They had endured such a turbulent eighteen months, that a little time of settled peace and quiet would have been very welcome. And she had hoped that Jason and Anna's wedding would have been the very first celebrated at the Grange. She gave a resigned sigh. There was no doubt that her son loved Anna and she was also certain that Anna would make him happy. But it seemed that there was to be one more hurdle to jump before she could settle down once more to a contented life at the Grange.

It was done! Everyone that mattered now knew her secret and Anna couldn't help feeling a great sense of relief. She closed the main door behind her and breathed in the fresh morning air, the sun warming her face. Ben and Mrs Wilby had been so wonderful. Their support had been overwhelming and she knew she would be eternally grateful to them. But what of Margaret? She had become quiet and rather subdued after the revelations in the parlour, finally taking herself off to her study to finish some paperwork for a seminar that was booked for the following week. Anna had so wanted her approval and the disappointment she felt cut into her. After Margaret had left, Ben and Mrs Wilby had told Anna not to worry herself over it. She would come round in time, she was an understanding woman and she only wanted what was best for her son. Thoughts of Jason filled Anna with yearning. How she wished he would come home. She decided to take a walk since the sudden downpour had stopped and the sun had finally made an appearance. As she was going out, she had volunteered to take Tess with her.

Anna had never taken a dog for a walk, but Ben had assured her that the old retriever only ambled along at her own pace and there wasn't any danger of her running off on her own. And so Anna had collected the dog's lead from the hallway cupboard and attaching it to her collar she ventured outside. Slowly they walked along the drive and through the small pedestrian opening that was adjacent to the main gate and out onto the main highway that ran past the grounds of the Grange.

The main road outside the grounds skirted the wall and was long and straight. When standing at the tall, ornamental gate Anna could see up the road for a good quarter of a mile in each direction but at each end the road then curved out of sight. Anna knew that she would be able to hear Jason's car first before it turned the corner and finally came into view. If she took Tess into the meadow and let her have some time to roam about, she would still be in earshot. Holding onto the lead tightly, she crossed the road and walked along to the wooden gate.

Everything seemed to be drenched with the torrential rain that had continued unabated while she had been in the parlour. Large drops dripped relentlessly from the leaves and huge puddles filled the ditches and gullies by the side of the road. The gate had a metal bar over the post to keep it closed and after pulling this back, Anna passed through and into the sweet smelling meadow, closing the gate after her. She removed the lead and almost straight away Tess went to investigate a rabbit hole and finding it discarded, went on to sniff out any interesting inhabitants in the hedges. Anna watched her and smiled. The old dog was obviously enjoying herself and she was relieved that her first outing as a 'dog walker' seemed to be going without any hitch.

Grinning at Tess's inept attempts to make friends with a frog, Anna began to form some kind of plan for the future. When Jason arrived home, he would have an appointment for her with the solicitor and then she would phone Dave and tell him that she wanted to start divorce proceedings immediately on the grounds of his adultery. It would be impossible for him to dispute his infidelities and he would be forced to admit his guilt. And then she would be free, free to marry the man she loved. Anna thought about the twins. She would invite them to Bishop Sutton and introduce them to everyone. She was convinced that her sons would understand and be happy for her.

She looked at her watch and decided that she had had enough and it was time to go. Calling Tess to her, she quickly attached the lead to her collar and made her way to the wooden gate and then back out onto the main road. Anna continued her stroll and although eager to be back in the security and warmth of the Grange, she didn't relish the idea of facing Margaret once more. She wondered if she had had time to think it over and perhaps, feel more comfortable with the idea. The roaring of a car engine in the distance interrupted her thoughts.

Anna thought that it must be Jason, but immediately realised that it didn't sound like his car and besides, it was travelling very fast. Anna sighed with annoyance that people should think it quite acceptable to speed on an open country road. The car turned the corner and was coming straight down the road towards her. The path she was walking was only narrow, some three feet in width and worried that Tess might take fright, she bent down and caught hold of her collar, speaking gentle words of encouragement to her.

She couldn't remember the exact moment in time that she thought the car was coming straight for her. Perhaps it wasn't even a thought, more an intuition, but suddenly she heard the engine rev into full throttle and the bonnet seemed to be on a direct collision course with her. She wasn't the only one who had the same idea. Tess might be old and her hearing and sight might be failing, but her instincts were still sharp.

Anna felt herself yanked forward and to the right as the retriever pulled her with all her strength. The force was so great that she was almost lifted off her feet and then she tripped and fell on her front in the ditch, the cold, muddy water seeping into her clothes and soaking her hair, making her gasp with shock. To make matters worse, the near side tyres of the vehicle hit a large puddle in the gully sending up a tidal wave of more filthy water to engulf her totally. And then the car was gone, its engine droning away round the corner and out of hearing.

Anna slowly got to her knees and then tried to lift herself out of the mud that held her captive. The fright at thinking that the vehicle was heading straight for her, plus the icy, cold water made her shiver. Tess watched her, whimpering and nuzzling her as if to bring a small amount of comfort. It was then she felt a pair of arms come round her and help her to her feet.

"Sweetheart, are you OK?"

Relief filled her from top to toe. "Yes, I'm fine. Just soaked to the skin," she said, grinning.

"Good Lord! I saw Tess first and immediately thought she'd got out of the gate."

"I offered to take her for a walk. But I didn't realise how strong she was." She raked her fingers through her hair trying to make herself more presentable.

Jason couldn't help laughing at the state she was in. "You poor thing, you look like a drowned rat. Let's get you inside and dry you off." He placed an arm tenderly round her and then took the dog's lead from her. He looked sternly at Tess. "I've not known her drag someone along for a long time, not since she was a much younger dog. She's usually so well behaved."

"Oh no, she hasn't been misbehaving. That car was coming straight for me, or I thought it was. And Tess must have thought so too because she pulled me out of the way."

"What car?"

They were walking towards the ornamental gates where Anna could see the Volvo parked as if just turning in, the driver's door still open.

She thought for a moment. "I think it was a Porsche. Black. And being driven far too fast!"

"And you thought it was coming straight at you?"

Anna felt uneasy. "Perhaps not. It seems a silly idea now I come to think about it. But its wheels did hit the gully and sent up a torrent of rainwater over me. I've always believed that kind of thing is a malicious prank by the driver!"

"Did you see the driver?"

"Afraid not. Tinted windows."

Jason remained quiet. There was one person he knew who owned a black Porsche and tended to drive it far too fast. Her name was Deborah Gilbert-Hines. And the direction she was taking was towards the golf club. But could Deborah really have meant Anna any harm? Was she really that wicked?

"How did your day go?" he asked, trying to release himself from his troubled thoughts.

"Not very well, I'm afraid. I don't think your mother is very pleased with me."

"Why, what happened?"

Anna paused before explaining light-heartedly, "I think she was …disappointed and upset that my circumstances were different from what she had been led to believe. And I suppose she has every right."

Despite her casualness he sensed her despair. "I can't believe that of Mother. What did she say to you?"

"Oh, nothing really. It was her manner and her expression. I don't think I'm the flavour of the month any more."

His eyes turned dark with anger. "I think I'd better have a word with her! This doesn't concern her and she has no right to make you feel uncomfortable!"

They had nearly reached the gates and although Anna was starting to feel the cold she stopped walking and turned to face him. She had never seen him like this and placed her hands on his arms to pacify him.

"Please don't be cross with her, Jason. You're her only child and she's looking out for your interests. She doesn't want you to be hurt again after all you've been through. I understand her perfectly. If it were Martyn or Chris I would feel just the same."

Jason smiled. His gaze took in her mud-splattered hair and the dirty marks on her cheek and chin. Even like this she was the most beautiful woman in the world. He took out his handkerchief and gently removed the smudges from her face.

"I've decided I want to start divorce proceedings as soon as possible. Did you speak with your solicitor?" asked Anna, taking the handkerchief from him to continue the cleanup.

"Yes, I did. And I've made an appointment for you."

Anna grinned as she suddenly remembered. "Oh, Jason, you should have heard Ben and Mrs Wilby. They were fantastic. They supported me all the way."

He nodded. "I would have expected that of them."

"But did you know that Ben was once married? And he just up and left his wife one day, without telling anyone?" She giggled as his expression showed utter surprise.

"He never talked about his family. I assumed he had none," he said.

Anna clicked her tongue. "And there's me thinking you know everything."

"Obviously not," he laughed. "But one thing I do know, we must get you indoors before you catch cold."

Tess agreed and began to bark loudly reminding them that the rain had started again.

Once inside, Anna spent nearly thirty minutes in the bathroom trying to wash away the mud and dirt that clung to her so relentlessly. She washed her hair three times until she felt it was absolutely clean and then changed into fresh clothes. She was ready just in time for lunch and ran downstairs to join Jason and the others in the dining room. She would face Margaret and deal with the situation, she thought ruefully, it was just a question of making her understand.

While Anna had been tidying herself, Jason had taken Tess down to the kitchen and given her something to eat. Then he went straight to his room to freshen up for lunch. He had neither the desire nor the patience to confront his mother on the matter of his future plans concerning Anna. She could not be blamed for making the wrong choice in the man she had married. Jason knew that his mind was set and he loved Anna with all his heart. She was all he wanted and no one was going to take her away from him.

"And Deborah is buying up more shares in your company? What's the implication of that?" asked Anna.

Jason nodded. "Only that she's now a shareholder and will attend meetings. I can't see there being a problem except that I really don't want her involved in any aspect of my life, either personal or professional."

They were in the parlour alone, since Ben and Mrs Wilby had gone to visit a mutual friend in Wedmore and Margaret had taken herself off to the study once more. Thankfully lunch had not been as tense as Anna had feared and in fact, everyone had kept up a happy banter during the meal. Margaret had tried to join in with the conversation, but often she would become unusually quiet. Sometimes Anna would catch her eye and knew she was being assessed.

Now sitting on the couch with Jason, Anna felt that her troubles were coming to an end, except for the problem with Margaret.

"What are you going to say to your mum?" asked Anna quietly.

He answered sharply. "Nothing! Absolutely nothing!" Seeing Anna's expression he smiled and took her hand. "I'm sorry that I'm cross with her when you asked me not to be. But I'm a grown man and I don't need my mother to make my decisions for me."

"I know and I understand. I just wish everything was settled and there wasn't all this uneasiness. I never meant for this to happen and I do so want her to like me again."

He kissed her hand. "You really worry about what people will think, don't you?"

"I guess I've always been that way." She wrinkled her nose. "My mum is exactly the same. She believes it's undignified to call attention to yourself and has strong opinions about 'making your bed and lying on it'. Hence the reason for hurrying me into marriage when I fell pregnant."

He looked down at her fingers, devoid of her wedding ring. "When are you going to tell your family about us? Why don't you call them now," he nodded towards the phone in the corner of the room, "and ask them to come down for a visit so I can meet them."

Anna couldn't hide her excitement. "I was thinking that myself. It would be wonderful, but could they stay? Is there room at Bishop Sutton?"

"We'll put them up in a hotel in Bristol. That can be sorted out when we know the dates they can come down."

She licked her lips, her eyes shining. "Perhaps they could come for just a weekend. It will give me a chance to talk to them and tell them what we're doing."

"Then do it." He smiled at her enthusiasm.

"Oh, Jason, I can't believe you're going to meet my boys." It was as if the floodgates had opened and the torrent could not be held back. Jason understood this and let her continue, smiling as she babbled on. "And then of course there's the rest of the family. Greg, my stepfather. We never thought Mum would marry again after Dad died, but suddenly Greg walked into her life and he's wonderful. He's had his own printing business for the last twenty years, so he knows what it's like to chase contracts. And then there's my little sister, Elaine and her husband, Terry. They've never had children which is so odd in a way, because Elaine is a midwife but I guess she's been too busy bringing kids into the world to have any of her own…" And then she ran out of breath and started laughing. "Oh goodness, where did all that come from!"

Jason began to laugh with her and pulled her close. "I hope from happiness. And as for meeting your family, I can't wait!" After a few moments he whispered, "I have a little gift for you."

She looked at him in surprise. "Another birthday present?"

"Not exactly."

He pulled a small box from his pocket and opened it. Inside was a ring, set with three diamonds mounted in gold, the middle diamond slightly larger than the ones on either side of it.

"Oh Jason, it's beautiful," she gasped.

"You said that when you took off your wedding ring, you would wear my ring. I'm holding you to that promise."

She held out her left hand and he slipped it on her third finger. "It fits perfectly! How on earth did you know?"

He grinned mischievously. "Actually, I cheated." He opened his hand and lying in the palm was her wedding band. "I found this in the sink when I handed you a towel this morning. I thought it would come in handy to get the right size."

"I threw it across the bathroom in a fit of temper! I thought it had gone in the sink, but when I looked for it, I couldn't find it. And you had it all the time!"

"Do you want it back?"

Anna hesitated, her mind spinning. "No, you keep it. This one is much better."

"You really like it?" he asked, putting her wedding ring back in his pocket.

"It's absolutely gorgeous. I've never had an engagement ring."

"So, you and Dave never got engaged?"

"Didn't seem worth it. Anyway, we needed the money for baby things." She gave a sad smile.

"I think the sooner you end this marriage of yours the better. Then we'll be able to make our own plans."

Suddenly she remembered her thoughts when she was taking Tess for a walk. "I'm hoping Dave will let me divorce him on grounds of his adultery. It only seems fair."

"Well, let's hope he plays fair."

His comment made her frown. "Do you think he won't?"

He blinked hard, realising he shouldn't have put doubts into her mind. "I don't know him well enough, sweetheart. What I'm saying is that it's a dirty business and emotions can be raw. But if he's sensible then he'll see that it's better all round for your marriage to end."

Anna snuggled against his shoulder, trying to hide her worried expression. Her hopes for a straightforward divorce were suddenly dashed, as Jason, despite not knowing her husband, had been more than astute. Dave would give her a hard time and she would need all her strength and courage to fight him.

CHAPTER TEN

They were on the eighteenth green and Anna was preparing herself for a long putt that would win her the game. The putt was about four metres but she had played far longer ones with great success. She steadied her balance, took careful aim and then tapped the ball sharply. They watched as the ball sped across the grass and then dropped with a satisfying clunk into the hole.

Jason gave a groan. "You win again!" he said.

"Only by a small margin," she answered, trying to soften the blow.

"Sweetheart, I gave everything I had and it still wasn't enough. What am I to do just to draw with you?"

Anna couldn't help grinning as they collected up their bags and started for the clubhouse. She was relieved he was a good loser. Her husband wouldn't have been. Anna hadn't yet contacted her sons about a visit, even though she had already had a text from them to say that they had returned from their holiday and had had a wonderful time. As excited as she had been about the idea, she had not found the courage to pick up the phone, so she had decided to delay the call until after they returned from their game of golf.

"I'll buy lunch, just to compensate," she said.

"I wouldn't hear of it!"

The restaurant at the clubhouse was very pleasant and they chose a table by the window so that they could watch the other players out on the course. The weather had turned truly remarkable and everyone around them seemed in high spirits now that the sun was out.

"Hi Jason. I'm sorry to interrupt you, but I wondered if I could have a word with your friend."

They looked up to see a jovial young woman with short hair and a ruddy complexion.

"Oh, Caroline, it's nice to see you again. Let me introduce you to Anna Stevens, Anna this is Caroline Beaumont."

The two women shook hands and Caroline slipped into the seat next to Anna.

"I won't take up much of your time. It's just that I'm the captain of the ladies team and I wondered if you'd like to join us in the next match?"

"Me?" said Anna, feeling quite stunned.

"I know this is short notice, but your reputation for being an outstanding golfer is already the talk of the club."

"I wouldn't call myself outstanding!"

Caroline winked at Jason. "She's quite modest, isn't she! The problem I've got is that we're playing a phenomenal club in two weeks' time and unless I can find some better players, then we are going to get our arses kicked."

"Oh, I don't know. I'm only a guest here."

"Well, that can be remedied," suggested Jason, smiling broadly at the turn of events.

"But we're going back to Bishop Sutton on Sunday. And I'll be too busy."

Caroline looked crestfallen. "Oh well, I can only ask. Our best player is Deborah Gilbert-Hines and she pales into insignificance compared to you. If you change your mind, ring the club and they'll contact me."

She was gone in a moment, walking quickly through the restaurant and out into the foyer.

"Well, fancy that! Being invited to join the team," said Anna, in great amusement.

"You did say you were captain for the team in Wakefield. I think you should do it." Anna shook her head. Jason continued his argument. "Not even to give Deborah a good thrashing?"

Anna wagged her finger at him. "Now then, when you play in a team you play together. Personal rivalries should be put aside for the greater good. Those sorts of battles are better fought in the individual matches."

"Mmm," said Jason into his wineglass. "Well, I'll be in the front row!"

It was mid-afternoon when they arrived back at the Grange and Anna decided to make the phone call to the twins. Jason thought this was a good time to tell his mother about his future plans with Anna and clear the air somewhat. He disappeared to the study, where Margaret seemed to be hiding herself these last few days.

Anna walked into the parlour and finding it empty crossed the floor to the phone. Her hands shook as she lifted the receiver and dialled the number, her heart thudding as the phone rang at the other end, but no one answered. Finally, she decided to ring her sister.

"Hello." It was Elaine's voice.

"Hi, it's me, Anna."

"Anna! How are you?"

"I'm very, very well. How's everyone there?"

"We're fine too, but missing you very much, especially the boys."

"That's what I'm ringing about. I've called Mum, but there's no answer."

"Ah, I remember now. They've all gone into Leeds to pick up books and some stuff for living in halls."

Guilt flooded through Anna. This was something she should have been helping them with. "Has their dad gone with them?"

She heard Elaine give a chuckle. "Dave's in Germany on business. The lads will be home soon, or why don't you call them on their mobiles?"

"I'd rather not speak to them while they're on the move. I want them to come down for another visit, only this time for longer, perhaps for a weekend. If you and Mum come too, then you can stay in a hotel and we can have a chat about everything."

Elaine didn't answer for a moment but finally said, "Are you really staying in Bristol? Aren't you ever coming back here?"

"Of course I'll come back for a visit, but I won't be living there again."

"Mum was saying how happy you seem now."

"Oh Elaine, I am. Very, very happy."

"It sounds like you've got a good job." She paused before adding, "And what's your plans regarding Dave?"

Anna licked her lips before replying. "I'm going to ask Dave for a divorce."

She heard Elaine let out a huge breath. "We wondered about that. Well, I can't say I'm surprised. I know what you've had to put up with."

"Thanks for your support. Once my marriage is over, I can move on with my life."

Anna heard someone enter the room and turned to look. Jason was hovering on the threshold not quite sure if he should intrude, but Anna beckoned for him to come in. He walked over to the drinks' cabinet and poured himself a whisky.

"So, what happens now Big Sister?"

"Ask the boys to ring me and we'll take it from there. I'll give you this number, since I'm not at Bishop Sutton at the moment." She gave the number of the Grange.

"I'll do that. I'm passing their door later 'cos I've a patient round the corner. Talk about busy, all the Christmas babies are starting to arrive…If you know what I mean."

Anna gave a giggle. "I'll talk to you later. Bye." She put the phone down and ran over to Jason who was still standing by the cabinet nursing his drink.

"How did it go?" he asked.

"The lads were out, but it was lovely talking to Elaine. It's a busy time of the year for her."

"Why's that?"

"I told you Jason, she's a midwife and people get very careless at Christmas time."

He suddenly realised what she was talking about and gave a chuckle. "I can imagine. Now, what would you like to drink? Why don't you try a vodka and orange?"

"Are you trying to get me drunk! Because if you are…it will certainly work!"

He made her the drink and passed the glass to her. "I've talked to Mother and told her that her attitude is out of order."

"Oh, Jason, you didn't upset her did you?"

"I really didn't care if I did or not."

"But I don't want her upset over me!"

"Well, she insisted that she had to get it off her chest."

Anna began to feel faint and took a sip of her drink. "So, how does she feel about me?"

"Well, she believes that you should have told me the truth right at the beginning, perhaps at your interview."

"But I wouldn't have got the job."

"I told her that, but she thought that irrelevant."

She shrugged. "That interview seems such a long time ago now. So much as happened since then."

Jason smiled. "That's exactly what I said. I told her that I took you on as a personal assistant not as my future wife."

Anna put down her glass and wrapped her arms round his middle. He responded with a gentle embrace.

"Perhaps she's right. I should have told you the truth when we first met," said Anna.

"And where would you be now?"

"Not with you that's for sure."

"And still unhappy?"

"Yes." She swallowed the rest of her drink in one gulp.

"Hey, steady on!" he said in alarm. "You're not supposed to do that."

"I needed it!"

"I feel as though I'm corrupting you," he said, shaking his head.

"I know. And it's wonderful," she giggled. The telephone rang and Anna gave a cry of delight "It must be the boys!"

Anna was overjoyed to hear from her sons and listened intently as she was told how they had enjoyed Ibiza, how brown they were and the girls they had met. Jason made himself comfortable with the newspaper. But after ten minutes, it had been agreed that a weekend visit would be arranged and they would ring back with details of how many people would come. By the time she put down the phone, she felt exhausted with the emotional stress and flopped onto the couch next to him. "I fancy another drink," she said licking her lips.

Jason stood and pulled the bell. "I'll get Fran to bring up some tea."

"Spoilsport!"

"Did someone mention tea?" said Margaret, suddenly appearing in the doorway.

Anna felt a wave of apprehension pass through her, but was surprised to see Margaret smiling and looking more like her old self.

"Yes, I've just called for Fran," said Jason casually.

Fran finally arrived with the tea and although Anna felt extremely uncomfortable in Margaret's presence she tried to relax and appear at ease.

"I need to talk to you two," said Margaret, putting her cup down on the tray. Anna's gaze turned to her, although she noticed that Jason wasn't too happy about this and was staring intently at his mother, the muscles in his jaw tensing. "I hope you can both forgive a silly old woman who should have known better. Anna, I had no right to treat you the way I did."

Anna felt stunned at such a confession, but it was Jason who answered. "It's OK, Mother. Don't worry about it."

Anna grimaced at his coldness and her heart went out to the elderly lady sitting opposite them. She stood and went to sit next to her.

"It's fine, really it is. Please don't fret. Mothers will always worry about their children even when they're big enough and ugly enough to look after themselves."

Jason looked startled. "Big and ugly! I beg your pardon!" But then he smiled and came to sit beside his mother.

"I've just had a phone call from Sarah Orchard," Margaret said awkwardly. "We're trying to finalise my birthday trip to London and also she and the doctor are coming for dinner tomorrow evening. I hope you don't mind Anna, my dear, but I needed to confide in her."

"Oh, for goodness sake...!" started Jason, but Anna felt the need to stop him.

"No Jason, other people are going to find out sooner or later. What does it matter now."

Margaret took her hand. "You're very understanding. However, Sarah has known me a long while and she decided to tell me a few home truths. Especially about the time I told your father, Jason, that I was...pregnant so that he would marry me."

Jason stared at his mother in astonishment. "You did what?"

Margaret shrugged her shoulders. "It was during the war. I was only seventeen when we got engaged and we decided to get married when peace came and Tom came out of the Navy. But it seemed to be dragging on for years and I had the impatience of youth."

"So, you told him you were expecting a baby?" said Anna.

"Yes, and he came home on leave and we married by special licence."

"But didn't that cause a scandal in your family, expecting a baby before you were married? I thought girls in those days waited until they were wearing a wedding ring."

Margaret started laughing. "My dear, you won't believe how many illegitimate births there were in those days. It was an unsure time, your man went off and you didn't know if you'd see him again. People lived for the moment. Yes, there were a lot of war babies. So, we married in January 1945. Of course the war ended in the May. If I'd known, I would have waited. I was only eighteen."

Jason felt puzzled. "But didn't he get suspicious when a baby didn't arrive?"

"I was going to tell him that I'd made a mistake, but then I fell pregnant on my wedding night. So, I was expecting a baby after all. And Tom, the poor love, never realised. It never occurred to him to count up the months."

"That's because he trusted you," said Anna sadly.

"I know. And it was very wrong of me to deceive him like that."

Jason had remained quiet, counting up the years. "But that can't have been me. I wasn't born until 1956."

She patted his knee. "No, my dear. You came along eleven years later. I was nearly thirty before you arrived and by then we'd given up all hope of having another child. That's why you were such a blessing."

"But what about your first baby?" His voice was hushed.

"She would have been your big sister. She was stillborn. I carried her for nine months, but it all went wrong when I went into labour. I shouldn't have been allowed to deliver her, you see. I'm too small to have a normal delivery and I nearly died too. I should have had a caesarean. That's why you came into the world that way."

Jason's face turned white, the revelation shaking him to the core. "You never told me anything of this."

His mother brushed away a silent tear. "There didn't seem to be any point. I was going to call her Christina after your grandmother." She turned her gaze towards the window, her thoughts distant. "It's strange to think she would have been in her fifties by now and most probably with children and grandchildren. And I would have been a great-grandmother." She turned to Anna. "So, you see, Anna. We are all capable of deception and I'm no different."

After Margaret had left, Anna and Jason sat quietly together.

"I might have had a sister," he whispered after a short while.

She hugged him close. "Your mother was very brave to tell us."

"Christina. That's a beautiful name." He pulled Anna closer to him, holding back the tears.

Nigel Barnes was very happy to take on Anna as his client and when she kept her appointment with him, he greeted her warmly. Jason had suggested accompanying her but Anna had different plans. She wanted to do some shopping and spend some time on her own.

Anna travelled to Bristol with a great deal of apprehension and yet excitement. It was the first time she had driven alone in her new car and she was enjoying every minute. She felt independent and totally at ease as she picked up the main road. But she wondered what the solicitor would say to her and what he would advise. When Dave came back from his business trip, she would have to speak to him about the divorce and she wasn't looking forward to that.

Once in Bristol she found a parking space and following Jason's directions she made her way to the offices of Barnes, Atherton and Gill. Nigel was waiting for her and in his polite and professional manner made her comfortable and offered her a cup of coffee. And then they got down to business.

"It's important that my marriage is ended as soon as possible," she told him. "I'm hoping to divorce him on grounds of his adultery."

"As long as he admits to it, then there shouldn't be any problem."

Anna pursed her lips. "I caught him out three times. The first two he admitted to, but he denied the third."

Nigel sat back in his chair. "Did he admit his guilt in front of witnesses? I mean, besides you."

Anna shook her head. "No, he was always defensive and even the first two were difficult for him to admit."

"That could be a problem. It will be your word against his."

"Is there any other way I can get a divorce?"

"Well, there's unreasonable behaviour, but you'll have to give a statement listing reasons why you think your husband behaved unreasonably."

"Despite his adultery, he was a good provider and an excellent father."

"Then there's irretrievable breakdown of marriage. But you'll have to wait two years for that to happen. When did you leave your husband?"

"End of June, but that seems such a long time to wait."

Nigel linked his fingers together. "If you want a quick divorce then I can only suggest you…let him divorce you on grounds of your adultery."

Anna squirmed uncomfortably. "But that doesn't seem fair! He cheated on me while we were married while I…" She knew she was blushing, it seemed so strange to be talking like this to a relative stranger.

"It would be the easiest way," he said kindly. "Have you talked to your husband yet?"

"Not yet. But I will when he comes back from his business trip."

"Excellent! If he's willing to admit he committed adultery then I will need to know the name of his solicitor then we can start communicating all the details. Also, your husband will have to tell his solicitor the time and place when it happened."

Anna nearly dropped her cup in her lap. "I'm sorry, I don't understand. What do you mean, time and place?"

Nigel put his elbows on the desk and clasped his hands together. "Mrs Stevens, if your husband is going to admit adultery then I will need verification." Her embarrassment showed in her face. Nigel had seen this many times before and smiled sympathetically.

"Is that really necessary? I mean, what would happen if I admitted adultery?" said Anna slowly.

"Then it would be the other way round and your husband's solicitor would need the date and place when it happened." He spread his hands on the desk. "I know it sounds harsh, but it's only a question of your husband providing a date and place of his own choosing."

"Do you need photos too?"

He couldn't help laughing. "No, that won't be necessary."

Anna put down her cup and sighed. "It seems such a degrading business. Why can't he just admit it and leave it at that?"

"I assure you there's nothing to worry about. It's just a formality. If everything goes smoothly and your husband doesn't contest it, then your divorce should go through in four or five months. That would make it February."

"That would be good. The sooner the better."

"What about a settlement?"

"I haven't thought about that. We have a house but it's mortgaged and I think a few investments."

"In an amicable divorce the property is usually shared and if your husband sells the house you will be entitled to half. Unless your husband buys you out."

Anna shook her head. "Would it be easier if I just killed him?"

Nigel gave a chuckle. He had really warmed to Jason's new lady friend. "Well, if you decide to do that, I will have to pass you on to our Mr Gill. He deals with criminal law, I only deal with family law."

After she had left Nigel's office, Anna found a café and bought a cup of coffee. She watched from the window as shoppers hurried past carrying their purchases. All these people, she thought, going about their business. All with their own worries and plans and dreams. And quite a few of them will have gone through a divorce. Well, she thought feeling more confident, if they can do it so can I.

Anna found the shop were she had bought her dress for Margaret's party. She wanted to buy another for this evening. Doctor Orchard and Sarah were coming to dinner and Margaret had requested a more 'dressy' occasion, although not too formal. Anna made a selection from the rail and after trying on a few, finally settled on a red lace cocktail dress, knee length with pretty embroidered shoulder straps. The assistant was very helpful and found some matching shoes and a handbag. She only needed to buy some 'bits and bobs' and then she was on her way home.

She was nearly ready. She had done her hair and makeup and was sitting at the dressing table, her kimono wrapped round her, the dress still hanging on the wardrobe door. Her thoughts returned to her appointment with Nigel Barnes. She had liked him and if he was Jason's friend as well as his solicitor, then there was no reason why she shouldn't have absolute faith in him. But if Dave refused to co-operate, it would be down to her and she would have to give the time and place when she had committed adultery! Time and place indeed!

There was a quiet knock on the door and she went to open it just an inch to see who it was. Jason was standing outside; his hand already raised as though he was about to knock again.

"Good evening. I thought I'd escort you downstairs. The good doctor and his wife will be arriving in just ten minutes."

"I've got a better idea," she murmured.

Before he could say another word, she pulled him into the room, slamming the door shut behind him. She leaned up against the wall, entwining her arms round his neck and forcing his face down towards hers. Her kiss was passionate and took him unawares.

"What a surprise! I didn't expect this when I knocked on your door!" he gasped.

"Well, I know I'm a bit late but I've just thought of another birthday present I'd like."

With one hand, she unfastened her robe and let it slide with a soft swish to the floor. Underneath she was wearing a satin slip in pale pink.

He let out a cry of dismay. "Anna! We haven't time for this. We're expected downstairs."

She started unbuttoning his shirt, watching with joy as he struggled with her, his features twisted with bewilderment and desire, as he tried to understand her sudden actions, even if her intentions were quite clear. Once his shirt was undone, she slid her arms round him and caressed his back, continually kissing his neck and throat, delighting in her role as temptress.

He breathed faster, pressing her close. "Oh, God! It's a shame we haven't got time," he murmured. He hooked his finger under the strap of her slip and slid it off her shoulder, kissing her bare skin.

"Who says we haven't got time?"

"I told you, they're waiting for us downstairs."

"Then you'd better hurry up and get on with it." She started unbuckling the belt on his trousers.

He gabbed her hand to stop her. "Anna! You know I don't do this kind of thing in such a hurried manner. I've always prided myself on a little finesse and care to detail."

She had managed to get his belt undone and now aimed for the zip. "I do know! But as you say, we haven't got time. And if you think ten minutes isn't long enough, then I disagree."

He groaned and his hand went down to her thigh and then up under her slip. He jerked back from her. "Dear Lord! You're wearing stockings!"

She gave a giggle knowing she had him now. Pushing his trousers over his hips and exposing only the necessary parts of his anatomy, she ran her fingers lightly over his buttocks and then pulled the small of his back towards her. He breathed heavily through his teeth, squeezing her up against the wall, his face showing the strain of mounting tension.

"Five minutes and counting," she whispered in his ear.

With a moan of relief he finally surrendered. Lifting her up onto the chest of drawers he ripped off her panties. She drew her knees up round his waist and he lunged forward, his mouth covering hers as if he wanted to devour her.

It was frantic and wild and very wonderful. His breathing becoming faster and more rasping, his skin sticking damp and hot against her slip. She moved with him, not thinking of her own pleasure, but instead simply enjoying the fury of his passion. Exhilaration overwhelmed her as she relished her power to tantalise and satisfy.

Within minutes, his body heaved and then stiffened, the ecstasy and vigour of his orgasm making him rise up on his toes to absorb the intoxicating sensation that shot through him and threatened to rip him apart. Sucking in his breath, he released it with a groan and an anguished cry of gratification.

The madness passed and he stood quietly, taking in huge breaths to calm his pounding heart.

And then they were laughing together.

"Wow!" he said his voice hoarse and hardly able to leave his dry throat. "The car wasn't enough for you, then?"

"What were you saying about people waiting for us downstairs?"

"To hell with them!" He stared at the ceiling, concentrating his mind on the ornate cornices.

Anna stroked his face. "Poor love. You look as though you've run ten miles."

"Sweetheart, I feel as though I've run ten miles. I've never experienced anything like it."

"Never mind. You'll feel much better after you've had a cup of tea."

He threw back his head and laughed. "A double whisky would be more appropriate. I think I'd better go to my room and sort myself out, although the way I feel, I'm wondering if I'll be able to walk." He quickly adjusted his clothing and helped her down. He picked up the robe from the floor and she held it against herself. She looked so lovely and innocent that he couldn't help pulling her close and holding her in his arms once more. "See you in a minute," he whispered, opening the door and stepping outside. Before leaving, he kissed her hand.

As she slowly closed the door, she lowered her eyelids seductively. "Bye, sailor. Call on me any time. You know where I live."

He tried to answer, but instead blew out a long breath and made his unsteady way to his own room.

Anna gave a chuckle as she scurried to the bathroom. She completed her toilet routine and tidied herself up, before slipping into her new dress and putting on her shoes. As she left her room she couldn't help laughing. How about Thursday evening, on top of the chest of drawers? Mr Barnes ought to like that, she thought with amusement. In minutes, she was in the parlour demurely kissing the doctor and his wife and taking a cocktail from Ben. She watched the door for Jason but there was no sign of him.

It was Margaret, who asked irritably, "Where is Jason? He's not usually this late. We can't start until he arrives. Anna, have you seen him at all?"

Anna looked up from talking to Sarah, who was telling her about their holiday to Jamaica.

"I did see him, Margaret. I think he went to his room."

Jason suddenly appeared at the door. His hair was damp from taking a shower and he had changed his clothes. But his smile was more apologetic than guilty.

"Jason! What have you been doing! We thought you were never going to come down!" his mother reprimanded him, as she poured him a drink.

He murmured 'sorry' and took his place beside Anna on the couch.

She leaned towards him and whispered, "Yes, Jason. Why don't you tell your mother what you've been doing? I'm sure she'd be interested to know."

"Shh!" he answered, almost choking over his glass.

"Don't tell me you're afraid of what she might say?"

He grabbed her hand and squeezed hard, turning his face away to stop himself laughing.

That night Anna snuggled down next to Jason, happiness flooding through her. Everything was going so well. The boys were paying her another visit, her divorce was in the pipeline and she was engaged to a wonderful man.

He rolled over and raised himself up on his elbow to look at her. "So, what time is milady leaving me in the morning? Shall I set the clock for the wee small hours?"

"No, you can leave it. I'll get up when you do and then pop to my room to have a shower and get changed."

"What! You're staying the entire night?"

"Yes."

"But what happens if Ben or Mrs Wilby, or perish the thought, Mother sees you leaving my room? Aren't you afraid of what they'll say?"

"No, to hell with them!" She closed her eyes and sighed contentedly.

He smiled and reached over to turn off the light.

CHAPTER ELEVEN

It was the last day of their holiday and Jason had insisted that they play another game of golf before their departure back to Bishop Sutton. He needed to discover just once and for all if he could match Anna's skill, although he had a suspicion that he couldn't. Anna ran upstairs after breakfast to collect her jacket as the weather had changed yet again. There was no rain, but the wind had started up and the trees were already swaying with its force.

Margaret knocked on the door. "Could I have a word with you, Anna dear." She stepped into the room and Anna smiled. Margaret seemed contrite. "I know I've already apologised to you…" Anna started to say that another apology wasn't necessary, but Margaret held up her hand to silence her. "No, let me finish. I know you've just started divorce proceedings, but when it's all over, I want to give you a fantastic wedding here at the Grange? Did Jason tell you I've got a licence to hold weddings?"

Anna felt stunned at the offer. "Oh Margaret, I'd love to get married here. As long as Jason thinks it's OK."

"I'm sure he will. He and Kiera got married in a short ceremony in Vancouver. I thought that this time we could do it a little better. Have more of a celebration. As long as your mother doesn't mind and besides we have plenty of bedrooms for your family and any guests you invite from Yorkshire."

"That sounds lovely."

"Oh good. Well, I'm glad that's decided. I wanted to make amends for the way I treated you and if a lovely wedding eases the hurt I caused, then all is well."

Anna put her arms round her. "Please don't upset yourself over it! It's all forgotten now. I'm just so glad that I met Jason in the first place no matter how it came about."
Margaret returned her hug and smiled happily.

Outside, Anna told Jason about her conversation with his mother and what she had suggested.

At the conclusion he was beaming. "I think it's a wonderful idea to get married at the Grange. I was going to put the idea forward myself," he said.

Anna sighed. "I have my divorce to get through first."

"It will pass. Still, I see no reason why we can't make a few plans of our own while we're waiting."

"We can't set a wedding date."

"No, we can't. But let's make a promise. As soon as your decree nisi comes through we set a date?"

"And that's about six weeks before the absolute?"

"Yes. We could be married two months after you're divorced. How does that sound?"

"Lovely!"

"How would you like to go to Mauritius for our honeymoon?" He gave her a sidelong glance. "Or Blackpool if you wish? I've heard you northerners love Blackpool." She gave him a withering look for his impudence. He quickly changed the subject. "Well, are you ready to be beaten into the ground?"

"Fat chance!" she answered, opening the car door.

He gave a smile. "No, I think today is my lucky day."

"It might be. But not for playing golf!"

Jason was just about to climb into the driver's seat when Margaret came rushing out.

"Anna! Phone call for you," she panted, her face red with the exertion.

"It'll be the boys," said Anna. "I bet they've organised a date when they can come down. Won't be long." She closed the car door and hurried excitedly back into the house. Anna picked up the receiver lying on the small table. "Hi there."

There was a short pause before the reply came. "Anna, it's me, Dave."

Her heart almost stopped beating with the shock. "Dave? How did you get this number?"

"Your mother gave it to me."

She felt as though she had been thumped in the stomach. "Why did she do that?"

"Because I asked for it."

Anna took in a breath. She needed to speak to him, but now wasn't a good time. "In a way I'm glad you phoned. There's lots for us to discuss, except that I'm just on my way out, so would you mind if…"

He interrupted sharply. "Anna! I'm sorry you haven't got time to talk to me. I realise you have a busy life now, but at least let us get a few things sorted out!"

"Yes, of course."

"Your mother said you wanted a divorce?"

"Yes…Yes, I do. I need the name of your solicitor so that we can get started."

"Is that really necessary? Can't we talk about it first?"

"I don't think there's anything for us to talk about."

"You've made up your mind, then?"

"Yes, I have."

There was silence at the other end and Anna wondered if he was still there. "The boys said you're very happy in your new job."

"I am happy, Dave. And I want a divorce and then I intend to stay down here."

"Look, I know I've not treated you well in the past, but going away like you did made me do some soul searching."

"It's a bit late after all these years."

"Yes, I realise that. Although I don't know why you left in the first place. What reason did you have?"

Anger welled up inside her. How dare he act all innocent. "I told you in my letter. Don't tell me you've forgotten that incident in the pub? That redheaded woman you seemed to be very friendly with."

His voice was husky. "Woman with red hair?"

"Oh, for goodness sake! You were at the bar and you grabbed hold of her hand."

She heard him suck in a breath. "Are you talking about Pam?"

"I didn't know who she was."

"Bloody hell, Anna! She works in the office and that evening she was meeting a bloke on a blind date. She'd been going on about it all day, nervous as hell she was. I had no idea she was going to the same pub and I took her hand to give her some moral support. It meant nothing."

Doubts began to creep into Anna's mind. "Is that the truth, Dave?"

"Absolutely. I've been good as gold since before you did your college course."

Anna realised he was talking about the last time she had found him out when the boys were twelve. "I'm not sure I believe you."

There was silence again and Anna knew her husband was struggling with his feelings. Displaying his emotions was never his strong point.

"If you're really happy working down in Bristol, then there's no reason why you should give up your job. I can easily find something in my line of work. In fact, I've been looking and I've already seen some good possibilities. I could sell this house and buy one down there. We could start again."

Anna felt stunned. "You'd come to live down here?"

"Yes, if that's what you wanted and it made you happy. The boys will be going soon so now is the ideal time."

"But I don't understand." She drew on her strength. "I heard that you phoned...my employer and gave him a hard time."

"I'm sorry for that. I bitterly regret it now. It's just that I thought you'd left me for another man. But I now realise you went to Bristol to start a new job and that guy I talked to really was your boss, but I was too jealous and stupid to listen to him." He gave a nervous laugh. "He must have thought me a rude bastard. I'm glad he didn't sack you."

"He's very understanding," she whispered.

"I know I've never shown you much affection, but I do love you and I don't want to lose you. Please, Anna, I miss you and I need you. I know I can make you happy if you just give me another chance. Please don't leave me."

The phone began to slip from her hand as the enormity of what he was saying and the fact she had misunderstood the situation that had driven her from him. The room spun round and she felt sick

"I can't talk now. I'll ring later." She didn't wait for his answer but put the receiver down.

She leaned on the wall trying to stem the tears that spilled onto her cheeks.

Anna knew that she was too quiet as they drove towards the golf club. Jason kept up a happy conversation for most of the journey, but eventually he fell quiet too.

He parked the car, but as she turned to get out, he caught her arm. "Sweetheart, everything is going to be OK."

"Is it?" she said brightly, trying to force a smile.

"Please don't worry if the boys can't come down for a visit. We can go up and see them."

Anna licked her lips nervously. "The boys can't visit?"

He smiled and nodded. "You were on the phone quite a while so I guessed that all the arrangements had fallen through. But it's not a problem."

She didn't answer.

To begin with, Jason felt elated that he was actually equalling Anna in his score and then finally he past her. But by the time they had reached the tenth fairway he knew that she was completely off her stroke and he became worried.

"You're not playing at all well today," he said kindly. "That phone call really upset you, didn't it?"

She tried to focus on the ball, but it kept swimming in front of her as if she was looking through a huge raindrop. She gripped the iron tightly and tried to concentrate. Playing golf was the last thing she wanted to do, as tears finally trickled down her cheeks and she let out a harrowing sob.

Jason hurriedly crossed the green, took the club from her and put his arms round her, alarmed at her sudden outburst of uncontrollable distress. He waved to the three men waiting their turn and pointed to the clubhouse. Gathering up the equipment, he guided Anna off the fairway and towards the building on the far side of the course.

The bar was virtually empty and it was easy finding a table in the corner, where Jason made her sit down while he fetched them both a drink. As she sipped hers, he watched her. Her expression was one he recognised, the one she had had at Bishop Sutton, when she had been trying to keep her secret from him. He had forgotten that look, but the last week had changed them both completely and they had found the kind of happiness that seemed too good to be true. His heart began to beat rapidly. Had it been too good to be true? Had something happened to snatch it all away?

"I think you'd better tell me what's going on," he said softly. "It wasn't your sons on the phone, was it?"

She shook her head. "No, it was...my husband."

Jason blew out a breath and leaned forward in his chair. He took her hand and noticed it was her left one wearing the engagement ring.

"Now I understand. You asked him for a divorce and he got nasty about it. That was bound to happen. There's going to be some animosity for a while. But you're not alone, we can see this through together."

Anna took another sip of her drink. "He wasn't nasty. Oh God, I wish he had been. If he had, then it would have made the situation easier."

Jason frowned. "Now I don't understand."

She took a big breath before explaining. "He said things to me he's never said in all the years I've known him. That he...loved me and that he didn't want to lose me. He said...that he missed me and that he could...make me happy if I gave him another chance. He even talked of selling up and joining me in Bristol."

He absorbed this information before asking softly, "And what did you say to that?"

"I didn't know what to say."

He began to feel uncomfortable. "Did you tell him why you wanted a divorce?"

"Yes...I think so," she said. Her thoughts became confused.

"What do you mean, you think so! Anna, does he know about us?"

"I...I...don't..."

Jason broke away from her and sat back in his chair, staring at her, his eyes dark with concealed anger and disappointment. "He doesn't know about us, does he?"

She licked her lips nervously. "I hadn't the courage to tell him. I should have, but what he said knocked the wind out of me."

Jason thought for a moment and then sighed. He sat forward again and put his hand on her knee. When he spoke his voice was reassuring but firm. "You really must face up to him. I imagine he'll be upset when he discovers about us and he'll probably feel jealousy and rage. God knows I felt the same way when Kiera left me for Peter. But you mustn't let him make you feel guilty, because that's what he's trying to do. Sweetheart, you have to insist on a divorce and not give in to this emotional blackmail."

Anna put her hand over his and tears once again filled her eyes. "He'll react badly when I tell him, I just know he will."

"Then I'll tell him."

"No, you won't!"

He cocked his head to one side. "What am I going to do with you?" He looked down at her engagement ring. "So, now you have to make a decision. Do you listen to your husband and start afresh with him? Or do you carry on with the divorce and stay with me?"

Anna's thoughts troubled her. "If Dave doesn't know about us then he must have been sincere on the phone. But he's never spoken to me like that before. Not in all the years we were married, not once."

"Can a leopard change its spots?" he asked, raising his eyebrows.

"I'm...not sure."

"It doesn't take a man nineteen years to tell a woman how much she means to him. And can you trust him? How do you know he'll not cheat on you in the future?"

Anna shook her head. "He said he hasn't done that since the boys were twelve. In fact, he told me that the incident I saw in the pub when I thought...He said it didn't happen."

"He would!"

"No, I mean he admits the incident, but he said it wasn't what I thought it was."

Jason sat back in his chair once more. The bar was starting to fill as players arrived for their pre lunch drinks.

"I can't comment on that. But I know that the brief conversation I had with him led me to believe he had little concern for you."

"He…apologises for that. He was angry…"

"Apology accepted."

She gave a weak smile. "I felt so sorry for him and guilty that I'd abandoned him and the boys. I've always tried to do the right thing and…"

"Anna, you can't go back to him because you feel sorry and guilty. That would be crass stupidity."

"I realise that."

"All right, let's assume he doesn't know anything about us. Either he is genuine and realises that he's lost something very precious, after all, sometimes a person doesn't know what they've lost until they've lost it. Or it could be that he thinks of you as a possession and wants you back only for that reason."

"And if I go back to him?"

He closed his eyes for a moment. "Then we're back to the leopard changing its spots."

"I don't know what to do."

"Do you love me?"

"With all my heart."

"I'm glad about that, I was beginning to wonder."

Anna leaned forward and took his hand. "I do love you but I've been married to him for most of my life. He's the father of my boys," she said desperately.

Jason glanced around the room. "So, you don't know what to do?"

"I just wish someone would tell me that I'm doing the right thing."

He stared at her intently. "I've just thought of something. We'll toss a coin." He reached into his pocket and took out some loose change.

Anna felt horrified. "What do you mean toss a coin?"

"Heads you stay with me and tails you go back to Wakefield and your husband."

She began to panic. "Jason, we can't make a decision about my life on the toss of a coin!"

"Why not? It seems a good a way as any."

"But we should discuss it."

"We've already done that!" He held the coin between his fingers for a moment and stared at her, his eyes cold and dark. She stared back numbly. Anna watched mesmerised as he skilfully tossed the coin in the air and then catching it with one hand, slapped it down on the back of the other. "Are you ready? Shall I look?"

"This isn't right," she whispered.

He lifted his hand and peeped underneath. His expression became resigned as he blew out a long breath.

"Well, it looks like you'll be on that train as soon as we can arrange it."

Anna's heart beat rapidly and she gasped. "It's tails? Oh no, it can't be. Fate couldn't be so cruel." She took a quick sip of her drink. Her voice was almost pleading. "Please Jason, don't send me away. Please don't send me back to that awful man. I'd rather die than do that." He started laughing. "Why are you laughing? It's not funny tossing a coin to decide something!"

"Sorry, sweetheart." He squeezed her hand. "It was something my father taught me. When you can't make a decision then toss a coin and let fate decide."

"It seems an odd way to go about things!"

He grinned. "Ah, but it's not the result that matters, but how you feel about the result." Anna stared at him in bewilderment. "I told you the coin said you had to go back to your husband. It was obvious by your reaction that it was the last thing you should do. If anything, it told me and I hope you, exactly what you thought about that."

She took another sip of her drink. "Well, I guess it worked. It looks like the last thing I should do is go back to my husband."

He leaned towards her and caressed her face. "The trouble is, I cheated," he whispered.

"How did you cheat?"

He opened his hand. "It actually came down on heads. So the decision should have been that you stay with me."

She snatched the coin from his hand. "But why didn't you tell me that?"

His expression became serious. "Because I didn't want any doubts. I had to know for sure that you wanted to stay with me."

She looked at the coin in the palm of her hand.

"You're a tricky one. I can see I'm going to have to watch you!"

The bar was now getting quite full.

"Shall we go and have our lunch?" he said, smiling.

"Yes, but can I keep this coin?"

They stood up.

"Why?" he asked, puzzled.

"It'll remind me of how stupid I am and how I nearly lost you."

They had a pleasant lunch at the club, sitting at their favourite table by the window. It seemed the weather was getting worse and the wind was becoming stronger, causing the trees to bend alarmingly. Many of the players were abandoning their game and coming in for an early lunch. Among them were Caroline Beaumont and her friend who took a table close to Jason and Anna.

But when Caroline spotted them she came over to them. "Anna, are you OK? I heard that you took poorly."

Anna smiled. "I felt…dizzy. That's all. Nothing to worry about."

Caroline frowned at Jason. "I hope you're being careful! I'm intending to break down Anna's resistance until she joins my team. But it'll all be for nothing if she's unavailable for the next nine months!" She left them, laughing with amusement.

Anna felt stunned. "Was she talking about a baby?"

Jason looked up from the menu he was studying. "It seems so," he smiled.

"Good heavens!" She glanced around at the other diners. "How did she know I'd felt…ill? I'm amazed how news gets round this place. It's a hive of rumour and speculation."

"That's a golf club for you. But it's something to think about."

"What is?"

"Having a baby."

Anna's mouth fell open with surprise. "I think I'd rather concentrate on the current problems, if you don't mind!"

He leaned towards her, resting his elbow on the table, his hand cupping his cheek. "I'd love to have another child. A brother or sister for Hollie sounds wonderful."

She was saved from answering by the waiter coming to take their order.

They were just finishing their coffee when Jason received a call on his mobile, a fact that caused annoying stares in his direction since he had forgotten to turn it off and they were forbidden in the restaurant. He quickly headed for the foyer, apologising to everyone as he past them. Anna sipped her coffee. It was then that she noticed that Caroline was bending her head very close to her companion and they seemed to be discussing something in great depth.

Jason reached the spacious foyer and took the call. He was just concluding it when he saw a woman come out of the bar and start climbing the stairs, obviously on her way to the ladies room that was on the next floor. He called her name, loud enough to hear but not enough to attract attention. She halted her climb and looked down at him. A satisfied smile spread across her face as she came slowly down the stairs.

He took her arm and pulled her into the well of the stairs where they couldn't be seen.

"I want to know what's going on!"

"What are you talking about?" Deborah smiled a slow smile.

He pushed her roughly against the wall. "Tell me now, why you have it in for Anna!"

She smiled again. "I don't know what you're talking about."

"Did you frighten her the other day? Did you deliberately drive your car at her?"

She threw back her head and laughed. "Why are you so upset that your sweet, little girlfriend got a drenching? I was just having some harmless fun."

Disgust overwhelmed him as he confirmed his suspicions about the driver of the black Porsche.

"So, that was you?"

"Yes, it was. Hope she didn't catch a chill."

"Why did you do that? What has she ever done to you?"

She pulled a face and sighed. "Well, you know what they say about a woman scorned."

Jason squeezed her arm. "You evil…!"

"Let go of me." Jason closed his eyes and regained control. He released his grip. He stared at her, hatred pouring from his eyes. For some strange reason his anger seemed to excite her. She reached up and put her arms round his neck. "We were always good together, weren't we Jason?" She pressed herself against him. "I'm sure you don't get as much…pleasure with her as you did with me. I can understand why you want to have a little fling with your secretary, but when are you going to forget all this nonsense and come back where you belong?"

He pulled her arms away. "Oh, it's a lot more than a little fling. I've asked Anna to marry me."

Deborah's lips twitched, her eyes dark with envy. "Have you really? Now, why would you want to do that when you can do so much better?"

Her meaning was clear, but Jason had heard enough and turned away as if to leave. "You're nothing compared to her," he said with loathing. "Absolutely nothing."

He turned his back on her and walked away. In the dining room, he ordered another drink.

"Sorry to have left you so long. It was Graham, finalising the next contract."

"Are you OK?" His flushed complexion and glistening eyes alarmed her.

He nodded. "Certainly." He took in a breath, thankful that his anger was ebbing away.

Anna's gaze was drawn to Caroline and her companion, who were still engrossed in conversation, although now and again their eyes would turn in Anna's direction.

"Jason, I get the feeling that they're talking about me."

"Who, sweetheart?"

"Caroline and her friend."

Jason smiled. "Probably discussing your illness on the golf course."

Anna looked towards Caroline and her companion. "Somehow I don't think that's what they're talking about."

But Anna's fears were confirmed when she went to collect her jacket. As she slipped her arms through the sleeves, she overheard them as they were collecting their equipment.

It was Caroline's friend who seemed offended. "Of all the terrible things to do! To say she's a widow and nursed her husband through a terrible illness and all of a sudden she's a married woman. How can Jason accept all her lies?"

Caroline answered with a contemptuous click of her tongue. "Well, I think we should give the girl a chance. We don't know the full story and it's very wrong of Deborah to go round spreading gossip like that."

Deborah! Anna bit her bottom lip anxiously. Had Deborah now resorted to causing trouble for her at the club? She fastened her jacket and sighed. They were going back to Bishop Sutton the following day and she would have some distance between herself and all this hostility. She breathed a sigh of relief and went to meet Jason who had gone ahead to put their bags in the car.

During their journey home they talked about their future and Anna's spirits lifted, as she thought about their wedding and their life together. But then she remembered Caroline's conversation with her friend.

"They were talking about me. I overheard them," she sad sadly.

"Eavesdropping again?"

She tapped him on the leg. "You should talk!"

He gave a chuckle. "All right, what were they saying?"

"Well, they've heard I'm not a widow."

Jason shrugged it off. "Let them talk. Next week they' have found something else to bitch over."

"But how do they know so quickly? I only told the oth on Monday."

"It's strange how these things get around. It could have come from Fran or even Irene. Not John though, he wouldn't spread gossip."

"They heard it from Deborah."

Jason frowned. "Did they now?" He shook his head. "That woman is beyond belief. If I didn't mind going to prison, I'd strangle her."

"I'd come and visit you every day," she said, smiling.

When they arrived home Anna decided to take a quick shower. The trauma of the day had literally brought her out in a cold sweat and she needed to freshen up. She was just coming into the bedroom when Jason knocked on the door and came into the room. They were so secure in one another now, that waiting for permission to enter a room seemed unimportant.

He grinned cheekily. "Irene has made us a pot of tea."

"I shall be ready in two ticks."

He studied her. "Good." He lifted her chin with his forefinger and briefly kissed her lips. "Hurry up. I'm finding it very difficult to concentrate knowing that you're naked under that towel."

She gave a giggle and changed the subject. "After our tea I'm going to phone Dave."

"You can use the phone in my room if you want. It'll be more private."

Anna took the stairs once more to Jason's room to make the call to her husband. She sat on the bed for some time staring at the phone trying to pluck up the courage. Finally she picked up the receiver and dialled the number.

Dave's voice was quiet when he answered. Anna paused for a moment before saying, "Hi Dave, it's me." It seemed ages before he replied. She detected a chilly tone in his voice and she was relieved. Now he sounded like the old Dave and not the one she had spoken to that morning. "I said I'd phone back."

"You didn't waste any time. So, have you thought about what I said?"

"I have but...I'm sorry Dave, I still want a divorce. Please can I have the name of your solicitor?"

There was a long silence before he answered. "Didn't you listen to a word I said! I said I would move down there. I said I would give up everything for you."

"I know that, but I can't...trust you. I shouldn't have put up with your behaviour all those years."

"What the hell do you want me to do? I've said I'm sorry."

"I want you to give me my freedom."

She heard him suck in a breath. "I'll use that one in Wakefield. The one I went to when I bought this house."

Anna thought for a moment. "I remember it." She knew that she would get no more from him, not even the address. But she didn't care. It would be easy to find the information she needed.

"Are you absolutely sure about this? Don't you want us to talk it over some more?"

"No Dave, my mind is made up."

"Why don't you come home and we can discuss it face to face."

Anna was suddenly filled with dread. Although she knew Dave was an excellent father and would never hurt the boys, she wasn't so sure about her own safety. Once inside the house he might be capable of anything. She tried to dismiss these terrifying thoughts from her mind.

"No, I don't think so. We can communicate through our solicitors from now on. Have you got a pen handy? I'll give you the details of mine." She looked down at the card in her hand; the one Nigel Barnes had given her and carefully read out the name, address and telephone number. She hoped that Dave was writing it down.

"This is stupid, Anna!"

She ignored him. "I want to divorce you on grounds of your adultery."

"What? Do you mean from…six years ago?"

"My solicitor says that as long as you admit it, then everything should go through smoothly."

"Forget it."

"Please Dave." She was answered with a cold silence. She took in a steadying breath. "OK, then you…you can divorce me for…adultery."

"What do you mean?"

"Do you want me to draw you a picture!"

"You've met someone else?" Anna tried to speak but her throat dried up. "Anna, have you met someone else?"

"Yes…Yes I have. And I love him and he's asked me to marry him and I've said yes." Anna could almost feel the anger at the other end of the phone.

"How long has this been going on? Who is he?"

"That doesn't matter. And you can't judge me after your behaviour. Anyway, I met him when I came to work in Bristol."

"Oh no, you didn't! I was right wasn't I? You went down there because you already had another bloke!"

"No, I didn't. I came here to work," she said defiantly. "Me and Jason only…I mean I.…"

"Jason? Wait a minute, when I phoned Harrington Rhodes in Bristol, they gave me the number of a Jason Harrington. Is that him? Is it the man I talked to?"

Anna began to curse her stupidity. Why, oh why, had she left her CV and her application letter on the computer? It would have only taken a second to delete them.

"I don't want to talk about him. I just want to get this divorce out of the way."

"Oh, do you! Well, you'll not get anything out of me. I'll fight you all the way!"

"I don't care about the money. I can support myself. I have a good job."

A bitter laugh erupted at the end of the phone. "Well, I'm sure you've got a good job if you're screwing the boss!"

"Goodbye Dave."

"You slut! I'm glad to get rid of you.…"

She didn't want to hear any more and slammed down the phone.

Anna sat for a while, hugging herself and rocking gently backwards and forwards. She closed her eyes and tried to calm herself. She mustn't let him get to her. She would ring Nigel on Monday morning and pass on the details of her husband's solicitor. And then everything can go ahead, even if it meant admitting her adultery. Life wasn't fair, she sobbed, but it was only for four or five months and that wasn't so long to wait. Then she and Jason could get married, here at the Grange. She would be happy with Jason, she knew it. And the boys would meet him and little Hollie too. They would love her new family. And perhaps in time, she would have another baby. Jason said he would like another child. Perhaps in twelve months' time she might be pregnant. And they would all live happily together, for the rest of their lives.

Jason stuck his head round the door. "All done?"

Anna nodded. "I've got the name of his solicitor and he knows about us."

He came to sit on the bed with her. "How did he take it?"

She turned her face away in embarrassment. "You were right about the animosity. And, damn it! You were right about the leopard." She turned to face him again and he could see the pain in her eyes. "I'm trying to decide if it's better to be a whore or a slut. I mean, what would you choose?"

"Oh, sweetheart." He put his arm round her and pulled her close, kissing her hair.

She went into the pocket of her jeans and pulled out the coin that Jason had used.

"I think I'll put this on a chain and hang it round my neck!"

He took it from her and put it in the drawer of the bedside table.

"You must forget it now. Let Nigel do his job and all this will come to an end soon."

She leaned against him, finding comfort in his nearness. For quite a while they didn't speak, as she breathed deeply trying to control her agonised trembling. It felt so good to feel the warmth of his body close to hers, to smell the aftershave he liked to wear.

She lifted her face and he kissed her lips. "I need to know that you love me," she said softly.

"You know I love you very much."

"Show me," she whispered.

They undressed slowly. Being with Jason was always wonderful but it seemed for Anna, that this time was even more exquisite. Their kisses and caresses were gentle and unhurried; the tender murmurings of their lovemaking soothed and comforted her. She loved him desperately and she needed to feel part of him, to feel that she was truly his.

And when he slipped inside her, she lifted her body to meet his, crying out in pleasure and the anguish she had endured seemed to melt away. She closed her eyes and let herself be carried to a place where only that instant counted and nothing else mattered. Jason held back until the last possible moment and only when he saw the warm flush spread across her breasts and neck did he join her in that special place.

CHAPTER TWELVE

She was running, running so fast that she thought her heart would burst. Dave was right behind her, his face twisted in rage, his hands reaching out to grab her. She ran from room to room desperate to find an escape, a place to hide, but there was none. Suddenly she felt the force of his body on top of her and his hands were round her neck. She was choking, crying, pleading for her life, but he wasn't listening. He was intent on her destruction and nothing was going to save her. Anna jumped out of sleep with a scream and sat up in bed.

Jason came hurrying out of the bathroom. "Dear Lord! What is it?" His face was white as he sat on the bed next to her.

"Bad dream. Just a bad dream," she gasped, reaching out and holding him close.

He wrapped his arms round her and kissed the top of her head. "Wow! You gave me a fright."

"It was nothing. You go and finish shaving."

Anna watched him go feeling ashamed, she really must pull herself together. Their holiday was over and they were travelling back to Bishop Sutton to pick up the threads of their lives and Anna knew that Jason was keen to get back and resume his normal life. How strange it would be to work in the office once more, she thought and yet how wonderful too. She had been happy staying at the Grange and it seemed that the last week had been the most eventful of her life. Anna slipped out of bed, drew back the curtains and smiled at the scene outside the window.

It was going to be a beautiful day now that the rain and gusty winds had moved off to the east. The telephone rang and Anna ran swiftly across the room. She answered in a hushed voice and to her delight discovered it was Martyn. Keeping her voice calm, trying to hide her excitement, she confirmed the details of their visit in just three weeks' time. Anna told her son that arrangements would be made for their overnight stay and how much she was looking forward to seeing them again. As she replaced the receiver she saw Jason standing at the bathroom door.

"Your turn," he smiled.

"Sorry, for frightening you like that."

"We all have bad dreams, sweetheart. So the visit is all sorted?"

She nodded. "Saturday the twenty-eighth. But only the lads. The others can't make it. Martyn has just told me that he's passed his driving test, so he and Chris are coming down in my car."

Jason gave a quizzical look. "Your car?"

She squirmed in embarrassment. "Yes, the car I used at home. It seems his dad has put him on the insurance and now he's driving it. I'm pleased about that. It was only sat idle."

"Oh, so you did have a car," he smiled. His smile faded. "Oh, dear, the twenty-eighth? That's the weekend I'm going to Vancouver to pick up Hollie." He saw her face blanch and quickly added, "But don't worry I'll make other arrangements."

"But what? Hollie needs to go back to school, so you must go and collect her."

"No, I want to meet your sons, so I'll ask Ben to go."

"Will he mind doing that?"

He threw back his head and laughed. "He'll love it. He's been to visit the Macintoshes many times before. He's one of the family."

"Oh Jason, I'm so sorry for upsetting your plans. I should have checked with you first, but I was so excited about seeing the boys again."

"Don't worry, it's not a problem." He smiled. "Well, if it's just the two of them visiting, they can use your room." Seeing Anna's quizzical expression, he added, "We must decide which bedroom we're going to sleep in when we get back. We can't be running backwards and forwards between rooms like we've done here. I know it's been fun but…"

Anna couldn't help giggling. "That would be confusing." She gave it some serious thought before saying, "Yes, I'd love to move in with you."

He bent forward and kissed her. "Wonderful," he murmured.

Back in her room, Anna packed the last of her things. Then she made her way down to breakfast. Ever since her phone call with Dave, she had been filled with resignation. There was nothing to do but see it through and hope that her husband would put aside his bitterness and realise that their marriage was over. She really wanted to get on with the process of ending it once and for all and she prayed that Dave would see his solicitor as soon as possible and not cause any hindrance to her plans.

After breakfast, there was the hustle and bustle of bags being collected and taken out to the cars. The realisation that she really was leaving the Grange made her sit on the top step of the staircase and lean her head against the banister, deep in thought. Jason came through the main entrance and started up the stairs. He stopped when he saw Anna sitting at the top.

"Everything's loaded and we're ready to go. Ben and Mrs Wilby are just saying goodbye to Mother." He grinned. "I used to sit there when I was a small boy. I liked to watch all the comings and goings."

"It's a nice place to sit," murmured Anna.

"May I join you?"

Anna nodded and shuffled over to give him room. "I'm just collecting my thoughts before we set off. I feel that this is a new beginning for us. We're going back to Bishop Sutton changed people."

"Why's that, sweetheart?" he said, glancing around.

"Exactly that. When we left you weren't calling me sweetheart."

"I guess not."

"And I wasn't wearing your ring."

"It was on my mind, though."

"And we weren't lovers."

"And that was definitely on my mind."

Anna took in a breath. "I used to sit on the stairs when I was a little girl and wait for my dad to come home from work. And when he came through the door I would run down and throw myself in his arms."

Jason smiled and put his arm round her. "I can just imagine you doing that. To lose your dad at twelve years old seems too much to bear."

She gave a sad smile. "But even after he'd gone I would sit there, waiting. Part of me knew he wasn't going to come home any more, but part of me wouldn't believe it. I thought that if I just sat there long enough he really would come through the door again."

Anna's reflections brought a lump to Jason's throat. "I lost my father two years ago, but I was lucky to have him for so long since his health was very poor for years." He gave a grimace. "But I don't know how your family coped."

"We had no choice. Dad used to call Elaine and me 'his little women'. He was such a good man, so kind and gentle. I never knew him to be angry."

He squeezed her shoulder trying to bring some comfort. "You've been through a lot, but I promise that you'll be happy from now on. I'll do all I can to make you happy."

"I know I shall be happy with you, despite having to go through a divorce with a despicable man." She remembered her phone call to her husband. "When I asked Dave for a divorce I could almost feel his hatred, even though he was hundreds of miles away. I felt afraid and I was so grateful I wasn't in the room with him. I hope to God that Nigel can do what's necessary without me having to set eyes on Dave again."

"Your husband wouldn't dare hurt you, not while I'm around," said Jason, his eyes turning dark.

She grinned. "My hero."

He grimaced and then burst out laughing. "Oh dear, is it old-fashioned now for a man to want to protect his lady? Perhaps it smacks too much of chivalrous knights and damsels in distress. And you've proved how strong and self-reliant you can be."

"I don't think I'm a damsel in distress, but every woman dreams of a knight who will fight for her honour."

He smiled with her. "Now, are you ready? Ben is champing at the bit to be gone."

The following morning, Anna rang Nigel Barnes and gave him the information regarding her husband's solicitor. He reassured her that once they had made contact, events would start moving. However, he wanted to make another appointment for her for the following week.

And there was a great deal to do during the following week. Anna soon moved her things into Jason's room and made herself comfortable. Not only was it the largest bedroom in the house but also boasted a king's size bed and huge built-in wardrobe that Anna loved on sight.

They had arrived back to a mountain of mail that included a wedding invitation from Sharon. She was to marry just eighteen days before Christmas Day and everyone was invited just as she had promised before leaving. Anna sent an immediate acceptance and included a short note telling her that the invitation might be reciprocated in due course. She smiled as she put the stamp on the envelope knowing that Sharon would be agog with speculation.

Working together again turned out to be exciting as well as exhilarating. They soon fell into their normal routine and Jason's life picked up once more with his endless meetings and trips abroad. But there was one marked difference and that was their time in the office was punctuated with the occasional kiss and caress.

"You've heard nothing?" said Anna in dismay.

Nigel leaned forward in his chair and put his forearms on the desk. "I would have expected something from your husband's solicitor by now."

"I don't understand. That was the name he gave me."

"We can only wait until the paperwork arrives. I'm sure it's on its way," he said, smiling with confidence. "Are you sure he said he would file for divorce?"

"He told me to forget the idea of divorcing him, so I assumed he would file." She squeezed her hands together. "Can't you write to them and ask them to hurry up?"

He grinned. "I've often had those thoughts myself but unfortunately it's unethical."

"What do you mean?"

"Your husband might have decided to choose another firm of solicitors. And if he is filing for divorce then his solicitor must approach me first. I'm afraid my hands are tied until I hear something."

Anna glanced over to the window and watched two pigeons strutting on the ledge. This was the second time she had sat in Nigel's office and she had hoped this appointment would just be a formality since she had told him the information he required.

"What happens if I file?"

"Then I could approach this firm of solicitors. Do you want me to do that?" Anna licked her lips. "Unless you can talk to your husband once more and find out what his plans are?"

She shuddered at that request. "Oh dear, I don't fancy doing that again."

"It would move the situation along a bit if you could summon up the courage."

She pulled a face but then became more practical. "What would happen if you didn't hear from any solicitor?"

Nigel sat back in his chair. This was an awkward question. "Then I will write to the one you gave me and say you're filing for divorce. However, I think we'd have a long battle on our hands if your husband denies adultery."

"And I wouldn't get my divorce."

"Well, you could still go for unreasonable behaviour."

Anna grimaced. "I'll have to think about that one, it just seems so much more complicated." She gave a sigh. "I suppose I could wait the two years."

He nodded, understanding. "I would start proceedings as soon as the two years were up. Unfortunately, if he contests it, you'll have to wait five years."

Anna considered this for a while before saying, "That could be what he's after. He's already told me that I'm not going to get a penny so making me wait sounds just like him."

"You have a right to a share of the property."

Anna left Nigel's office with a heavy heart. What on earth was Dave up to? Was he so vindictive that he would fight her every inch of the way? As she walked towards the car she wondered if she could pluck up the courage to phone him once more. But she winced at the thought of giving him another opportunity to insult her.

If Anna thought her appointment with Nigel was disappointing then this turned out to be insignificant compared to the news she received just five days later. Chris phoned to say that they had to cancel the proposed visit at the end of the month. It seemed that both the boys had decided to move into halls that weekend in preparation for their first term at university and since their lives were so busy at the moment, he suggested that they postpone their visit until Christmas. Anna tried to take it bravely, understanding that they would need to settle in and if they didn't have time to see her then so be it, she had walked out of their lives and it was unfair to expect them to accommodate her. But she had looked forward to them meeting Jason. Then she wondered if a visit to Wakefield would be in order, to catch them before they left.

"Sweetheart, I'm up to my gills in work too so I can't take you at the moment," said Jason sadly, when Anna asked him.

"I suppose I could travel up there and visit them myself. I could stay with Mum."

"What about your husband? Is there any chance of your paths crossing?"

Anna glanced up at him and saw the worried expression in his eyes. Since their conversation on the stairs at the Grange, he had become very concerned about her safety.

"I don't think he would hurt me," she said.

"I wouldn't like to give him the opportunity," he replied tersely.

She didn't want to cause Jason any worry and decided to wait until Christmas.

There was one thing they didn't have to wait for and that was the arrival home of little Hollie. Ben had travelled to Vancouver the weekend the boys should have come to visit and spent the next four days there before bringing her home. She bounded into the house carrying a huge bag of presents and telling everyone a month's worth of news in five minutes.

She gave everyone a big hug and then ran upstairs to see that her room was OK. Their meal that evening was more chaotic than they were used to as Hollie told them about Ben's promise to build her a Wendy house in the garden. It seemed that she had played in the one her mother had had when she was a girl and had taken a serious liking to it. In fact, the entire visit had been a great success and Hollie had visited many of the places linked to her mother's childhood.

After the household had calmed down, Jason told his daughter that very soon she would have a stepmother.

"But not a wicked one!" laughed Anna.

"Are you really, really going to get married?" said Hollie, her eyes sparkling with surprise.

Anna nodded. "We've decided to get married at the Grange."

"When?" she asked.

Taken aback by the question, Anna turned to Jason for help.

"We're not sure yet, sweetie. There's lots to sort out," he said.

"But Grandma Harrington says it'll be OK?"

"Oh, yes. It's just that we've not set a date yet."

"Is everyone invited?"

Ben answered with a sharp retort. "Do you think we're going to stay away? Not likely!"

Mrs Wilby agreed wholeheartedly without taking her eyes from her knitting.

"Can I be a bridesmaid?"

Anna felt startled. "Goodness, I've not thought of that." She studied Hollie for a moment as if pondering the matter. "What do you think?" she said winking at Jason.

"She'll scrub up OK," he said nonchalantly.

Anna held out her arms to the little girl. "Of course you can." Hollie ran to her and Anna held her in a tight hug. "Now, I wonder what colour your bridesmaid's dress will be?"

"Pink! Pink!"

"What a surprise!" said Anna.

Anna didn't feel so gleeful when they went to bed that night.

"Sometimes I wonder if we'll ever get married," she said.

"Now what's brought this on?"

She let out a sigh. "Nigel said he'll phone me when he gets the paperwork from my husband's solicitor. But I've heard nothing yet and the waiting is killing me."

Jason rolled over and raised himself on one elbow, looking down at her. "Impatient to be my wife, eh?" he chuckled. "Even if things don't start moving until the summer after next, we can still get married as soon as."

"But I was hoping for May when it's your birthday."

Jason opened his eyes wide in horror. "Dear God, forty-one!"

"Oh, well that convinces me. I'm not marrying a decrepit old sod like you!"

"You cheeky...old am I!"

He grabbed her and pinned her down while she struggled, squealing with delight. But within seconds his mouth was on hers and she surrendered. What was it about this man that he could arouse her desire so spontaneously? The thought lasted a second only. His tongue was exploring, making her melt with wanting, needing. She met his passion with a moan of welcome.

Hollie duly returned to school the following week, pristinely dressed in her winter uniform of black pleated skirt, blue blouse and black sweater with the school's motif emblazoned on it. She was very reluctant to go and only Anna's entreaties that it wouldn't be long before Christmas, encouraged her to climb into the car with her father. Anna waved her off every morning and then would have a quick cup of coffee with Ben and Mrs Wilby before resuming her own work in the office. The work seemed relentless with Jason chasing contracts all over the world. There was even talk of him travelling to Singapore to start negotiations for a job that would last for the next five years. Harrington Rhodes Shipping Agents was going from strength to strength.

During the next few weeks, Anna received numerous phone calls from her family. Although not able to make a visit, her mother, sister and sons kept in touch regularly and after every phone call, Jason thought Anna glowed with a vivaciousness that added to her beauty. Unfortunately, her happiness was short-lived, since no news came from her husband. Finally, Anna plucked up the courage to ask her mother about Dave. Her mother had to admit that Dave had been sullen and moody for quite a while, snapping at anyone who so much as mentioned Anna's name. As for him instructing a solicitor? Her mother was completely in the dark about that, but she offered to broach the subject with him. Anna found she had no choice, but to leave it in her mother's hands.

Jason was away on one of his interminable business trips and Anna missed him terribly. He had often suggested her accompanying him but she felt she should stay behind and care for Hollie, so keeping her promise to Kiera. The personnel in the main office in Bristol now knew that she and Jason were engaged and after an initial week or so of rumour and innuendo over her 'widow' status, the news fell into history and was overtaken by other events on the world stage.

Anna stood at the window looking out at the garden. She noticed how the trees were starting to turn bright gold and orange and sometimes an occasional leaf would flutter to the ground. It wouldn't be long before all the leaves would be falling and winter would be on the way. The garden, as well as the cars, were Ben's pride and joy and even now, she could see him cutting back a few late summer roses. He looked up, spied her and gave her a wave. Anna smiled and raised her hand in acknowledgement. She took in a lungful of air and then collected up her jacket and bag. She had an appointment with the doctor and she didn't want to be late.

It was Hollie's bedtime. A routine had developed were Anna would see to her bath and then spend some time with her, brushing her hair and talking with her. She would let her babble on about anything, her school, her mother, and her visit to Vancouver. But soon the conversation came round to Anna's wedding.

"But why don't you know when it is?" said Hollie irritably.

Anna sighed. "It's a bit complicated. But as soon as we set a date you'll be the first to know." She stopped brushing the long, dark hair. "It might be a few years before we get married."

"Years!" puffed Hollie in disgust. "Well, we'd better not buy my dress just yet or I'll be too big for it." The little girl studied this morsel of information a moment longer. "Is it because Mummy died? Aren't you allowed to get married for a while?" Anna pursed her lips and decided that she would tell the truth. And so she told Hollie about her marriage and how she needed a divorce before she could marry again. At the conclusion, Hollie frowned. "So, your husband didn't die?" Anna nodded shamefully. "But why did you say he'd died?"

Anna nearly choked on her reply. "It was silly of me...I should have told the truth."

"Was Daddy cross?"

"No, he wasn't. And I was so glad."

Anna couldn't help feeling downhearted the following day and worked tirelessly trying to banish the thoughts of hatred for her husband from her mind. But events turned even worse when she was turning off the computer for the day and her mother phoned. She had indeed broached the subject with Dave, but all he had said was that his wife could 'go to hell!' Anna went to have a shower, since they were having dinner with Nigel and Sophia Barnes that evening. She let her tears be washed away with the warm soothing water.

Dinner with Nigel and Sophia Barnes was a delight. Anna was introduced to their three children, a boy and two girls. Sophia Barnes turned out to be a wonderful cook and Nigel an entertaining host. They sat round the table for hours after the children had been put to bed and talked about everything and anything. Anna liked Sophia on sight. Tall and slender with red hair, her green eyes sparkled with the joy of life. Her work as a psychologist kept her busy but next to her family and occupation, Sophia liked meeting new people. Anna offered to help her wash the dishes and was greeted with a howl of amusement.

"Wash up! Goodness me, I've had a dishwasher for years. But come into the kitchen away from the menfolk and we can talk."

They left the 'menfolk' to their discussion and went into the kitchen. As Sophia put the dishes into the machine, Anna helped her tidy up.

It was Anna who mentioned the sorry state of her marriage. "I can't understand why he won't divorce me. I'll agree to everything he wants and I'm not going to fight for the house. He can keep everything, I just want to be free to marry Jason."

"Perhaps he doesn't want to give you up?" ventured Sophia.

Anna took in a breath. "It's a ridiculous situation. I've given him grounds and it made me…" she struggled to find the right words. "…feel dirty. And I don't want to feel like that. Jason and I have a wonderful relationship and Dave is spoiling it."

"You said he cheated on you?"

"Quite a few times."

"Men like that can often be the possessive kind."

"I believe you!"

"He'll treat you as property and I'm afraid jealousy can lead to violence."

"Jason thought he might be like that. I wanted to go to Wakefield to see my sons but he's reluctant to let me go in case I meet Dave."

"Does Jason think your husband might harm you?"

"He doesn't want to give him the chance."

Sophia slammed the door shut and set the machine going. The kitchen filled with the gentle sound of gushing water.

"I wouldn't advise you being alone with your husband. If you do decide to see your boys then always have someone there with you."

"Well, I've got family who would help. My brother-in-law is in the CID and he's huge. Any man would think twice before they tackled him."

Sophia threw back her head and laughed. "Good. As long as you're chaperoned, I can't see any harm coming to you." She reached out to touch her hand. "Keep faith. I'm sure Nigel will hear something soon."

Anna gave her a half-smile.

Sharon's wedding in Dublin gave her the opportunity of getting away for a while. They decided to fly since Mrs Wilby had no mind to travel on a ferry in winter. They planned to stay at a hotel for two nights and see a few sights of the city at the same time.

It was lovely seeing Sharon again who hugged them all and introduced them to her fiancé, Aengus who spoke little but smiled a great deal. As Anna surmised, she was surprised but so very pleased when she saw the engagement ring on Anna's finger. However, they decided not to tell her that the future bride must await a divorce, although Anna wondered if she already knew. After all she had colleagues at the main office in Bristol and someone must have spread the gossip. In fact, Anna saw two or three of them at the wedding and even had a few courteous words with them. But if Sharon knew that Anna wasn't a widow, she was polite and caring enough not to mention it, preferring instead to concentrate on her own happy nuptials.

The wedding that Saturday was a traditional Catholic affair with everything included. The ceremony seemed to last a long time.

"What's those funny words they're saying?" whispered Hollie.

"It's Latin," came back Anna's reply.

Hollie pulled a face. "Can't they speak English here, then?"

They arrived back at Bishop Sutton the day before Hollie's eighth birthday and just over two weeks until Christmas Day. Since Jason would be leaving for Singapore in a few days, it was decided that they would decorate the house and have a party for Hollie. Now a happy and wonderful atmosphere filled the rooms as the festive season approached. Anna and

Hollie decorated the living room with holly and ivy and scented candles. Jason and Ben lugged in a huge fir tree that took pride of place in the hall and which Anna, Hollie and Mrs Wilby spent hours over, trimming with baubles, lights and tinsel. When they finished, Hollie clapped her hands and jumped up and down like a jack-in-the-box. It really did look magnificent, thought Anna and much better than the artificial one she would pull out of the loft every year.

Mrs Wilby spent a great deal of time in the kitchen and soon the house was filled with the wonderful smell of baking sausage rolls, mince pies and fruitcake, distracting everyone from their normal duties and leading them literally by the nose to sample any tasty morsels.

Anna had had many calls from her sons, now separated for the first time in their lives with Martyn at Warwick and Chris at Loughborough. They had settled down as students and were thoroughly enjoying the life of lectures, campus and the bar in the Students' Union. But Anna missed them and Christmas couldn't come quickly enough.

Shortly before Jason was leaving for Singapore, Ben made a startling revelation. They were gathered in the kitchen one afternoon enjoying a coffee together.

"I meant to tell," said Ben. "I won't be coming to the Grange for Christmas."

Jason put down his mug and frowned. "But you've not missed in seven years."

Ben agreed. "Yes, I know. But I think I'll go and visit my sister instead. She's been inviting me for years and I've hardly seen my nephew and niece."

"You have a sister?"

"She's younger than me by three years and my nephew and niece must be ten and eight by now."

"What's changed your mind?" asked Mrs Wilby, startled that Ben had more family than he had admitted to.

"It's silly really. It was when I was in Vancouver; I suddenly began to miss my kin. As you can imagine all the talk was of family and I began to think of mine. So, it looks like it's up to Nottingham for me this Christmas." He gave a chuckle.

It was their last night together. Jason's trip would last one week and it seemed an age for Anna who had not been separated from him for more than two or three days at the most. That night their lovemaking was like their first time again and Anna clung to him as if she couldn't bear to let him go. Suddenly she longed for Christmas when he would be back and they would travel to the Grange once more. As Anna fell asleep in Jason's arms, she reassured herself that seven days wasn't long. She would spend it working and finishing her Christmas shopping. Time would pass quickly and he would soon be home.

The first two days were the loneliest Anna had ever known. The phone calls from her sons helped the heartache and plans were made to see one another. To her utter joy, Margaret phoned and suggested they come to the Grange for part of the holiday. Yes, she thought, to introduce them to the family and show them round such a beautiful place would delight her. She had finally told them that there was a new man in her life and their reaction had been mixed. Martyn was pleased, but she could tell his mind was more on his new life at university. Chris was hesitant and wanted reassurances that she wasn't on the rebound. Anna had smiled at her cautious younger son and told him that she certainly wasn't and that Jason was the man for her.

Jason phoned when he reached Singapore and told Anna he had had a comfortable flight, sleeping most of the way in club class, his only preferred way of travelling by air. He was seven hours in front of GMT and the weather was very different from the bitter cold he had left behind in Great Britain. He told her it was hot and sticky and he was already missing the rain.

Hollie had finished school for the holidays and spent most of her time in the garage where Ben was working on her Wendy house. But for everyone else, preparations were made for their trip to the Grange. They planned to go only five days after Jason returned from Singapore and two days before Christmas, the twins joining them when they could. Ben would leave the same day to spend some time with his family in Nottingham. Anna felt excited about visiting the Grange once more, since it was over three months since she was there last. Although Jason had visited his mother regularly with Hollie, Anna had never accompanied him.

It was after lunch on Friday when she decided to call it a day and go into the city to do some Christmas shopping. She still had a great deal to buy and had not been able to decide on anything for Margaret yet. She also wanted to go to HMV and buy her sons some vouchers. It would be easy to pop them in an envelope and send them. Anna had now got into the routine of leaving the car in the car park belonging to Harrington Rhodes. Since it was a working day the place would be full, but she always used Jason's space, a fact she was eternally thankful for, as there would be no chance of parking in Bristol.

She manoeuvred the Peugeot into the bay and got out. She glanced up at the third floor and saw Graham Rhodes standing at the window. He raised his hand in a friendly wave and Anna waved back. And then she set off to walk the short distance into the city centre, a matter of five minutes. Graham watched her and frowned.

It had been ten o'clock that morning when his secretary had pointed out a man sitting in a car just across from the car park. Graham had kept an eye on him since then and although he wondered what he was up to, he really couldn't see he was doing any harm. His secretary had thought it very suspicious that he should be sitting there all that time, but again, Graham and simply shrugged and said it was a 'free country'. But now he felt slightly uneasy. As Anna past the end of the road, the man got out of his car and started following her. It seemed strange that he should move from his place as soon as Anna arrived, but in all probability it might be just a coincidence. Perhaps he should contact her on her mobile and warn her? But not wanting to alarm her and realising she was heading for the busy part of the city centre, to join the throng of Christmas shoppers, he turned back to his desk.

Anna didn't know where to start her shopping. The streets and shopping centre were crowded to capacity, people hurrying backward and forwards carrying their treasures in bags from every possible retailer. The fairy lights twinkled and glowed making a colourful display in the shop windows. Swinging over the road in a gentle breeze, a cascade of rainbow lights stood out against the darkening sky. It looked like it was going to rain and it was bitingly cold. The rain might turn to snow and if not, it would definitely turn to ice. Anna wrapped her scarf more closely round her and pulled the hat over her ears. She went into the Broadmead shopping centre and pushed her way through the heaving mass of bodies. She smiled at the faces of the children as they pointed upwards and laughed at the huge displays hanging from the roof depicting Santa in his sleigh his bag overflowing with gifts. The children's joyful laughter mingled with the melodious voice of Aled Jones singing *Walking In The Air* from the sound system.

Anna bought a few items and then made her way to HMV to buy the vouchers for her sons. She lingered long enough to look through the rack of 'new releases' since she knew Jason had mentioned a particular one he would like. She picked up a case and started reading the index of songs on the back.

"I don't think Chris was thinking of that one," said a cheery voice from her left.

She turned her head sharply and gasped with surprise, for standing there was the last person she expected to see.

"What are you doing here?"

"I thought I'd surprise you," said Dave.

"You've come all this way to surprise me?"

"Well, not on my own. The boys are with me."

Anna nearly dropped the CD case with shock. "The boys are here?"

"They certainly are," he grinned.

"But they were coming to visit in a few weeks."

Dave nodded. "Oh, they still are. This is a special Christmas present for you." Anna quickly looked around as if expecting to see them. Dave noticed. "They're not here. They're back at the hotel waiting for you."

"How did you find me?"

Dave gave her a surprised look. "You're not going to believe it but it was pure chance. I forgot to pack a shaver and I was buying a new one." He held up the Boots bag. "And then I saw you disappear into this shop."

Anna still felt puzzled. "I don't understand. Why didn't the boys phone me and tell me they were coming down?" She pulled her phone from her bag and checked it for messages.

"They did, but you weren't there obviously, so they left a message and the hotel number. They hoped you'd phone so that we could all meet up. The boys can't wait to see you."

Anna realised that they must have phoned the house in Bishop Sutton and left a message with Ben or Mrs Wilby. Although why they didn't contact her on her mobile was a mystery.

"I don't wish to sound ungrateful, but why did you come with them?"

Dave looked down at his feet. "The boys made me see sense. I treated you abysmally and I thought this was a way of making amends. We could talk about our divorce with the boys and settle everything before we leave."

Relief flooded through her. "Which hotel are you staying at?"

"The Marriott. It's not far. I've booked a table for a meal so I hope you could join us. We can spend the evening catching up on all the news."

Still stunned but hardly able to breathe for excitement, Anna allowed him to take her arm and guide her through the crowds and into the street. The hotel certainly wasn't far since he had chosen one almost in the city centre. As she passed through the massive entrance door and into the impressive foyer she marvelled that Dave had had the enthusiasm or sentiment to accompany the boys. And to have a change of mind about their divorce was wonderful. The boys had worked wonders.

Deborah parked her car and headed for her office. There was a lot to do before she finished for the weekend and she was also having dinner at the Marriott Hotel with a client, so she needed to get home to change. She was just about to climb the few steps to the main door when two figures caught her attention. She looked closer, squinting against the glare of the Christmas lights. She recognised the woman instantly even thought she was shrouded in a thick coat, scarf and hat. That was none other than Jason's sweet little fiancée, but who was with her? He was obviously very friendly with her since he placed an arm protectively round her as they disappeared into the hotel across the road. He's quite a good-looking guy, thought Deborah with disdain. I wonder if Jason knows his lover is frequenting hotels with other men? It would be information worth remembering for the right occasion.

How Anna wished that Jason wasn't in Singapore at that very moment. How wonderful it would have been if he could have shared in the surprise. Dave collected the key from the receptionist, a fact that puzzled Anna, since surely the boys could have opened the door? Shrugging the incident off as unimportant and her face bright with anticipation, she followed her husband to the lift and soon they were being whisked to the third floor and then a short walk down a thickly carpeted corridor took them to the room. He opened the door and let her go in first.

She went in smiling, ready to enfold her sons in her arms once more, after an absence of five months. Anna quickly glanced around the room and saw it was empty and then she heard the door slam behind her.

CHAPTER THIRTEEN

She spun on her heel and confronted her husband. "They're not here, Dave. What the hell do you think you're doing?"

He smiled smugly, threw the key and carrier bag on the table and removed his coat.

"Couldn't get you to see sense, so I thought I'd come down and confront you. You know what they say about Mohammed and the mountain?"

"I don't want to talk to you. That's a cruel trick to play on me! To say Martyn and Chris are here and it's all lies."

He stepped closer and she took a step back. "Don't talk to me about lies! That's all you've done from the very beginning. A widow indeed!"

"I'm sorry for doing that. I should have told the truth, but I wasn't thinking straight at the time."

"Not a very good excuse for brushing me off as insignificant…or dead."

"I needed to get away. Can you imagine how I felt, never being able to trust you?"

Dave walked over to the fridge in the corner. "You needed to get away?" he mused. He took out two small bottles of wine. "I take it you mean from me? Take off your coat and let's talk it over."

Anna remained still for a moment and then decided it would be better to comply than antagonise him. She removed her coat, hat and scarf and lay them over a chair. Dave poured out two glasses of wine and handed her one and then went to sit down on the bed. Anna chose a chair by the door and sipped her drink gently.

Dave studied her for a few moments. "So, you were saying, you felt the need to get away?"

Anna nodded. "I wasn't…happy…I decided that I'd had enough of your flirting, cheating ways. I know you said that woman in the pub wasn't who I thought she was, but right from the start I've lived a life on the brink…I shouldn't have stayed with you in the first place."

"So, why did you stay?"

"For the boys, of course. How could I break up their home?"

"Not to mention the comfortable home and life you had."

"What are you talking about?"

"I was a good provider and you didn't have to go out to work. All right, I admit that I had a few affairs, but I told you they meant nothing."

"I don't care that they meant nothing. The fact that they happened was enough."

"And what about your affair with your boss? Or is it one rule for me and one for you?"

His tone sounded sneering, but when she glanced at him he was taking a drink and the glass obscured his features.

"It's not the same thing. I was separated from you when Jason and I started a relationship."

"You didn't leave me for him?"

"No I didn't! I left you to work in Bristol."

"I'm glad about that. Didn't like the idea of you going off with another bloke."

"But I hadn't." Now that she felt the air was cleared, she started feeling better. Surely Dave would understand?

"You're not wearing your wedding ring."

She took a big gulp of the wine. "Didn't seem any point."

"I see you're wearing his ring. God! He must be rolling in it. But there again he's got his own business. It's doing very well too from what I've read."

"Jason works very hard."

"Jason Harrington," he said quietly. He rolled the name round on his tongue as if savouring it.

She tried to explain, feelings of panic rising up inside her. "We didn't mean to fall in love. His wife died and he needed my help."

"His wife died! How very convenient. And I guess you were more than ready to comfort him." He gave a strained laugh and Anna saw the jealousy in his face. "Did he still think you a widow then? How long after starting work for him, did you feel it necessary to mention your husband?"

"I told him on my birthday," she whispered.

Dave frowned as he made a quick calculation. "I make that two months! Goodness, you can keep a secret!"

"But he knows now. And he loves me and I love him."

"You've got a nerve to get engaged while you're still married."

"But why won't you file for divorce? My solicitor is waiting to hear from yours. I've told you that you can divorce me on grounds of adultery."

Dave put down his glass. "Adultery," he murmured. "The very idea of you sleeping with someone else made me feel sick!"

"How dare you! What do you think I went through all those years? No, Dave, our marriage is over. It's been over a long time and it would be better if we made it legal. I want rid of it."

Anna realised she had said the wrong thing as Dave's eyes flashed with anger.

"You want rid of it! Is that what you think of our nineteen years together, something to be rid of!"

She put her glass on the floor and stood up, trying to steady her trembling. "I think I'll leave now. I've had enough of this." She walked quickly to the chair and snatched up her coat.

Dave jumped up and grabbed her arms. "Oh no, you don't. I'm not finished yet."

"Well, I'm finished. Let me go."

He clasped her hands behind her back, holding them together with his left hand. Anna struggled trying to release herself. She hadn't realised he was so strong.

His face was close to hers. "You're still my wife and I have more claim over you than he does."

"No you don't! We don't live in the Victorian times. A husband hasn't that kind of power over his wife any more."

"Hasn't he!"

He started pulling at her clothes with his free hand, undoing the button and zip on her trousers.

"What are you doing?"

"Showing you what rights a husband has." His grip on her hands became painfully tight, his face twisted with fury. "I'll teach you not to walk out on me and embarrass me in front of my family and friends. Do you have any idea what it's like to have people talking about you behind your back!"

Frightened, she tried to struggle away from him. "No! Dave, please...don't!"

He didn't hear as he forced his mouth over hers, crushing her lips in a harsh and cruel kiss. Burying his face in her neck, he bit into her throat. She struggled to free herself, but her squirming only seemed to excite him more. Bending her backwards, he leaned on her so heavily, she lost her balance, causing them both to come crashing down onto the carpet. Pinned down by his full weight, Anna's slender body became trapped.

Covering her face and lips with hard, brutal kisses, he was unaware of her fight to catch her breath. She felt and tasted the blood trickling from her cut lip and nausea overwhelmed her. With mounting alarm, she felt him tug at her clothing and although she tried to kick him away it seemed to have no effect on him whatsoever.

Anna couldn't remember how she ended up in her underwear. She was only aware of his hands on her breasts and thighs, hurting her, bruising her. Inside her head, she screamed and then the scream reached her throat and she opened her mouth. But nothing came out. She struggled against him but he didn't notice, didn't care that he was hurting her, as he tore the rest of her clothes from her.

He was forcing himself between her legs, gripping her knee to bring it up round his waist. She tried to cry out, but his weight crushed the breath out of her lungs and made her gasp for air. When he thrust inside her, the pain seared like a hot poker, burning with agonising intensity with each frenzied heave.

She sobbed with pain. "Dave...please.... please stop!"

Her husband didn't hear her tearful cries. She raised her arms to push him away, but he caught her wrists and pinned them down on the carpet behind her head. His face became taut with pleasure as he took what he believed was rightfully his. His breathing gulped faster and faster, until finally, his body stiffened and he let out a muted groan, his head thrown back, his teeth clenched. Slumping on top of her, his writhing became calmer until they ceased altogether.

Anna lay still, waiting for the pain to ease itself. As the burning slowly ebbed away, the anguish started to well up from her throat, ending in quiet, uncontrollable tears that came in soft choking sobs. Dave raised his head, a look of triumph in his eyes. He pulled himself to his knees, fastening up his clothing. Once released from his weight, Anna sprang to a kneeling position, pulling her discarded clothing towards her trying to hide her nakedness.

He watched her. "Where's he now, this new guy of yours? If he was half the man you say he is, then he would have been with you, looking after you. This is all his fault for not being around to protect you. Too busy making money I should think." Anna tried to put on her shirt. Why, oh why, did Jason have to go to Singapore? If he had been home then this wouldn't have happened. Or would it? Jason didn't accompany her everywhere! She didn't need a chaperone. Suddenly Sophia's words came into her mind. *Don't be alone with your husband*, she had warned. Dave reached out and pulled the shirt from her hands. "You don't need that yet."

"Don't touch me! Keep away from me!" she shrieked. She shrank from him, crawling along the carpet, trying to make for the door. He jumped to his feet and pulled her up with him.

"Do you want to use the bathroom?"

"Don't want the bathroom," she whispered. "I want to go home."

"Not yet. Lie down on the bed." Anna gave out a scream and he clapped his hand over her mouth. "Shut up, you idiot! Do you want the neighbours to hear?"

He pushed her onto the mattress, pinning her down with his weight once more.

"Let me go home."

His face twisted in a smile. "Soon."

"I'll call the manager and he'll call the police."

"And what will you tell them?"

"That you…you…"

"Raped you?"

"Yes," she gasped.

"They won't believe you. You came to this room willingly, the receptionist will testify to that. And you've been drinking."

"I haven't drunk much."

"It doesn't matter. I'll deny everything. I'll say you came up here so we could have a little chat and we got a bit amorous. You're still my wife."

"Everyone knows I want a divorce."

"Whose going to believe anything you say? You've already proved yourself a liar." He rose from the bed and walked over to the wardrobe. Taking out the spare blanket he wrapped it round her, smoothing out the folds. He then disappeared to the bathroom. In minutes he came out with a bundle of damp tissues and sitting on the edge of the bed, used some to wipe away the blood from her lips and then others as a cold compress for the bruises that were starting to appear on her chin and neck. He winced. "Oh dear, you'll have rather a big love bite tomorrow."

He was unusually gentle after being so rough and Anna wondered if he would be sympathetic to her plight.

"Why don't you let me go?" she said quietly.

"I'm not finished with you yet."

She recoiled from him. "I promise I won't tell anyone."

He gave a smile. "Oh, I know you're not going to tell anyone." He scooped up her glass from the floor and held it to her lips. "Take a drink." She gulped the wine thirstily. Being drunk or a little tipsy seemed to be a good idea at that moment in time. He placed the glass on the side table and picked up the bundle of wet tissues once more. "Now then, let's sort out the rest of you." He pulled the blanket away and Anna let out cry and clung onto her only means of cover.

"No, leave me alone!"

Dave stared at her in amazement. "Have you forgotten you're the mother of my children? I've seen you naked before." Keeping a tight rein on her fears, she tried to relax and allow him to bathe her private parts, all the time talking to her in a soothing voice that belied his true intentions. When he had finished, he wrapped her in the blanket once more and took the tissues to the bathroom. He was gone quite a while and she looked desperately towards the door leading to the corridor, wondering if she could make a run for it. "I know what you're thinking, Anna," he called. "And I can move faster than you."

He came out of the bathroom wearing only his shorts and T-shirt and made his way over to the bed. Anna shrank from him in dread. He clicked his tongue in disapproval when he saw the large globules trickling from the corners of her eyes. He lay beside her and started talking. At first, she was stunned and then amazed as he reminisced about their married life together and their two sons. He spoke about the boys when they were small, reminding her about the happy times they had had when they had been a family. All through his reflections, Anna remained silent. She listened impassively, not wanting to pass comment that she had been bitterly unhappy during all that time and that he had been the reason for her unhappiness.

She let her mind wander and thought of Jason so far away in Singapore. She guessed it would be the middle of the night for him and he would be fast asleep, having no inkling of what she was enduring at that precise moment. She wondered if Ben and Mrs Wilby were worried about her now that she was so late in arriving home. Would they call the police and report her missing? Suddenly she had the terrifying idea that Dave might murder her. Surely Dave wouldn't end her life, he would be caught in no time. She blinked in horror.

"Feeling tired?" said Dave quietly.

Anna didn't dare look at him. "Yes I'm very tired. Please can I leave?"

He turned towards her and pulled away the blanket. She tried to hold onto it. He moved over her as she gave a cry of alarm, but he shushed her by putting his forefinger on her lips. He pushed inside her for the second time and she let out a cry of pain.

"The reason why you're not going to the police is because if I'm arrested, I could go to prison." His mouth was close to her ear. He began to move, enjoying her humiliation, building up the momentum. "And if I go to prison…what are the boys going to...think about having a father in prison. Their university chums...will love that. I can just imagine all the...snide comments. Now I don't think you'd want to put...your sons through that, would you?"

He started to breathe heavily. It wasn't so frenzied this time and Anna closed her eyes and prayed for it to finish. And then it was over with a groan and shudder of pleasure. Even then, she kept her eyes closed. He lifted himself from her and she heard him go to the bathroom. Moments later he came out and when she opened her eyes she saw he was dressed. He looked down at her, as he pulled on his coat and then picked up the key and threw it next to her.

"Well, that was fun. You're certainly a very beautiful woman. Enjoy the room. I've paid for the night." And then she heard him slam the door behind him.

Anna couldn't move, her tears drenched her face, her body ached. The soreness between her thighs throbbed and she felt defiled and unclean. But much worse than the physical pain, was the knowledge that the man who had fathered her children had violated her. A man who had resorted to taking what he believed was rightfully his because of their marriage vows. All she had asked was her freedom and he had treated her with derision.

But then Anna was filled with horror. What would Jason say when he came home? Would he say she deserved everything she got, since she had gone willingly to the room with him? Why had she placed herself in such a risky situation? She should have had more sense. How could she face him? How could she face Jason, knowing she had been so stupid? She wouldn't tell him. She would keep it a secret. If she told him he would insist on getting the police involved and Dave was right. She couldn't let her boys go through the embarrassing ordeal of seeing their father sent to prison.

Anna climbed off the bed and tried to stand. She would clean herself up and then she would get a taxi home. It didn't matter about the car. She could come back and collect that later. She just wanted to go home.

Deborah leaned forward and lowered her eyelids seductively. Her companion was certainly very attractive and if he hadn't been a client she would have suggested skipping dessert and spending the rest of the evening at her apartment. She sighed with regret; she never mixed business with pleasure. She turned her head to watch the people coming and going in the foyer. And then the lift doors opened.

At first she was startled to see Anna coming out of the lift that led to the bedrooms but then she smiled. Well, well, well, she thought, Jason's intended wasn't above having a bit on the side when she fancied it. How absolutely delicious! She looked at her watch and raised her eyebrows in appreciation. And she took her time about it, this was a woman after her own heart. What a pity she despised the very ground she walked on. In better circumstance she might have suggested a *menage a trois*. Jason had always repelled the idea in the past, but with his naive little secretary, he might think differently. It would be interesting to put it to him, next time their paths crossed.

The nightmare seemed to go on and on. Anna was horrified to see how late it was when she finally looked at her watch. Somehow Dave had managed to keep her prisoner for nearly six hours and it was already gone ten o'clock. To make matters worse the office Christmas parties were in full swing and the street thronged with people enjoying a night out. The deafening noise of disco music poured from the doors of the bars and clubs and partygoers milled about in all manner of festive clothing. The commissioner was very kind and tried repeatedly to call a taxi, but it was a good thirty minutes before one became available. Falling back against the seat, Anna was grateful to be on her way home. It was only when the city lights had faded in the distance did she realise it was Friday the thirteenth.

She arrived home just after eleven and was dismayed to see the light still on in the kitchen. Ben and Mrs Wilby were sitting at the kitchen table and as she opened the door they jumped to their feet in relief.

"Anna! Where have you been? We were thinking of calling the police!" said Ben, helping her off with her coat.

"I got held up. The city's bedlam," she answered lamely.

She couldn't hide her cuts and bruises.

"What's the matter with your face?" said Mrs Wilby. She tried to take a closer look but Anna rebuffed her and went to the fridge for a drink of milk.

"Oh, I fell over. Slipped off the kerb."

"We should put something on that."

Anna shook her head. "No, I'll be OK. Must go to bed, I'm very tired."

Ben and Mrs Wilby exchanged worried glances.

"Jason must have rung three times," said Ben. "The last call came about six. He was just off to bed and he wanted to speak to you."

Anna licked her lips nervously. "What did you tell him?"

"What could we tell him? That you hadn't come back from your Christmas shopping," said Ben.

Anna smiled. "No doubt he'll phone again tomorrow. I'm off now."

She made her escape leaving a very perplexed Ben and Mrs Wilby standing in the kitchen.

Anna spent the next forty minutes in the shower. She felt that all the soap in the world would never make her clean again. Finally, she climbed into the large bed and pulled the covers over her. For the first time she was glad to be alone. If Jason had been with her that night then she wouldn't have been able to hide her injuries or distress from him. She would have had to confess everything and there was no doubt that he would have reacted fiercely. There was no way she could have prevented him getting the police involved. She lay on her back staring at the ceiling, her feelings numb. She would try and forget it. Surely it would be easy to dismiss it from her mind? All she had to do was pretend that it had never happened.

If Anna thought she could put it out of her mind, she was very much mistaken. She had a fitful sleep, tossing and turning all night, her dreams filled with the horror of her ordeal.

"Anna, wake up! Daddy's on the phone." Hollie was tapping her on the cheek.

Anna pulled herself up in a sitting position and took the receiver from her.

"Hi Jason. I'm sorry, I seem to have slept in."

She heard him chuckle at the other end of the phone. "I hope you haven't been at the Christmas sherry, sweetheart."

She tried to smile. "No, I'm just a bit tired at the moment."

"Well, you've been working very hard. I'm afraid I need some information for this meeting I'm just going into."

Anna eased herself gently out of bed. "I'll get it for you now. What is it you want?" He told her and she nodded. "Yes, I know where to look. Won't be a minute." She passed the receiver back to Hollie who had remained standing by the bed. "Talk to your daddy and then put the phone down when I pick up the extension in the office."

Hollie blew out an indignant breath. "I know what to do!" She watched as Anna struggled into her dressing gown and rushed out of the door. "Silly Anna! She's such a sleepy head this morning."

"Perhaps she didn't sleep very well last night," said Jason, trying to make conversation while he shuffled some documents into a file.

"I was so cross with her last night for coming in late! She wasn't there to read me my bedtime story," said Hollie.

In Singapore, Jason stopped shuffling the papers. His daughter went to bed at eight-thirty. "She was shopping that late?"

His daughter went to make a comment, but was prevented by Anna coming back on the line.

"I'm here, Hollie. Say bye to your daddy." She heard the soft 'goodbye' and Jason responding with an equally tender farewell. "I've got the information. Have you a pen ready?" Anna gave him the details he wanted.

"I should be home on Wednesday afternoon," he said tenderly. "I've missed you so much."

Anna swallowed hard. "I miss you too. It seems ages since you left."

"It won't be long now. Must go, sweetheart, they're waiting for me. Love you."

Anna put down the phone but didn't move from her position by the desk. She tried to shrug away the tears that stung her eyes. A feeling of desperate loneliness swept through her, followed by overwhelming yearning. Just hearing Jason's voice made her feel like splintered glass.

"Please come home. I need you," she whispered.

Her thoughts were in turmoil. Everything she had suffered the night before was as fresh as though it had just happened. She ached in every joint and her head was splitting. She must find some aspirin before it got any worse. She remembered what Dave had said to her, his threats and the mind shattering knowledge that he knew exactly how to control her. He had known her better than she had ever guessed. She took in a huge breath and shivered.

Anna tried to pull herself together. She would work in the office today, even though it was Saturday and catch up on all those little jobs she never seemed to have time to do. By the evening, her memories will have faded.

Ben rushed into the room. "Anna! You're not going to believe it, but your car's been nicked!"

"What!"

"It's gone! From its usual place," said Ben.

Anna suddenly remembered. "Oh, it's not been stolen. I left it in the car park at Harrington Rhodes." She smiled weakly. "I ran out of petrol so I got a taxi home."

Ben wiped his hand across his forehead. "I wish you'd told me! I nearly had a heart attack when I saw it missing."

"Sorry, I should have, but I was so tired when I came in, it went completely out of my mind."

Ben mused for a moment. "You ran out of petrol?"

Anna nodded. "I should have filled up on my way into Bristol, but I forgot. I only remembered when I went to start the car and realised there wasn't enough to get me to the petrol station."

"Well, if you get dressed, we can go and sort it out," said Ben, watching her. Anna was usually the last person to run out of petrol. She liked to fill up as soon as the gauge reached halfway.

Anna did as she was told and forty minutes later she was sitting next to Ben en route to Bristol. They didn't talk much on the journey and Anna was relieved. She thought he might question her about her late night and she didn't want to go through the ordeal of having to lie. She had already started telling untruths and it sat uncomfortably with her. On the way, they pulled into the petrol station and Ben filled up a can, but as they drove into the car park, Anna was dismayed to see Graham standing by the Peugeot. He gave a look of relief as he saw her.

"Thank goodness for that, Anna! I was getting quite worried. I thought you'd not come back all night."

"Ran out of fuel," she lied.

He pulled a face. "Well, I'll leave you to it. I've got a lot of catching up to do and Saturday is the only day I get the chance, when the phones stop ringing." He disappeared into the building.

Anna unlocked the petrol cap and Ben began to pour the fuel into the tank.

"Jump in and give it a try," he said. Anna slipped into the driver's seat and turned the key. The engine exploded into life immediately. "Well, that should be enough until you fill up."

"Yes, I'll go now," said Anna, jumping out, locking the petrol cap and hoping he wouldn't notice the fuel gauge that stood at three-quarters full.

She climbed back in, waved and sped away. Ben watched her with a frown.

When Anna reached home, she went straight to the office. She worked the entire day only stopping for a short lunch break. Ben and Mrs Wilby exchanged concerned words during the afternoon, but decided that Anna was missing Jason and everything would return to normal once he was home. Even so, they worried at her ruthless determination to work herself into the ground.

Jason phoned again at three o'clock. He was off to bed as he was exhausted, but told her that everything was going well and the five-year contract was almost 'in the bag'. Anna decided to go to bed early too and soon after reading Hollie her bedtime story, she was under the covers, squeezing her eyelids shut in an effort to forget everything in sleep. It didn't work and she spent most of the night listening to the house as it creaked and groaned.

Sunday found her exhausted and unable to do anything but her washing and ironing and then sit listlessly watching television. Ben and Mrs Wilby became even more concerned. Before Jason had left, he had confided in Ben that Anna's husband was none too pleased about a divorce and he might cause trouble. Ben had been left with strict instructions to keep an eye on her, a fact he winced at, since he had let her go shopping alone in Bristol on Friday. But he had been busy finishing off Hollie's Wendy house and felt that a shopping expedition hardly needed his attention.

Sunday night came and once again, Anna hardly slept. By the time she went into the office on Monday morning, she was screaming inside. She walked up and down agitated, her only thought that she needed help. By mid-morning she went into her bag for Nigel Barnes's card. The receptionist told her that he was with a client but would pass on a message as soon as possible. An hour later Nigel returned her call. When he discovered that Anna wanted an appointment he went into his diary and suggested the end of the week. But when Anna let out a cry of dismay and begged him to let her see him earlier, he became alarmed and kindly gave up his lunch hour, telling her to come for one o'clock.

The drive to his office seemed interminable. Finally parking and climbing the stairs to his office came as a great relief to Anna. But waiting her turn suddenly made her panic. What was she going to tell him? Why had she asked for this appointment? She didn't have time to put her thoughts together before he came out of his office and beckoned her in.

"Thank you for seeing me at such short notice and giving up your lunch time."

He waved his hand in a gesture of dismissal and offered her a seat. "In my line of work I get used to working all hours," he smiled. "Now what can I do for you? And before you answer that, I'm afraid I've not heard from your husband's solicitor."

The receptionist came in with a steaming mug of coffee and Anna held it between her hands drawing comfort from its heat.

"I didn't think you would," she murmured.

He watched her curiously. "I really wish you'd consider the other choice I gave you."

"Unreasonable behaviour?"

"Yes. Then you could file for divorce." He suddenly noticed the shadows under her eyes and the paleness of her complexion. "Are you OK, Anna?"

She didn't seem to hear him. "What would I have to do to get a divorce on grounds of unreasonable behaviour?"

Sighing with relief he sat back in his chair. "All that's needed is a short list of things you believe your husband did to cause you unhappiness. It doesn't have to be anything specific. The fact that he neglected you or his behaviour caused you distress..." He stopped talking as he noticed tears trickling down Anna's cheeks, her face creasing in despair. "Oh, my goodness," he said in alarm. He rose from his seat and pulled another chair closer so he could sit next to her. "What's the matter?"

She turned a tear stained face towards him. "Is raping me, good grounds for divorce?"

He stared at her hardly understanding. "Your husband...raped you?" She nodded. "Anna, why didn't you tell me this when you first came to see me? You have a very strong case to end your marriage. When did it happen?"

Anna took a sip of her coffee and tried to summon her courage. "Last Friday," she whispered.

Nigel's face blanched with shock. "I think you'd better tell me what happened."

For the next thirty minutes, Anna told him about meeting her husband and her subsequent ordeal in the hotel bedroom.

When she had finished, she pleaded with him. "Please don't tell Jason. I couldn't bear it if he knew. He would want me to press charges."

"And he'd be right!" said Nigel. "Anna, no man, husband or not, has the right to violate a woman like that." He thought rapidly. "Did you see a doctor?" She shook her head. "You should have! For the sake of your own health and also a doctor's report would have gone a good way in helping your divorce."

"I just wanted to try and forget it ever happened."

"I think that would be impossible," he said softly.

"But by this morning, I knew that I needed help," she sighed.

Nigel took her hand. "Listen, Anna. Do you trust me?" She nodded. "First of all, we must get you examined by a doctor." She made to protest but he patted her arm to calm her. "I know someone who will go with you and also counsel you. She's very good and very understanding.

"Who is she?"

"My wife Sophia."

"Sophia?"

"She's a rape counsellor and she'll help you through this. At the same time I'll start divorce proceedings on your behalf."

"Will I get a divorce on the grounds that Dave…That he…"

"Absolutely! No judge in the country would turn down your application. Now, I want you to go home and get some rest. I'll get Sophia to phone you as soon as possible and she'll make a doctor's appointment for you at the clinic."

"You won't tell the police will you?"

"Anna, everything you've told me and what you tell Sophia will be in complete confidence. We won't do anything you don't want us to do."

Anna drove home with her mind a little easier. Sophia did indeed ring that evening after making an appointment for her to attend the clinic the following day. After exchanging some gentle and comforting words, she reassured Anna that she would be with her and that she mustn't worry. For the first time Anna slept better, although still not soundly. At least she had shared her burden with others and the very fact that she didn't feel alone any more, gave her some peace of mind.

Sophia met her at the clinic and taking her arm, accompanied her inside. The doctor examining her was kind and sympathetic, only passing a concerned comment that perhaps it would have been better if she had consulted her sooner.

Sophia took her back to her office and there, Anna was able to tell her everything that happened that dreadful Friday evening. It was only when she reached the conclusion that she became distraught. Up to that point, she had remained calm, telling the details as they happened without any emotion.

She held her head in her hands. "I tried to fight him off, Sophia, I really did. But he was too strong for me."

Sophia put her arms round her. "A woman can't possibly match a man's strength. You mustn't blame yourself."

"But why did he do it?

Sophia gave a sad smile. "He was treating you as property. To be used as he saw fit."

"He seemed so jealous of Jason, even though I left him long before we fell in love." Her expression turned to anguish. "He sent me a letter ages ago and he threatened to hurt Jason...well, not Jason exactly, but any man that he thought I had left him for."

Sophia frowned. "Anna, your husband is a dangerous man, are you sure you don't want the police informed?"

Anna opened her eyes wide in fright. "Oh, no, please don't even suggest it. I just want to put this behind me. I get the feeling that it's over now, my husband has done all he can to hurt me, although why he wants to hurt me, I can't imagine. I've never done him any harm."

"He's not thinking of you. As far as he's concerned you had a good chance of going back to him until another man came on the scene."

"I never would have! I was deluding myself all those years, trying to make my marriage work."

Sophia grimaced. "You were very brave to leave him, but unfortunately rape is an act of violence not of love. It's used as a means of power and control."

"I went willingly into that hotel room with him," Anna whispered in horror.

"You were a victim," said Sophia. "He tricked you. It wasn't your fault."

Anna left feeling more confident and with a further appointment in her diary for the New Year, she drove home more relaxed. The following day Jason would be returning from Singapore and his very presence would cast some light into the dark place that was her life at the moment. But when she arrived home, she discovered she had missed his phone call once more. The one he had made just before boarding his flight.

CHAPTER FOURTEEN

Jason arrived home the following afternoon, tired and jet lagged. He hugged everyone but left Anna until last, enclosing her in a tight embrace and smothering her with soft, warm kisses. It was wonderful to have him home again and she clung onto him for a long time. He seemed to fill the place with his presence as he told her that the trip had gone very well and after some difficult negotiations, he had completed a deal worth millions. He made a joke that he could retire at fifty, but Anna knew it was all nonsense, Jason thrived on the cut and thrust of the business world and couldn't live without it.

Hollie went to bed at her usual time and Jason spent thirty minutes with her, telling her a story and tucking her in. Although he had slept on the plane, his body was still set at Singapore time and it was the early hours of the morning for him. He decided to go to bed early.

"Would you like me to sleep in my old room?" Anna asked, as he started up the stairs.

"What on earth for?" He had just put his foot on the first step and stopped in surprise.

"I thought you'd like to have the bed to yourself, so you'll get a good night's sleep," she said quietly.

He reached out for her and drew her close. "Certainly not! Sweetheart, I've slept alone for the last week and I've missed the comfort of feeling you next to me. But you come to bed when you're ready."

It was gone eleven when she finally slipped in beside him, but he didn't stir. She watched him for a few minutes and then bent to kiss his lips. It was strange to be sharing a bed with him again. He had been away only seven days but it might as well have been seven years. She had missed him and yet she felt uncomfortable being so close to him. It had never been like that in the past.

Anna awoke early with Jason still sleeping peacefully. She carefully removed herself and dressed. By eight o'clock she was in the office working.

Mrs Wilby appeared at the door ten minutes later. "Are you coming for your breakfast, or are you giving it a miss again?"

Anna detected a note of disapproval and smiled. "No, I'll be there in a few minutes."

"Thank goodness for that. I thought you were on a diet or something."

As she turned to go she collided with Jason. "Who's on a diet?" he smiled mischievously.

"Not me," she said. "My husband always liked the fuller figure in a woman. Not string beans that you can't see sideways on!" She stomped off to the kitchen.

Jason came into the office and made his way to Anna who was sending a fax.

"Did you sleep in your old room?"

"Now, what makes you think that?"

"You weren't there this morning and I just wondered."

"I slept with you all night," she said warmly. "But I doubt you noticed since you were so tired."

He gave a grin and caressed her cheek. "I'll notice tonight, though," he murmured.

Anna answered with a half-smile.

After lunch, Jason drove to a meeting at the main office to discuss his trip to Singapore with Graham. The meeting lasted most of the afternoon and it was only at its conclusion that Graham mentioned Anna's car.

"Poor girl, she must have been so embarrassed to run out of petrol."

Jason chuckled. "She doesn't like to be a bother to folk, which is probably why she hasn't told me about it."

"It was sorted in no time. To be honest, by the time I got to my office and looked out of the window, they were leaving. Mind you, gave me a right shock to see it still parked there when I arrived Saturday morning. I thought something had happened to Anna."

"What time did she leave it?"

Graham thought for a moment. "It must have been about three. Obviously she got a taxi home when she realised she couldn't get to a petrol station."

Ben was in the garage with Hollie, when Jason arrived home. The Wendy house was now finished, complete with striped curtains, a small piece of carpet and dainty little furniture.

"Do you like it Daddy?" she asked, her eyes aglow with enthusiasm.

"It's lovely, sweetie. But where's it going?"

Ben gave a chuckle. "She hasn't decided yet and I'm not moving it until she does. My days of moving stuff about on the whims of a female are long past!"

"I can hide in it when you're cross," she said. She went through the small door and looked out of the window.

"So, Anna ran out of petrol?" said Jason to Ben, his lips twitching.

"Ah, I see there's been a bit of gossip from Graham. Well, yes, but at least it wasn't stolen like I thought it had been."

Jason nodded. But he would have to mention it to Anna, he couldn't let her get away with so obvious a chink in her efficiency.

Anna was in the office and just finishing off for the day.

"How did the meeting go?" she asked, as Jason threw his briefcase on the desk and sank into his chair.

"Very well. At least the folk at Harrington Rhodes will have employment for the next few years." He stared at her for a few seconds. She seemed very engrossed in her work. "Why didn't you tell me your car ran out of petrol?" he smiled.

Anna spun round and moistened her lips. "It wasn't a problem. Please don't laugh at me, it'll not happen again."

"That I'm sure about. So, you had to get a taxi home?"

"Had no choice."

"That must have been difficult at this time of the year." He wasn't asking a question, more speaking his thoughts out loud.

"I waited ages, but finally got one."

"You were very lucky." She didn't answer and walked over to the cabinet, replaced a file and slammed the drawer shut. Jason tried not to ask the next question, but failed. "You were shopping quite late?"

"That's how it is at Christmas," she smiled.

"Didn't realise the shops were open that time of night."

She clicked her tongue in despair. "Well, that doesn't surprise me. Shopping isn't exactly your favourite pastime. Why all these questions?"

He caught his breath. Was he interrogating her? If he was then he must stop immediately and yet his thoughts were troubled. What was wrong with him? It was perfectly acceptable for Anna to stay out on an evening, she was a grown woman and if she needed to shop late, that was absolutely normal at Christmas. He mustn't grow too possessive of her or he'll ruin everything he had.

He changed the subject. "Oh, I've got some good news and some bad news." She walked across to him. "Remember the Harrington Rhodes Christmas dinner dance?" She nodded. "I'm afraid the hotel has double booked and can't take us."

Her mouth dropped open in surprise. "But Jason, it's on Saturday night!"

"I know and they've given us a full refund."

"So, it's cancelled. Oh dear, I was looking forward to it. I was going to wear the dress I wore for your mum's party."

"Were you! Wow! Well, the good news is that Graham has pulled a few strings and he's got us another venue. The Marriott Hotel." He saw Anna tense and her face become pale.

"We're going there?" she whispered.

He reached out for her, but she moved away. "It's a beautiful hotel. You'll have a lovely time," he said softly.

The phone ringing on her desk allowed her a means of escape.

Anna spent the evening feeling very subdued. She dreaded the idea of going back to the Marriott, back to the place where she had been imprisoned and assaulted. She wondered if she could make an excuse? Perhaps she could say she didn't feel well. But then she realised that Jason might decide to keep her company and as the Managing Director he would be expected to attend a company function.

Later on, Anna went to soak in the bath. She took a long time over it, so long in fact, that Jason was forced to take a shower in one of the spare bathrooms and was in bed while Anna was still bathing.

"Have you fallen asleep in there," called Jason in amusement. "Because if you have, you'll get all wrinkly."

Anna had finally pulled herself from the soothing water and had dried and dressed herself in a pair of royal blue satin pyjamas. She stared at herself in the mirror. She still had a bruise on her neck where Dave had cruelly bitten her, but for the last six days she had worn a polo-neck jumper or a shirt with a pretty scarf. The previous night, Jason had been too tired to notice anything, but would tonight be different? She took her powder compact and tried to hide the blue and black blemish.

She came out of the bathroom. Jason was sitting up in bed. "I thought you'd taken up residence," he chuckled.

"Wanted to look nice for you," she said.

He held out his arms to her. "Sweetheart, you always look beautiful to me. Come here."

Normally, she wouldn't need a second invitation but now she hesitated. She walked across the carpet and instead of sliding in beside him, she sat up against the pillows, her leg tucked underneath her. She could see the desire in his eyes and thought of all the times they had made love in the past. They had always been such wonderful moments and taking in a large breath she convinced herself that this time would be no different. She loved him passionately and that very fact would make everything all right.

Taking her time, Anna started undoing the buttons on her pyjamas. Jason watched her mesmerised while she undid the first two, trying to control his breathing that was coming in short gasps. He found her so alluring and sensual that he thought he was going to explode with yearning.

"Let me do that," he whispered. He undid the remaining buttons and then pulled her down into his arms, kissing her hair, then her forehead and then her lips. "God! How I've missed you."

He caressed her shoulder and then ran his hand tenderly down her body. He felt hungry for her, like a starving man suddenly offered a delicious plate of food. But he sensed something was wrong. Anna wasn't responding in her usual way, she was tense and nervous. They had been parted only one week, but it was as though they had never made love before. He would have to be as gentle as possible. And unhurried. Perhaps just by loving her he could help her relax. He slipped the pyjama top over her shoulder, kissing her bare flesh. But it was when he tried to remove the top she tensed even more.

"Can I keep it on?" She clutched at the garment, pulling it to her, trying to cover herself.

He lifted his head, puzzled. "Are you suddenly feeling shy?"

"No, just a bit cold."

Jason gave a smile and drew her closer. "It looks like I'm going to have to warm you up," he murmured.

He helped her out of her pyjama bottoms and then pressed his lips on her neck and throat and mouth, his body aching with sexual tension. Anna tried to relax, tried to think of Jason and their love for each other. But her husband's face kept floating into her mind.

She didn't know if she imagined it but Jason seemed to enter her with a violence he had never used before. Anna let out a muted shriek of pain and held onto him, burying her face in his shoulder. Pain and pleasure are often indistinguishable and for Jason, Anna's cry only meant enjoyment. Not for one moment did he believe he was hurting her. And not for one moment did he think that each urgent thrust into her made her grit her teeth and bring tears to her eyes. Only after he had fallen asleep, did Anna slip from the bed and go into the bathroom to apply the soothing cream prescribed by the doctor.

The following day brought some remarkable news from Nigel. He phoned to say that he had received the paperwork from the solicitor representing Anna's husband, since now he was divorcing her on the grounds of adultery.

"Are you OK with that?" he asked.

"He's got a bloody nerve!" she said crossly. "He puts me through hell and then calmly divorces me on grounds of *my* adultery."

She quickly glanced round. Jason had just gone to the kitchen to make them some coffee. She didn't want him to come in and catch her in the middle of this particular conversation.

"I was surprised, to be honest. But it'll be a lot quicker if you allow him to divorce you. It should be straightforward from now on and you could get your divorce by April or May. June at the very latest."

"I would like that very much!"

"Then I will get on with it immediately."

"Thank you."

"There's also some good news on the financial front. He's agreed to buy you out, so you should receive a cheque when your divorce is finalised."

Anna felt stunned. "He has? Now I'm really confused."

"It looks like he's being amicable and we have to be thankful for that." He gave a nervous cough. "Listen, Anna. I'll do everything I can, but are you sure you don't want to press charges?"

But Anna was adamant. The situation was totally impossible. "I can't do that. I don't want to hurt my boys."

She heard Nigel sigh. "Very well. But let me know if you change your mind." There was a slight pause before Nigel added, "I know I'm your solicitor but I'm also a friend. Ring me if you ever need to talk. And Sophia says the same thing. Don't be worried about ringing us at home if you really need to."

Anna bit her lip. She could hear Jason coming through from the kitchen. "Thank you. I'll bear that in mind," she whispered. "Must go. Bye."

She quickly put down the receiver as Jason appeared. He had heard her talking and noticed her abrupt stop when he entered the office.

He put the mug down in front of her. "Who was that?"

"Nigel. It seems I'm going to get my divorce after all. Dave has agreed to go ahead. Nigel thinks it'll all be completed by the late spring."

Jason's face became radiant as he pulled her onto her feet and swung her up in his arms.

"That means we can have a summer wedding at the Grange," he said, laughing with delight.

She didn't feel like laughing with him. "Yes, that would be wonderful."

He gently put her back on her feet, his heart melting. "I know it's been tough for you, but let's look forward now. There's Christmas and your boys visiting and then all the plans we can make for our wedding."

Although tears threatened she was determined not to give way to them. She had spent enough time crying over her husband's despicable behaviour. She gave a watery smile and shook away her tears. "Yes, of course," she said briskly. "Must finish this letter so it can be posted tonight."

She sat down at her desk and started typing.

Jason returned to his desk, his thoughts grim. While making the coffee he had had a conversation with Ben and Mrs Wilby who felt duty bound to tell him of Anna's terrible wretchedness while he had been away. They put it to him that she was missing her boys to the point that she could make herself ill, something that he had already concluded. Thank goodness a visit was imminent.

They carried on working for the rest of the day. It was now Friday and it was a week since her ordeal with Dave. The memory will fade, she thought confidently. Jason was right, she must think of the summer and the wonderful life she and Jason would have together. She would take each day as it came. Her thoughts turned to the night before when she and Jason had made love. She had still felt some pain, but of course she was still a bit bruised since she hadn't quite healed yet. But she would, she convinced herself and then everything would be as it was before. All she had to do was be patient.

The next day was Saturday and that evening they were to go to the Marriott Hotel for the Christmas dinner dance. That evening, Anna dressed feeling very nervous, but the fact that they were in one of the suites eased her mind somewhat. She only had to walk through the main door and into the foyer. After that she would be in a room that had no association whatsoever with her husband.

She dressed with care, wearing her hair as she had that night of Margaret's party. In fact, she decided to wear the same jewellery. It had been a wonderful evening and she and Jason had made love for the very first time that night. Perhaps she could capture some of that magic again. But she had forgotten the love bite on her neck. It was slowly fading but was still noticeable. There was nothing for it but to wear a scarf. She selected a silver one to match the trimming on her dress.

Hollie came bouncing into the room. "Do I look pretty?" She was wearing a pink party dress and Anna had already done her hair, tying it up with a ribbon.

"You look wonderful. The belle of the ball."

"What's that? The bell and the ball?"

Anna couldn't help laughing. "No, sweetie, the belle of the ball. It means the prettiest young lady there."

"You look good too," she said, skipping round the room and then out of the door.

Jason appeared. "Goodness! You look great. And that scarf really sets it off."

Anna pulled the silver taffeta more closely round her. "Thought it would look more Christmasy."

Anna didn't look to either left or right when she entered the hotel. She kept her eyes firmly ahead, her hand through Jason's arm. And before she knew it she was in the suite, decorated with balloons and garlands with the tables set with silver cutlery, shining wineglasses and Christmas crackers and party poppers.

The evening turned out to be very pleasant and the meal was delicious. She and Jason watched with amusement as Ben and Mrs Wilby did a 'turn' around the floor and then spent the next ten minutes fanning the large lady with their menus as she panted with the exertion. During the evening, Anna started enjoying herself as she danced with Jason. There was always something so wonderful about being in his arms and seeing him smile at her. It was if she was the only woman in the room and he always made her feel very, very special. She was so desperate to recapture what they had shared that she was unaware that she was drinking too much.

Jason noticed. "That's your fourth glass of wine, sweetheart. Be careful, you know you can't hold your liquor."

She leaned towards him. "Oh, can't you handle me when I'm drunk?"

He gave a smug smile. "Of course I can. I'm just thinking of you."

He put his arm round her shoulders, pulled her close and gave her a quick kiss on the lips, relieved that she seemed more relaxed. The alcohol was certainly helping.

Graham crossed the floor towards them. "I wondered if Anna would care to dance?"

"Love to," said Anna, rising unsteadily to her feet.

Jason smiled with amusement.

It was gone one in the morning when they finally arrived home. Although Hollie had been allowed to stay up just this once, she had fallen asleep and her father carried her upstairs and Anna undressed her and put her to bed. It had been quite a wonderful evening and with the wine inside her, Anna felt more relaxed and happier than she had been for the last week.

She went into their bedroom and fell backwards onto the bed.

"I'm absolutely pooped."

Jason was just starting to undress. "It's all that alcohol you drank. I'm going to have to watch you, or you're going to turn into a drunken sot."

"Cheek!"

He lay down next to her, leaning on his elbow. "Well, is milady going to get undressed?" He caressed her cheek. "Or do you need some help?"

She gave a sleepy smile. "I can undress myself."

He slipped the straps off her shoulders and started kissing her. Anna began to float away on a pink cloud and when he kissed her lips she responded passionately, flinging her arms round his neck and pulling him down towards her. He ran his hand up her leg to her thigh. Suddenly she was aware of his weight pinning her down. This seemed so strange as Jason never positioned himself so that his full weight was on her, he was always considerate of her comfort. At first she thought she was imagining it, but he felt very heavy. His kisses became more ardent and she found it difficult to breathe. She began to struggle against him.

Jason lifted himself up and grinned. "Now what's going on here?" he murmured. "Are you wanting to play a little game?"

Anna had never suggested 'games' in their lovemaking, but there again, she had had very little experience in sexual matters.

"I…want to get up," she said. She tried to push him off.

Completely misreading the situation, Jason pushed her back and held her hands in a vice like grip behind her head.

"Oh no, you don't. You're not getting away from me!"

She struggled more violently. "Jason, please don't!"

He pulled her dress up to her thighs and started unfastening his own clothing. Anna gave out a muffled scream and he saw the fear in her eyes. He stopped immediately and sat upright, frowning in bewilderment.

"Sweetheart, I'm sorry. I thought you…"

She jumped off the bed. "Don't ever do that again!"

He got up slowly. "I won't, I promise you."

"I'm sleeping in my old room tonight. I'll get my things," she said, heading for the bathroom.

He caught her by the arm. "Please don't. I said I'm sorry."

"Leave me alone!"

His eyes turned dark with anger. "Then go if you must!"

Anna collected up her nightwear and toiletries. In minutes she was back in her old room, feeling very frightened and so alone. She climbed into bed, hid her face in the pillow and tried to smother her sobs.

Jason lay in bed, staring at the ceiling. Whatever had gone wrong, he thought bitterly, was much worse than a lovers' quarrel. For when he had caught her arm to stop her leaving, he had inadvertently pulled the scarf away from her neck. There he had seen the shadow of a love bite and he knew beyond any doubt that he wasn't the cause of it.

It all looked very different in the cold light of day. Jason stared at his reflection as he shaved, his thoughts on the night before. He had definitely seen a love bite on Anna's neck and he abhorred love bites. He thought them unsightly. Suddenly his mind drifted back to the previous Thursday night when they had made love for the first time since his return from Singapore. He knew he had lost control, his desire for her had been phenomenal. Could it be possible that he was the cause of the bruising on her neck after all? Even through his desire, he had still sensed a tension in her, a nervousness that he had never known before. She wasn't relaxed and he might have been too rough. Perhaps he had hurt her?

There was no doubt that since his return from Singapore she had been quieter and more subdued. He had seen a glimpse of the old Anna the night before after the Christmas party, but then she had had a few glasses of wine in her. At first, she had responded passionately until everything suddenly went pear-shaped. He sighed as he tapped the shaver in the sink and placed it back on the shelf.

Anna wrapped a towel round her and then twisted a second one round her damp hair. She was still in her old room and knew that she must venture to the one she shared with Jason in order to get dressed. Padding across the landing she opened the door and breathed a sigh of relief when she saw the empty bed. She chose some underwear from a drawer and then collected together a jumper and a pair of jeans, throwing the entire bundle on a chair. Sitting on the edge of the mattress she bent her head forward and began to rub her hair vigorously with the towel.

"That's one of the many images I had of you, while I was away," smiled Jason, coming out of the bathroom.

Anna jerked her head up and stared at him through a tangled mass of blonde hair. "Thought you were downstairs."

"Well, I'm not. And I didn't think you'd be back so soon."

She gave a grimace. "Unless you want me to go down to breakfast like this, then I had to come back to get dressed."

She sat at the dressing table and carefully combed her knotted hair.

Jason watched her as he pulled on a T-shirt. "What do you want to do today?"

Anna hesitated before replying. "But it's Sunday. Aren't you going to the gym?"

He shook his head. "The hotel in Singapore had wonderful facilities. I worked out and went swimming nearly every day. Thought I'd give it a miss this morning."

"Well, I need to do some more Christmas shopping, I'm afraid."

He suspended his action of pulling on a jumper. "More! I thought you'd be finished by now?"

"I've sent off those for the family." Her appointment with Nigel had allowed her to return to the music store and buy the CD vouchers. It had been a dreadful experience, causing her to rush in and out as quickly as possible. "And I've bought for everyone except your mother. I can't seem to find anything for her. I'm really stumped."

"Shall we go together? Perhaps I can give you a few ideas."

Jason expected her to reject the suggestion out of hand, but her immediate response took him off guard.

"I'd really love that. As long as you don't mind trailing round," she smiled.

He nodded taken aback by her enthusiasm. "Then that's what we'll do. Perhaps we could take Hollie with us? There's a fair on and she'd enjoy going on the roundabouts."

"That sounds wonderful." She plugged in the dryer and started drying her hair, bending her head forward and rubbing her fingers through blonde curls. The whirring noise prevented any further conversation.

Jason had finished dressing and wondered if he should go down to breakfast, but then he hesitated. He felt reluctant to leave her after their quarrel the night before. He sat down on the bed and waited for her to finish.

"I think we need to talk," he said, when she lifted her head and switched off the dryer.

"What about?" She turned to the mirror and brushed her hair.

He stood up and walked across to her, placing his hands on her shoulders. "I feel I've done something very wrong."

She looked up at him. "Why do you think that?"

"These last few days you've not been yourself. I wondered if anything had happened while I've been away. If you've had any problems."

Anna felt her heart pounding. "What sort of problems?"

"Anything. With your family or at work? I appreciate you're missing your sons, but…"

"Yes, I am missing them, but I'll be seeing them soon."

Jason took the brush from her and placed it down on the dressing table. He gently raised her to her feet and put his arms round her. She spread her hands on his chest as if to keep him at a distance.

He closed his eyes momentarily, summoning up his courage. "As I said, I feel that I've done something to upset you. Anna, if you've changed your mind about us, then please tell me. If you want to break off our engagement then I must know. I can't live my life pretending that everything's OK when it's not. I had to do that too many times with Kiera."

Anna stared at him, panic welling up inside her. He looked so lost as his deep blue eyes searched her face for reassurance. He wasn't smiling but she needed him to smile, to be happy. It meant everything to her to make him happy.

She slowly lifted her arms round his neck; wanting to tell him everything, needing him to understand the horror she had endured. And then he would be there to comfort her and give her the courage to make it through each day.

She pressed herself against him. "No, it's not that. I couldn't live without you, I love you too much," she whispered.

He gave a moan of relief as his mouth covered hers. She was hardly aware that the towel had fallen to the ground or that Jason was lifting her over to the bed, covering her face with tender kisses. There was no pain this time, not even a sensation of discomfort. Only the joy of their lovemaking and the wonderful knowledge that they were together again filled her conscious thoughts. And her only cries were those of pleasure and happiness.

The following morning and only two days before Christmas, they all piled into the Mercedes and set off for the Grange. Ben had left that same morning for Nottingham, but he would return in good time to celebrate the New Year. At first they struggled through heavy Christmas traffic, but finally they were out into the countryside. It was a sparkling winter morning, with a touch of frost in the air. There wasn't going to be any snow for Christmas, the weathermen had said, and Hollie had felt very disappointed.

"Snow isn't a very good thing to have, where we're going," Jason told her. "If it's really bad, the country roads get completely blocked and then we can be cut off for days."

Hollie said she didn't really care if they were cut off, if it meant she didn't have to go back to school. She sat next to her father gabbling away ten to the dozen, while Mrs Wilby and Anna had a peaceful journey sitting in the back.

At regular intervals, Jason would glance at Anna in the mirror, marvelling at the sudden change in events. Their shopping expedition had been wonderful. After lunch, they had gone to the funfair and taken Hollie on the rides, laughing with her as they whizzed about or scrambled up the helter-skelter. The ride on the Ferris wheel had been a delight as they viewed Bristol from on high. It was as if all the problems since his return from Singapore had simply evaporated and Anna was more like herself. He grimaced when he thought of the last five days and prayed they would never experience anything like it again.

When they reached the gates, Hollie jumped out to swing them open. She had always enjoyed doing this job, but then she saw Grandma Harrington waiting for them by the main entrance and set off to run into her arms. Jason drove through the gates and Anna got out to close them, shaking her head at the whimsical little girl. They dove up the drive and into the forecourt where Margaret stood, holding Hollie's hand.

"Anna! Where've you been for the last three months?" chastised Margaret. "I've missed you and you should have come to visit with Jason and Hollie." Anna apologised and followed everyone indoors and into the warmth of the parlour. "My dears, we are going to have a lovely Christmas together, but what a shame Ben couldn't join us this year." Suddenly, Hollie saw Tess lying peacefully on the hearthrug in front of the fire and bounded towards her. Flinging herself on the floor, she gave a shriek of delight as she put her arms round the retriever's neck. "Don't be too rough, Hollie dear. She's an old dog and can get bad tempered if she's man handled too much."

"Old!" Hollie screamed. "She was here when the dinosaurs were about."

It was wonderful being back and Margaret had already discussed the sleeping arrangements, putting Anna and Jason into his room at the top of the flight of seven stairs.

They had their coffee and then went up to their rooms to unpack. Anna couldn't help stopping halfway up the grand stairway to survey the immense hall below her. Yes, she thought, being here will help me forget. It was here Jason and I fell in love. She smiled at the gigantic Christmas tree standing in the corner, glittering with lights and tinsel.

Jason caught up with her. "Guess who's coming to lunch tomorrow?"

Anna thought for a moment.

"It can't be Doctor Orchard and Sarah. Margaret said they've gone to Spain for Christmas."

"No, it's Nigel and Sophia."

"Wonderful," smiled Anna, in absolute delight.

And it was a delight for her. After they had eaten, they all took a walk outside, even though the light was starting to fade.

Sophia came to Anna's side. "I know this is a social visit, but I was just wondering how you are," she said, keeping her voice low.

"I'm fine. My bruises have healed."

"You certainly look better," said Sophia. "You've got more colour in your cheeks."

"Yes, I feel better and more positive. My husband...he's finally agreed to a divorce."

"Good! Get plenty of rest over the holiday and you'll soon be your old self." She looked about her. "It's so pretty here."

Above the main entrance a cascade of Christmas lights trailed over the stonework and to the left of the door was a spruce weighed down by tinsel and blue and white lights. These twinkling lights were repeated in the trees along the drive. The air seemed filled with the scent of moist pine needles.

"Yes," breathed Anna. "It's magical."

"Have you thought any more about telling Jason?" Sophia hoped that Anna couldn't see the eagerness in her eyes; informing Jason would solve so many problems.

"No and I never will," said Anna adamantly.

"Why not?" Sophia couldn't hide her disappointment.

"Because he'll be appalled and he'll want to do something about it. And he'll also think me an utter fool to trust a man like my husband."

"I think you underestimate him. If you explained it all to him, I'm sure he'll understand."

"Yes, I'm sure he will. After he's got Dave banged up in prison!"

Sophia couldn't help laughing. "Well, I'll leave that up to you. But you're going to need a lot of support and understanding over the next few months and no one can give that better than the man you love and who loves you."

"I think he'll give me that anyway," said Anna softly.

CHAPTER FIFTEEN

Christmas Day started at five-thirty, much to the displeasure of the adults who were forced to stumble, bleary-eyed downstairs to open their presents. Hollie had made it her duty to wake up everyone, ringing a bell that had been found in the kitchen.

"Who the hell gave her that?" groaned Jason, pulling on his dressing gown.

"I think it was Fran," said Anna, from beneath the bedcovers.

"Come on! Get up everyone. It's Christmas Day!" came the cry around the house.

Margaret tried to shush her and told her not to wake up John and his family who were still sleeping in their apartment.

"Lucky old John and family," muttered Anna. She tried to snatch a few more minutes but finally had to give in and join the others in the parlour.

It turned out to be a very wonderful two hours as they opened their presents in front of the fire. Margaret went down to the kitchen and brought up a pot of steaming coffee and as they let the caffeine bring them to life, they marvelled at the gifts that littered the floor. There seemed to be everything; clothing, books, toiletries, jewellery, tapestry frames and numerous other treasures, some requested and some given as a surprise. Jason's gift to Anna was a beautiful and very expensive watch bought from Harrods. Anna began to wonder if all his gifts had to come from only the exclusive department stores and if he had ever chased a bargain as an astute Yorkshire lass would do. Margaret's gift to Anna was a wonderful set of golf clubs in a leather bag.

"We'll have to try them out as soon as we can," Jason smiled.

"Isn't the club closed over Christmas?"

"Only today and tomorrow. We can play on Sunday after the boys have left, if you like?"

Anna nodded, her heart skipping a beat at the impending visit.

A short time later, everyone made their way upstairs to get dressed and then back downstairs for breakfast. And after breakfast, Anna and Jason took Hollie outside to try out her new bike, courtesy of Grandma Harrington.

Christmas Day at the Grange was always spent quietly and for the first time in many years, Anna wanted to attend the morning service with Margaret and Mrs Wilby. Jason expressed surprise at this, but not wanting to be left behind, agreed to accompany everyone to the beautiful medieval stone church of Saint Mary's where he had been christened. The service was pleasant and Anna enjoyed singing the carols and listening to the sermon on the meaning of 'love and trust'.

And then it was back to the Grange for lunch. This was also an unhurried, quiet affair with turkey, Christmas pudding and all the trimmings. Being with Jason's family made Anna's heart twinge. This was the first Christmas Day she had spent away from her sons, the first Christmas she had not been with her mother and sister and after lunch, Anna paced the floor waiting for the call that would lift her spirits. When it came, she bubbled over with delight as her sons confirmed their arrival for the following day. As she put down the phone she was convinced more than ever that not telling Jason had been the right thing to do. Pressing charges would not have helped the situation one bit. Why spoil Jason's happiness? Why spoil her sons' life?

The twins arrived on Boxing Day about mid-morning, after setting off very early and making good time. Not that Anna could wait to see them since she had spent the time since breakfast, going backwards and forwards to the window, until Hollie shouted that they were finally parking outside the house. Anna was out of the front door in seconds, her arms round her sons as they climbed out of the car. And then they were surrounded by the rest of the household, shaking hands and receiving kisses, before being bundled into the warmth of the Grange.

"I said they must be fine young men," said Jason, as they drank their coffee in the parlour. "And I was right."

"I do believe they've grown," Anna smiled. "Although Martyn needs his hair cutting…and that beard!"

"Beards and long hair are part of life at uni."

"Does that apply to the girls too?" laughed Anna.

She couldn't describe her feelings over the next three days, having her sons close. But it wasn't just that, it was the fact they fitted in so well with life at the Grange and they obviously approved of Jason, telling their mother that he was a 'great guy'. She showed them round the house and grounds and listened to their many stories of life on campus now that their first term was over. On an evening, she, Jason and the twins would escape to the billiard room and play snooker, the happy banter between the men she loved, lifting her heart out of the mire of depression she was apt to sink into at unexpected moments.

Anna loved every room in the Grange, delighting in their unique style, but the billiard room was her favourite. It had hardly been touched for centuries and harked back to the time when the gentlemen would leave the ladies to pursue their own interests. Masculine in design, with oak beams, lime green walls and brass light fittings, the soft furnishings were upholstered in plush olive green velvet and very comfortable. Stepping into the room, Anna always got the impression that she was entering an exclusive gentlemen's club.

Anna leaned on her cue and narrowed her eyes. "Is this true, Martyn? Are you telling me there wasn't a washing machine in halls?"

Her elder son squirmed with shame. "I didn't have time to do my washing."

Chris grinned. "So, he brought it all home for Grandma to do, even his bed sheets, the dirty sod."

"Thanks Bruv," said Martyn, rubbing his chin.

Jason bent to take his turn, trying not to smile. "I remember it well."

Anna turned on him in disgust. "Not you, surely?"

Jason straightened his back as the red ball disappeared into the side pocket. "I tried to get home every few weeks and I must admit I hauled my washing with me."

"Poor Margaret."

Jason winked at Martyn. "If you want to keep on the right side of your mother, then I suggest you use the laundry facilities."

"Well, I don't suppose it matters to me," Anna sighed. "I'm just thinking of my mum. She's getting on and doing a whole term's worth of washing isn't going to help her bad back." She cocked her head to one side. "Unless you move back in with your dad. I'm sure he could cope with the washing." She caught the boys' wary side-glance at each other. "What is it?"

Chris cleared his throat. "Dad has a girlfriend. Well, a woman friend actually. She's just moved in with him, so we decided to stay out of the way while they settled down."

Jason looked at Anna and noticed a blush come to her cheeks.

"Oh, that's fine," she said nonchalantly. "Why shouldn't he? Anyone I know?" She didn't care that she was being curious.

"Her name's Pam," said Chris. "Someone from work, I think, but we haven't met her yet."

Anna closed her eyes as a cold wave passed over her, followed by a pang of jealousy as she imagined another woman using her kitchen, sleeping in her bedroom. But then a sense of relief flooded through her. She had been vindicated, the woman in the pub was exactly who she thought she was. Now she knew for certain, she started laughing.

Jason came to her side and put his arm round her shoulder. "Are you OK, sweetheart?"

She nodded vigorously. "Oh, yes. I said she could have him and so she can."

After the boys had left, the heavens opened and it rained continually, saturating the garden and drumming down on the roofs of the cars like a hail of bullets. Jason had proposed a game of golf but now it would have to be abandoned.

"It's such a shame," said Anna, peering out of the window, while Jason sat reading his newspaper. "I was so looking forward to beating you again. Never mind. It might brighten up later."

But it didn't. In fact the rain turned to a fine, chilling drizzle that had the power to seep into clothing and soak a person right through. Most of the day was spent in the parlour either watching television or playing board games and cards.

Eventually, Jason looked at his watch and glanced across at Anna. "Do you fancy going to the club anyway? We could have a drink in the bar."

She looked up from her magazine and smiled. "That sounds great. We've been cooped up too long."

"My fees are due on the first, so I'll be able to pay them while we're there."

She gave him a withering look. "Oh, Jason, I reminded you about that before you went to Singapore!" She smacked his hand in playful annoyance.

"I know but it slipped my mind," he said guiltily.

They were about to leave the parlour when Hollie burst through the door carrying a large vanity case. She was in her dressing gown after having her bath and her hair hung down her back in dark, damp ripples.

"I'm ready now, Anna," she cried, her face aglow with enthusiasm.

Anna stopped, a look of disquiet spreading across her features. "Oh, I forgot! I promised Hollie I'd put her hair in ringlets."

Jason chuckled. "Looks like I'm not the only one with a bad memory."

Anna bit her lip apprehensively. "I'd better keep my promise." She looked towards the little girl emptying the contents of the vanity case on the table. It had been a present from Mrs Wilby and she treasured all the paraphernalia associated with hair and beauty. "She'll be terribly upset if I let her down."

Jason gave a sigh. "You're probably right. But I must go to the club and pay my fees."

"Can't you send a cheque tomorrow?"

He shook his head. "It won't get there in time."

"I'll come to your car with you."

Despite his protestations, she insisted on walking with him into the hall while he pulled on his coat. Outside it was dark and bitingly cold. Anna hugged her arms as she stood in the porch out of the driving rain.

He noticed she was shivering. "Sweetheart, go inside. You'll catch your death."

She watched him climb into the car. "What a pity I can't come with you."

He waved his hand. "I'll be an hour at the most." He suddenly added, "Shall I pick up an application form for you? I think it's about time you became a member and you've still not made use of Mother's birthday present to you."

"Yes, do that. If I'm going to beat you into the ground, it might as well be official."

Jason gave a grin and drove away. Anna watched him go. Whenever she thought of that moment in the future, she bitterly regretted her promise to Hollie. If she had accompanied him, perhaps events would have turned out so differently.

Jason pulled into the car park and looked towards the lights streaming from the windows of the club. The folk inside were obviously enjoying a Christmas drink and he suddenly felt disappointed that Anna had had to stay behind. It would have been nice to get away from the Grange for a few hours. Sighing heavily, he climbed out of the car and ran through the rain and across the shining tarmac. The warmth and comfort of the building enclosed him.

There were very few people in the foyer, as they all seemed to be in the bar. Jason walked over to the desk and the smiling receptionist brought up his details on her computer and prepared to take his payment on his credit card.

"Well, hello stranger." The husky voice was unmistakable and he quickly glanced to his left.

"Hello Deborah. Merry Christmas," he answered politely. She sidled up to him and came far too close. He used the excuse of signing the receipt to move away from her. "Could I have an application form, please," he asked the receptionist.

Deborah smiled seductively. "Don't tell me Anna's becoming a member at last?"

Unsmiling, Jason took the form, folded it and put it in his inside pocket.

"We thought it was about time."

"Be warned! Caroline will be after her. She still wants her to join the team."

"I'm not surprised. Anna is an excellent golfer and I think she'll be a credit to the club."

He said it in a way that would sting her and when her dark eyes turned even darker with jealousy, he found it difficult to hold back his enjoyment.

"Yes, well." She glanced around the foyer as if trying to control her temper and then turned her attention back to Jason. "So, have you had a pleasant Christmas?"

"Very nice, thank you."

He knew his coldness would cause rancour, but for some reason he couldn't help goading her. If there was one thing he had learned about Deborah Gilbert-Hines it was that she thrived on the heat of passion and anger. He remembered the last time he had confronted her and how his rage had 'turned her on'. He wasn't going to fall for that again.

"I heard you've been away?"

"Yes, to Singapore on business."

"Gone long, were you?"

"Just a week."

Deborah feigned thoughtfulness. "Would that be round about the thirteenth of December?"

Jason frowned. "I guess so. I left on the eleventh, so yes, I was away then."

"Didn't take Anna with you then?" She didn't let him answer. "Of course you didn't. Because that's the day I saw her with her friend at the Marriott Hotel"

"You saw her where?"

She knew he had heard her and decided to ignore his question. "Mmm. Probably having a nice, cosy Christmas drink with him."

"Him?"

Deborah smiled in triumph. She knew what buttons to push. "Very attractive man, actually."

He scowled, trying to stem the suspicions that were rising up inside him.

"There's nothing wrong with Anna having a drink with a friend, male or female!"

"He was certainly very friendly, the way he had his arm round her."

Jason didn't want to hear any more and decided to leave. "I'm going. I don't want my Christmas spoilt with your innuendoes."

"Innuendoes! Certainly not! I saw them go in and I saw her come out…about six hours later!"

Jason froze on the spot. "You were watching her for six hours?"

"No, of course not," she said coyly. "I was just returning to the office when I saw them going through the door of the hotel. And much later on, I was in the restaurant with a client and I saw her leave. On her own of course."

"She left on her own?"

"I think she was on her own. But you know how crowded the lifts to the rooms can be." Now Jason's eyes turned dark and it was Deborah's turn to gloat. She pushed the dagger in to the hilt. "Oh, don't worry about it. As you say, there's nothing wrong with her having an intimate, cosy Christmas drink in a hotel bedroom."

She turned to go but Jason caught her arm. She smiled in exaltation at his angry but pained expression.

"You're lying!"

"Lying! Oh, come on, Jason. Get real! If anyone's good at lying, it's that fiancée of yours. Remember her story about being a widow? That was a pearl."

"She…She had her reasons for doing that," he stammered.

"I'm sure she did." She patted his arm. "And I'm sure she's got a valid reason for going to a hotel room with a male companion." She smiled smugly. "Why don't you ask her?"

"I will and she'll have a good reason." Somehow he knew he didn't sound convincing.

Deborah had won and now she was satisfied to leave, but not before sending a parting shot.

"You've always been rather blind when it came to choosing your wife, haven't you? Well, as my dear old grandmother used to say, 'you can't half pick 'em'." She made her way through the foyer to the bar, laughing as she went.

Jason drove back to the Grange in a state of turmoil. The demons of suspicion travelled with him and although he tried to rationalise everything he had heard, he found he couldn't. If Anna had been for a Christmas drink with a friend, then they would have stayed in the bar. There was no reason for her to go up to the bedrooms. He tried to stay calm, convinced that Anna would set his mind at rest.

He arrived at the Grange and as he locked the car, a feeling of nausea swept over him. He remembered the love bite on her neck and the strange coldness she had shown him after his return from Singapore. And then there was that particular day when she was out late. The day her car ran out of petrol.

He went straight into the parlour without removing his coat and scarf.

"Where's Anna?" he asked, quickly glancing round at the faces present.

"Upstairs," said Hollie, munching on some chocolates.

He took the stairs two at a time. Anna was in their room sorting out a dress for the New Year's Eve party.

She smiled brightly as he came in. "I don't know whether to wear this one." She held up a blue dress. "Or this one." She held up a black one. Her smile faded when she saw his expression. "What's the matter? You look as though you've had some terrible news."

He moistened his lips. He was a businessman and was used to getting to the point quickly.

"I want to ask you a question, Anna. And I want a truthful answer."

She opened her eyes wide in surprise. "What is it? What's happened?" She took a step closer to him.

"While I was in Singapore, did you go to the Marriott Hotel?" He saw her reel back in shock.

Anna felt as though she was going to faint, the colour draining from her face. "I...I don't think so."

He stepped forward and grabbed her arms. "Did you go there with someone?" She stared at him in horror. "Answer me!"

"No, I didn't," she stuttered.

"You were seen going into the hotel with a man!"

She had known him angry before, but never like this.

"They must be mistaken. It wasn't me." Her voice became stilted with fear.

Jason moved away from her, staring with fresh eyes at the woman he loved. She seemed so different, so alien.

"You're lying to me!"

"No, I'm not!"

He took hold of her once more. "Anna, look me in the eye and tell me that it wasn't you going into the Marriott Hotel."

She slapped his hands away. "No, I won't! I don't have to justify my actions! How dare you! Just because we're engaged doesn't give you the right to question me like this. I'm not your property, your possession."

He advanced on her, his expression thunderous. For one awful moment she thought he might hit her and put up her arms to ward off a blow.

Her sudden defensive action startled him. "I ask very little of you. But I do expect faithfulness in a woman," he said softly.

"Do you think I could…Why don't you trust me?"

"I want to, but you've lied in the past." He winced at her hurt expression. He stepped a little closer, desperately wanting her to understand his position. "But when I hear something that unsettles me, then I have to know the truth."

"And you'd rather listen to vengeful gossip than to me?"

He held her arm, but this time his touch was gentler. "Anna, just tell me the truth."

She twisted her head away, her heart thudding wildly, tears of humiliation spilling onto her cheeks.

"I don't want to say anything to you when you're in this kind of mood."

His grip tightened. "Deborah told me that she saw you coming out of one of the lifts to the bedrooms…"

Anna turned on him angrily. "Deborah! You've been listening to someone like *her*. A woman you despise! Oh, Jason, I expected better from you!"

"Yes, it does seem ironic," he said, smiling wryly. "So, prove her wrong. Prove her to be the malicious gossipmonger she is."

Anna knew she was caught in a trap. She couldn't refute the allegations but there again, there was no way that she wanted to confirm them. Jason watched her closely.

She was desperate to escape. "I'd like to go downstairs. Perhaps we can talk about this later."

He shook his head vigorously. "Not until we get this sorted out." Anna stared at the floor for a few seconds, but then her sharp glance in his direction made him gasp. He had caught her look of deceit. "Was Deborah right? Did you go…to a hotel bedroom with…another man?" His arms fell to his side and he backed away from her, his eyes showing the agony of his feelings. Biting his lip he stammered, "I thought my suspicions were just…!" He passed a trembling hand over his face. "No! I can't handle this."

She heard the door slam and everything went quiet. She stood motionless, waiting, hoping that he would return.

The door opened quietly and Margaret's anxious voice drifted into her consciousness.

"What is it, my dear, what's happened? Jason has just left as though the devil was chasing him."

Anna slowly turned towards her and then for the first time in her life, she fainted.

Jason couldn't remember how he got home. He drove instinctively and pulled up outside the house in Bishop Sutton with the rain beating down relentlessly. He was surprised to see lights on and realised that Ben must be home from his Christmas visit with his family. He rushed through the door and almost collided with him in the kitchen.

"Oh, you're back," said Ben. "I was going to set off to the Grange tomorrow." Jason's black expression alarmed him.

"Decided to come back early. I'm off to bed. See you in the morning. Don't forget to lock up."

He left Ben standing alone, puzzlement etched across his face.

Jason reached his room and immediately went to the bathroom, where he vomited into the toilet. He had never felt so ill in his life, his insides churning round, his head fit to burst. Stumbling back into the bedroom, he threw himself on the mattress fully clothed and stared about him.

He had shared this room with Anna for over three months and now it seemed forlorn and empty. He knew why he felt so unwell. The shock to his system had been on the scale of an earthquake, since every fibre of his being had trusted her, because he loved her so deeply. It was as if his very vital signs, his breathing and heartbeat, depended on her. And now that she had betrayed his trust, his body rebelled at the idea. He noticed the phone beside the bed. He would call the Grange and tell his mother he was back at his own house. There was no point in worrying her.

Anna awoke with Margaret leaning over her, pressing a cold flannel on her forehead. She was lying on the bed and in the background she could see Mrs Wilby and Fran hovering near.

"Just lie still, my dear. You gave me such a scare fainting like that. Thank goodness John was around to lift you up." She turned to the others. "You two go downstairs. She's fine now, we don't need a doctor." Anna tried to sit up but Margaret pressed her back. "No, stay where you are for just a few minutes more."

Anna obeyed, she felt so weak. "Where's Jason?" she asked quietly.

"No idea."

"We had a row."

"Well, that's obvious," said Margaret sadly.

There was a brief pause as Anna gathered her courage. "He accused me of having an affair," she whispered.

Margaret suspended her actions of offering Anna a cup of tea. "An affair! That's preposterous. Not you."

"I'm glad you've got so much faith in me."

Margaret started laughing. "My dear, I can read people's characters very well. And the moment I set eyes on you I knew you were the faithful kind."

"Even though I lied about my husband?"

"I said I knew you were faithful, not truthful."

"The trouble is, my lies have made him doubt my fidelity."

Margaret shook her head. "I'm sure that's not the case. How can he doubt you?"

Anna struggled up onto the pillows. "I haven't had an affair, Margaret. You're right, it's not in my nature. I was married a long time and I never considered it then, even though I was bitterly unhappy."

"And Jason will realise that, when he comes to his senses."

"That might not be for a while."

"He'll cool down eventually," said Margaret soothingly.

Anna glanced around the room. "I don't think he'll be back tonight. He'll have gone to Bishop Sutton."

"Well, I hope he phones. Do you want to come downstairs?"

Anna shook her head. "I think I'll have a bath and go to bed, if you don't mind."

"That sounds like a good idea. You drink your tea and don't worry. Everything will be sorted out tomorrow."

Yes, thought Anna as she sank into the bubbles, everything will be OK tomorrow. Jason will come back to the Grange and laugh at the stupidity of it all. He will take her in his arms and tell her he shouldn't have believed someone like Deborah. Surely he will realise that her information couldn't be relied on. And yet she had been telling the truth! Anna couldn't blame Jason for thinking she was having an affair, it must have looked that way. But deep down she knew the situation was dire. He had come very close to finding out the truth about her. Had Sophia been right all along? Should she have told him everything? Her heart ached with yearning.

Sleep came only spasmodically for Jason and he awoke the following morning feeling washed out and weary.

"You look a bit the worse for wear," said Ben, as he poured him some coffee. In fact, he felt quite worried about his boss. He had never seen him looking so ill.

"Drank too much at Christmas," Jason lied. He picked up the mug and took a gulp. "I'm going into the office. Got to catch up on a few things." He turned to go but then turned back. "Do you remember when I was in Singapore and I was trying to contact Anna?" Ben nodded. "She was out quite a bit, wasn't she?"

"She did a lot of shopping if I remember right."

"Was there any time when she was out for most of the day…or evening?"

Ben thought carefully. "On the Friday, she was out for a good part of the day," he said hesitantly.

"You know beyond any doubt it was the Friday?"

"It was actually Friday the thirteenth. You know how superstitious Mrs Wilby can be and she mentioned the date in passing."

"What time did Anna get in?"

Ben took a sip of his coffee. "Late."

"How late?"

Ben felt extremely uncomfortable and made a non-committal answer.

"Late enough."

"I asked what time she arrived home!"

"We had to stay up for her. She got in about eleven."

"Eleven o'clock! Did she say where she'd been?"

"We asked, but she said she'd been held up. Didn't seem to be any point in making a fuss about it. We were just glad she was home safely."

"How did she seem?"

Ben hesitated once more but could see by Jason's angry expression that he had to answer.

"Her lip was cut and bruised. She said she'd slipped and hit her face on the kerb."

Jason frowned while he considered this for a moment. "I…I won't be going to the New Year's Eve party, but you go as you planned. I'll ring the Grange this morning and tell Mother."

"She'll be upset," ventured Ben.

"Can't help that. Perhaps you could bring Mrs Wilby and Hollie back on the second of January?"

Ben turned in his seat. "What about Anna?"

"Anna can do what the hell she likes," Jason muttered, making his way to the office.

In his office, Jason stared down at his desk. Her lip was bruised, he thought bitterly. He remembered his time with Deborah. There had been no love between them and when they went to bed it was purely for sex. And Deborah had liked the rough stuff. Not that it was Jason's preference but he had complied with her wishes and found it interesting although rather alarming at times. Why a woman would want to be treated violently was beyond him.

It had never been that way with Anna. Sex with Anna had always been an expression of his love for her and he had cherished that, since he had never experienced such a powerful force of emotion with anyone else. Being with Anna had been tender and gentle, but unbelievably exciting. The feelings he had known had been mind blowing. And he knew Anna had felt the same. In fact, he knew beyond any doubt that he had aroused passions in her that had lain dormant for so long.

Perhaps that was it! Perhaps he had awakened her to the point where she craved more variety and she had searched further afield. Her lip was cut. Deborah had experienced many cuts and bruises to her lips when he had pressed harsh, brutal kisses on them. But Deborah had enjoyed that.

He rose from his chair and wandered across to Anna's desk. He felt sick to his stomach. Why had she cheated on him? Of all the women he had known, he would never have thought it of her.

"I'm off now," said Ben, from the doorway. "Do you want me to pass on any message?"

Jason shook his head. "I'll phone my mother so she'll expect you."

"You're not staying here by yourself, are you?" said Ben. "You can't spend the New Year on your own."

"I'll be fine. You go and enjoy yourself." He heard the door slam and then a car driving away.

He returned to his desk and picked up the phone. A few minutes later he was talking to his mother, explaining that he wouldn't be joining them for the New Year's Eve party, but Ben was on his way and would bring back Hollie and Mrs Wilby at the beginning of January.

"I think you're being very silly," his mother reprimanded him. "Why don't you come back and talk to Anna?"

"I've done enough talking," he said angrily.

Margaret paused for a moment. She knew there was no reasoning with her son when he was like this.

"And what shall I tell her? Is she never to go back to Bishop Sutton? She does work for you, Jason. What about her job?"

Bitterness suddenly overwhelmed him. "Working together will be impossible. Tell Anna...tell her I'll sort out her wages...and her P45 will be sent to her."

CHAPTER SIXTEEN

Margaret didn't have the heart to tell Anna that she had lost her job and by implication, her home also. It could wait until after the New Year, she decided, let the poor girl have a few days of peace. And besides, everything might change once Jason had had the chance to think things over. At the moment he was like a wounded animal, biting and snarling at everyone. But she knew her son loved Anna with all his heart and that alone would bring him round.

The arrival of Ben brought some news of Jason, but only that he was determined not to return to the Grange for the celebrations. Anna listened with a lump in her throat. How could things have gone so terribly wrong? They had travelled to the Grange only one week ago and she and Jason had been so happy and so full of plans for their future.

By the time the final day of 1996 came, Anna had convinced herself that she would never see Jason again. She was almost on the verge of asking Ben to take her back to Bishop Sutton so she could confess everything, when something else began to occupy her thoughts. Something that filled her with ecstatic hope and yet at the same time, with the most awful dread.

Anna dressed for the party and then joined the others in the ballroom. She hadn't been in this room since Margaret's party and her memories nearly overwhelmed her. Thick, velvet curtains were drawn across the bay windows, the deep colour enhancing the polished floor and plush red and gold wallpaper. Fires had been lit in the two huge white marble fireplaces at each end of the room and the warm flicker of the flames was reflected in the chandeliers. Margaret had organised a lavish buffet that was spread on a long table against the far wall. There was going to be a live band followed by a disco and the players were already taking their places.

The arrival of the guests caused a great deal of chaos as coats were discarded and drinks were served. Nigel and

Sophia followed on the heels of Doctor Orchard and Sarah and it seemed Jason's absence was immediately noticed. Standing next to Ben, with Hollie holding her hand, Anna became the focus of attention. Margaret diplomatically made some excuse why Jason was missing, waving her hand in a gesture of casual dismissal. Anna tried to reflect her nonchalance and threw herself into the celebrations as though she hadn't a care in the world.

The room began to fill and it wasn't long before the band started up. The party had begun, but as time passed, Anna began to feel the strain of smiling and trying to appear happy. Eventually, she just couldn't summon up any more enthusiasm to join in. When the buffet was served she used it as an excuse to go outside for some fresh air.

She stood just to the right of the main entrance, looking up at the stars. It was a beautiful clear night but very cold. She pulled her scarf round her chin and focused on the blue and white lights that decorated the trees along the drive. In two days' time, Ben would be taking Mrs Wilby and Hollie home, but she had no idea about her own future. Ben had told her that Jason was in a foul mood and had not been specific about her return to Bishop Sutton. She took in a huge breath and closed her eyes.

"The lights are lovely, aren't they?" said Sophia.

Anna turned round. "Yes, they are. Have you come out for a bit of fresh air too?"

Sophia lit up a cigarette. "I've got three hours to smoke myself to death before I give it up," she laughed.

"Another New Year's resolution?"

"I try every year. One time I actually got as far as March."

"Perhaps it's the job you do."

Sophia nodded. "It's a rather harrowing occupation. But I like helping people."

Anna slipped her arm through Sophia's. "And you've helped me so much. I don't know how I'd have managed without you."

Sophia gave her a wry smile. "I know what you're going through."

"You know?"

Sophia turned her head away and sighed uneasily. "I was raped when I was nineteen while at university by a man I had come to trust."

Sadly, Anna absorbed this information. "I'm so sorry."

"It was a long time ago."

"But it must have been difficult for you, being so young."

Sophia nodded. "It was difficult and I dropped out of uni. But then I met Nigel and he was so wonderful. He was the turning point in my life."

"So, you told him all about it?"

"Yes and he encouraged me to go back and finish my degree." She turned to face Anna. "That's why I want you to tell Jason. He loves you very much and he'll understand, I know he will."

"Are you saying this as a friend or a counsellor?"

Sophia laughed. "As a friend."

There was silence once more as Anna thought this over. "I think I'm pregnant," she said softly.

Sophia stubbed out the cigarette. "You only think?"

"I've not had a test or anything. But I've been here before and I've started feeling a bit unwell, just like I did with the twins."

"That's probably because you're missing Jason. When he's back you'll feel a lot better."

"I don't think he will be back. We had an awful row."

Sophia took in a huge breath. "Is that why he's not here tonight?" She pulled a face but then smiled. "Then go to a chemist and buy a test and get it confirmed."

Anna couldn't help smiling with her. "I've already got one in my bag."

"That's very organised of you."

Anna grimaced. "I was fitted with the coil about three years ago. But I had the doctor remove it when I realised that Jason would love another child and… well, I'm not getting any younger. I didn't have any trouble falling pregnant before, so I hoped it would happen straight away. I had this wonderful idea of surprising him with the news as a special Christmas present. I bought the pregnancy kit a few days after seeing the doctor. I was so excited about it all."

Sophia put her arm round her. "Then do the test as soon as it's necessary and then for God's sake, tell Jason."

Anna tried to hold back the tears. "I can't tell him. I don't know if he's the father!"

Sophia considered this. "When was your last period?"

"Twenty-sixth of November. I'm actually seven days late."

"So, your husband could be the father too?"

"Yes, I'm afraid so."

Sophia licked her lips. "You can have a termination, if you wanted."

Anna shook her head in horror. "No! This child has a right to live." She put her hand to her forehead. "I just pray that it's Jason's, but no matter what, I will still love it." And then she added quietly, "But please, please God, let it be Jason's."

Anna sat on the edge of the bath and waited patiently. The instructions told her that it would take a few minutes before she would know and the time seemed endless. But when she glanced down again she had her answer. She was disturbed from her thoughts by Hollie calling her from the hallway. It was now the second of January and the others were leaving to go back to Bishop Sutton. Margaret had invited her to stay at the Grange for as long as she needed, a kindness she had greatly appreciated. At the moment, Anna needed the comfort of its walls round her, for she never felt so much at home, as she did in this ancient manor filled with history.

She ran downstairs and scooped Hollie up in her arms. "Bye sweetie. Be a good girl for me."

Hollie shuffled uncomfortably. "But why aren't you coming with us?"

"I'm staying here for a few more days," said Anna gently.

She hugged Mrs Wilby and Ben and then went outside with Margaret to see them off. She felt her heart would break as she saw them drive away and kept waving until they had turned at the gate and were out of sight.

Margaret put her arm round her. "I've something to tell you."

"And I've something to tell you."

Margaret gave a chuckle. "Then let's go into the parlour and sit comfortably by the fire."

She thought afterwards that it was only a quirk of fate that Anna happened to break her news first. And because of Anna's information, Margaret found it quite unnecessary to tell the poor girl that the man she loved had sacked her and thrown her out of her home. Had it been the other way round then Anna would have had to cope with two distressing problems instead of one.

"Are you absolutely certain?" asked Margaret.

Anna snuggled into the armchair and tucked her legs underneath her. "The test is supposed to be very reliable, but I'll do another in a week just to be sure."

Margaret couldn't help smiling with glee. "Oh, another grandchild. I really thought that Hollie would be the only one. And if you have a boy, that means a Harrington to carry on the family name."

Anna hated to disillusion her. "I'm not married to Jason."

"That doesn't matter! A child can still have his father's name. What did Jason say? I would have thought he was over the moon!"

"He doesn't know."

"You haven't told him yet?"

Anna watched the flickering flames of the fire. "I'm not going to tell him. I don't want him to know."

"But why not, my dear? If anything will bring you together, then this will."

Anna shook her head. "He accused me of having an affair. If I told him and he said that this wasn't his child, then I wouldn't be able to cope."

Margaret could see the logic in her argument. "I see." She gave a sigh. "And the way he is at the moment he's liable to do just that."

"I'm so glad you understand."

"When's the baby due?"

"Early September I think."

"You'll have to see Doctor Orchard and you'll have hospital appointments to attend."

Anna began to laugh. "You're really thinking ahead, aren't you."

Margaret poured a second cup of tea for them and handed a cup to Anna. "I'm thinking that you should stay here while you wait and see how things go between you and Jason."

Anna sipped her tea. "Thank you, I'd love that. But I must do something. Perhaps I could help Irene in the kitchen or Fran?"

Margaret shook her head. "No, I've thought of something much better than that." She pursed her lips. "Have you ever helped a bride plan her wedding?"

"No, not really."

The elderly lady made a noise with her tongue. "Brides are an absolute pain in the butt." Anna grinned with amusement. "They fuss about this and that until you want to tell them to shove their nuptials up their…!"

"I take it they're hard work?" laughed Anna.

"That's an understatement! So, I thought it would be just the job for you. You're much younger and will be more on their wavelength."

"Me? A wedding planner! But I wouldn't have the first idea."

"A wedding planner. How very American. I think it would be right up your street. Working for my son has given you plenty of experience." Margaret began to warm to the idea. "We'll set you up in an office. No, you can use the library. That's where my late husband used to work and he always found it comfortable. It's got a wonderful old desk in there just waiting to be used again. Prospective couples will be very impressed being interviewed in such a pleasant room."

Anna leaned forward swept along with enthusiasm. "Do you really think it would work?"

"Absolutely. I'll tell you what I've been doing and then you can take it from there. Any new ideas you have will only improve matters. All wedding enquiries can go straight through to you and I can concentrate on the seminars and business conferences." She gave a sigh. "Businessmen are so much more amenable." Anna wasn't sure if she would agree with that.

"It sounds great."

"You accept the job, then?"

"Yes, of course."

"I shall pay you a wage…"

"My board and lodging will be adequate."

"Certainly not! A fair day's pay for a fair day's work, as my dear Tom used to say."

Anna suddenly saw a problem. "But what about Jason? He visits regularly and I don't want to keep bumping into him."

Margaret frowned. "Do you really want to avoid him?"

"Yes. Until I know he feels differently about me."

"Then that will be a problem." Margaret tapped her chin with her forefinger. "He knows what a busy woman I am so he always phones to make arrangements to visit. When I get the call, then you'll just have to…hide somewhere."

"Hide?"

"Well, just go somewhere while he's here. It's a big enough place to get lost in. But we'll deal with that problem when it arises."

Anna thought of something else. "Would it be OK to move back into my old room? I can't stay in Jason's room."

"Yes, of course. I'll get Fran to make the bed up."

"Oh, my goodness! What about the staff? They might say something to him."

"I shall have a word with them. They've worked for me for years and they can be very discreet. Fran will love it! She will find it all very romantic, you hiding from your…sweetheart."

Anna gave a sad smile but then said, "Oh, what was your news?"

Margaret shrugged. "It isn't important any more."

That evening, Anna transferred her possessions back to her original room. She had to admit that she was glad to be back. The wide four-poster bed and the marvellous Victorian bathroom had always been an absolute delight to her. Before she closed the door on Jason's room she decided to search through all the drawers and cupboards to make sure she hadn't left any incriminating evidence behind. She winced at the sight of his shaver and other toiletries that he always left in the bathroom and the bits and bobs in the drawers. And then in the small drawer of the bedside table she found the coin.

Anna sat there for a long time, holding the ten pence in her hand. Her thoughts went back to that afternoon at the golf club when Jason had tossed it in the air to decide her fate. It seemed such a long time ago and she shuddered that she had even considered going back to her husband. If only she had known the future, how different things would have been. Holding the coin tightly in her hand, she picked up her bag and after giving the room a quick glance, she closed the door behind her.

Jason was pleased and relieved when the others arrived home. He had spent three days on his own, either in the office, or sitting watching television. He had got through a phenomenal amount of work and felt pleased that the New Year would start with no backlog whatsoever. He had tried to keep his mind free of any negative thoughts, but memories of Anna were harder to block out. She seemed to be everywhere.

Every room in the house echoed with her presence, but the bedroom was the worst. Her cosmetics and toiletries littered the dressing table and bathroom and her clothes still hung in the wardrobe. Alone in bed, he could almost imagine she was close since her perfume lingered on the pillow that he hugged every night. There was no doubt that he still loved her, even if he found it impossible to be with her. His dreams were filled with her and he would wake up in the early hours of the morning with a yearning that almost bordered on pain. He would remember her smile, her laugh, the way she walked, her wonderful passion when they made love and the sensual look on her face when she came. But then he would remember that she had given all that to another man and his heart would turn to stone.

Even so, when Mrs Thompson arrived and began to vacuum and polish the house and strip the beds, he feared that she would sweep away the memory and watched with mounting alarm as she removed the sheets that Anna and he had last shared. The bed wasn't the same after that.

"So, what happens now?" asked Ben, as they sat down for lunch round the kitchen table.

Jason shrugged. "I'll have to ring Graham and ask him for a new PA, I guess."

"You're not going to advertise like you did before?"

"No, I think there's enough staff at the main office and someone might be willing to transfer here."

Mrs Wilby looked around the kitchen. "It'll be strange being without her." She sighed sadly. "And everything seemed to be going so well for you both."

Hollie had stayed quiet, taking small sips of her milk and nibbling at her lunch. Most of the adults' conversation had gone over her head, but one thing she did understand and that was Anna was not coming back.

"Why don't you go to Grandma Harrington's and fetch her home?" she asked her father, when there was a lull in the discussion. "Then she can work in the office with you again."

"Because Anna doesn't live here any more, sweetie," he said softly.

"Did she say she doesn't want to live here?"

"Not exactly. We had an argument and it's better if she stays with Grandma."

"Whose fault was it? The argument."

"No one's fault. Grown ups fall out sometimes and then everything has to change."

Hollie stood up, pushing her chair back with a grating noise that jarred everyone's nerves. Anger creased her face. "No! It's your fault! It's always your fault!"

Her father reached out to her trying to bring some comfort. "No, Hollie. You don't understand."

She glared at him. "Yes, I do. You made her go away, just like you made me and Mummy go away!" Her dark eyes were liquid with tears. "And then Mummy got sick and died. And if Anna doesn't come home she'll get sick and die just like Mummy did!"

Jason felt startled, while Ben and Mrs Wilby exchanged worried glances. They had never seen her so distressed before, not even at her mother's funeral.

"Anna's not going to die. Come here, sweetie," said her father, holding out his arms to her.

She stepped to one side as if she couldn't bear to be near him. "I want you to go and get her! I want her to come home before God takes her soul to heaven."

Jason shook his head in bewilderment. "You've got it all wrong. Anna is perfectly fine, nothing is going to happen to her and I can't go and get her..."

"You could if you wanted to." Hollie had now become completely distraught. "But you won't cos you don't want to. I hate you! I hate you!" She ran out of the kitchen and headed for her bedroom.

A stunned silence followed, as the adults tried to come to terms with what had just happened.

"I'll go and see if she's OK," said Mrs Wilby, rising from her chair.

Jason stopped her. "No, this is my problem. I'd better sort it out."

After he had left, Ben and Mrs Wilby remained silent, not daring to express their concerns. They knew that Anna had been an integral part of the household and without her, their life might be in danger of coming apart at the seams.

Jason phoned his mother that evening. He hadn't been able to console Hollie who had spent the rest of the afternoon in tears. Only Ben had been able to persuade her to play outside on her new bike while there was still a bit of light left in the sky.

After a few minutes of conversation Jason asked hesitantly, "Is Anna OK?"

"She's very well," said Margaret.

He detected the cold tone in her voice. "I know you're upset with me, but I had my reasons for leaving so abruptly."

"Everyone at the party wanted to know where you were. I had to make excuses for you."

"What did you tell them?"

"What could I tell them! That you'd been called away, of course."

He bit his lip. "I'll come and see you in a few weeks. I'll bring Hollie with me."

"Well, don't forget to phone before you do. You know how busy I am."

"I always phone before I make a visit, you know that!"

"Could you sort out Anna's clothes and her other stuff. I'll send John to pick them up."

"Yes, I'll...do that." His heart lurched at the finality of everything. He paused before asking, "Did you tell Anna what I said about her job?"

"No, I didn't."

"Why not, for heaven's sake!"

"Because circumstances have changed."

"What are you talking about?"

"Anna has other plans," she said nonchalantly.

"You mean she's leaving the Grange?"

"She's got a new job," she said, avoiding the question.

"Already?"

"So, if you could send her P45 to me, I'll make sure she gets it. Her new employer will want it as soon as possible."

Jason put down the phone feeling stunned. So, Anna was leaving to start a new job. He wondered if she had plans to go back to Wakefield. It seemed incredible, but there again it was her home. Jason looked around the office in desperate loneliness.

CHAPTER SEVENTEEN

"I'm sorry Miss Warren, but we can't change the décor."

The bride-to-be pursed her lips and quickly glanced round the ballroom. "Red and gold isn't exactly me."

"We can offer you the dining room for your reception if you wish. That has more muted tones."

Miss Warren was still not impressed. "No, I don't think so. It's far too small." She gave a theatrical sigh. "I think I'll choose another venue if you don't mind."

Anna held the clipboard against her breast. "Well, that's your prerogative, of course," she smiled politely.

In the library, Anna threw the paperwork down on her desk and walked over to the window. Miss Warren and her intended were just getting into their car arguing fiercely. He obviously liked the place, thought Anna with amusement, but she is much more difficult to please. Margaret had been so right. Prospective brides could be a pain! Not all of them, of course. In the week since she had started the job, she had met one lovely young lady who glowed with enthusiasm. Hanging onto her fiancé's arm, she had *Ooh'd* and *Aha'd* her way round the Grange, delighted with everything she saw. And Anna felt more confident now, adversity had made her stronger, despite her heartbreak and she was enjoying herself. She had a few ideas of her own to improve the system. She had a good rapport with the registrar and other officials needed to solemnise a marriage and she had established deals with two good catering companies. Irene might be happy to cook for twenty or thirty businessmen, but two hundred wedding guests filled her with horror.

Anna smiled as she saw John pulling up in front of the main door and went out to meet him. He had just returned from Bishop Sutton after collecting her possessions and he carried them in, in three cases and four boxes. She was surprised that she owned so much, but at least she had some clothes now. For the last week she had been washing and wearing the same outfits over and over again.

The in-house staff had been informed of the situation and their discretion was promised, with also a reassurance that nothing would reach the ears of the part-time employees. Margaret's speculations about Fran had proved to be absolutely correct. She thought it very romantic that Miss should want to hide from her sweetheart. It was a lovers' tiff and nothing more, they all agreed. But neither Fran nor John and Irene knew about the baby yet. Margaret had suggested that that little morsel of news should remain a secret for as long as possible.

Anna had seen Doctor Orchard who had agreed that two positive pregnancy tests were conclusive and had arranged an appointment for her first visit with the midwife. His patient was strong and healthy and he could see no problems except for the fact it was a pregnancy many years after her last one.

John had said very little when he had arrived at Bishop Sutton to collect Anna's possessions, simply concentrating on the job in hand. And subtle enquires by Jason about Anna's new employment had been met with a noncommittal answer. Jason had not been able to bring himself to pack Anna's clothes and when Mrs Wilby had kindly offered, he accepted it with relief.

Now the bedroom was devoid of all her possessions, Jason had found it difficult to sleep, tossing and turning until the early hours. And although she was constantly on his mind, his pride would not release him from his lonely prison.

A few days later, Jason was forced to ring Graham to ask for a new PA. To say that the financial director was surprised about the change of events was an understatement. He didn't ask any intrusive questions but said that he would ask around for any volunteers. On the following Monday morning, Natalie arrived.

Tall and wiry and with a dour personality she was, nonetheless, a good worker. She and her family had moved into the neighbouring village and she thought it more convenient to travel the few miles to Bishop Sutton instead of into the city centre. However, she only took the job on condition that she worked a strict nine to five and definitely no weekends. Jason's entreaties that lunch was part of the hospitality of his home was greeted with a grimace and a reassurance that she was quite happy to sit in the office eating her packed lunch.

"I'm surprised she accepts our coffee," said Mrs Wilby sourly. "And you couldn't buy a smile from her!"

In many ways, Jason was happy that Natalie kept herself apart from them. He didn't want any gossip to reach her and then be passed on to the staff at the main office. There was some advantage in having an aloof PA even if her coolness seemed to chill the entire house. Sometimes he would forget that Anna was gone and would glance across the room expectantly. And then it was like a bullet hitting him when he saw Natalie sitting at the computer, instead of Anna. He missed her desperately, but even his grief couldn't heal his wounded pride or soften his steadily hardening heart.

"What shall I do with Anna's things?" Natalie's monotone voice broke into his concentration.

Jason looked up, puzzled. "What things?"

"There's a few items in the drawers. Not much, but they're getting in my way."

He gave a sigh. "Put them in a box and I'll sort them out later."

He was due to go on a business trip the following morning, the first since the New Year and he was very relieved to be getting away from the house for a few days. Perhaps throwing himself into the ruthless world of negotiating for contracts would focus his mind and give him an objective to aim for.

Natalie did as she was instructed and put Anna's remaining possessions in a box previously containing stationery and placed it on Jason's desk. That evening after dinner, he returned to the office to finish off for the trip and noticed the box. Slowly he went through it, smiling at the objects a woman kept in her desk drawer. There was some perfume, lipstick and a comb. There was hand cream, a small packet of mints and poignantly, the photo of Anna's boys that Natalie had removed from the desk and shoved into the drawer. The one item that intrigued him was a diary from the year before. He didn't want to pry but he found himself flicking through the pages of the final few months of 1996.

Jason knew what he was looking for and the disgust he felt with himself churned up his stomach and made him feel ill.

He was relieved to find nothing untoward. He saw that she had a doctor's appointment in early October and there were a few visits to Nigel. One appointment that caused him surprise was the one for Sophia Barnes in mid-December. It was written in capital letters and underlined. Jason thought it surprising that she should be seeing Sophia socially and yet, never mention it to him. He smiled, pleased that Anna had found a friend in Sophia and wondered if they were still in contact. Perhaps Sophia might know her whereabouts since he knew Nigel wouldn't divulge any information like that.

Thoughts of his mother suddenly came into his head. She had been very reticent about Anna's circumstances and even his offer to send her P45 directly to her new employer had not fooled her. She had insisted that it came to the Grange and she would deal with it. When it came to his mother, he was sure he sensed a conspiracy.

Fran rushed into the library in a whirl of agitation. "Madam's just said that Mr Harrington has phoned about a visit. He's on his way, miss. So, you'd better hide quick!"

Anna threw back her head and laughed gleefully. "There's no panic."

But Fran wouldn't listen and hurried her out of the room and down to the kitchen. It had been agreed that Anna would stay in the apartment when Jason visited, since John and Irene's home was one place he never ventured. At the same time, it was Fran's job to run upstairs and lock Anna's bedroom door. Not that Margaret anticipated Jason going into that particular room but she didn't want to take any chances.

From the kitchen, Anna climbed the back stairs up to the apartment that overlooked the forecourt. It was a spacious, modern flat and carrying a couple of files of paperwork, she knew she could spend the next few hours gainfully employed.

His first visit had been quite harrowing and she had positioned herself so that she could peek through the curtains as he parked the car. Her heart sank at the sight of Hollie jumping out and hurtling into the building, but the glimpse of

Jason set her pulse racing. She longed to reach out for him and hold him close, to feel secure and happy in his arms once more. But then she would remember the look in his eyes that evening he came back from the club. It still haunted her, the way he had backed away from her as though she had been an object of scorn.

From then on she had tried to keep away from the window when he visited and concentrate on her work. Only once had she weakened and gone to the window, just as he was leaving. She had been horrified when he had suddenly glanced up and she had pulled back abruptly, almost taking the curtain with her.

Anna was determined that this visit was going to be treated as just routine and settled herself at the table with the files in front of her. She started working and twenty minutes later she heard the familiar crunch of gravel and a car pulling up in front of the main door. She struggled with her desire to go to the window and leaned her elbows on the table to prevent herself moving. When everything went quiet she continued working for a further hour. There was plenty to do, bookings were coming in at a fast rate and the first wedding was to be held in mid-February.

After a while, she lifted her head and stretched herself. It was then that she saw a small table in the corner that seemed to be covered with shiny bits of metal. She decided to give herself a breather and wandered over. To her surprise she saw that it was an improvised workbench for making jewellery.

"It's my hobby, miss," said Irene, coming in with a steaming mug of coffee. "Thought I'd bring a drink up for you. No point in you going thirsty."

Anna took it from her. "You make jewellery as a hobby?"

Irene looked down at the table. "Done it for years. I make earrings, pendants and necklaces. Some are special jobs for folk in Wedmore, for birthday and anniversary gifts. But I do sell them at craft fairs too."

Seeing that Anna was showing interest in her pastime, Irene then described how she made the jewellery using all kinds of stones and mounting them in frames and attaching chains. She even brought out a box containing finished products. Anna had never seen anything so lovely and wondered if she should buy something for her sister and mother, or even for herself.

Suddenly she had an idea. "You couldn't make this into a pendant for me, could you?"

She took the coin from her pocket and showed it to her.

"But it's a ten pence, miss," said the cook, looking very bewildered.

Anna laughed. "I know, but I wondered if you could make it so I could wear it round my neck."

Irene took the coin in her hand. "Seems to me this is more than just money."

Anna felt embarrassed. "Yes…Yes it is. I know it sounds silly but it would mean a lot to me."

"I can put it in a frame and attach a chain. Would that do?"

"That would be perfect."

They heard voices drifting up from below and Anna wandered to the window keeping carefully concealed behind the curtain.

"You ought to tell him, miss," said Irene thoughtfully.

"Tell him what?" said Anna, not taking her eyes off the man getting in the car.

"That you're expecting a baby."

Anna spun round. "Expecting a baby! What makes you think that?"

Irene gave a knowing smile and tapped her nose. "Fran said she found ginger biscuits in your room. And ginger is a good remedy for sickness."

"I like ginger biscuits," said Anna scornfully.

Irene shrugged. "OK, I admit it! I saw you coming out of the doctors and I knew it was antenatal day."

Anna groaned. "Oh, Irene, I need to keep it a secret."

"I won't tell, miss. I won't even mention it to my husband. But it's going to get very awkward as you get bigger. Someone in Wedmore is going to notice and news travels fast round these parts."

Anna thought for a moment. "Then I'll not go out unless it's absolutely necessary. I shall stay in the Grange and never go further than the grounds."

"Well, the grounds are big enough for you to get plenty of fresh air and exercise," said Irene pursing her lips. "But that kind of secret is bound to come out soon."

Shaking her head sadly, Irene took Anna's empty coffee mug and they both made their way back down to the kitchen.

The first wedding at the Grange turned out to be a great success. The day was beautiful, crisp and clear with a vivid blue sky. The bride looked stunning and the groom looked handsome. All in all it was a perfect day and when the guests departed and the staff were clearing up, Anna went to the library feeling satisfied.

"Well done!" said Margaret from the doorway. "You should be very pleased with yourself."

"I really enjoyed it," smiled Anna. "There's no more now until March, but after that they come thick and fast."

Margaret came further into the room. "I've just had a call from Jason. He's decided to take Hollie on a trip to Florida, to visit Disney World for two weeks."

"Sounds lovely."

"So, how about you phoning your family and asking them to visit?"

Anna could hardly speak with surprise. "I would love to see them."

"Then it's decided. It's about time you saw your sons again."

Anna was suddenly filled with doubts. "Please don't tell them about the baby. I want to tell them in my own time." She bit her lip hoping that Margaret wouldn't be offended, but all she received was a complacent nod.

The second weekend that Jason and Hollie were away, Anna's mother, sister and two sons arrived at the Grange.

Her mother and sister were impressed with the Grange and Anna spent hours showing them round and telling them about her work. Enquiries about Jason made the situation a little uncomfortable, since obviously they wanted to meet the new man in her life after hearing so much about him from the boys. But Anna kept her secret and said that he was out of the country, which was the truth. Thankfully, no further questions were asked.

The talk round the dinner table that first evening was convivial at first.

"Why are you working here now?" asked Martyn, glancing round the impressive dining room, decorated in soft creams and beige. "Not that I begrudge you, it's a beautiful place."

His mother smiled. "I'm helping Margaret sort out the weddings. She has lots to do what with the business seminars and such like."

Margaret grinned at the boys. "And while your mum is here you must come and visit any time you wish. You'll always be welcome."

The twins nodded in appreciation. But then the conversation turned to their parents' divorce.

"How long do you think it'll be?" said Chris. Martyn had already told her that of the two of them, Chris was taking the divorce a little harder.

Anna grimaced. "I've been told it will be over by the summer." She put her arm round her younger son and brushed the blond hair from his forehead forgetting that he was nearly nineteen. His expression told her how sad he felt and her heart ached. "I'm sorry to have to put you through this."

"But you still did!" laughed her mother sarcastically.

"Mum!" said Elaine sharply. "We agreed it would be a pleasant visit and no bad feelings."

Her mother shrugged. "It needs to be said."

Anna turned on her. "Elaine is right. Please don't spoil your visit. And besides, I did what I thought best."

Her mother grimaced. "I know you're enjoying this new life of yours, Anna. And I can see why. But I think it's better to persevere with a marriage. It's for better or worse, you know."

Margaret felt she ought to intervene. "But sometimes it's better to end a marriage that makes a woman unhappy and it's worse for the children if she struggles trying to make it work."

Anna cast her a warm smile.

"Dave's not a bad husband," insisted her mother. "He's always been a good provider and she's never done without. She didn't need to work!"

"Mum, I told you. He's a womaniser," whispered Elaine.

Her mother gave an exaggerated sigh. "Well, it was different in my day. You just got on with it no matter what your husband was like. A woman was happy just to have a husband what with the war and everything."

Anna was glad when Margaret suggested driving the boys and Anna's mother to see the farm and she was able to have a peaceful chat with Elaine. Since Elaine was a midwife and they had always been close, Anna decided to tell her about her pregnancy. They were walking round the garden when she made her confession.

"I'm due at the beginning of September, but I haven't told Mum or the boys yet."

"But you must tell her. She'll love being a grandma again."

"Perhaps, but she's not pleased about my divorce and I can't imagine her being delighted about me having a child out of wedlock. It will be too much like the first time!"

Elaine gave a gentle laugh. "Mum can be old fashioned that way."

"I wondered if you'd tell her, but a little later on?"

Elaine squeezed her hand. "Of course. I can't wait to meet this new man of yours." A thought suddenly occurred to her. "I suppose you're going to have to postpone your wedding if you're pregnant?"

Anna nodded not wanting to get into any conversation about Jason. "I'll be going for a scan in April, so after that you can tell Mum."

"Are you going to ask the sex of the baby?" said Elaine, her eyes shining.

"I'm not sure. Probably not."

"Oh well, keeps it a surprise I suppose." She studied the Grange and gave a low whistle. "Mind you, if it's a boy, he's going to inherit one hell of a fortune when he grows up."

Anna smiled. "Perhaps." She swallowed hard at the thought of how things should have been. "I'd like to have the baby here."

Elaine turned abruptly to face her. "No, Anna! You need to be in hospital."

"I'll be well looked after, better than any hospital."

"You haven't had a baby for a long time so your body is starting from scratch. It'll be like having a first baby again and the doctor won't know what's going to happen."

Anna was adamant. "I know it will be OK."

Elaine shook her head. "You're risking your baby's life as well as your own! You're a lot older now, there might be complications."

"Can you come down and deliver it?"

Elaine smiled and linking her arm through Anna's, they carried on walking.

"I can't I'm afraid. I'm not authorised to deliver babies down here. You'll have your own midwife."

"Sister Davenport is very good, very competent."

"And the doctor?"

"Doctor Orchard is wonderful. He's a friend of the family."

"Then I suggest you talk to him and see what he suggests. But I reckon he'll advise you to book into a hospital where there's the facilities in case anything goes wrong."

"Nothing is going to go wrong."

"Well, let's hope not!"

After her family had left, Anna had to reflect that the visit hadn't gone as she had thought. She had not realised that her mother would be so hostile to her divorce, or Elaine so against her having a home birth. On the subject of her giving birth at the Grange, she knew everything would be fine. But more than that, she had convinced herself that if she had the baby in Jason's boyhood home, then Jason would turn out to be the father.

"I think it definitely looks like a boy," said Margaret, bringing the car to a halt at traffic lights.

"How can you tell?" laughed Anna. "It could be just as much a girl."

"No, it's the way he's punching the air with his fist. Reminds me of Jason at school when he won an event on sport's day. He used to do just that."

Anna smiled and looked down again at the scan picture. The trip to the hospital had gone very well and the radiographer had confirmed that she was expecting a healthy child with nothing to worry about. But she had declined his offer of knowing the child's sex. That could wait until the birth.

"I want the baby at the Grange," she said quietly.

This sudden statement caused Margaret to grind the gears. "But I thought you were booked in at the hospital?"

"I am but I've told Doctor Orchard and the midwife that I want a home delivery. The hospital is only a precaution in case anything goes wrong during my pregnancy."

Margaret stayed silent for a good thirty seconds. "I really don't like that idea, Anna."

"Well, you're not the only one. Doctor Orchard and Sister Davenport felt just the same."

"I don't blame them. In fact, I can imagine Colin being very reluctant. It was his father who tried to deliver my first child and we all know how that went!"

Anna was more positive. "Ah, but the sister finally agreed that I'm having a text book pregnancy and I'm very healthy. She had to admit that she couldn't see any problems with having the baby at the Grange and she told Doctor Orchard that."

"So, Colin agreed?"

"Not exactly. He said he's not going to promise anything until two weeks before the baby is due. If everything is OK then, he'll make his decision." She thought for a moment. "And you mustn't forget I've given birth to two babies in the past and I was fine with them."

"But I'm sure you didn't have the twins at home."

Anna shook her head slowly. "No, I didn't. But they could have been born at home, labour and birth were very much straightforward."

"You sound as though you've made up your mind."

Anna stroked the coin now hanging round her neck on a silver chain. "I really would like this baby at the Grange. But I want you to be happy about it."

Margaret gave a sad sigh. "My little Christina didn't live long enough to draw her first breath."

Anna looked down at the photo again. "I realise that. But that was over fifty years ago and it's different now. Doctors are better trained. And besides, it'll only happen if my pregnancy gives no cause for concern. That's Doctor Orchard's very words."

Margaret smiled. "It would be nice to have a baby born at the Grange. And a boy!"

"You're obsessed with boys," giggled Anna.

Margaret hesitated for a moment before saying, "You're still wearing your engagement ring."

"Can't get it off. My fingers have swollen a little."

Margaret gave a half-smile. "Any more thoughts about telling Jason?" she said, after a minute of silence.

Anna looked out of the window watching the people rush by on their various errands. She decided to answer a question with a question. "Does he ever mention me when he visits?"

"Never. Although Hollie talks about you constantly."

Anna smiled. "I miss her so much."

"And Jason?"

Anna glanced at Margaret. How could she admit that she missed him with a longing that drove her crazy? That she ached for the man she loved and yearned to feel him close, especially at night when she was alone in bed. How could she explain how much she had wanted to run into his arms every time he had visited and confess everything?

"He still thinks I had an affair."

"But he never speaks of it. Perhaps he's had second thoughts. Perhaps he's realised that he misjudged you terribly."

"Somehow, I don't think so. If he'd changed his mind, then he would have said something to you."

"I might be his mother, but he doesn't tell me everything."

They had reached the gates of the Grange and Anna smiled as they passed through. Spring had arrived, the bluebells and primroses carpeting the meadows and woodlands, the daffodils and tulips blooming either side of the drive and in the garden. All around her the world was bursting into life, the trees just starting to bud with cherry blossom. But then her smile faded at the thought that Jason had put her into the past along with Kiera. He thought her a faithless woman and he would never forgive her.

"You've lost another one!" Graham studied his business partner with concerned eyes, this state of affairs couldn't go on for too long.

"I'm sorry, I did my best," said Jason dryly.

"I don't think you did. You've not been right since Christmas. In fact, not since you and Anna separated."

"Anna has nothing to do with it! It's more difficult to win contracts now. There's more competition."

Graham knew he was making excuses. "That's not the case!" He checked the computer. "We've lost three contracts in as many months. If this carries on, we'll all be looking for new jobs."

"We've got the Singapore contract."

"Thank goodness for that! But it won't keep everyone occupied. The last thing we want is to start laying people off."

Jason was sitting in Graham's office. The trip he had just come back from had been an unmitigated disaster. He had not clinched the deal and worse than that, their main competitor had won it instead. He glanced through the glass partition separating Graham from the main office. The employees of Harrington Rhodes Shipping Agents were going about their business as usual. He knew most of them by name and his heart sank at the thought of them losing their livelihoods. They depended on him and he was letting them down.

"I'm going for another in a few weeks."

Graham shook his head. "It's only a small one." He studied his partner carefully. "You don't seem to be motivated any more. It's as though you've completely lost interest in the business."

"That's not true!" Jason leaned back in his chair rubbing his forehead, trying to ease his splitting head. But deep down he knew Graham was right. He had lost his ambition, his drive to achieve.

Zahra, Graham's secretary came in with some aspirin and Jason took them from her gratefully, swallowing them with a glass of water Graham had poured for him.

Graham let out a breath. "Well, at the moment everything's just steady. Harrington Rhodes is still doing OK. But we can't afford to lose any more contracts."

"I know, you don't have to tell me that," Jason sighed.

Graham stared down at the document on his desk.

"We've had an offer. From Matthew Gilbert in San Francisco. A very good offer actually, to buy us out. Of course, we would stay on as directors, but we would be fairly rich men…"

"You want to sell the business?" Jason sat forward in his seat.

Graham shrugged. "It is a good offer. It will certainly solve our current financial problems."

Jason narrowed his eyes at him. "Matthew Gilbert? Isn't that an advertising firm run by Deborah's father?"

Graham nodded. "A huge advertising company. Its turnover is billions per year."

"Why are they interested in a shipping agency?"

"I'll remember to ask next time they call. But it's something to think about."

"No, it's not! Sell our company! We started this business from almost nothing and we've done well."

"Up to now!"

Jason stood, wanting to go home. "No, Graham. We'll bounce back. I promise you that. It won't be necessary to sell us out, especially not to the father of Deborah Gilbert-Hines."

But he didn't go home. Instead he stopped at a wine bar just near the city centre. He craved some peace and quiet, a moment to himself. Going back to Bishop Sutton didn't hold the attraction it once had and besides, if he waited a little longer, Natalie would have left. He couldn't face her sombreness, not today, and certainly not after Graham's proposals.

Jason made himself comfortable at the end of the bar and absorbed himself in his newspaper, trying to forget the terrible day he had had. Ten minutes went by before a light touch on his arm brought his attention back.

"Would you like to buy me a drink?" He looked up to see a woman with large, almond eyes smiling at him. "A gin and tonic would be nice." Jason frowned slightly, the woman looked familiar. "Have you forgotten me? It's Thalia!"

Jason smiled back, folded his newspaper and ordered the required drink. "Now, fancy meeting you here after all these years."

"I've been trying to get your attention for the last five minutes," she laughed. "But you seemed to be in a world of your own."

They talked for the next forty minutes. Jason and Thalia had met at university when he was in his final year. They had been an item for only three months since Thalia was of a restless nature and couldn't seem to settle with one man for too long. And it seemed she hadn't changed. With two brief marriages behind her, she still had that haunted look of a woman on an endless quest for happiness. But Jason was starting to enjoy her company. As they reminisced over old times, he suddenly realised that she was flirting with him and he was enjoying that too. He had missed the male-female teasing and she was distracting him from his problems, easing the pain. And for that, he was very thankful.

By the end of an hour she was leaning against him, her hand on his shoulder. He knew that she was sitting too close, he could smell her perfume and the softness of her body filled him with desire. He desperately wanted to forget the last four months, wanted to fill his mind with new images instead of the constant ache he had for a certain blonde who was now hundreds of miles away and perhaps, with someone new.

He slipped his arm round her waist and pulled her closer. She brushed her lips against his and he closed his eyes, gasping at the excitement that surged through him. She had always been a seductive creature. When she suggested going back to her place for old time's sake, he nodded and gulped down his drink, while she paid a visit to the ladies room.

Suddenly, a young couple rushed through the door laughing with delight. The man was carrying a car seat and snuggled in blankets a small baby, only a few weeks old, slept peacefully. They were greeted by friends who had been waiting for them and who crowded round the infant, eager to see the new arrival. Jason watched as if hypnotised.

The young couple beamed with pride and answered the barrage of questions with delight.

"The house is unrecognisable," said the young father with a chuckle. "I keep tripping over stuff and there's strange smells and sounds everywhere. And as for a good night's sleep; forget it!"

Out of the corner of his eye, Jason saw Thalia coming towards him, looking so beautiful and oozing sex appeal, but yet her entire demeanour smacked of emptiness. It wasn't so long ago that he and Anna were planning their future, a wedding and even talking about having a baby. He hesitated. Was this what he really wanted, a one-night stand with a woman he had just met again after twenty years? And there was no doubt it would be just a brief fling, Thalia didn't do permanency. It would be a moment of pleasure and then it would be gone and the pain would return. He wanted more than that! He wanted a life with meaning. He had found that meaning with Anna and now that he had tasted it, he couldn't tolerate anything less. Thalia slipped her arm through his.

Jason shook his head apologetically. "I'm sorry…I've just realised…I can't go with you. My daughter will be waiting…" He gently removed her arm. "Sorry…I must leave."

He left her standing alone, bewildered and frustrated and with the conviction that she had been right about men all along.

Jason sat on the bed, his head in his hands. Life was shit. He could lose his business just as he had lost Anna. He lifted his face and looked around the room. Mrs Thompson had done too good a job. Every trace of Anna had been swept and polished away. He had tried to find something of her, a strand of hair; a small possession left behind, even an item of clothing overlooked in the wardrobe or drawer. But there was nothing, only his memories and some photos were left. He was full of regrets. He regretted ever interviewing her for the position of PA, or offering her the job in the first place. But she had stepped into his office and with one look she had ignited something deep inside him. And that fire, dampened down for a while, was starting to burn brightly once more.

He had been attracted to her from the moment he saw her. And it wasn't just her loveliness, but the wonderful innocence he had sensed almost immediately. He stood up abruptly, clenching his hands in a tight fist. But she had shattered his dreams; she wasn't so innocent after all. She had betrayed his trust and he couldn't forgive her for that. She was out of his life and he would accept it. If only he could forget her. Forget the feel of her, smell of her, taste of her. Sometimes he thought he would go insane with the memories that haunted him. He heard Hollie calling him and glancing quickly round the room, he went to read the obligatory bedtime story.

The phone call came at the end of April. Anna was overjoyed when Nigel told her that her decree nisi was on its way with the absolute following six weeks later.

"Your husband has already sent the cheque to buy you out of the property and I'll forward that on." He hesitated for a moment. "It's only fifty-seven thousand, but I can try for more if you wish."

Anna sighed. That would work out at three thousand for every year she had been married!

"I'll go with that. Were the boys mentioned?"

"He's agreed to pay all relevant expenses for their university education."

"Oh, good. But somehow I thought he would do that."

Nigel could sense her sadness despite her agreeable manner. "Is everything OK with the baby?"

"Yes, I'm fine. Quite healthy actually. But pregnancy always did suit me."

Margaret had decided to host a special lunch in celebration of Jason's birthday that was in early May. Anna listened to Margaret's plans with dismay. Jason would be at the Grange all afternoon and for most of the evening and she would have to go to John and Irene's apartment while he was there. Suddenly, Anna felt frustrated. She had so wanted to be with Jason on his birthday and the yearning became more acute.

She had a busy time ahead of her, with three interviews and two weddings at the weekend. The bookings seemed endless with her phone ringing every minute of the day. At the moment she was coping well, since she was still in the second three months of her pregnancy and she had always considered that the best time. Her sickness had passed and she had not yet reached the uncomfortable, back aching stage. Even so, Margaret had insisted that she rest as much as possible and when she did get too cumbersome, she must pass some of the workload onto her. Anna felt very reluctant about doing that. Planning the weddings was her responsibility and she would relinquish the work with a heavy heart.

The guests arrived for the birthday lunch and Anna was hustled out of the way by Fran.

"I feel like Cinderella," she said, as she made her way to the apartment, with numerous folders tucked under her arm. "And I've not been invited to the ball."

Once there, she absorbed herself in her work while the family greeted one another just below her.

She was roused from her concentration by a gentle knock on the door. Anna was delighted to find Sophia waiting on the threshold and drew her into the living room.

"I thought we could have a chat."

"Won't the others miss you?"

Sophia shook her head. "They've all gone outside to enjoy the garden before sitting down to lunch. The weather is so beautiful today. I told them I had to pop to the loo."

"Is everyone OK?" asked Anna wistfully. "Ben and Mrs Wilby?"

"They're absolutely fine. But I know they miss you, especially Hollie"

Anna gave a strained laugh. "Well, you'd better not spend too long on the loo, or they'll think you've got a gippy tummy." She drew her down to sit next to her on the couch.

"You look very well, positively radiant," smiled Sophia

"I feel well and everything's going great."

"How's Margaret been?"

"Unbelievable. So kind and caring. I don't know what I'd have done without her help. She's convinced I'm having a boy to carry on the Harrington line."

"So, she doesn't know that…"

Anna looked at her aghast. "Of course she doesn't know! How can I tell her anything like that? In fact, only you and Nigel know the real truth."

"What will you do after the baby's born? Jason will have to know then."

"I'm not thinking that far ahead."

"He could have a DNA test. Then you'll know if he's the father."

"But then I'll have to tell him *why* he might not be the father. I couldn't bear that."

Sophia reached across and took her hand. "Whatever happens, Nigel and I are still here for you. We'll give you every support."

Anna squeezed her hand in gratitude.

Jason left the others to go back inside and fetch his sunglasses. As he passed the door of the morning room, he couldn't resist peeping inside. The room was made up for the marriage ceremonies, the chairs in tidy rows, with the end ones decorated with a white, silk ribbon. Huge pedestals of flowers stood either side of the large oak table where the register was signed and the air was filled with the fragrance. Jason liked the way white, silk material had been draped over the walls giving the room a soft appearance and as he looked about him, he could see the hard work that went into organising these events. He couldn't imagine how his mother managed since she still had the business seminars and conferences to cope with.

Jason felt restless and wandered out into the hall. He didn't know what made him start climbing the stairs; it was as though he was drawn to Anna's old room. Standing outside the door, her delightful laugher echoed through his mind. He closed his eyes and remembered how much they had shared on their summer visit to the Grange. How they had made love for the first time after his mother's party. His hand reached out for the handle and he slowly turned it. But it didn't give and then he realised it was locked.

Fran appeared, a look of complete horror spreading across her face when she saw him standing outside the door.

"Why's this room locked?" he asked.

She came to stand beside him, staring at the door as if she had never seen it before.

"Madam must have done it."

"But why?"

Fran shrugged. She wasn't very good at making up stories. Suddenly she remembered when the morning room had been locked during its renovations for the wedding ceremonies and Madam's instructions then.

"Because it's been painted and there's ladders and equipment all over the place. And we don't want people to go in and trip over and have an accident," she mimicked, smiling in triumph that she sounded just like Mrs Harrington.

Jason raised his eyebrows in surprise. "Got the key? I'd like to see what they're doing."

"Madam's got key," she murmured, shaking her head.

He grunted in frustration and decided to give up. At the bottom of the stairs he met Sophia just coming through the door that led to the stairs down to the kitchen.

"Where've you been?"

She gave him a bright smile. "Been talking to Irene. She's making you a wonderful meal." She didn't wait for further comment but skipped across the marble floor to the main door. Jason followed her outside into the bright sunshine, completely forgetting why he had gone inside in the first place.

Sophia was right and the meal was wonderful, but Jason felt the need to bring up the subject of Anna's room.

"The door was locked. Why is that?"

Margaret shrugged nonchalantly. "Thought it needed decorating. And I didn't want anyone going in there and getting hurt. Ladders and things." She was grateful that Fran had told her about her son's curiosity.

"May I see what you're doing?"

"Oh, it's a mess at the moment. Perhaps after it's finished."

Jason took a sip of his wine. "The morning room looks lovely. The white material on the walls is very effective."

"Oh, that was Ann…another good idea from Sarah." She quickly took a drink of water. "She's got quite a knack for interior design. Should have taken it up as a career."

Jason watched his mother keenly. She seemed to have developed a stammer, although he knew that normally she was a very articulate woman. He also noticed that Nigel cast her a warning glance. He narrowed his eyes. There was something going on at the Grange and it seemed he wasn't in on the secret.

CHAPTER EIGHTEEN

"He's still hurting terribly," said Sophia, as they drove home after a night out at the theatre.

"You're right there."

"And I don't think he's doing very well at Harrington Rhodes."

"What makes you think that?"

"A little bird told me that he's losing business. He's not winning the contracts like he used to."

Nigel blew out a breath. "Well, that state of affairs can't go on for too long."

"So, I think you should tell him!"

"Why me?"

"He can't carry on the way he is. He needs to know about Anna and the baby."

"And how will that help him?"

"At least he'll know the truth. It's terrible keeping him in the dark like this."

"But that's how Anna wants it. And I ask again, why me?"

"Because you can have one of those 'man to man' chats."

"No, I can't! I was told in confidence, as you were. It's unethical to go around breaking client's confidences."

Sophia thought for a moment. "You're dealing with Anna's divorce and that has no bearing on what happened to her. So, you'll not be breaking a confidence."

"Well, that's cockeyed reasoning for you! And besides she told me as a friend as well as a solicitor and that still makes it a confidence."

She sniffed in disgust. "I can't tell him. I'm her counsellor. And you've known Jason a lot longer than you've known Anna. Doesn't your friendship with him mean anything?"

Nigel shook his head in exasperation. "Why don't you send him an anonymous letter? From a 'well wisher' or 'interested friend'."

"Don't be facetious!" She paused before adding, "I've invited him to dinner next week."

"Oh, joy! I shall look forward to that!"

"Let's see what happens then." She lit up a cigarette and sighed. "So much for trying to give it up. But there's always next year."

The evening was very pleasant, as it always was when he visited Nigel and his family. His last two business trips had brought about a modicum of success. He had won the contracts but only just. He felt confident that the next few would be a lot easier. His life was getting easier now that he had established a routine of living from one day to the next and not thinking too far into the future. As for the offer from the American company? He had managed to persuade Graham to put that on hold for the time being.

"How's your new secretary doing?" asked Nigel, as he poured Jason another glass of wine.

"Oh, Natalie. She's fine. She gets on with her work and then rushes home at the end of the day."

"Doesn't like putting in the extra hours, then?"

"No, she likes to be gone as soon as she can and she can't do Saturdays. But I took her on with that understanding. I can't expect any more from her since she has a family to care for."

"Very different from Anna, who left her husband to work for you," said Sophia sharply.

Jason peered at her over his wineglass. He had never seen her so tense. "But Anna lied to me about her husband. And unfortunately, she couldn't stop lying." He gave a sigh. "I'm glad she's gone back to Wakefield!" He thought that if he said it enough times he would eventually convince himself of the truth.

"But Anna isn't…!" she started.

"Sophia!" interrupted Nigel. Sophia started at the angry tone of her husband and even Jason gave him a sidelong glance with surprise. In all the years he had known the couple, he had never heard either of them speak harshly to one another. Sophia rose from her seat and Jason could see tears in her eyes, a fact that also made him look on in amazement since she had always seemed a woman not given to emotional outbursts. She left the room hastily. "Sorry about that," said

Nigel, giving a grimace. "I'll go and see if she's OK. Won't be a minute."

"Take as long as you need," said Jason. Somehow it seemed comforting to see another man suffering strife in his relationship and although Jason wouldn't have wished it on anyone, it made him smile that he was not the only one in the world with problems. But then his thoughts went back to Sophia and her outburst. Why did he get the impression that her tears came from frustration, rather than emotional upset? Nigel was gone ten minutes and returned rather subdued. He took his seat next to Jason and poured himself another glass of wine. He offered some to Jason, who declined politely. "How is she?"

"Angry with me."

Jason threw back his head and started laughing. "The trials and tribulations of married life. Don't I know it well!"

Nigel shook his head. "We've had our spats in the past but not like this one."

"It must be bad. I know it's none of my business, but if you want a friendly ear..." said Jason, smiling.

Nigel studied him for a few seconds. "Actually, the argument is about you and whether we should break a confidence."

Jason frowned. "That's a tough decision. However, if it's about me, then I'd rather know."

"I thought you might say that. Sophia believes you ought to know about a certain someone and that I should be the one to tell you."

Jason shuffled uncomfortably in his chair. "If you're talking about Anna, then it's not really a topic I would care to discuss."

"And I understand that. But you know my wife!"

Jason took a sip of his wine, nodded and placed his glass carefully on the table. "Then let me make this easier for you since I wouldn't want to come between you and your wife. You've both been worried about me since Anna and I parted and I appreciate that. I imagine that the 'confidence' you've heard is the fact that I accused her of having an affair and you want to assure me that Anna couldn't possibly have behaved that way since it isn't in her nature."

Nigel frowned. "You think Anna had an affair?"

Jason raised his eyebrows in surprise. "Oh, it's not about that, then? Well, I don't think she had an affair, I jolly well know she did! And nothing will convince me otherwise, so don't even try!" He reached for his wineglass and nearly tipped it over with his shaking hands.

Nigel sat back in his chair. "Why did you think she was having an affair?"

"Because I can read the signs."

"And the signs are…?"

Jason thought his friend was becoming irritating. "I asked her if she'd met someone else and she couldn't give me a straight answer. And she couldn't look me in the eye."

"And you built your case round that information only? I'm glad you're a shipping agent and not a solicitor. You would be sending innocent folk to prison every day!"

"Ah, but I had a star witness."

"Who?"

"I'd rather not say. But this person saw…" Jason took another gulp of wine and tried to steady himself. "Saw Anna going into the Marriott Hotel with a man. And leaving quite a long time later." He turned his face away, so that Nigel couldn't see the pain in his eyes.

"Did you establish the identity of this man?"

Jason turned back and cleared his throat. "Does that matter?"

"She might have met a friend and just gone to have a drink with him."

Jason shook his head slowly. "That's what I said until I discovered she was seen coming out of the lift leading to the bedrooms."

Silence followed as Jason tried to control his emotions.

"Did your star witness tell you that this man could have been a family member from her home town?" said Nigel softly.

Jason put down his glass and stared at his friend. "A relative?"

Nigel nodded. "And somehow he managed to track her down."

"Track her down! What on earth are you talking about?"

"In my experience an irate husband is very cunning at finding a missing wife, hence the hundreds of injunctions I have to apply for each year."

These revelations made Jason's head swim. "You're saying this man could have been her husband?" Nigel made no comment. "And he came to Bristol and…found her!" He gasped with shock. "But she wouldn't go to a hotel with him. She hated him and I know she was afraid of what he might do."

Nigel took in a breath, feeling uncomfortable and yet knowing this was for the best. He began to tell Jason everything and Jason listened, leaning forward in his chair, his elbows resting on the table. When Nigel came to Anna's ordeal at the hands of her husband, Jason felt himself shaking, his heart beating in his throat. He leaned on one elbow and slowly cupped his hand round his mouth, as if to stifle the cry that was erupting inside him. At the conclusion, Nigel took a sip of wine and kept silent. Jason found he couldn't speak, his mind filled with memories of his return from Singapore and the fact that, for a while, Anna had changed towards him. She was so tense and nervous that he knew something was terribly wrong.

"My wife's been counselling her," Nigel said, breaking into his horrified thoughts. "Sophia is very good at her job. Sometimes she must hear worse things than I do."

Jason found his voice. "Why didn't Anna tell me?"

Sophia appeared in the doorway. "Because women who are raped are also brutalised into believing that those they love will be hurt if they speak out." She took a seat at the table. "And if anything keeps them quiet that does."

"He threatened her sons? That's despicable."

Sophia nodded. "Not physical violence you'll understand. The simple fact that their father might be arrested and sent to prison is an awful burden for a young person to have to carry. Anna didn't want to lay that on their shoulders."

Jason gave a low moan and sank back into his chair. "Oh, Lord! I was thousands of miles away! I wasn't there to help her. And then I go and accuse her of having an affair, after all she'd been through!"

"But as you say, she kept it from you," said Nigel.

Jason reached out for his wine and gulped it down. "I would have insisted on calling the police and that would have been the last thing she wanted." His ideas were turning, as he became oblivious to the people sitting with him. "I must find her and tell her that I know and that I'm so sorry for behaving the way I did." He shook his head in frustration. "But I don't know where she went. I assumed she went back to live with her mother in Wakefield." Nigel and Sophia exchanged wary glances. Jason noticed. "Oh, come on you two! Is there something else?"

"Well, I think I'll go and answer the call of nature," said Nigel, rising from his chair.

Sophia and Jason were left alone. "I'm afraid there were consequences," said Sophia.

Jason shook his head slowly. "You might as well tell me everything."

"She's expecting a baby."

He stared at her in disbelief. "No, that's impossible. She told me she'd been…"

"Fitted with the coil?" said Sophia. Jason nodded. "And she had been for some years. But she had it removed, when she realised that you'd like another child."

He gave a groan. "Yes, I remember our discussion."

Sophia smiled sadly. "She wanted to give you the news at Christmas. As a very special present."

He felt so wretched that nausea engulfed him. "And because she did that for me, she left herself vulnerable. My poor sweetheart."

Sophia reached out and took his hand. "But you must remember that this child could be as much yours as his."

"She doesn't know for certain?"

"No Jason, she doesn't. How could she know?"

He licked his lips. "I've got to contact her. Please, please Sophia, if you know where she is then please tell me."

She smiled but suddenly became serious. "If I tell you where she is, you must promise me something."

"Anything!"

"Don't go putting any pressure on her. She's been through a lot and she needs to move at her own pace. You're going to have to start at the beginning and win her confidence and her heart all over again." Jason nodded slowly. She studied him, thinking. "Anna told me about a letter she received from her husband shortly after starting work for you?"

"Yes, she burnt it."

"Did she tell you what was in it?"

"No, not really, except that it wasn't pleasant."

"It contained an indirect threat against you."

He leaned forward, clenching his fists on the table. "What!"

"I said an indirect threat. I believe he was trying to intimidate her by threatening the man he believed took her away from him. At the time it didn't matter since you weren't together, but now circumstances are different."

"He won't hurt me," said Jason, giving a crooked smile. "I'd like him to try."

"That's as may be, but please remember that he doesn't have to use his fists to hurt either Anna or you, or even her boys." She sighed sadly. "I've been a rape counsellor for a very long time and of all the hundreds of women I've tried to help, unfortunately I've lost three."

"Lost?" he queried.

Sophia nodded. "Two took an overdose and one cut her wrists."

"Women have actually committed suicide over what happened to them?"

"Oh yes. People often don't realise the dreadful consequences of an assault on a woman. It devastates her life and can destroy her relationship with her partner. And sometimes it becomes too much for her to handle and she finds another way to free herself from the pain."

Jason shook his head. "I never realised this."

"Men often don't." She paused and carefully folded her serviette. "I reminded Anna that she could have an abortion, but she turned it down flat."

"She would," he sighed.

"What I'm trying to say is that Anna has somehow remained strong throughout all this. And I believe that the only thing that's kept her going is that she hopes this child is yours. When you meet up with her, you must keep that hope alive for her."

"I certainly will," he whispered.

Sophia thought for a few seconds more but then nodded in satisfaction. "She's living at the Grange with your mother."

Jason had to force himself to drive straight home and not go to the Grange. Lying in bed that night he formed a plan. He needed to go to the main office in the morning and talk to Graham but after that he would set off and this time he would not phone beforehand. He would make an unexpected visit and catch them unawares. He rolled over and pulled Anna's pillow towards him, holding it close.

He had sensed a conspiracy many times, but had put it down to his imagination. Jason remembered his mother stumbling over her words at his birthday lunch. She hadn't stammered at all, she had made a slip of the tongue, nearly saying Anna's name and had stopped herself just in time.

His mind drifted back to Christmas and his return from Singapore. Things had been very strained between Anna and him. It was as if she had been repelled by intimacy and he had assumed it was because she was seeing someone else! Jason gasped in horror. Intimacy must have been so physically painful for her. She must have been bruised and hurting every time he made love to her and he hadn't even realised. It had never crossed his mind that anything like that had happened to her. And then he remembered the night of the Christmas party when he had totally misunderstood the situation. He had thought she wanted to play a little game, but in fact she was terrified of him because she thought he was going to force himself on her. He would never do that sort of thing, but after what she had been through, she had reacted instinctively.

Sleep came reluctantly and Jason was very relieved when morning came and he could start his day.

"You're a little more cheerful this morning," said Mrs Wilby.

"Am I?" came back his vague reply.

"Must be the lovely weather," said Ben.

"Yes, it is a beautiful day," Jason agreed with a smile.

Hollie poured milk over her cereal and watched as it turned a muddy brown colour. "That's what you've been like," she sniffed. "Like a pond filled with dirty water."

Jason looked up from the document he was reading. "Have I? Well, I'm hoping that things will be different from now on." He threw the file into his briefcase and snapped the catches shut. "Are you ready, sweetie? You don't want to be late for school."

Hollie gave him a withering look. "Daddy, does it look like I'm wearing my uniform! It's half-term!"

"Oh, I didn't realise that. Well, I'd better get myself off."

He strode towards the door and gave a cheerful wave as he disappeared. The others watched him until he was out of sight.

"Something's afoot," said Ben and then he glimpsed Natalie. "Oh Lord, here comes the wet weekend to spoil everything!"

Jason had a good meeting with Graham, there were at least three contracts in the pipeline and if Jason could pull them off, things would start looking up. At first, Graham was startled and then pleased that his business partner seemed more motivated. There was an earnest look on his face that he hadn't seen for many months, an energy and vitality that gave him hope.

At the conclusion of the discussion, Jason got up to go. Why this idea suddenly occurred to him he had no idea, but it was as if it jumped into his head.

"Did anything strange happen at Christmas?"

Graham stared at him in surprise. "Strange? In what way?"

Jason tried to be nonchalant. "Did anything happen that gave you cause for concern?"

His partner gave a soft chuckle. "Jason, I can barely remember what happened last week, never mind at Christmas."

"Well, if anything does occur to you, then let me know."

Zahra was just clearing away the coffee cups and had been listening in on the conversation.

"There was that man in the car, Graham."

"What man in what car?" said Jason curiously.

"He was parked across from the car park. I noticed him about mid-morning. Sitting there for hours he was and I thought that very suspicious. But then when I looked sometime in the afternoon, he was gone."

"He'd driven away?"

"Oh, no," said Zahra. "His car was still there, but he'd gone."

"Thank you, Zahra. Don't forget to send that fax, will you," said Graham quietly. Zahra left the office muttering something about having worked there for years and still couldn't be trusted to do her job. Graham smiled as he closed the door after her. "She won't forgive me for that insult for months."

"Do you know anything about a man in a car?" said Jason, frowning.

"That's why I wanted to get rid of her so I could tell you. I'd forgotten all about him to be honest. I was watching him too. Couldn't understand why he was sitting there like that, but I didn't want to jump to any conclusions."

"And you saw him leave his car?"

"Yes I did and it made me quite jittery. You see, Anna pulled up and parked in your space as she normally did. She set off walking towards the city centre and that's when this guy got out of his car. It looked like he was following her."

Jason took in a big breath. "You're sure about this?"

"Well, that's what it looked like, but it might have been a complete coincidence."

"But he was parked there a long time?"

"Oh, yes. Zahra first noticed him about ten o'clock and Anna arrived about three. So he was there a good five hours."

"You didn't see him come back?"

"No, I left about six-thirty and his car was still there. As was Anna's, of course. And that's when I came in on the Saturday morning and saw Anna's car still parked. Gave me a terrible jolt, when I remembered that man."

"I take it he was gone by the time you came in Saturday morning?"

Graham nodded. "There was no sign of him."

"What kind of car was it?"

"A dark blue BMW." Graham opened the office door for him. "All just a coincidence, thank goodness and no harm done."

Jason sat in his car for a while trying to absorb this new information. Her husband must have looked up the details of Harrington Rhodes and discovered the office address. That would be easy enough to find. He would have assumed that she worked there, since the family had been told not to tell him that she actually worked in a small office in a private house. He must have sat there hoping to see her, perhaps when she left the building for lunch or to go home. It was just a terrible coincidence that Anna decided to go Christmas shopping that afternoon. If she hadn't then his vigil would have been futile. Reversing out of his space, Jason headed for the Grange.

Jason drove up the drive and parked in the forecourt, determined that he would not leave until he had spoken with Anna and promised the protection and support he had failed to give her in the past. He entered the hall and taking off his sunglasses, glanced up the stairs to the landing and then towards the parlour door listening for voices.

Fran was mopping the marble floor, humming a little tune.

Jason bent over her. "Where is she, Fran?"

She jumped with fright and staggered slightly, making him reach out to steady her.

"Who? Who?"

"You sound like an owl! I'm talking about my fiancée. Where is she?"

The look of horror on the young girl's face made him smile. "I don't know who you're talking about, I'm sure sir!"

"Fran! I know you know. So, come on and tell me."

Margaret appeared at the parlour door. "Oh, for goodness sake, Jason. Leave the poor girl alone, you're terrifying her."

He strode across to her. "I'm not leaving until I see her!"

She could see by the look on his face that he meant it. "Very well, she's in the rose garden." As he turned to go she caught his arm. "Be kind and gentle with her!"

Jason raised his eyebrows in surprise. "I have no intention of being anything else."

Anna had spent her most peaceful moments in the rose garden, sometimes bringing out her work so that she could enjoy the late spring sunshine. The garden was starting to bloom and even at the end of May, the roses were showing their cascade of vibrant colours. It would soon be summer and she was filled with hope. The Grange had kept her safe and her secret was part of its fabric now. Somehow that seemed comforting. That morning, her files and paperwork were scattered over the small table Margaret had found for her. She lifted her eyes from her work and looked about her, blinking hard against the glare of the sun. There was someone coming along the path. A man, but not John, he was too tall and then with a muted cry she realised it was Jason. Anna jumped to her feet and headed for the kitchen door. She didn't get far.

Jason increased his stride and caught up with her. "Anna! Please don't run away. We must talk." She stopped and turned to face him. His deep blue eyes looked into hers with fierce determination. "I know what happened. About your husband and what you went through." She turned her head away in embarrassment. "And I want to say sorry for hurting you and making the situation worse." He raised her face with the edge of his forefinger. "Please say you forgive me for saying all those dreadful things. I should have trusted you and realised there was more to it." She closed her eyes as if she couldn't bear to look at him. "Anna, in God's name, please talk to me, before I go out of my mind."

She squinted at him. "Who told you?"

"It doesn't matter. All that does matter is that I love you."

Anna frowned. "I didn't want you to know."

"But if you had told me, I could have helped you."

She shook her head vigorously. "I couldn't tell you."

He decided not to pursue the argument. "Does it change things now that I know?"

She moved away from him. He made no attempt to stop her, but stood patiently waiting.

"I don't...Let me think a minute." She trailed her fingers through her hair. He noticed that it had grown and now she dressed it with a pretty band letting the soft blonde curls fall over her shoulders. She looked so lovely and yet vulnerable. "Everything's so different now. Everything has changed."

He wanted her to understand. "I still love you so much," he repeated.

She stepped closer to him and he resisted the urge to reach out for her. "But Jason, I'm carrying a child and I don't know who the father is."

"I don't care about that. I know who the mother is and that's more important to me."

Anna looked at him and her heart melted. "You really want to be with me?"

He laughed softly. "Anna, please, please let me back into your life. I can't function without you. Only you can make my existence bearable."

He slowly reached out for her and she stayed quite still. "I don't seem to be able to think beyond tomorrow," she whispered.

"Well, then that's what we'll do," he smiled. We'll think only of tomorrow and let the future take care of itself." He raised her hand to his lips and kissed her fingers. "You're still wearing my ring." She didn't answer. "And what on earth is this?" He lifted up the pendant round her neck. "You're wearing a ten pence coin!"

"It's our coin, the one you used in the club. I never take it off."

He shook his head in disbelief. "I've bought you some expensive gifts and you cherish something so mundane?"

"It's not the price of something that's important, it's the meaning behind it." Anna stared at him hardly believing that he was standing there.

He pulled her closer. "Oh, Anna, please let me help you through this."

She put her arms round his waist. "You were so angry with me."

"Yes and now I'm angry with myself. I've been unbelievably cruel."

"I used to peek through the curtains when you visited," she giggled. "I tried not to but I couldn't help myself."

He gave a chuckle that was so good to hear. "You've been here all the time and I didn't know. Where were you when I came with Hollie?"

"Hiding. In John and Irene's apartment."

Jason threw back his head and laughed. "The one place I would never go. And you were using your old bedroom, weren't you?"

She nodded. "Yes, but Fran had to lock the door every time you came."

"I thought I felt your presence. But I put it down to wishful thinking." Jason looked down at her and smiled. For the first time he saw how she bloomed with health. Pregnancy enhanced her beauty. It suited her. "When's the baby due?" he whispered.

"Beginning of September."

He glanced around the garden that was starting to fill with the heavenly colour and scent of roses, clematis and a variety of other summer plants.

"I haven't been to this part of the garden for a long time."

"Actually, I spend most of the day here if the weather is fine and I want to work outdoors."

"You work here?"

"Yes, your mother employed me. I've been her wedding planner." She pointed to the table laden with files.

He sucked in a sharp breath. "She knows?" Anna shook her head. "I have a lot to make up for. Whatever you want us to do, then I'll do it gladly."

She felt reluctant to ask the next question but needed to know. "How's everything at Harrington Rhodes?"

He became serious as his smile faded. "Not so good. I've been losing contracts. Can't seem to get my head round the business and if I don't pull myself together I'm certain it's heading for bankruptcy." He pulled her closer and smiled. It was wonderful feeling her in his arms again. "I exaggerate slightly, but I have been losing contracts."

Anna opened her eyes wide in surprise. "But in all the time I worked for you, you never lost one."

"That was when you were working for me. Now Natalie sits at your desk."

"Natalie?"

He grinned at her jealous tone. "Mmm! She needs to be seen to be believed."

"That perfect, eh!" He teased her by not answering. "Well, I'm pleased you found yourself another PA." She turned her face away.

Jason waited a few seconds and then cupped her face in his hands. "But she's not you. I've missed you terribly."

"And I've missed you." She paused for a moment. "In a few weeks I'll not be married any more."

Jason jerked back in surprise. "Your divorce! It's finalised?"

"The decree absolute will be through very soon."

"That's wonderful." He rubbed his cheek on top of her head. "I hope I never meet your husband. I'm liable to do him some harm."

She pulled away from him. "Oh, no you won't. He's done enough damage to us. Make me a promise that you'll never let him come between us again."

"I promise," he whispered.

Fran appeared. "Madam says are you friends now? And do you want to come in for coffee?"

They smiled at each other.

"Yes, we'll come in," said Anna, taking Jason's arm.

CHAPTER NINETEEN

The next three weeks were unbelievable. Jason established a routine of coming for dinner every Wednesday evening and he and Anna would walk round the garden, or if it rained, they would stay in the parlour, talking endlessly, while Margaret kept herself busy with her cross-stitch. Sometimes she would raise her eyes from her work and smile at Anna snuggled comfortably in the armchair with Jason sitting on the floor at her feet. The fact that her son was now reconciled with the mother of his child, filled her with absolute delight. And then at the weekend, Jason would try and stay overnight, depending on his business commitments, sleeping in his usual room and leaving on Saturday or Sunday evening.

The change in events affected everyone. John, Irene and Fran could now breathe a sigh of relief that they no longer needed to hide Anna. Although news of their reconciliation had not reached him yet, Graham Rhodes saw a complete upturn in the business as Jason started winning the contracts again.

"The boy is back," he said, rubbing his hands in satisfaction.

And the news hadn't sifted through to the people living at Bishop Sutton either. Jason had decided he wanted to get used to the idea himself, before he broke it to them. But they couldn't help noticing the radical change in his manner and temper. He filled the house with his presence once more and the only conclusion they could come to was that their boss had a new lady in his life. This would certainly account for his regular absences from home and his overnight bag. They didn't ask questions and discouraged Hollie from doing the same.

"He'll tell us when he's ready," said Mrs Wilby sadly. She knew Hollie had never stopped missing Anna.

For Anna, life began to take on a whole new meaning. She looked forward to Jason's visits and would wait at the door for his arrival. Sometimes they would travel to Bristol and go to Mothercare to buy items for the baby, including the pushchair, cot and car seat, laughing as they struggled to pack them into the boot.

"I'd forgotten how cumbersome these things are," Jason grinned.

He had kept his promise to Sophia and had let Anna set the pace of their reconciliation. Gradually he began to win her trust and confidence and when the moment finally arrived when he found the courage to press a kiss on her lips, he was surprised and overjoyed that she responded passionately. He didn't dare hope that they would share the same bed just yet, but there was no doubt that their love was as strong as ever. And that alone was enough for him.

Anna's divorce came through and she was now a free woman. The enormous relief that flooded through her when the notification arrived was overwhelming. She was in the library when Margaret gave her the letter and although she knew what it was, her hands trembled as she opened the envelope.

"That's it," she said, giving a half-smile. "I'm no longer married."

"Thank the Lord for that. Perhaps you and Jason can make some plans of your own now," said Margaret with relief.

After Margaret had left, Anna sat down at her desk and for the first time in months she could see into the future. She and Jason had not discussed marriage, as they had kept to their strategy of taking life one day at a time. But now everything seemed so different. Without realising it they had planned for the baby's arrival and she knew that Jason was now in the same frame of mind as she, that beyond any doubt the child she was carrying was his. They were both convinced of it and nothing it seemed would shake their belief.

It was a wet Saturday just a day after Anna had received her decree absolute. Jason was away on business, but he hoped to arrive at the Grange in the late afternoon and spend the night. Anna was very busy with yet another wedding and she felt sad for the bride and groom that the weather was being unruly and threatening to spoil their special day. Although photos in the garden were impossible, Anna had put 'Plan B' into operation, that is, photos in the large conservatory filled with flowers and an abundance of natural light. This plan had always been welcomed in the past and today of all days it was viewed with relief by the agitated mother-of-the-bride who had fretted over the weather. The photos completed everyone made their way to the ballroom to start the reception. Anna needed to collect some invoices from her desk and quickly hurried to the library.

She met Fran en route. "Gentleman waiting to see you, miss."

Anna pulled up short. "Oh, Fran, I'm too busy to see anyone today. And he hasn't got an appointment."

The young girl pulled a face. "He said it wouldn't take long. Sorry, miss."

Letting out a sigh Anna went into the library determined to get rid of this unwanted intrusion.

He was standing at the window, his back to her.

"I'm so sorry, but I really can't see anyone without an appointment, especially today."

He turned slowly and Anna gasped with shock.

"I'm sure you can see me," he said, smiling.

Anna stood completely still as though paralysed. "What do you want? You shouldn't be here. We're divorced now."

"Your mum told me that you're pregnant and that you're due in September." His gaze dropped to her expanding waistline as he took a step forward.

Anna moved so that the desk was between them. "What's that got to do with you?"

"Because I've got an inkling that you're carrying my kid."

"No, I'm not! This is Jason's baby."

"Are you absolutely sure of that?"

"Yes, I'm positive."

He moved round the desk and Anna quickly changed her position. It was though they were in some bizarre dance. He moving forward and she moving back.

"I don't think you are. Let me think." He stroked his chin, his eyes never leaving her face. "We were together at Christmas…"

"Together! How dare you call it that, as though I agreed to it!"

"What else would you like me to call it?"

"You forced me…you kept me a prisoner…!"

He waved his hand in dismissal. "Whatever! As I was saying, December to September is nine months, so there's a strong possibility that I could have fathered that child."

Strength began to surge through her body and she clenched her fists in anger. "You are *not* the father of this child. And I would appreciate it if you would leave."

He pursed his lips. "I only popped in as I was in the area. But I'll be making a special trip in say…three months."

"Don't you come anywhere near me!"

"Oh yes, Anna, I will. I want to know if this is my child. So, you'd better warn that bloke of yours, because if it does turn out to be mine, I'll be applying for access."

"You can't do that. I don't want you anywhere near this baby."

"Is that so? A judge can't bar me from seeing my own child."

"He would if I spoke up and told him what you did."

He gave a mischievous wink. "Ah, but you won't do that, will you?"

Anna sat at her desk for a long time after he had left. She would have to talk to Nigel, surely her husband couldn't intrude into her life and make a nuisance of himself? Then she remembered that Dave was her ex-husband by only twenty-four hours and he was still causing trouble. But the baby was Jason's she knew that for certain, she felt it. Suddenly she remembered the wedding reception and hurried into the ballroom.

Jason arrived just as the guests were leaving and had to stand aside as they spilled out of the main door. One exuberant lady emptied the remnants of her confetti box over him and when he finally entered the hall, he was brushing it from his hair and clothing.

"Look what they're doing! What a chuffing mess!" said Fran in disgust. "They've been told to get that biological stuff, but do they listen? And then I've got to sweep it all up."

"Where's Anna?" he said, grinning.

"Oh, she's in the library. Must be worn out, poor lamb."

He had to admit that she was right. Although Anna was in the best of health, she looked very tired and there were shadows under her eyes.

"Why don't you go upstairs and lie down?" he suggested.

"I've just got to finish off here first," she said, looking down at the pile of paperwork.

He would have none of it and gently helped her to her feet. "Lie down for an hour and then I'll bring you a cup of tea."

She put her arms round him. She had already decided that she must tell him about Dave's visit and his threats to her, but not at the moment.

"OK. But just for an hour, then you must wake me."

Anna climbed the stairs with relief and once on her bed, fell into a dreamless sleep. The hour flew past and soon Jason was there with the promised cup of tea.

She patted the mattress. "Come and lie down beside me," she whispered, shuffling over to give him some room.

At first Jason was surprised, as they hadn't done that for a long time. But the invitation was very welcome and he made himself comfortable beside her.

"I've been talking to Mother," he said as he kissed her. "She's absolutely overjoyed about this baby of ours. She wants a grandson."

"I know," laughed Anna. "She's convinced it's a boy. I hope she's not disappointed if it turns out to be a girl."

"She'll be delighted whatever the sex of the baby." He thought for a moment. "I'm going to have to tell the others soon. And Hollie will need to know about her little brother or sister."

Anna smiled mischievously. "Would you like to see a photo and then you can decide for yourself whether it's a boy or girl."

He turned to face her. "A photo?"

"Look in the bedside table."

He rolled over, opened the small drawer and took out the scan picture.

"Wow! This is him or her?"

Anna smiled at his enthusiasm. "Your mum thinks it's a boy because he's punching the air like you did at sports day after you'd won an event."

Jason frowned. "I don't remember doing that."

"But a mother always remembers."

His smile appeared again. "He's beautiful," he murmured. "I wish I'd been with you when you had this done."

"Margaret came with me. She's been absolutely wonderful. But there again she doesn't know that…" For the first time in months, Anna felt tears stinging her eyes.

He noticed. "Hey, this won't do!" He gathered her up in his arms. "This baby is mine. I just know it."

"I really hope so."

"There's no doubt about it." He gently stroked her stomach. "This baby will have my name and when you're ready I want us to marry. Then we'll be a family."

She looked at him; her eyes filled this time with happy tears. "Then you'd better tell Hollie so we can buy her a bridesmaid dress."

Anna knew she should have told Jason that her ex-husband had visited the Grange and threatened her. And she had meant to when she had invited him to lie down beside her. But his sweet endearments and his tender kisses had proved too much for her. She just couldn't spoil the moment or the absolute joy of planning for their future once more. She decided to tell him after dinner but the evening had been so wonderful that she let the opportunity pass.

Anna tossed and turned restlessly. She had fallen asleep almost straight away but then had awakened with a start. Glancing at the clock she realised it was only two o'clock. Anna grimaced and remembered that this was nature's way of preparing her for all the nightly feeds. It would be strange coping with a small baby again. She had really thought that her childbearing days were over. Anna rolled onto her side and still not able to get comfortable finally slipped out of bed and walked across to the window. She drew back the curtains and let in the bright moonlight that filled the room with a silvery sheen. Then she wondered if Jason was awake too.

Trying to hold back her giggles, she tiptoed down the corridor and up the short flight of stairs. She turned the handle gently and entered the room that seemed in complete darkness. As her eyes became used to the gloom, she saw him lying peacefully asleep and hesitated for a moment. But then closing the door silently, she hurried across the carpet and climbed into bed beside him.

It was strange feeling him close like this. He was lying on his back and as she watched him she remembered all the nights she had missed this closeness. She felt safe with him and lying next to him she felt that nothing and nobody in the world could harm her. Anna placed her hand on his chest stroking his bare skin. Her hand floated over his stomach and she felt it ripple under her touch. Her fingers drifted lower and he gave a low moan, hardening immediately. This was very naughty of her, she thought mischievously, she really ought to let him sleep.

His eyes flickered open and he gave a gasp. "Who's that?"

Anna sniffed indignantly. "Should I be offended at that question?"

He reached out and switched on the light. "Good God! What are you doing here?"

She pulled a face. "I was sleep walking and when I woke up I found myself in your room."

He smiled and pulled her closer. "And in my bed it seems."

She cuddled down against him. "I woke up and couldn't get back to sleep."

"So, you thought you'd wake me up too."

"It's your baby keeping me awake."

He adjusted his position. "Well, you're very welcome."

"You don't mind me sharing your bed tonight?" He raised himself up on his elbow and his eyes flickered over her rounded shape. She noticed and suddenly felt embarrassed. "That's unless you find me very ugly and repulsive. In which case, I'll go back to my own room."

She tried to sit up, but he gently pressed her back against the pillows. "There's something very erotic about a pregnant woman," he smiled. Slipping his hand under the covers, he caressed her over her nightdress, passing tenderly over her breasts until he reached the new life growing within her. "I've imagined being with you every single day," he murmured against her ear.

Jason thought he would die from happiness, that his heart would burst. Life was about giving and loving and everything he and Anna shared. And seeing Anna smile up at him was all he wanted. They enclosed each other in their arms and for what seemed a long time they didn't speak. They were content to kiss and caress, allowing the tender enjoyment of their lovemaking to linger for as long as it could.

They stared at him in surprise hardly believing what he had just told them. For the last month they had steeled themselves for meeting the new lady in his life and instead they were hearing something completely different.

"It's Anna you're seeing?" said Ben incredulously.

Jason nodded. "Yes, she been living at the Grange with my mother."

"How come you didn't bump into her when you visited?" said Mrs Wilby.

Jason let out a breath. "She didn't want me to know she was there."

"Was she playing hide and seek?" chimed in Hollie, her dark eyes sparkling with delight.

"Yes, sweetie. I guess she was."

Hollie jumped up and danced round the kitchen. "Yes, yes, yes. Anna's coming back! Anna's coming back!"

Jason tried to stem her exuberance. "I'm not sure about that. At least we've not discussed it."

Hollie took her seat a little more subdued. "But this is her home, Daddy. She has to come home."

"Well, she's working for Grandma Harrington planning the weddings and she's very busy at the moment."

Ben gave a chuckle. "Planning the weddings. That would suit her."

"So, when will she be unbusy?" Hollie was determined to keep to the point.

Jason decided to divert her attention. "We'll be visiting the Grange in August as usual and then you'll see her again."

This seemed to pacify her. "That'll be nice." She jumped down from her chair. "I'm going to play in my Wendy house."

Jason was glad when the adults were left alone, now he could tell them the rest of his news.

"Actually, there's a little more to it."

"I thought so," said Mrs Wilby. "I could tell by the look on your face you hadn't told us the whole story."

He cleared his throat. "Anna's expecting a baby in early September."

His news was like a bombshell and at first they didn't know how to answer. Jason prayed that they would assume the obvious and not ask any questions. And he breathed a sigh of relief when they did just that.

Mrs Wilby gave him a hug and Ben shook his hand. "Congratulations," he said and then added, "Although I'm rather disappointed that we can't get rid of old misery drawers!"

Jason gave a laugh. "Sorry, but you'll have to put up with her for the foreseeable future."

Anna adjusted her position. She was seven months pregnant and for the last week, the baby had insisted on kicking her beneath her rib cage. The only relief she could get was by pressing her hand over the place and stopping her ribs from moving up and down with the tiny punches.

A waiter suddenly appeared.

"Would you like a cushion? You could put it behind your back."

Anna smiled and took it from him. "That's so kind. I'm waiting for my fiancé but he's a bit late." The waiter nodded in sympathy.

Her appointment at the hospital had gone well and she and Jason had agreed to meet up at the restaurant for lunch. She was waiting for him at one of the small tables by the bar and had already received a call on her mobile to say he would be another ten minutes. But sitting on the hard chair was causing her discomfort.

"I see you're pregnant," said a husky voice behind her.

She turned to see Deborah smiling at her. But the smile looked false like one a snake might give before devouring its prey.

"Yes, I'm due in two months."

"Who's the father?"

Anna was caught off guard. "Jason, of course."

"Really! I was told that your husband, or should I say, your ex-husband could be the father."

Anna suddenly began to feel faint. "Who told you that?" she whispered.

"I have my sources. Does Jason know that he might not be the father?"

Anna didn't want to answer. "He is the father," she said quietly.

Deborah's smile widened when she saw Jason coming towards them. Anna rose to her feet and he put his arm round her, his face showing concern that Deborah and Anna were alone together, like an angel and a demon.

"Sorry I'm late, sweetheart." He turned to Deborah. "Hello Deborah. Are you eating here?"

"Business lunch, but just leaving." She glanced towards Anna. "Congratulations. I see you're going to be a father again."

"Thank you, but we must go. Our table is booked for one o'clock." He quickly guided Anna away. Deborah watched them for a few seconds.

"I haven't finished with you two yet," she murmured.

Anna was acutely aware that she had kept many secrets from Jason in the past, but Deborah's remarks to her in the restaurant, could not be ignored. And so Anna decided to tell him about it.

For a few seconds, anger flared in his eyes. "That woman is unbelievable!"

"But how did she know about my ex-husband?" she said, biting her lip anxiously.

"I've no idea," Jason said. "Who actually knows about…?"

"Well, besides you, me and my ex-husband, there's only Nigel and Sophia."

He pursed his lips. "Would you mind if I mentioned it to Nigel? I'm having a drink with him tomorrow evening. He might have some inside information."

Anna felt much happier after telling Jason about Deborah's cruel remarks. Suddenly she began to realise that sharing some burdens actually made the situation easier. Even so and despite the fact that her reunion with Jason had given her added strength, she still couldn't summon up the courage to tell him about Dave's visit or his threats against her.

At first, Nigel was as much in the dark as Jason.

"I can't see how she would know. Except that she's a devious creature."

"I'll drink to that," said Jason, raising his glass.

Nigel picked up a beer mat and turned it about between his fingers. "Of course, if you look at it logically, who would want to pass on information?"

Jason thought for a moment. "Not Anna and I. And her ex-husband, I assume, doesn't know Deborah. So, that seems to leave you and Sophia."

Nigel pressed his lips together and continued playing with the beer mat. After a short while he said, "I think we can count out Sophia, so it's down to me."

"I don't think so! Why would you want to pass on any information to that woman?"

"I passed confidential information on to you," he said, grimacing.

"Don't be too hard on yourself. You did it with the best of intentions and I'm glad you did."

Nigel threw the mat down on the table. "Glad you feel like that."

Jason was in no doubt. "I might have gone on indefinitely, not knowing Anna's true circumstances or, perish the thought, about the baby."

"I take it you'll be having a test to establish that you're the father?"

He was answered with an expression of disdain and a sharp retort. "I will not! The baby is mine, I'm sure of it and so is Anna. We're going to leave it there. The child will have my name and in due course we intend to marry."

Nigel smiled. "Good for you. I hoped you'd say that. I'm up to my ears in paternity suits."

Jason watched him with interest. "So, go on. Why do you think you've passed on information to Deborah?"

Nigel leaned back in his chair and sighed. "I'm not thinking of me personally. I've been going over the staff in my office that have to sign a confidentiality agreement. Quite a few of them have been with me some time, so I feel fairly happy with them. But there are at least two of them who have been with me only a short time. I think I'll check them out and see what I come up with."

Jason opened his eyes wide with surprise. "You think you have a spy in your midst?"

"How very MI5. But it's a possibility and it's better if I eliminate them."

"And if you don't find a culprit?"

"Then I'll ring Deborah and ask her outright where she got her information from!"

Anna was interested in Nigel's notion of a 'spy' and waited eagerly for further developments. However, she had decided to ignore Dave's threats to her and the baby. She grimaced when she thought about her marriage and how alone she had been. In the past, she had never been able to tell Dave anything, or share anything with him. He had been too disinterested in her to make the effort and if she did attempt to bare her soul, he would tell her to 'stop whining'.

Of course, she now realised how much he could control her and how well he did know her. Like threatening to apply for access to the baby. He knew that that was enough to distress her and spoil her happiness. And she knew for certain that that was his motive. He resented her happiness. But he was hundreds of miles away in Wakefield and she was sure that he wouldn't make a journey down to Bristol in September, just to verify that the baby was his. It was all bluff and nothing more than empty threats. The baby was Jason's and her ex-husband was out of her life forever.

With these thoughts firmly entrenched, Anna continued with her life happily preparing for the baby's arrival and wading through the pile of paperwork that accumulated with every wedding she planned. It was now mid-July and there was only six weeks to go before the birth. She had received a postcard from the twins in Benidorm and when they returned from their holiday, Martyn was coming to Bristol to work for Harrington Rhodes for the summer. Chris had opted to stay in Wakefield to work for an engineering company and thereby continue his gliding interests in Rufford.

She and Jason had bought all the necessary baby things and although she had to prevent Margaret from trimming up the Moses basket in blue lace, she felt contented and ready. The doctor had been more than pleased with her progress, but he wouldn't make his decision about a home delivery for another month.

Jason hadn't been surprised that Anna wanted to have her baby at the Grange, but he did share his mother's misgivings.

"It doesn't sound safe, sweetheart," he frowned. "What happens if anything goes wrong?"

Anna turned on him in annoyance. "Why does everyone assume that something is going to go wrong!"

He smiled and held up his hands in defeat. "OK, OK, you win. Have the baby here, as long as I can be present."

"At the birth?"

"Absolutely."

"That will be interesting."

But during the next two weeks Anna began to believe that happiness was like a soap bubble. Very beautiful but very fragile and liable to be popped at any moment. And as the saying goes, bad news comes in threes.

The first thing that happened was that Tess, Margaret's golden retriever, passed away peacefully in her sleep. Irene found her one morning, lying in her basket, her head over the side. She hadn't been well for quite a few months and a visit to the vet had confirmed that she was going blind and her liver was failing. Margaret rejected the vet's suggestion of having her put down, as she believed that if she wasn't suffering then she should live out her life until its natural end.

Anna missed her a great deal. Tess had followed her around continually and had often lain at her feet in the rose garden, while she worked. All the household of the Grange attended her funeral held in the pet cemetery on the estate. Hollie came with her father and together they placed some wild flowers on the mound of earth.

Jason thought this a good opportunity to tell his daughter about the baby. Anna's reunion with Hollie brought tears to his eyes as he watched them hugging each other. And then there was the excitement of showing her all the baby things and telling her their plans for a wedding, including the proposed shopping trip for her bridesmaid's dress.

"When will it be?" she asked, jumping up and down.

Anna didn't know how to answer and turned to Jason for support.

"Oh, after the baby, sweetie. Perhaps January or February?" he cast a hopeful glance at Anna who smiled and nodded.

But then news arrived that Fergus Macintosh, Jason's father-in-law had also died.

"I remember he was ill," said Anna, cuddling up in bed with Jason on one of his weekend visits.

He nodded. "When I last talked to Gaynor, she said that he didn't have long. The poor lady, to lose her daughter and then her husband." He slipped his arm round her. "I'll be flying across for the funeral with Ben, but we'll be away only for as long as it takes. Four days at the most."

"Shall I come with you?"

He turned over and his gaze swept over her swollen body. "I don't think there's a plane big enough to carry you!"

She hit him with a pillow. "Thank you, kind sir. Isn't it bad enough that I feel like a beached whale!"

His laughter echoed round the room. He pulled her close and kissed her hair.

"I think you look beautiful. Although I'm looking forward to getting my arms right round you again." He chuckled at her expression but then became more serious. "No, I think you'd better stay here. I don't think an airline would be happy about carrying someone in your condition on such a long flight. And you don't want this baby to be born Canadian, do you?"

"I suppose not. Is Hollie going with you?"

"I've told her about Granddad Macintosh and she had a little cry. But she didn't say anything about going so I decided not to mention it. She's barely got over her mother's death."

Jason and Ben left for Vancouver two days later. It really would be a quick visit as they only planned to attend the funeral and then fly straight back. Jason's business was doing very well and he didn't want to be away for too long, as well as not wanting to leave Anna now that she was starting her ninth month. But it was while Jason was in Canada that the third and most devastating event occurred.

Anna had had a very busy day and the mid-week wedding had been tiring. She was glad when the guests had departed and the Grange fell quiet once more. It had been a gloriously hot day and for the bride and groom that had been marvellous but for Anna, the heat had only made her condition more uncomfortable. Her back ached and she needed to keep going to the toilet as the baby was now sitting on her bladder. Jason phoned in the late afternoon and it was wonderful to hear his voice and also hear that Mrs Macintosh was bearing up well. She was surrounded by some amazing friends and neighbours who were all rallying round to give her support.

After his call, Anna climbed the stairs to her room for a lie down. She made herself comfortable on the bed and stared up at the ceiling, smiling at the fact that she only slept in Jason's room when he stayed overnight and for the rest of the time she would sleep in her own room. It was as if she had two lives. She was just about to doze off when there was a gentle knock on the door. She called a soft 'come in' and was surprised to see Fran standing on the threshold.

"Madam says can you go down to the parlour, miss."

Anna struggled to her feet. "Of course. What's happened? Is it Mr Harrington?"

"I don't think so, miss. But Mrs Harrington doesn't seem very pleased."

Anna made her way down to the parlour where Margaret was standing by the fireplace. She looked up as Anna entered the room.

"I've just had a phone call. And what I've heard has really disturbed me."

Feeling alarmed, Anna took a seat on the couch. "You'd better tell me," she said, her heart in her mouth.

"I've been told...that the baby you're expecting...might not be my son's...might not be a Harrington."

Anna felt her mouth dry up. "Who told you that?"

"It doesn't matter. But I want to know the truth. Is that my son's child?"

Indignation welled up inside her. "Of course it is! Whoever you've been talking to has got it all wrong. Who were they?"

"Is there a chance that this baby might be another man's?" Margaret asked, brushing the question aside.

"N...No. No, of course not! That's a terrible thing to say."

Margaret came to sit beside her. "Anna, I told you before that I thought you faithful but not truthful. I need to know the truth now."

"I...I know it's Jason's. Oh God, who would say such terrible things?"

"I've been looking forward so much to another grandchild, a grandson to carry on the family name. Jason is the last and if he doesn't have a son, then that's the end of the line. The Grange will go to Hollie and I doubt she'll stay a Harrington once she's grown."

"This is Jason's child," Anna whispered.

Margaret wasn't happy with her reassurances. "You and Jason had a fall out at Christmas and that's when this child must have been conceived. I want to know if you had an affair and Jason was right all along?"

"I didn't have an affair. It wasn't like that."

"Like what?"

"It wasn't an affair."

Margaret pulled back from her in horror. "What was it then? A one-night stand? A fling?"

"No! No!"

Margaret's expression told her everything. "Anna, you've become very dear to me over the last year and your help in the business has been invaluable. But if you've lived here under false pretences, if you've taken advantage of my kindness and hospitality then I cannot tolerate that."

"I wouldn't do that," said Anna, turning desperate eyes towards her.

Margaret paused before asking, "But could this child be someone else's?" Anna looked down at her hands, her fingers twisted together in agitation. She couldn't answer. "Then let me ask you another question. Does my son know that this child might not be his?" Anna nodded slowly. Margaret stood. "When Jason returns, he can take you back to Bishop Sutton. It seems he's more liberal in his ideas than I can be."

Anna climbed the stairs heavily, her heart breaking. She had been asked to leave when Jason returned, but she knew she couldn't spend another night under Margaret's roof. But she couldn't go back to the house in Bishop Sutton, she hadn't seen Ben and Mrs Wilby since New Year. What would they say if she suddenly turned up on the doorstep?

In her room, she packed a few things in a small bag and then made her way back down to the hall, down the few steps that led to the kitchen and then up the flight that finally took her to the apartment. John answered her gentle knock.

"Why, miss. What's the matter?"

"Could you give me a lift to the home of Doctor and Mrs Orchard, please."

"Of course, miss. I'll just get the car keys."

John asked no questions as he drove her to Wedmore. He pulled up at the gate and frowning, watched Anna make her way up the path of the modern bungalow and knock on the door.

Sarah answered. "Anna! What are you doing here?"

A steady stream of tears poured down her face. "Margaret has asked me to leave the Grange and I've nowhere else to go. Please could you help me?"

CHAPTER TWENTY

Sarah Orchard accepted the situation at face value, and like John, didn't ask any intrusive questions. Being a doctor's wife for many years, she had plenty of experience in dealing with the traumatic side of life but had always tried to keep a positive attitude. She made Anna as comfortable as possible and when her husband returned from a house call, he was concerned enough to give Anna a thorough examination. Except for her blood pressure being slightly elevated, he confirmed that a good night's sleep would be beneficial. As for any other problems, they could be dealt with in the morning. He prescribed a mild sedative and told her to rest.

The following day, Anna spent the time in Sarah's beautiful garden, wrapped in a blanket on the lounger. But one thing Sarah felt obliged to do was ring Margaret. The two friends talked for ten minutes and Margaret had to admit that she had been surprised when John had told her where he had taken Anna, but was satisfied with Sarah's reassurances that she would take care of the mother-to-be. When Margaret asked if Anna could stay there until Jason returned from Canada, Sarah felt disturbed.

"She talked as though Anna was a package to be kept until its rightful owner collected it," she said to her husband that evening.

The doctor frowned. "Jason will be home soon and she's very welcome to stay here. I'm sure it's all a terrible misunderstanding and will be sorted out when he gets back."

Sarah was starting to have misgivings. She was quite concerned by the desperate look in Anna's eyes and the way she couldn't seem to focus or concentrate on anything. She knew that she was in a deep state of depression and that didn't bode well with childbirth being so close.

Anna was grateful for Colin and Sarah's kindness and she knew she should be showing her gratitude, but there was something dragging her down into a pit of misery. She remembered Sophia telling her that the memory of her rape ordeal wouldn't vanish overnight; that it would be with her for a long time to come and she would need constant support.

But Anna hadn't believed her. Since Jason had come back into her life, she had never felt better or happier. The nightmare of that terrible evening in the Marriott Hotel had slipped into the background as she and Jason planned for their baby. And it really had been their baby as he had helped her to believe that the child was his.

And only now, with Margaret's accusations, did the awful truth dawn on her. She could be carrying her ex-husband's child and the very thought filled her with horror. Suddenly she wished that she had taken Sophia's suggestion and had the pregnancy terminated and then there wouldn't have been any repercussions from her ordeal. For the first time since it had happened, Anna wished she could die. It suddenly crossed her mind to disappear, to live in the fields and woodland until her baby came and then perhaps she would give birth out in the open and she and the baby would die together. And then she noticed the photos of the numerous Orchard grandchildren and common sense prevailed.

"What do you mean, she's not here?"

Margaret took in a breath. She knew that look on her son's face all too well. "I told her she must leave after your return, but she left on her own accord. She's staying with the Orchards."

"And why did you ask her to leave?"

"I had a phone call. I was told things that I didn't like to hear."

"Such as?"

"That she's not carrying your child. That it might be someone else's."

Jason closed his eyes in shock. "And who was this person who decided you needed to know this?"

"I have no idea. They didn't give me their name."

"You had an anonymous phone call?"

"Yes."

"Mother!   How can you believe gossip from…!" Suddenly Jason remembered his conversation with Deborah at the clubhouse at Christmas. She had levelled accusations at Anna and he had believed them.

Margaret started to feel uncomfortable. "She admitted it. Sort of."

"Sort of?"

"She told me that you knew she might be expecting another man's child." She caught his sidelong glance and knew she had hit a nerve. "And I must say I'm surprised at you. After you accused her of having an affair, you then decide to take on another man's child! I don't know whether you're very gullible or just plain stupid."

Jason had heard enough and turning on his heel rushed out of house, ignoring the cries of his mother as she called his name. Within minutes he was on the road to Wedmore.

Sarah's greeting was much kinder and her relief at seeing him was overwhelming.

"She's in the garden, but she's hardly spoken two words since she arrived. My husband is not too worried about her physical health, but she's very depressed. It's as if she's lost the will to live."

Jason stepped into the garden and saw Anna standing underneath a beech tree, looking up into its branches. He quickly went to her and put his arms round her. She sank against him and started shaking, her sobbing taking her over, her tears soaking into his clothing. He knew that it was better for her to get it out of her system and held her tightly, caressing her back and murmuring comforting words. Her body finally calmed and she stood quietly, still clinging to him.

"Dave will never let me go. He's going to harass me until I die."

"Please don't say that. If you believe it then he's won."

"He's already won. I can't fight him any more."

"Then don't. Let me do all your fighting for you."

She looked up and searched his face. "He's going…to come back. When the baby's born…he wants to know if it's his. And if it is…he's going to apply for access."

Jason stared at her in disbelief. "He's been to see you?"

"Yes. About six weeks ago."

Jason couldn't hide his horror. "Why didn't you tell me!"

"I didn't think it was important. I thought it was an empty threat."

He thought rapidly. "We'll get Nigel to apply for an injunction."

"Do you honestly believe that'll keep him away! An injunction will only goad him."

"But he can be arrested if he comes anywhere near you." She shook her head. "Then come back to Bishop Sutton with me. It's your home."

"I don't feel I belong there any more and besides, I was hoping to have this baby at the Grange."

He smiled and gently put his hand on her stomach. "Our baby."

"Do you really still believe that?"

He nodded. "With all my heart."

They held each other close for a few minutes until Anna said, "The last few days I've wanted to die."

Jason's heart went into his mouth as he remembered Sophia's grim description of the fate of some of her clients. *Two took an overdose and one cut her wrists!*

"Then there's only one thing for it!" He held her away from him so that he could look her in the eyes. "Knowledge is the best defence, they say, so you must let me tell Mother what happened to you. We'll admit that you could be carrying your ex-husband's child and…"

She pulled away from him. "No! I don't want her to know. I would feel so ashamed."

"But it wasn't your fault, sweetheart. She'll understand. Then you can move back into the Grange in time for the baby and also everyone will be aware of your ex-husband and he won't be allowed on the premises. You'll be well protected."

"Are you thinking of telling John and Irene too! And Fran? What about the rest of the staff?"

"No, of course not. What I'm saying is…"

Anna couldn't believe what he was suggesting. She moved away from him. "Oh, why not tell everyone! Tell the whole bloody world, why don't you! I know, why don't you put it in the paper? Make it official that your fiancée was kept prisoner in a hotel bedroom and raped twice by her...!"

"Twice!"

She stopped short suddenly realising what she had just said. "Y...Yes."

He stepped closer to her. "You never said that...! Oh, God, what have you been through!"

She put her hand over her mouth, trying to choke back the tears.

"I...I don't want to think about it."

He reached out for her. "Sweetheart, please come back to Bishop Sutton with me."

"Please go, Jason. I need to be on my own."

He shook his head. "I'm not leaving you on your own. I'm too scared for you."

She gave a wry smile. "Why? Do you think I'll do something silly?" His eyes turning dark told her she was right. "I won't. So you don't have to worry."

He glanced around the garden. "OK, I'll go. But I'm coming back tomorrow and the next day and the next, until I can persuade you to leave with me." He reached for her hand and kissed her fingers.

He left her standing under the beech tree. Sarah was waiting for him.

"Will she be OK?" she asked anxiously.

"I don't know. I hope so, but is it all right for her to stay?"

"Oh yes, absolutely. We'll look after her."

"I'm coming back tomorrow. By then she might have changed her mind and be willing to come home with me."

Anna stared up at the beech tree. She remembered climbing one when she was a girl. But a bee had started pestering her and she had scrambled down, frantically trying to get away from it. She had cuts and bruises all over her legs and hands and her mother had laughed.

"You've done yourself more damage than the bee has."

Was this happening now? Was she doing as much damage to herself as her ex-husband had done? She had sent Jason away at a time when she needed him the most and forbidden him to tell his mother her secret. But if Margaret knew everything, then she would understand. And what's more she would take the necessary actions to protect her and her baby. Ignorance didn't protect a person. Ignorance made a person vulnerable. Knowledge is the best defence, Jason had said. And he was right.

Suddenly she began to panic. She fled out of the garden and round the side of the bungalow just as Jason was pulling away from the kerb. He saw her, brought the car to a halt and climbed out. She hurried towards him as fast as her growing child would allow and flung her arms about his waist, pressing her face so hard against his chest, she could hear the steady beating of his heart. He had opened his arms to receive her and once entwined held her tightly, stroking her hair. For many minutes they didn't speak, as she clung to him.

"I'll come back to the Grange with you," she whispered. "And you can tell Margaret everything."

He smiled. "Go and get your things."

Jason wanted to speak to his mother alone and so he sent Anna upstairs. She went to soak in a hot bath, leaving Jason to do her fighting, just as he had suggested. He went into the parlour and while his mother sat quietly, he told her about Anna's frightening experience at the hands of her ex- husband and how the child she was carrying could be either man's, but he hoped it was his.

Margaret couldn't hide her horror. "The poor girl. If only I'd known the truth."

Jason nodded. "And she needs our love, support and protection now. Her ex-husband is still threatening her even though they're divorced. He wants access to the baby if it's his."

"Then after the birth, you must have a test."

He groaned. "That was something I wanted to avoid. I was going to take on the child as mine. He was going to have my name."

"It seems you have no choice now. At least a test will make it certain who the father is."

"But if it's his, then he'll apply for access and Anna's life will become intolerable."

"We'll have to face that problem when it comes. But one thing's for sure, he's doing it to cause trouble for you too."

"Me?"

"Oh, yes. I think you're his target not Anna. His jealousy of you has warped his mind." She patted his knee. "If this had been two hundred years ago it would have been pistols at dawn. But in the twentieth century it comes down to a DNA test. That's progress for you. But however you look at it, you're in a deadly duel with this man."

"Dear Lord, I hope you're wrong!"

"Well, if it comes to a fight in a courtroom, you've got a good solicitor."

Jason smiled and his respect for his elderly mother soared. She was a powerful force at seventy, goodness knows what she must have been like at forty. Anna appeared and the look on her face showed her apprehension. Jason took her hand and drew her down on the couch with him.

Margaret stood and came to sit next to her. "My dear, I'll tell John and his family that no strangers must enter these premises without a prior appointment. Your ex-husband will not get through the doors of the Grange I promise you."

Anna leaned against Jason's shoulder and closed her eyes with relief.

"Thank you, Margaret. But I should have told you at Christmas when I found out I was pregnant." She looked at Jason and grinned. "Me and my secrets!"

Nigel's phone call came unexpectedly one scorching hot afternoon. Ben had opened all the windows and doors to allow any welcome draught of cool air to circulate round the house. Mrs Wilby had made her special lemonade and Hollie had been given the task of supplying it to anyone who needed it. Even the ice cold Natalie seemed to be melting under the heat.

Jason looked at his watch. "I think we'll call it a day. It's far too hot to work."

Natalie turned in her seat, her blouse damp between the shoulders. "It is hot, isn't it! I wouldn't mind going if it's OK with you."

Jason smiled. "Get yourself off."

After she had gone, he decided to phone Anna.

She answered with a soft laugh. "I hoped you'd phone too. I've had a call from Chris. He went gliding this afternoon and said he thoroughly enjoyed being up in the blue sky. How's Martyn doing?"

"Graham is very impressed with him. He's become an asset to the company and giving Graham a run for his money telling him all the new economic theories he's learnt at uni."

"It seems strange that he's sleeping in my old bedroom."

"He's won Mrs Wilby's heart and enjoys helping Ben with the cars. Hollie adores him and keeps reminding him that they will be stepbrother and sister."

"Well, don't indulge him too much."

Jason chuckled. "I shall be there tomorrow for dinner as usual and this weekend, we'll be descending on you for our summer visit."

"I can't wait to see everyone. I can't believe it's eight months since I last saw Ben and Mrs Wilby. Do you think they'll notice a difference in my appearance?"

"Just a bit. They've bought something for the baby."

"Oh, Jason. That's so kind. I'll be seeing the doctor next week and I'll find out for definite if I can stay here for the birth or I must go into hospital. Will you come with me? He's sure to be agreeable if you're sitting there working your charms on him."

"Of course I'll come but I don't think my charms work on Colin."

She chuckled. "I'm in the rose garden at the moment and it's lovely and cool."

"Wish I was with you, sweetheart."

"We'll see each other tomorrow."

"Wonderful! There's something I need to discuss with you."

"Goodness, that sounds intriguing. Can't wait."

After speaking to Anna, Jason sat quietly, looking around his office. He had lived in this house since he and Kiera had married and that was over eleven years ago. Jason shook himself from his reflections. That was the past and now he had someone else to think about and another child to care for. His life was changing and soon he would have quite an extended family. He had a plan but had kept it to himself until he could discuss it with Anna.

The telephone rang and it was Nigel. He seemed in a jovial mood and asked if Jason could meet him for a drink, with it being such a hot day. Jason agreed wholeheartedly.

"I've actually got you here under false pretences," said Nigel, taking a gulp of lager.

"Suits me on a day like today."

Nigel leaned forward, keeping his voice low. "Remember our discussion about how Deborah knew about Anna's circumstances?" Jason nodded. "I think I might have found the person who's been passing information from my office to Deborah."

Jason felt intrigued. "Go on, then. Tell me!"

"My secretary, Maureen, has been with me for years and I trust her implicitly. I mentioned my concerns to her and she said that she had seen one employee in the general office, pop a computer disk into her handbag. Of course, that meant nothing since the disk could have belonged to the employee and contained personal information, bank accounts and such stuff. But I thought it worth investigating, so I had to put my trust in Maureen more than usual by asking her to go into the aforesaid handbag when the employee was out of the office and find out what was on the disk."

"I take it you found what you wanted?"

Nigel nodded. "Yes I did. The disk contained confidential information about you and various other clients.

"Well done!"

Nigel smiled smugly. "My secretary deleted everything on the disk and then put it back so that the employee wouldn't suspect. I also checked into the suspect's background and found some interesting information. Now, let's go back to my office and we'll confront her together. If she admits to it then I think Miss Gilbert-Hines is going to be in for one hell of a shock." Their drink finished they made their way back to Nigel's office and once there, he picked up the phone and when answered he said, "Yes, could you send her in now. And take any calls, will you?"

There was a gentle knock on the door and Nigel called 'come in'. A young girl entered, with mousy brown hair and grey-blue eyes. She seemed very timid and Jason frowned with misgivings about this 'suspect'. Surely this reticent, shy little dormouse of a creature couldn't possibly be an informer? Nigel asked her to sit down. And she did, taking off her spectacles and wiping them nervously on her sleeve.

"Have I done something wrong, Mr Barnes?" She had an American accent but it was quiet and soft.

Nigel didn't answer her question. "You've been working here, what, twelve months?"

"Yes, Just over twelve months. And I've been very happy…"

"And before you came to work for me, you worked for a company in New York?"

"Yes…yes I did…as a secretary." She looked at Jason and smiled.

Nigel narrowed his eyes. "Are you sure that was your last employment, Ellen?"

She seemed taken aback at his question. "Of course."

"I believe your last employment was with Deborah Gilbert-Hines."

"No, it was not."

Nigel sat back in his chair. "I know that you came to England to work for Miss Gilbert-Hines."

She gave a bitter laugh. "Actually, I came to England to get married. But it only lasted a few months. He left me for another woman."

"Oh, yes. You might still call yourself Ellen Hoffman and many women still use their maiden names at work. However, you married Peter Shelby in December 1994 at Reading Register Office."

Jason stared at her. Was this Peter's wife?

Ellen looked uncomfortable. "Yes, but as I said, it didn't last."

"And your husband turned out to be a good friend of Miss Gilbert-Hines and he found the job for you in her company?" She nodded. "Why did you leave her employment?"

"I wasn't happy."

"Why did you omit it from your CV?"

"There didn't seem any point in mentioning it. Like my marriage, the job only lasted a few months."

"I don't think so. I've had someone watching you and your husband. And it seems you still live under the same roof." She remained quiet. "And you've also been discovered copying confidential files." His expression started to show anger that Jason had never seen. "Have you been passing information on, Mrs Shelby? Have you been divulging confidential facts about my clients?"

"No...No, I haven't!"

"I think you have. And that's a criminal offence. You could go to prison."

Tears welled up in her eyes. She turned to Jason. "Are you a police officer?"

Jason smiled and shook his head. "No, I'm not. But I think it would be in your best interests to tell Mr Barnes the truth."

His smile did it and Ellen feeling totally disarmed, began to cry.

The next thirty minutes consisted of a very blubbery confession as Ellen Shelby admitted she had been completely controlled by her husband and intimidated by Deborah. And when they had 'persuaded' her to take the job with Barnes, Atherton and Gill in order to pass on information, she had done it reluctantly. She was besotted with her much older and worldly-wise husband and his threats to leave her again, were enough to make her comply with his wishes.

At the end of her narrative, Nigel sighed. "I won't be pressing charges but I suggest you go and see Miss Gilbert-Hines immediately and tell her you quit." He gave a slow smile. "Oh yes, and you're also fired from this company too!"

She left the office dejected.

Jason couldn't help laughing. "God, you can be evil when you want to!"

Nigel picked up the phone. "I haven't finished yet." He dialled a number and asked to be put through to Deborah.

The next few minutes were a sheer delight to Jason as he listened to Nigel calmly telling her that she should expect Ellen Shelby on her doorstep very soon and he was also contemplating calling the police and having her arrested with dire consequences for Deborah.

At the conclusion of the conversation, Jason shook his head in disbelief. "And I thought I worked in a dog-eat-dog world!"

Nigel gave a grin. "Oh, we're just the same. It's just that we do it with a little more charm than you."

Jason had a thought. "But how did you know that Ellen had worked for Deborah?"

"I didn't. I just took an educated guess. It just seemed logical when I discovered that she had married Peter Shelby. I knew that Shelby and Deborah were old friends."

"And the fact Ellen and Peter were still living as man and wife? Did you really have them watched?"

"No, but I figured that Shelby would want to keep an eye on her."

Jason sighed. "So that was the young woman Peter abandoned to be with my wife?"

"I'm afraid so. However, it was after Shelby left Kiera and went back to Ellen that Deborah persuaded her to come and work for me and indulge in a bit of spying."

"She can be so manipulative. She's buying up shares in my company and I'm sure she's behind the offer from her father."

"No doubt. She's like a parasite. Destroys everyone she meets."

"But what would Shelby get out of it?"

"Oh, Deborah would have offered him something. If your company did accept the deal from Matthew Gilbert, I doubt you and Graham would have been directors for long. Your contracts would have been terminated and perhaps Shelby would have sat at your desk."

Jason shuddered at the very idea. But then another thought occurred to him. "My mother had an anonymous phone call telling her that Anna might not be expecting my child. I wonder if that was Deborah?"

"More than likely. Although Deborah seems to get others to do her dirty work for her. Chances are it was that lonely soul who was persuaded to do it."

Jason was delighted to tell Anna about Deborah's fall from grace, when they met the following evening. And it was during the conversation that the phone rang and Jason went to answer it. His tone was first one of surprise, then anger.

He shook his head as he came to sit next to Anna. "That was Nigel. It seems Deborah is on her way to San Francisco to work for her father. But before she left she accused me of ruining her life as she's having to sell her business."

Anna took his hand. "It's certainly not your fault that her life is in shreds. That's her doing."

"Yes, you're right. She's not worth wasting breath over and I hope she stays in America."

Anna let the subject drop and spent the rest of the time before dinner, telling Jason about the groom who had passed out during the ceremony and the bride who had nearly caused Margaret to have a fit when she suggested transplanting some of the flowerbeds in the garden. Although Jason laughed at her stories, he felt deeply sad.

Watching Anna's animated face, his eyes scanning her misshapen but fruitful body, he knew he should be the luckiest man on earth. But Deborah's part in all this had shaken him. In her own inimitable style she had sullied a wonderful time in his life, by spitting hatred at both Anna and him. But she was a nasty piece of work and he couldn't have expected anything better from her. Unfortunately, it had made him realise once again, that there were still many problems ahead of them. And problems that could mar their happiness.

Before Jason left, he and Anna took a walk in the rose garden and Anna remembered his previous phone call.

"What was it you wanted to discuss with me?"

He gave a grin. "Coming to live back at the Grange."

At first Anna felt stunned. "You want to sell the house in Bishop Sutton?"

"Yes," he nodded. "I feel as though my time there is finished and I know you're happy here."

"But what about your business?"

"It's just as easy to get to Bristol from here as from Bishop Sutton. I can jump straight onto the M5. It's nearer the seaside for Hollie and she'll get more fresh air and exercise."

"What about her school?"

"It's still within easy travelling distance."

"And Ben and Mrs Wilby?"

Jason couldn't help laughing. "You think of everything, don't you! I haven't mentioned it to them, but Mother is in desperate need of more help. The Grange has really taken off this last year." He chucked her under the chin. "And then, of course, there's you."

"Me?"

He suddenly became serious. "Sweetheart, I've often thought of what you told me down by the lake that day. Of your dreams to go to university and then become a teacher. I want you to do just that. I want you to follow your dream."

Anna looked down at her swollen stomach. "But I'll have a baby to look after."

"We can all help look after the baby. Mother's said that Fran is very keen to become an unofficial nanny."

"I don't…know. Those plans seemed a long time ago. I was a different person then."

He blew out a long breath. "OK, but the teaching profession will be poorer for it."

Anna struggled to explain. "Those were the dreams of youth. Being with you has changed all that. I've found more happiness with you than I've done for many years and I'm content in that happiness."

"I'm so glad to hear it," he smiled. He pressed a kiss on her lips. "I'll still need a PA."

"Ah, but I'm a wedding planner now."

Jason thought for a moment. "There's plenty of time to decide. I'll leave it up to you whether you stay as a wedding planner or become my PA."

"Will I get a pay rise?"

"I'll check with Graham." He tilted his head. "So, milady agrees that we should all move into the Grange?"

"Milady?"

"One day you'll be mistress of the manor."

Anna felt uncomfortable. "One day. But at the moment it's only my home because it's yours, but yes, it would be lovely for us all to be together again."

"Then it's settled. I'll put the house on the market straight away. It should sell easily enough."

When everyone arrived the following Saturday, they came in two cars, as Ben followed the Mercedes driving the Peugeot, with Martyn sitting next to him.

"Thought it might come in handy," Jason beamed. "I'll get the seat fixed up so it'll be ready for baby's arrival. Then you'll be able to pay us visits at Bishop Sutton until the house is sold."

The week turned out to be full of enjoyable moments, including a visit to Doctor Orchard who gave them the all-clear for a home birth, much to Anna's relief. She was told that the baby's head was fully engaged and that it might come earlier than expected. And when everyone left the following Saturday, Anna knew that their next visit would be to see her new baby.

"So, it's all systems go," said Nigel.

Jason nodded. "Yes, just one week to the happy event. Mother's going to phone me should anything start happening."

"And you're going to be there at the birth?" He couldn't hold back his smiles.

"I wouldn't miss it for the world." Jason had made an appointment with his solicitor to start proceedings for selling his house. Nigel hadn't been surprised that Jason wanted to move back to the Grange. After all, it was his boyhood home and his mother was getting on. "I think everything's going to be OK. Especially since Deborah left. I'm glad she's buggered off to America. At least she's not around to cause any more trouble."

After a slight pause, Nigel said, "I've given Ellen her job back."

"Have you? After all she did?"

Nigel breathed a heavy sigh. "It wasn't her fault. I've taken her back on some very strict conditions. And Sophia has found her an apartment."

"She's not living with Peter any more?"

"No, she's left him. She can start afresh now and I thought she deserved a second chance."

"You've got a soft heart."

Nigel shrugged. "I think we all deserve a second chance in life."

Jason took a gulp of coffee from his mug. "Do you remember what you said about being up to your ears in paternity suits?" Nigel nodded, his heart in his mouth. "Anna's been threatened by her ex-husband. He's wanting to know if the baby is his and if it is, he's going to apply for access."

Nigel's legal mind jumped into action. "Has he been to see her?"

"Yes, about mid-June I think."

"He has no right to hassle her! I can apply for an injunction if Anna wishes it."

Jason shook his head. "She doesn't want that."

"Then he'll have to be prevented from setting foot on the premises."

"Already sorted. Mother has informed every member of staff. I doubt he'll get past the gate."

Nigel nodded again. "You must have a DNA test as soon as possible and then the matter will be cleared up. But if it is his child then I'll do all I can for you."

CHAPTER TWENTY-ONE

It was Saturday again and Anna was looking forward to Jason's weekend visit. He was due later that afternoon and with the baby expected in only four days' time, Anna's hopes were high. Everything was prepared and Sister Davenport was on standby. The thought that her ex-husband might pay a visit had dwindled to the back of her mind. She was happy, contented and secure. The front gate was now permanently locked and fitted with an electronic system. Visitors had to speak into an intercom and announce themselves before being admitted. The buzzer had been installed in the kitchen and John or Fran had been given the job of checking every visitor with the appointment book. They had also been asked to look out for a dark blue BMW.

Although Fran gave a little moan at having to perform yet another duty, she secretly enjoyed talking into the intercom and had acquired a 'cultivated' voice to go with the task. Their most important role was to make sure that Anna was happy with the client before leaving her alone with them. On no account must a visitor go into the library unaccompanied.

However, that particular Saturday afternoon, Fran was in no mind to trek up and down the stairs.

"Have you got an appointment?" she asked sullenly, when the intercom buzzed.

"Yes, my name is Jackson. I have an appointment at three o'clock with the wedding planner. I want to book this venue for my daughter."

"Go through the main door and you'll find Mrs Stevens in the library. First door on the right," said Fran, as she pressed the button that swung the gates open. She leaned back in her chair and put her feet up on the chair opposite. She was having her break and nobody was going to disturb her.

Dave Stevens parked his car and walked through the main entrance. He soon found the library and after knocking sharply, he entered.

"Mrs Stevens," he said with a grin. He slammed the door shut and quickly turned the key in the lock. Anna rose slowly from her chair. "I see you've kept your married name. That's very civil of you."

"You shouldn't be here," said Anna. Although frightened she tried to stay calm. "Why did Fran let you in?"

"Who's Fran? The gates were opened for me but I saw no one."

Anna looked down at her diary. "I have an appointment at three with a Mr Jackson."

"Yes, that's me. David Jackson. Thought I'd use my mother's maiden name."

Anna's mouth went dry. "What do you want?"

"I told you I'd come back. You can't have long now." She refused to answer as his eyes swept over her. "Did you tell your fiancé what I intend doing if that kid's mine?"

"Yes, he knows."

He gave a cruel laugh. "I bet that gave him a shock. I can just imagine that a man like Jason Harrington is used to having anything he wanted. Even exclusive rights to another man's child."

"This is not your baby! This baby is Jason's. Please will you leave."

"We shall see." He stepped closer. "I must say you look positively blooming. But there again, you always seem to thrive on pregnancy. Perhaps I should have given you more kids, then you would have been too busy to run away from me."

"I should have left you when the twins were babies. When I first found out about you."

"That unhappy with me, eh?"

"I was bitterly unhappy. Your behaviour made me miserable."

He clicked his tongue. "How come? I provided for you. You had everything you wanted."

"Except you disrespected me with other women. And you told lies about this Pam. You were seeing her weren't you?"

"All right, I was. But it wasn't serious at the time…"

"I don't care! Your behaviour made me feel insignificant. As though I wasn't important." Anger began to rise up inside her. She hated this man, hated everything he stood for. Her hand brushed against the handle of the scissors lying on her desk. "You treated me like a scivvy as if I was there just for you, while you amused yourself when and where you liked."

"Perhaps if I'd had more attention from you, then I would have stayed at home."

She stepped closer to him. "Don't you dare blame me for your infidelity. I was a good wife to you and loyal. You didn't deserve me."

"And he does? Harrington?" His eyes swept round the library. "Yes, he can give you anything you want, but I'll still be around. I'll want to see my child regularly."

Her fingers curled round the handle of the scissors.

Jason arrived at the Grange a little later than expected. He had hoped to be there for lunch but now it was gone three o'clock. Grinning, he pressed the button on the remote control and the gates swung open with a smooth hiss. This new system with the gates was much more convenient and he couldn't understand why they hadn't done it sooner. He drove down to the main entrance of the house, but immediately saw a second vehicle parked to one side. It was a dark blue BMW and he started panicking. As he hurried to the main door, he almost collided with Fran racing out of the porch, a look of terror on her face.

"Oh, sir. I went to ask miss about some coffee for her visitor and the door's locked. The gentleman said...said he had an appointment."

Jason steadied her, his heart racing furiously. "Go and find your father."

"I've been looking for him."

"He might be in the workshop," he said, licking his dry lips. Fran set off down the path, while Jason ran inside and across the hall to the library. He tried the door but finding it still locked, banged on it with his fist. "Anna! Anna! Open the door," he cried.

Then he heard a muffled scream and his heart leapt into his throat. He was just about to yell again but stopped abruptly when he heard the key grating in the lock. Jason turned the handle and pushed the wood with a resounding crack, sending it flying back on its hinges, to crash against the wall.

What he saw made his blood run cold. Anna was bending over the desk, one arm across her stomach, her face twisted in pain. A man stood a few feet from her staring grimly. With a cry of anger, Jason lurched forward, his teeth gritted, fists clenched. The man turned to look at him and then backed away, putting up his hand to ward him off.

"What have you done!" yelled Jason.

"Steady on, mate! I've not touched her!" The man put the desk between him and his assailant.

Seeing that he couldn't escape without passing him, Jason went to Anna and put his arms round her, looking for signs of injury.

"Are you OK? Did he hurt you?"

The man gave an incredulous laugh. "Me hurt her? Perhaps you ought to check out who's holding the scissors and who's been injured." He went into his pocket and pulled out a handkerchief, wrapping it round the gash in the heel of his hand.

Jason noticed the scissors. "Give me those, sweetheart." He took them from her and placed them on the desk.

The two men stared at each other. Jason was finally facing the man who had imprisoned the woman he loved and subjected her to a terrible assault.

For Anna's ex-husband, it was interesting to see his adversary in person. He had seen his photograph when searching for information about him and he hadn't expected him to be so young. How did a man that age get so successful? It made him feel even more bitter and angry.

Anna let out a small groan and doubled up again. "I think the baby's coming. I've started having contractions," she gasped. Jason's arms tightened round her and she held onto him.

Her mind confused, she tried to remember what had happened. It was as though she had been in some terrible nightmare as her fingers curled round the handle of the scissors. She saw Dave slowly advancing on her and although his lips were moving she didn't take any notice of what he was saying. She didn't care what he was saying. All she wanted was for him to leave her alone.

The contraction had been quite strong and had made her wince. The baby was due and this could have happened at any time, but seeing her ex-husband standing there in a place where she had felt so safe, so protected, caused a cascade of emotions to well up inside her until her eyes and mind couldn't focus. Anger, hatred and fear swept over her; she had to protect herself. When he had come within striking distance, she had grabbed the scissors and sliced towards him. But she had been too slow and he had raised his arm in defence, the blades lacerating his hand.

Dave gave a smug laugh. "Goodness me! Looks like we won't have to wait much longer."

"Get out!" said Jason, trying to keep his voice steady.

"Oh, I'm going, but not far. I noticed a hotel in the village, so I might as well make myself comfortable while I wait."

"Wait?"

"I'm seeing this through with you, mate."

Anna gritted her teeth as another contraction took hold of her. "Please make him go away."

"I'll call the police," breathed Jason through his teeth.

Dave shrugged indifferently. "Call them, but don't forget it's me that's been assaulted. But I get your point and I'll leave your premises. Wouldn't want to be done for trespassing."

John appeared at the door with Fran just behind him.

"Show this gentleman out, will you," said Jason quietly.

When the room became calm, Anna breathed a sigh of relief. "I suppose I'm lucky, really. I could have killed him."

Jason frowned. "Are you in labour? You seem to be in pain." He looked her up and down.

Anna shook her head. "It could be just a reaction to the shock of seeing him. The pains might go away. I'll just take it steady and see how things go."

"Shall I get Mother?"

"Please don't. Let's keep this between you and me for the time being."

"Another little secret of yours," he smiled.

"Not really. There's no point in bothering her about it just yet. Shall we take a walk in the garden and just enjoy being together." She gave a half-smile. "After the baby, we might have very few moments to ourselves."

Jason's grin became wider. "Yes, I remember it well." They met John outside who assured them that the gentleman had been seen off the premises. "Make sure he doesn't come back," said Jason, as he guided Anna round to the rear of the house.

The weather was perfect for having a stroll and once in the rose garden they sat on a bench.

"I love this place," smiled Anna, looking about her.

"How are you feeling?"

"I feel very well. A bit shaky, though."

"I'm not surprised. I was scared to death when I saw him standing there."

Anna shook her head slowly. "I really thought he wouldn't come back. This last month, I was so convinced that he'd forget it and leave me alone."

Jason watched her. "I really wish you'd go into hospital. You might be safer there."

"I don't think so. He'll be able to get into a hospital."

"You're still determined to have the baby here?"

She nodded and put her hand over her stomach. "Well, the contractions are coming every five minutes. I think I'll go in and phone Sister Davenport," she said, looking at her watch.

They took a slow walk round to the main entrance, Anna leaning heavily on his arm and stopping at regular intervals to take in big breaths. As they went through the door, another contraction tightened her stomach and she timed its duration. She picked up the phone and dialled Sister Davenport's number.

Jason made a phone call of his own. Unknown to Anna, he had decided to ring Nigel and tell him about the incident with her ex-husband. Nigel suggested contacting the police and asking their advice but Jason declined, not wanting a police presence while Anna was having her baby. However, when Nigel said he would come to the Grange immediately and give support, Jason was more than relieved.

"What could be better than a black belt in kick boxing," he said with a grin.

Anna was delighted when Nigel and Sophia turned up and she took Sophia off so that they could have a little chat. They were in Anna's bedroom when the sister arrived and after giving her a brief examination, concluded that the baby was going to take some time and she would return later that evening.

That night Anna and Jason slept in the four-poster bed and Anna managed to get some rest, aided by the pain relief administered by the midwife. Jason slept only spasmodically, his thoughts on the man now sleeping at The George Hotel in Wedmore Village. Why didn't he go home? What did he think he was doing, waiting for the birth? And then Jason realised that it was a way of spoiling the occasion for them. Dave Stevens had no intention of letting Anna have her baby in peace and wanted to be an ominous presence throughout the process. The very idea gave Jason murderous thoughts.

The morning brought Sister Davenport who again nodded in satisfaction at Anna's progress.

"Has she slept?" she asked Jason.

"Yes, for most of the night," he said, trying to stifle a yawn.

She frowned. "But you didn't? I suggest you go and get some shut eye. You'll need your strength later on."

Jason stumbled gratefully to his own room and fell asleep immediately on top of the bed. Nigel and Sophia arrived and Sophia sat reading as the mother-to-be dozed after an injection of pethidine.

Anna awoke with a start sometime late morning, the contractions now coming in quick succession. Holding onto Sophia's hand she walked about the room, gasping her way through each pain that made her feel that some giant boa constrictor was tightening its grip round her and squeezing her to death.

Jason also awoke and after a quick shower made his way to Anna's room. He took over from Sophia while she went to get him a cup of tea and something to eat. While she was gone, Anna opened her eyes as she faced another bout of pain.

She gripped the hand offered to her and then realised it was Jason sitting beside the bed.

"I'd forgotten how bloody painful it is," she panted, laughing and crying at the same time.

"You're doing very well, sweetheart. Sister Davenport is coming back shortly and will give you some more painkiller." He smiled brightly. "She's already delivered two babies. A boy and girl, so she says you have the casting vote for today's tally."

Anna suddenly remembered. "Is he still here? My ex-husband?"

"I'm not sure," he said hesitantly. "But don't worry, he'll not get anywhere near you."

She couldn't remember the next few hours, only the frequent contractions kept bringing her back to the present when she was aware of movement round her. Jason fetched a cool, damp flannel and gently wiped her face as each agonising pain made her cry out.

Sister Davenport arrived at twelve-thirty and a quick examination confirmed that Anna would soon go into the second stage of labour. And when it started half an hour later, both Jason and Sophia were there to encourage her. With Jason supporting her from behind and Sophia's arm to grip onto, Anna began the exhausting task of bringing her baby into the world.

It took twenty minutes of sheer pushing before Anna decided she had had enough.

"I can't any more," she groaned. "I'm so tired."

The sister gave an encouraging smile. "Give me your hand." She helped her feel that the baby's head was almost born. "A few more pushes and you'll be there."

Jason rubbed his cheek against her hair, his arms tightening round her. "You're doing so well and soon we can start thinking of a name."

Anna gave two more pushes until the sister cried, "That's the head, now one more little push and...!" Anna did as instructed and then felt the warm, wet body flop out between her knees. "And you have a boy! Congratulations, the pair of you."

Anna fell back against Jason and closed her eyes in relief. When she opened them again a few seconds later she saw that, although he was smiling, he had tears in his eyes. The midwife wrapped up the baby and immediately put him into Jason's arms while she concentrated on the mother. For the next ten minutes, Jason stood beside the bed holding the small bundle and staring in absolute wonder at the tiny features on a beautiful child.

"Hello there," he murmured, suddenly filled with overwhelming pride. This had to be his son. Surely fate couldn't be so cruel as to take that away from him now.

Margaret entered the room, her face alight with expectation. "Was I right? Is it a boy?"

Jason nodded. "Yes and he's beautiful."

She studied the child. "I don't think you need to worry about who the father is." Jason glanced at her in surprise. "I'll have to get out some photos of you when you were born. I think you'll see the likeness." The baby suddenly opened his eyes as if trying to focus on the man holding him. "Oh, goodness me! He's got your eyes, Jason."

His heart began to pound with excitement and he licked dry lips. But then Sister Davenport took the baby from him so that she could complete her examination and clean him up.

After a few minutes she said, "Absolutely perfect and he weighs in at eight pounds two ounces and that's not a bad weight at all."

She placed the baby in Anna's arms and for a while Anna and Jason spent time with the child that they hoped would be theirs, while the sister made up her notes. She snapped her bag shut as Margaret arrived laden with a tray of tea for everyone. The sister only stayed long enough to swallow hers quickly and after confirming a further visit that evening, left the patient in capable hands.

While Sophia bathed and dressed Anna in a fresh nightie, Margaret placed the baby in the Moses basket. "I knew I should have trimmed it up with blue," she said thoughtfully.

Although Anna was worn out, she found it difficult to sleep. Knowing that her ex- husband was prowling about set her nerves on edge. She tried to close her eyes but the thought of Dave, made them spring open almost immediately.

Sophia noticed and took Jason to one side. "I'm off to find my dear husband. But I think you're going to have to persuade Anna to get some rest. I've got a feeling she's fighting it and you don't need three guesses for the reason!"

Jason made himself comfortable beside the bed. "Now, I want you to sleep," he said firmly.

Anna gave an exhausted smile. "I want to but I'm scared to let my guard down."

He studied her seriously. "Now, listen to me. I'm going to sit here beside you and nobody is coming into this room unless they have the right. So, close your eyes."

She blinked hard, but then noticed the book in his hand. "What are you reading?" He held up the cover. "*Bringing up Boys*! Where did you get that?"

"Mother bought it, just in case."

Anna smiled and closed her eyes.

Dave Stevens ate his evening meal alone. He was sitting in a cosy corner of The George Hotel with a large plate of steak and kidney pie and vegetables in front of him. He found it difficult to handle his knife and fork because of the bandage round his left hand.

"Stupid bitch," he muttered. "Always the drama queen."

A couple came through the door and headed for the bar.

"Hi ya! Have you heard the news?" said the young woman.

The landlord nodded. "Bloody tragedy, I say," he said, glancing at the television, full of the news of Princess Diana's death in Paris.

"Oh, not that! Mrs Stevens up at the Grange had a lovely baby boy early on this afternoon. Mr Harrington is so proud."

Dave gave a contemptuous smile. He'll be proud OK, he thought, when he finds the boy is mine. He knew that Anna's fiancé already had a daughter and since he had produced two sons while Harrington had fathered a girl, then it stood to reason that Anna's son must be his. Convinced of his logic, he made his plan for the following morning.

Sister Davenport was pleased that Anna had rested and her evening visit was brief. The others had all gone down to dinner and Anna had insisted that Jason join them.

When Jason came up after dinner, he found Anna feeding the baby, a cashmere shawl across her shoulders.

He grinned. "You're feeding him yourself?"

Anna looked up and laughed. "I thought I would give it a try."

"Kiera didn't feed Hollie. We had to make up bottles."

"Yes, the twins were bottle fed, but having two babies at once was rather daunting." She added with a giggle, "At least this is free."

Jason thought for a moment. "Does that mean I'll get a good night's sleep? I won't have to get up and do my share of feeding him?"

She narrowed her eyes. "Well, you won't have to feed him. But whether you sleep or not will depend on what kind of mood I'm in! And of course, he'll need his nappy changing."

He gave a playful grimace. "It'll be strange dealing with a boy. But absolutely wonderful."

Anna nodded and sighed. "Well, if there's one thing I know about, it's bringing up boys." Her eyes lit up. "We ought to pick a name for him."

"What do you suggest?"

"I wondered about Thomas, after your dad and Jason after you."

He smiled. "Thomas Jason Harrington. Yes, that sounds just perfect." They both fell quiet, suddenly realising that their problems were not yet over. For ten glorious minutes they had forgotten the threat that hung over them and had been immersed in the absolute delight of the son they regarded as their own. Jason cleared his throat, emotion welling up inside him. He leaned forward and took hold of the tiny fist resting on his mother's breast. "He's mine, you know.

I'm absolutely certain and so is Mother. She says he looks exactly like I did when I was a baby."

Anna decided to be practical. "That could be wishful thinking."

"It's more than wishful thinking! Oh, Anna, this is the life I want. Nothing I have, my business, the Grange, means a thing if I don't have my family with me."

She knew he was fighting back tears. "Then let's just enjoy the moment," she said, leaning forward for a kiss and receiving one.

"But I'll still have that damned test, just to prove he's mine," he said sharply. He tried to regain his composure. "I think I've told everyone. Chris and family in Wakefield send their love and I've told the folk at Bishop Sutton. Hollie is jumping around with glee. She wants to visit as soon as possible."

"Let them come tomorrow. I'll be fine having visitors."

"Are you sure? You only had him today."

Anna nodded. "It'll be my birthday and I'd love to see them." Jason's shocked face was a picture and she couldn't help grinning.

He gasped in surprise. "Your...Your birthday!"

"First of September. Don't tell me you've forgotten?"

"I have...I did...!" he stammered.

She looked away in haughty disdain. "You didn't forget last year when you bought me the car."

His guilty look made her giggle. "Sweetheart, I'm so sorry. With everything that's happened it went completely out of my head. But I'll make it up to you, I promise. Tell me what you'd like, I'll get you anything you want."

She turned her head back and smiled. "You can't buy what I want. And you said it yourself, nothing is more important than your family."

He nodded and lifted up the coin round her neck. "I ought to have learnt by now that you value the meaning of life rather than its possessions."

She eased the baby from her and after fastening her nightgown, turned him round so that she could see his tiny face. "Did you hear that, Thomas?" she said tenderly. "It looks like your daddy now understands where true happiness really lies." She was answered with a soft burp.

Nigel and Sophia coming to say goodbye interrupted them. But their departure was delayed for another thirty minutes as they spent extra time with the new arrival.

"It makes you quite broody," said Nigel, holding the baby in his arms.

His wife pulled a face. "You can stop that! I think three is enough!" She took the baby from him and handed him back to his mother.

"We did talk of five when we married," Nigel insisted.

"Well, you can have the other two!" she said, pushing him out of the door.

Dave drove his car within a mile of the farm and walked the rest of the way. When he reached the low-lying buildings he could see the farmer feeding the pigs. Mr Durrant turned when he heard the footsteps in the yard. He studied the young man walking towards him. He was smartly dressed and his manner was brisk as if he was on an urgent mission. Under his arm he carried a hard hat, the kind a builder or engineer would wear.

The farmer returned his smile. "What can I do for you?"

"Could you tell me the way to the Grange?" He grimaced. "My car broke down about a mile away. I have an appointment with a..." He pulled a piece of paper from his pocket. "A Mrs Margaret Harrington. I'm a structural engineer and she wants me to look at the foundations of the house." He took out his identification badge and waved it in front of the old man's face, smiling smugly as the farmer scratched his head.

"You've got a goodly way to walk, young sir. It's over three miles to the Grange."

Dave gave an exaggerated groan. "Oh, dear! I need to get there quickly. I've another job on this afternoon."

The farmer thought for a moment. "I'm going up there in about ten minutes, to deliver some milk and eggs to the cook. I could give you a lift."

Dave climbed into the Landrover keeping up a lively conversation, until the Elizabethan manor came into view and the farmer parked at the side of the house adjacent to the kitchen.

"If you go through the door and up the stairs you'll come to the main hall. I'm sure you'll find someone about to help you."

Dave nodded and disappeared through the kitchen, thankful that there was nobody about. There wasn't anyone in the hall either although he could hear a murmur of voices from a room leading off the hall. He climbed the stairs, the sound of a baby crying directing his attention to a half-open door just along the corridor.

He stood on the threshold, peering in but keeping back so he wouldn't be seen. He could see Anna walking towards the basket on a stand. She was still in her dressing gown and as she picked up the small bundle and carried it to the armchair, he grinned.

Without making a sound, he entered the room and came to her side. She looked up smiling expectantly, but then her smile vanished and she opened her mouth to scream.

"Shh!" he said, putting a finger to his lips. "I'm not going to hurt you."

Anna felt faint. She hadn't expected to see him again, not when everyone was on the lookout for him. How had he got in? Jason had been with her only minutes before, but she had sent him downstairs to have coffee with Margaret and wait for Hollie and Martyn to arrive with Ben and Mrs Wilby. They would be here in a matter of moments.

Anna steadied her breathing. "Why have you come back? Jason has agreed to have the test. Why can't you wait for the result?"

"I wanted to see my son."

"That remains to be seen." She held the baby close to her. "There's people coming in a minute. Coming to see the baby and me. You'd better go while you have the chance."

"May I hold him?"

"No!"

"I'll be gentle with him."

"Please go away."

His eyes turned hard. "I mean to have access to him if he's mine."

"Then go back to Wakefield and wait."

He looked around the room. "It's a great place this. Centuries old. Must be worth a fortune."

"It's been in the family a long time."

He nodded in appreciation. "Of course, there might be no necessity for that DNA test."

"What do you mean?"

"If Harrington could make it worth my while, then I'll go away and never come near the boy."

Anna felt appalled. "Do you mean give you money? Are you talking about him buying you off? That's despicable!"

He shrugged. "He's loaded. Can't think he'll miss a million."

"A million pounds? Are you joking?"

He turned to face her and she could see he wasn't. "Seems a reasonable amount."

Anna thought rapidly. "But if Jason has the test and he's the father, then that's the problem solved. He wouldn't have to pay you anything because the baby would be his."

"I'm talking about dispensing with the test. It would be a business transaction. He would understand that."

Anna held the baby closer to her. "No! No!" She wondered if she could make for the door. But with the baby in her arms, she felt vulnerable. And she couldn't leave him in his basket while she went for help.

"Well, it's the test, then. May the best man win." She watched him walking towards the door, but suddenly he turned and winked at her. "By the way. Happy birthday."

After he was gone there was deathly quiet for a few minutes before she heard angry voices down in the hall and knew that Jason and her ex-husband had come face to face once more.

Fran appeared at the door. "Are you OK, miss? Master sent me to check on you."

Anna stood. "I'm fine, but there's something you have to do for me. And you must do it exactly as I say."

Anna carried her child out of the room and along the corridor to the top of the stairs. Looking down into the vast hall she could see Dave leaning against the banister, wearing a smug smile. Jason was shouting and Margaret held her son by the arm preventing him from hitting out. Slowly, she walked down the stairs and it was when she reached halfway, that Jason broke his hold from his mother and lunged forward to grab Dave by his jacket.

"No, stop!" Anna's voice echoed round the walls and the two men suspended their actions, staring upwards at the figure holding the baby in her arms.

She continued her descent until she reached the marble floor. She glanced at Jason and then at her ex-husband. And then undaunted, she stepped forward and placed the baby in Dave's arms.

Jason gave a muted cry with shock and Margaret murmured something inaudible under her breath. Fran appeared and hurried downstairs carrying the Moses basket and a large bag of baby clothes. She gave Anna a quick look and then placed them at the feet of the stunned man holding the child.

Dave frowned. "What's all this! What kind of game are you playing now?"

"No game, I'm deadly serious. He's all yours so you don't have to bother applying for access. I'm not going to fight you any more. You can have all his things. I've started feeding him myself, so you'll have to buy bottles and milk from a supermarket."

Jason groaned as if in pain. "Oh God, someone please tell me this isn't happening."

Margaret held him by the wrist. "Wait," she whispered.

Dave and Anna stared at one another and suddenly strength surged through Anna's body like an electric charge. Fate had brought her this far and for good or ill she had to let fate decide the next step. She had to have faith and finish this once and for all.

Suddenly, the baby opened his eyes and Dave's expression changed to one of complete surprise as he stared down at the child in his arms. For Anna, an eternity seemed to pass.

And then her ex-husband gave a lopsided grin. "There's no doubt who fathered him. I don't think a DNA test is necessary." He crossed the floor and placed the baby in his mother's arms and then took a step back, studying her. "Pam would be livid if I brought home a new baby for her to care for," he said, laughing with amusement.

Jason's expression showed utter contempt.

John appeared from the kitchen stairs followed by a figure that was red-faced and panting painfully.

The flustered farmer gasped for air. "Oh, I'm sorry, sir. I really am. I had no idea!"

"Is everything OK, Mrs Harrington?" asked John, as he scrutinised everyone standing in the hall.

Margaret stepped forward. "Yes, John. Everything is fine, but this gentleman needs to be shown off the premises once more."

John clicked his tongue. "You're like a bad penny, you are."

Dave could only smirk at the absurdity of the situation. He turned to the farmer. "You couldn't give me a lift to my car, could you?"

Mr Durrant nodded. "Aye, but no funny business."

"And I'll go with you and make sure you leave this time," said John.

The three of them turned to descend the steps to the kitchen.

Jason came to Anna's side and put his arm round her shoulders. "You've just taken ten years off my life!"

"That was an incredibly brave thing to do, to call his bluff," said Margaret softly. "I doubt I would have had that kind of courage." She followed John, determined to see their unwanted visitor gone from her property.

Fran had remained close by, her hand over her mouth. "Shall I take the clothes back upstairs, miss?"

Anna nodded.

Jason picked up the Moses basket and they went into the parlour. Anna lay the baby down and carefully tucked a blanket round him. She made herself comfortable on the couch.

Jason sat beside her. "What made you do that? He might have taken him!"

Anna smiled and shook her head. "I knew that once he saw Thomas and how like you he was, then he would change his mind."

He blinked hard at the horror of it all. "Well, I hope he's gone for good."

"Oh, I'm sure he has. He'll not bother us again." She paused slightly before adding, "Please don't ever tell the twins what happened at Christmas between their dad and me. Or what happened today."

"Now, this is a secret I understand."

She nodded. "It's bad enough that they know he was unfaithful to me, never mind the other. Despite the way he is, they love him and I don't want to set them against him."

Jason took her hand and kissed her fingers. "You have a good heart." And then he smiled mistily at the sleeping child. "I can't believe he's finally here and he's really mine."

She put her arms round his neck. "He's ours."

He held her face between his hands and kissed her lips tenderly.

Suddenly there was disruption in the hall as their visitors burst in.

"Where is he?" yelled Hollie, dragging Martyn by the hand. "Where's our little brother?"

* * * * * *

ALSO BY JULIA BELL

A Pearl Comb for a Lady
Songbird: (The Songbird Story – Book One)
A Tangle of Echoes: (The Songbird Story – Book Two)
Broken Blossoms
The Wild Poppy
If Birds Fly Low
Nyssa's Promise
To Guide Her Home
When Lucy Ceased to Be

These novels are available as ebooks on Amazon, but are currently in the process of being published in paperback

A LETTER FROM THE AUTHOR

Dear Reader,

Thank you so much for choosing to read **Deceit of Angels**. I love writing but having my books read makes them come alive. Until they are read, the characters are only in my imagination and they need to live and be enjoyed. So, I hope you enjoy reading all my novels and you're able to spare a little time in telling me about it.

You can do this via my website or by leaving a review on Amazon.

Julia Bell
JuliaBellRomanticFiction.co.uk